Cowboy
Casual

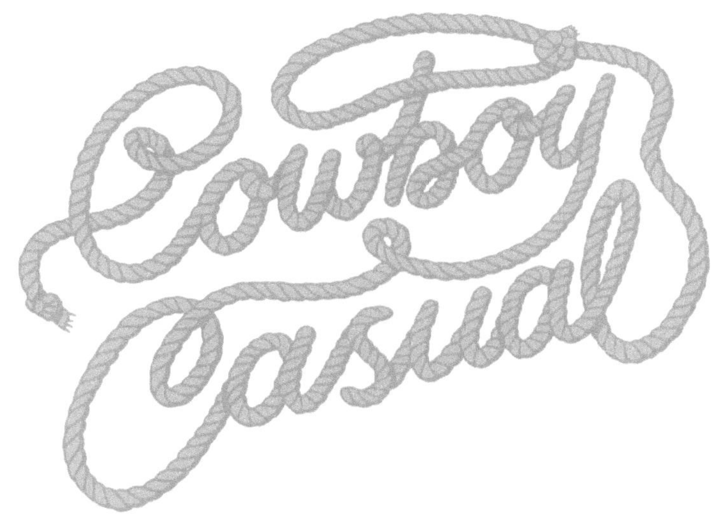

USA TODAY BESTSELLING AUTHOR
HOLLY RENEE

For my mama—
Who has loved cowboys for as long as she's loved me.

Content Warning

This book contains depictions of sexually explicit scenes, violence, and assault. It contains mature language, themes, and content that may not be suitable for all readers. Reader discretion is advised.

PLAYLIST

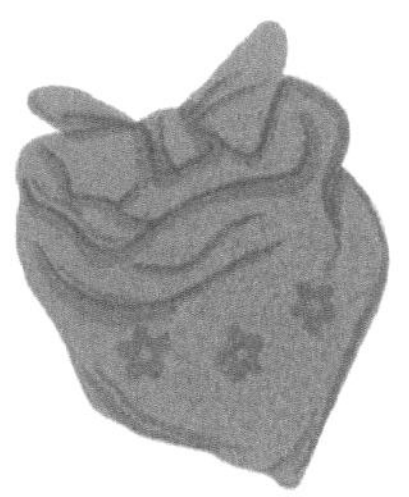

Down Bad by Taylor Swift
Worst Way by Riley Green
How Does It End by Taylor Swift
Don't Mind If I Do by Riley Green
LOML by Taylor Swift
Tears by Sabrina Carpenter
Dress by Taylor Swift
Ain't Nothing 'Bout You by Brookes & Dunn ft. Megan Moroney
False God by Taylor Swift
I Cross My Heart by George Strait
Treacherous by Taylor Swift
Cowboy Take Me Away by The Chicks
The Last Time by Taylor Swift ft. Gary Lightbody
Amazed by Lonestar
Sad Beautiful Tragic by Taylor Swift
You're Still the One by Shania Twain
You Are In Love by Taylor Swift
Neon Moon by Brooks & Dunn
That's the Way I Loved You by Taylor Swift
I'll Go on Loving You by Alan Jackson

CHAPTER 1
BLAIRE

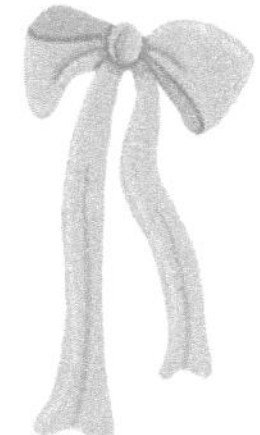

The photos landed in my inbox at 5:37 p.m. Another email, this one with the subject line URGENT: For Review-Grant Chandler Jr.

I barely blinked. Just another Thursday at Senator Monroe's office, where my job as press assistant meant I spent half my time putting out fires before they spread all over the internet. A few clicks, some carefully crafted lies, and by dinner, the world would be slightly less on fire and my father's re-election chances marginally more secure.

I spent four years at Duke getting my marketing degree, and here I was, a glorified janitor for my father's indiscretions and political messes. My professors would be proud to see that their star pupil's primary skill set had become making scandals disappear before they hit the trending page.

But the name at the top of the email wasn't my father's. It was my fiancé's.

The Chandlers had been bankrolling my father's campaigns since before I came to live with him, their hedge fund fortune buying the influence that kept both families comfortable. Four years ago, my father seated me next to Grant at a fundraiser. I was finishing my last year at Duke, and my father's eyes gleamed with approval every time Grant leaned in to whisper something that made me laugh.

Two hours and three glasses of merlot later, I'd mistaken his calculated attention for charm, and the next morning, roses crowded my tiny apartment doorway with a note that simply read, "Dinner? -Grant."

That one yes led to a diamond ring that had been on my finger for the last fourteen months, and now the wedding was a little over a hundred days away.

I opened the email, and the images loaded one by one. I noticed Grant first, then his assistant, who was splayed across his mahogany desk. Her blouse was unbuttoned, and his fingers tangled in her dark hair while the other hand gripped her skirt, wrinkling the expensive fabric I'd complemented her on last month. There was a hunger in his eyes I'd never seen in our bedroom.

More images followed as I scrolled, each one a blow. My stomach clenched. There they were in a D.C. hotel elevator, and the timestamp mocked me. Taken exactly fifteen days after the engagement party my father had thrown for us. Another showed them at some dimly lit bar. Grant wore a navy suit with a pale blue tie I'd tied for him the morning of his keynote speech. She draped her thigh across him, and his hand disappeared beneath the hem of her dress.

I scrolled through the evidence of his betrayal. In some, they were alone. In others, they exchanged secretive touches at campaign events where I stood just yards away, smiling for donors while his fingers found her waist.

The first photo was from thirteen months ago, and the most recent was from yesterday afternoon.

My vision blurred as I stared at the photos. A laugh from the bullpen made me flinch, and my gaze landed on the framed picture on my desk. Grant and I were at the Children's Hospital benefit. Grant's hand gripped my hip, his fingers digging in enough to remind me to stand straighter for the cameras. I'd wanted to wear the black dress I'd picked out myself, but he'd replaced it with the lavender gown that was hanging in our closet when I returned from work. "Trust me," he'd said, his voice firm.

I waited for the rage, for the tears, but found neither. Instead, my fingers shook against the keyboard as the room tilted and narrowed around me. In that moment, I felt the snap of that invisible thread that bound me to this life, to my father's ambitions and Grant's possessive hands.

In its absence came the rush, the flood, the name I'd locked away years ago.

Colt.

I physically recoiled from my own thoughts. *No. Not now. Not him.* I'd buried him beneath years of careful compartmentalization, sealed him away in the darkest corner of my heart where dangerous things belonged. He'd gutted me in ways Grant's betrayal couldn't touch, yet here he was, the first name my mind reached for.

The contradiction made me sick. Hating him and the physical ache of wanting him after all these years. I feared what that meant about who I really was beneath all these perfect, polished lies I'd wrapped around myself like expensive armor that suddenly felt paper thin.

I stood so fast my chair clipped the wall and made the edges of my vision pulse. There was a ringing in my ears as I willed myself not to look at the humiliating photos again. Everyone in this office would see them soon enough, and I should have been doing damage control. That was my job, but I suddenly couldn't give a shit about this job.

Instead, I walked straight out into the hall, closing my office door behind me with a soft click. My heels echoed on the tile as I moved, mechanical and purposeful, each step meant to keep the panic from overtaking me.

The hallway outside my office was lined with campaign posters, and today the images of my father felt like sentries watching me, silent and expectant. I tried to draw a full breath, but the air stuck in my throat and went nowhere.

I picked up my pace, crossing the bullpen and weaving past

the clutch of interns hunched over their laptops. Someone tried to get my attention, but I brushed past, offering only a brittle smile I hoped passed for apologetic. The elevator was slow as hell, so I ducked into the stairwell, grateful for the emptiness and the way the steps forced my body to move.

Three flights down, I stopped, leaning against the cool cement wall. My phone buzzed in my pocket, and I yanked it out, half expecting a message from Grant. But it was my father's assistant's name looking back at me.

Judy: Senator Monroe would like for you to meet him in his office immediately.

I stared down at the screen as if my entire future hadn't just imploded.

I should have been thinking about Grant. His betrayal. The years I'd spent smoothing his rough edges, convincing myself we were in love instead of two people playing assigned roles in someone else's strategy. I should have been furious or at least humiliated. But standing in that cold stairwell, an emptiness clawed through my chest, a ravenous, familiar void that didn't belong to Grant at all.

The realization ached inside me like a bruise pressed too hard, spreading from my sternum outward until even my fingertips felt tender with the truth I'd spent years denying. My body remembered what my brain had worked overtime to forget. His thumb tracing the freckles across my collarbone, the lake water dripping from his eyelashes as he surfaced beside me, the way my name sounded like a prayer when he whispered it against my neck at dawn. I hated how easily these memories returned, how they still burned beneath my skin while Grant's betrayal felt like nothing more than a paper cut.

I despised myself for it, for looking at evidence of my fiancé's infidelity and feeling only relief tangled with shame. The pain of losing Colt had carved hollows inside me I'd filled with pretty lies and my father's approval.

I started to turn back toward my father's office, because that's what the text demanded and that's what a dutiful daughter would do. But my body revolted. My hand hovered above the banister, knuckles white against the chipped paint, and I looked up the stairwell, concrete spiraling overhead.

Then my gaze dropped, my ears ringing, and saw an exit sign pulsing red at the base of the stairs like a dare. I pressed downward, footsteps echoing against the steps, and the farther I got from the office, the easier it was to breathe. My body was moving faster than my thoughts, and that felt like freedom.

By the time I hit the last step, my legs were numb. I didn't hesitate at the landing, didn't even process what I'd do next. Instead, I barreled toward the side exit, shoved open the steel door, and found myself in the narrow alley between the Monroe Senate offices and the looming black glass of Chandler & Chandler.

The sun hung low between the tall buildings, gilding the edges of everything it touched and forcing me to shield my eyes. When the door slammed behind me, I tried to breathe as my reflection fractured across the dark, mirrored windows of Grant's building. Three days ago, I'd walked through those same doors with his favorite sandwich and a smile, playing the role of the doting fiancée for an audience of receptionists.

I should've stopped to think and called my father. I should've done what I'd been trained to do. But all I could see was Grant's hand on another woman's thigh, and the way his smile had always held a flicker of calculation. For four years, I'd filed myself down, smoothed away any parts of me that might snag on propriety or expectation. Now something untamed and forgotten stirred beneath my ribs, screaming for me to be reckless, even as my father's voice in my head listed all the ways this would destroy everything I'd worked for.

I could feel myself being torn between the wild-hearted girl my mom had raised me to be and the dull woman my father had created.

Grant's building was emptying for the evening. Men and women in tailored suits filtered out the revolving doors, but I didn't slow down. I ignored the polite smiles offered by familiar faces. A few gazes caught on me, lingering a bit too long, and my skin prickled beneath their stares. The knowing glances made my stomach twist. Had they all seen the photos already? Or worse, had they watched Grant and his assistant slip in and out of his office for months while I'd been the oblivious fiancée?

I flattened my shaking hands against my skirt, smoothing wrinkles that had set in like permanent creases. My cheeks burned with each heartbeat, a flush I couldn't hide, but I lifted my chin and locked my shoulders back, marching into Grant's building before I could stop myself.

I passed the security desk, and the guard's eyes flicked up, then away. No need to check my ID when my father's face was on billboards and my fiancé's name was etched on the side of the building. I crossed to the elevator bank and jabbed my finger against the executive floor button, leaving a smudge on the polished brass.

The ride up was dizzying. Every surface in the elevator was a mirror, and three different women were reflected back at me. There was the Senator's daughter in her expensive suit and perfect posture purchased with years of correction. Then the jilted fiancé, with anger burning behind her trembling chin and firmly pressed lips where she'd learned to swallow her voice.

And then there was *her*. The one with wide eyes and color high in her cheeks, the one who looked like my mother. I wanted to scream at her, beg her to run, to fight, to do anything.

I'd let them kill her so slowly I hadn't even noticed she was dying.

The elevator groaned somewhere above me, the floor indicator ticking up, and I caught my mother's eyes in my reflection. Her dare and mischief flickered there, then disappeared beneath my father's careful mask. I touched my face, half-expecting to feel her sunlight warming my skin, but my fingers met only the sweat-damp foundation I'd applied that morning to cover my freckles.

My mother wouldn't recognize me if she saw me now, and I hated the way my mind still drifted to Colt, desperately wondering if he'd be the one person who could still see through to whatever remained of me.

What the hell was wrong with me? I should have been devastated about Grant, not feeling this treacherous relief.

The elevator jerked to a stop. I closed my eyes for a single, shaky breath, then wiped away a stray tear before it could mar my mascara. Just one tear was all I allowed myself to shed for the girl I used to be, the girl who'd been taught her worth came from men who never really loved her.

A soft chime announced my arrival as the doors parted to reveal a wall of windows framing the sunset-washed skyline. The remaining staff sat at their desks, sliding papers into briefcases and shutting down computers, their gazes carefully avoiding mine as I moved toward the frosted glass door that separated me from Grant's office.

Without knocking, I shoved open the door, and they sprang away from each other. His assistant met my gaze while her fingers straightened her shirt. Mascara tracks stained her cheeks.

Grant ran his fingers over his tie and offered his practiced smile. "Blaire, baby. What are you doing here?"

His assistant turned away, busying herself with paperwork on his desk, but I caught the way her hands shook.

I almost felt sorry for her.

"I thought we were meeting for dinner?" Grant's voice overlapped itself, the end of the sentence scraping against the beginning, like he was trying to race ahead of the silence I'd brought into the room. He took a step around her, positioning himself directly in front of me.

"Don't act like you don't know that I've seen the photos." My voice was steady, but my hands trembled so hard I had to dig my nails into my palms to hold them still. "How long has this been going on?"

There was a twitch in his jaw, but he kept his mask perfectly in place. "Come on, don't do this here." He tried to close the space between us, palm open, but I jerked away so fast I nearly toppled a crystal award he'd won for service to his community off his bookshelf.

"Do not make a scene," he hissed, jaw clenched tight, and eyes darting to the open door behind me.

The command landed like a slap, and my heartbeat thundered in my ears as that wild-hearted Blaire clawed her way out.

"Should I whisper about you fucking your assistant, Grant?" I didn't recognize my own voice, how it carried across the room. "Would that be more convenient for you?"

His eyes darkened as his shoulders squared. "We should discuss this at home. Privately."

He reached for my elbow, but I stepped back. "No."

"Blaire." He said my name like he was speaking to a trained dog, and I recoiled.

"Don't touch me," I said, and I heard the tremor in my voice, which only made me angrier, but the look on Grant's face told me the words landed as I intended. "Nothing you say will change what you did."

"Blaire," he tried again, gentler now. "Let's take some time to think about how we want to handle this, okay? I'll call your father—"

"Of course you will," I cut in. "You're such a fucking coward, Grant."

He flinched. Not enough that anyone else would notice, but I'd spent four years learning the tells of Grant Chandler. The tic in his jaw, the flicker behind his eyes when his composure slipped. I recognized the look of a man cornered, and it thrilled and terrified me that I was the one who'd put him there.

"This is my office. People are watching," he hissed as he angled his body like he was going to shut the door. "Let's be smart about this."

"Smart," I repeated, and the laugh that escaped me was raw and humorless. "Where were your smarts when you were fucking her on your desk? Did you think no one would notice? Or did you think I wouldn't care?"

"I never meant for you to find out like this," he said calmly. "I was going to tell you. I— I needed the right time. You know how your father is. How important this is for all of us."

I could hardly breathe as I thought of my father's ambitions, my own perfectly curated life, and the unyielding gravity of "all of us." It made me want to scream.

"My father." The words clawed at my throat as my gaze fell to the ring on my finger, the weight of the diamond suddenly crushing every bone in my hand.

"Yes, your father, Blaire," he said, drawing out each word as if I were too stupid to keep up. He leaned in, dropping the mask of concern for something infinitely colder. "Don't act fucking daft. He'll get a handle on this, and we'll figure it out."

"There's nothing to figure out." I shook my head. "I can't do this."

"Where the fuck else would you go?" He laughed, and his words hit hard, harder than I'd braced for. "You live in my condo, Blaire. You work for your father, whose campaign is funded by mine. The life you live is because of me, so don't act like you're better than this."

I had grown used to Grant's cruel words, but somehow, they still sliced through me like a blade. He was right, wasn't he? My clothes hung in his closet, my career existed at my father's mercy, and even my engagement ring had been passed down through generations of Grant's family. But I had built this life too. I had sacrificed for it, shaped myself to fit in it.

The phone on his desk rang loudly, making me flinch. His assistant lunged for it, her voice a distant buzz until she thrust the receiver in my direction, her eyes wide with fear. "Ms. Monroe, it's your father."

My stomach dropped as I brushed past Grant, my fingers clumsy as they closed around the handset.

"Dad—"

"Come to my office. Now." His tone was so measured and so infuriatingly calm that rage flooded me, making my teeth clench so hard my jaw ached.

"No." The word ripped from my throat, and I shook my head

even though he couldn't see me. "You don't get to ask me to swallow this. Not for you. Not for him."

"Don't be foolish, Blaire. Grant made a mistake. All men make mistakes." My father's voice slithered through the phone like poison. I locked eyes with Grant across the room, watching him watch me, and I felt like I was suffocating.

My fingers trembled against the ring, twisting it once, twice, before hesitating at the knuckle. The diamond caught the light, beautiful and cold. I yanked it off, wincing as it scraped my skin, then traced my finger over the pale indent left behind. I squeezed the metal in my palm until it bit into my flesh, drawing comfort from the pain.

"Go to hell, dad."

I hung up before I could hear my father's response, and the phone clattered into the cradle.

Grant's eyes darted between my face and the ring clenched in my fist. I thought he was about to plead, but instead, he said, "You're being childish."

I tried to move past him, but Grant moved faster. His hand shot out, catching my arm above the elbow. He held on like he thought he could will the moment backward, as if the world would reset if I stood still long enough.

The heat of his palm bled through my shirt, and I remembered every time he'd touched me gently for the camera, every time he'd squeezed my shoulder in public, always anchoring me to his side. I'd mistaken that pressure for security, but now it felt like a vise.

"You're not leaving until we talk about this." His voice dropped to a growl, low and ugly. He yanked me closer, pulling me off balance.

I twisted my arm, trying to pry him off, but his grip tightened, his thumb digging into the soft flesh inside my elbow.

"Grant," his assistant whispered his name from behind me, but he didn't acknowledge her.

"You're hurting me," I gasped, and this time, I wrenched free.

His face went slack with surprise, as if he couldn't believe I'd dare resist him.

"Never put your hands on me again," I said, my voice steadier than my heart, as the diamond's edge bit into my palm.

Ten years ago, on a night that still woke me up sweating, I'd stood in the gravel driveway of my grandmother's house and hurled Colt's necklace at his chest because I couldn't make him choose me.

But I couldn't bring myself to hurl this ring at Grant, couldn't bring myself to care enough. I opened my aching fist and let the ring fall to the ground, watching it bounce once before settling.

I thought he might grab for me again, but he just stared, mouth tight, as I stepped past him into the hall. I walked in a trance, the blood in my ears so loud I barely heard Grant call after me.

But his words chased me with a desperate, low chuckle. "You'll be back."

I forced myself to keep walking, and I didn't stop until I was jabbing my finger against the elevator button, then again, harder. I didn't want to think about what would happen if I didn't leave right now, if I let the old gravity pull me back toward the familiar controlling orbit of Grant, my father, and all the plans they'd fused around me like a glass cage.

The elevator doors finally slid open, and I stepped inside. Four years of my life stood behind me. Security, status, a future. I pressed my back against the wall and watched the doors close, avoiding looking at my reflection. My hands shook as I pulled out my phone and dialed my grandmother's number.

She answered on the third ring, her voice calm and steady as always. "Hello."

I opened my mouth, but nothing came out but a strangled sound somewhere between a gasp and a sob.

"Blaire?" Panic edged her voice, crackling through the connection. "What's wrong?"

"Can I come home?" The words tumbled out, raw and clumsy. I waited for the guilt, the flood of regret for throwing away everything I'd built, but all I felt was an overwhelming, dangerous relief that flooded through my chest like the first breath after nearly drowning.

"Always, baby." No questions, no hesitation.

I pressed the button for the ground floor. The elevator plunged downward, and with it came visions of Colt, the curve of his jaw, the calluses on his fingertips, the weight of judgment I'd find in his gaze. My lungs seized at the thought. I was going back to the place I'd fled a decade ago, back to where Colt Calloway's words had severed me from my roots, but now those same roots called me home.

CHAPTER 2
BLAIRE

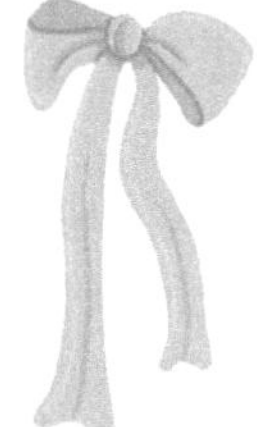

One of the very first things my grandmother taught me was that men ain't shit.

I considered getting those exact words tattooed across my forehead since, somehow, I kept needing the reminder.

But I hadn't really believed her then or when she told me I'd be back home someday.

She hadn't fought me when I packed my bags at seventeen, tears in my eyes and a fire under my skin, chasing the escape only a dumb, brokenhearted girl believed in. After months of resisting, I'd finally given in to my father's demand to go live with him, and she'd watched me go, steady and sure, while muttering, "You'll find your way back when you need to."

I'd laughed then, but I wasn't laughing now. Not with the Tennessee heat pressing in through my cracked windows, thick with the smell of honeysuckle and bittersweet memories. Memories that, no matter how hard I tried to forget, always found their way back.

My knuckles ached against my grip on the steering wheel as my car hugged each curve of the road I could have driven with my eyes closed. Willow Grove had always moved slower, softer somehow, and from the looks of it, not much had changed.

But I sure as hell had.

I drummed my fingers on the steering wheel, the weight of my whole life rattling in the back seat in two overpriced suitcases my father had gifted me as an engagement present.

It had only been a little over a week since I found out about Grant's affair, but I'd already boxed up my life and handed in my resignation. My father had told me that I was making a mistake, that I was making foolish emotional decisions because I was hurt. Maybe I was, but the anger felt cleaner and safer somehow. There had been so many times when I'd let my anger with him and with Grant dissolve into forgiveness, but I clung to it now, tight enough to make up for all the times I swallowed it down.

My mama had always said I was as stubborn as Grandma June, and that one day, it would come back to bite me. But I wished I'd held on to it tighter, so I didn't feel so lost.

Back with Mama and June, I'd never had to guess where I belonged. They'd carved out a space for me that fit just right, and the realization that I'd traded that certainty for empty promises left a gnawing pain beneath my ribs.

The urge to call June and tell her never mind clawed at me every hour of the last week. When I finally did, her, "Hello, my girl," knocked the wind clean out of me. I opened my mouth to beg her to tell me what to do, then closed it again, but June had always seen right through me anyway, straight to the parts I hid from everyone else, including myself.

She let out a breath, tired but knowing, and I pictured her sitting in that old kitchen chair, phone cord twisted around her finger like it used to be. "Sometimes you gotta face the music, even if it ain't your favorite tune," she said, and I both resented and clung to how she made it sound like the simplest decision in the world.

Like I wasn't headed back to a town that was not only haunted with memories of my mama, but of *him*.

The urge to ask her about Colt was a relentless itch beneath my skin, but I'd clenched my teeth and willed myself into silence before the words could tumble out. Because asking would've made it real. It would've admitted that I still thought about him, that I could still feel him in the cracks I couldn't quite close, and that his voice still echoed in my mind on nights when I drank too much and let myself remember.

It had been years since I said his name out loud, years since I heard the deep rasp of his laugh or the quiet hush of his voice in the dark, but my body refused to forget.

It was impossible to abandon the memory the way we fell into one another after years of easy friendship or the way he had touched me as if he'd been starved for me his entire life. But it was how he'd pushed me away that lingered the most, the way he had told me to leave, his voice cold and final, when my father came for me.

I told myself he didn't matter anymore. That I could steel myself if our paths crossed. But ever since I'd made the call to June, I'd been bracing for him.

Bracing for the anger, for the ache, for the boy that haunted my memories, and for the man he might've become that I no longer knew.

So when the town sign passed by in a blur, my breath caught without warning.

Welcome to Willow Grove. Population: Too damn small.

Small enough everyone would know my business by morning and have an opinion on it by lunch. They'd know I was back after years of running with nothing but a busted-up heart and a canceled engagement to show for it.

And Grant wouldn't be the only reason for the whispers that would follow me. This town had a long memory. They all knew I'd been broken before I ever left, that I was already damaged goods when I accepted Grant's ring.

I didn't slow down when I hit the split in the road. Right would take me to Main Street and left would take me past the Calloway Ranch, then to my grandmother's. I flicked on my blinker and veered left.

I didn't let myself look. I kept my eyes on the road, but I already knew what was there—the weathered fence line, worn soft from years of storms and sun, the fields that seemed to never end, and the glint of the lake in the distance.

Acres of land that had been built with blood, sweat, and generations of work. Land that Colt Calloway would never leave. I tried to force myself to forget what it was like to be loved on that land, but it was impossible.

A cluster of horses grazed in the distance, their dark shapes moving slowly across the fields. My stomach knotted at the sight that was too tied to him and every summer we'd spent on horseback. The Calloways had been our neighbors for my entire life, so I knew that land as well as I once knew Colt.

June's farmhouse appeared over the next hill, hunched beneath ancient oaks and weeping willows that were bigger than I remembered, their branches almost touching the ground.

The old mailbox came into view with *Cates* still painted on the side in June's messy handwriting, and a smile curved my lips as I pulled onto the long gravel drive.

The house hadn't changed a bit. Four rocking chairs lined the wraparound porch, though the wood was fading and the cushions flattened thin. Tangles of battered wind chimes hung from the eaves, tinkling in the breeze.

June was already waiting there, leaning against the doorframe.

She wiped her hands on the apron tied around her thin waist, and she looked exactly how I remembered. Her skin was kissed by the sun, and her gray hair was tied in two long braids with curls framing her face she couldn't quite tame.

She greeted me with a warm smile, her eyes crinkling at the corners, and waved like I'd only been gone for the afternoon. Even from my car, I could see the way she watched me with a fierce, steady gaze that was full of the strength born from years of loving deeply, enduring loss, and shaping the world around her with her bare hands.

I cut the engine and left the car door hanging open as I crossed the yard as quickly as I could. The screen door groaned with a creaky protest as she nudged it open with her hip, and I climbed the steps two at a time.

June caught me in a hug, and all at once, I was a kid again, skinny, barefoot, covered in dirt, and wrapped around her legs as she hulled strawberries.

She smelled like flour and lemons, and beneath it, a faint trace of a day spent with her hands in the dirt. I held on as long as she let me, until she pulled back, hands framing my cheeks and her eyes roaming over every inch of my face.

"There's my little strawberry." Her voice was like warm honey, but I heard the threads of worry that were stitched into her words where she thought I wouldn't notice.

Only three people ever called me that nickname, my mama, June, and Colt, and for a long time, I had hated it.

But today? It felt like coming home, and I clung to the way it fell from her lips.

"June." I sighed my grandma's name, which I'd started using when I was twelve. I still remembered the day I got my first period, and she told me I was a woman. And women, apparently, called her June. I'd felt so grown then, but I was nothing like the woman she raised me to be anymore. I placed my hands over hers and tried to take in every subtle change. "I'm twenty-eight years old. Don't you think I've outgrown that?"

Her eyes sparkled with mischief as she reached up and gently tousled my hair, now more muted auburn than the copper fire it used to be. "You're never too old to be my little strawberry."

For a moment, I let myself believe it, that I could find my way back, that I could be the girl I used to be, but then my phone vibrated in my pocket. I ignored it, rolling my eyes at my grandmother as if that vibration didn't course through every part of me until my stomach twisted. I already knew who it was without pulling my phone out of my jeans.

I wanted to ignore Raleigh and everything that came with it. But the weight of what I'd left behind tugged at me like an undertow. I'd have to face it all eventually, the broken engagement, Grant's betrayal, and my father's disappointment. Just not yet. I'd already called off the wedding and sent my resignation, but the fight would come anyway. My father and the Chandlers always turned "no" into a negotiation, but standing on June's porch, I wanted to pretend I could start over.

"If I'm old enough for Botox," I muttered, pushing my hair out of my face, "I'm too old for that nickname."

"You're still as stubborn as a mule," she said as her eyes scoured over me, and I did the same to her. The lines around her eyes were deeper, and there were new crinkles around the corners of her mouth, proof of a life well lived and well loved.

"Maybe even more so." I shrugged, trying to push down the lump rising in my throat. *I had been gone too long.*

"And even prettier." Her gaze swept over me, slow and measuring, like she was checking for the damage she knew I hid behind my smile.

"I'm pretty sure you're legally required to say that as my grandmother," I said, smiling as she swatted at my arm.

"No." She shook her head as she slowly moved past me and toward the steps I had just climbed. "Some people have ugly grandbabies. That's just the truth of it." She waved her hand over her shoulder for me to follow her, but she didn't wait for me as she moved down the steps. "I was fortunate I didn't. I could never fake it."

"June!" I laughed as I trailed behind her.

"What?" She looked back at me with those amber eyes, and being with her felt like finding shelter in a storm. "It's the truth. Let's all say a prayer that your babies are pretty like you. If they aren't, I'd have to lie to the ladies at my book club, and you know how I feel about lying."

The old wood creaked as she leaned on the banister, but she still moved with purpose, even if she was slower these days.

She paused on the bottom step, glancing up at me. "Well? You comin'?"

Something loosened in my chest as I trailed behind her, my feet remembering the path before my mind could catch up. "Where are we..."

But then I saw him.

He rose slowly, brushing his hands over his jeans, the sun catching on the sweat at the back of his neck. Heat flooded me until the only things I could focus on were the sound of my heartbeat and the sight of him. He shifted his weight, moving with the easy authority of a man who owned every inch of ground beneath his worn boots.

He looked carved from memory and like a stranger at the same time.

It didn't matter how much time had passed or how much he'd changed, seeing him was like a punch to the gut. I had left. I'd left because he'd told me to, and he was still here working away on his ranch, right next door to my grandmother's farm, as if he hadn't destroyed everything.

I took a small, instinctive step back, searching for something to hold on to, looking for anywhere to go but here. But then he turned, and I met his dark brown eyes. Eyes that didn't belong to the boy who'd broken my heart.

They belonged to his brother.

"Hunter." His name slipped past my lips, and he graced me with an easy, relaxed smile that seemed to light up his entire face as he wiped the sweat from his brow.

"Well, well, well," he drawled before he leaned against the fence. "Look what the cat dragged home."

His resemblance to Colt was like a physical blow.

Hunter was taller now, broader, his shoulders stretching the worn cotton of his T-shirt in a way they never had before. The lanky limbs and uncertain posture of Colt's younger brother had been carved clean away and replaced with a man with a chiseled jawline.

But the grin he flashed me over the fence was exactly as I remembered. One corner of his mouth hitched higher than the other, and a dimple appeared in his left cheek. It was the same smile I had watched him give girls to make their knees go weak, devilish in a way that promised trouble.

He swung open the gate that separated the two properties, boots crunching through the grass as he watched me.

"You're looking good, Blaire." He tipped his head in my direction, and I forced myself to stand straighter.

"Careful, Hunter. Compliment me too much and I might think you've missed me."

He laughed, and the sound curled through me. The deep rumble was warm and familiar in a way that made my skin prickle with warning.

He was far too similar to his brother.

"You wouldn't be wrong." His eyes traveled over me like he was taking inventory of the years between who I'd been and who I'd become. "We've all missed you. My mama still asks about you all the time."

I didn't answer. I couldn't.

I had missed them too, of course I had. Colt's family had once felt like where I belonged. His mother had been there for me when I'd lost my own, but they were little more than strangers now.

"Speaking of your mama, tell her I'll call her later once Blaire and I are settled," June said as she walked past him toward my car. "And make yourself useful and come carry her bags."

Hunter chuckled, but I quickly interjected. "You don't have to do that. I can manage."

"It's no trouble," he replied with a wink, lifting the hem of his shirt to wipe his face. "It will give me a break from this damn fence."

I glanced at June as Hunter pulled both suitcases from the back seat like they weighed nothing.

"I don't know where I'd be without you Calloway boys." June patted his shoulder, and I quickly looked away. "You can drop them on the porch. We'll handle it from there."

"Yes, ma'am," Hunter replied before he moved past us and up the steps.

June was watching me with the smug assurance of someone who could read my thoughts like an open book, and her eyes twinkled with amusement.

"Don't even start," I warned as I pointed my finger at her.

She used to bring Colt up all the time after I left, and again, once she found out I was engaged to a man she called as useless as tits on a bull. But I always shut down conversations about him. I had wanted to know nothing about his life here. I couldn't handle it.

"Didn't say a word," she replied, her tone light and teasing, but she didn't press. She slipped her arm around my waist and guided me back up the porch steps. "We'll talk later," she whispered, her tone half affection and half warning.

Hunter lingered by the front door, one suitcase in each hand, as he waited for us. "You sure you don't want me to take these upstairs?"

"That's plenty, Hunter," June told him before grabbing the door. "I appreciate your help, you handsome thing."

A slow smile spread across his face, his cheeks flushing. "You're good for my ego, Ms. June."

"That ego doesn't need no help." She rolled her eyes. "Never has."

Hunter chuckled before he finally set down the suitcases and ducked his head. "You need anything at all, holler."

"Thanks, Hunter," I managed, as we walked into the house.

It smelled of old pine floorboards worn smooth by decades of footsteps, strawberries so ripe their sweetness hung thick in the air, and the faint trace of June's perfume.

It smelled exactly as I remembered, like home.

We rounded the corner into the kitchen, and there were baskets overflowing with vibrant berries that bled out onto the table. Some had juice seeping out and creating dark, sticky patches while others had shriveled like the forgotten casualties of a harvest too heavy for one woman to manage alone.

"Been busy around here. Shorthanded," June said casually, wiping her hands on her apron, though her eyes lingered on me.

My throat tightened with all the things I could say, should say, but I couldn't force the words out. Instead, I tied up my hair with unsteady fingers and grabbed the nearest basket, the wicker cutting into my palm.

"Where do you want me?" I asked, already scanning the room for the worst of the disaster.

She gave me a gentle smile, the one meant only for me, that used to heal every scraped knee and mend every broken heart, but even June's magic couldn't reach the fracture Colt left behind. "Why don't you unpack your bags and get some rest? All of this can wait."

I shook my head. I was far too anxious to sit still. "I'll unpack later. I want to help."

She pointed out the kitchen window toward the rows of strawberries, their ruby flesh glistening under the merciless Tennessee sun. "Need to save what we can before the heat turns 'em all to mush. My farm hands are picking as much as they can, but the harvest has been heavy this year."

I kissed her temple, my lips brushing against the wisps of silver hair that had escaped her braids and moved to the back door. The hinges protested with a long, rusty whine as I stepped outside.

"I'm glad you're back, baby," June called after me. "It doesn't matter what brought you. It just matters that you're home."

CHAPTER 3
BLAIRE

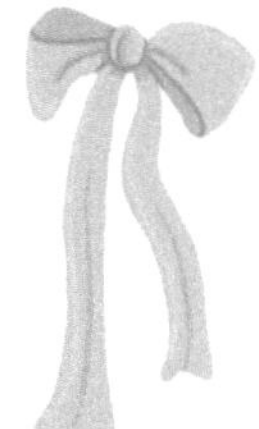

Heat shimmered over the rows of strawberries as I stared out over the farm.

I needed this: the dirt under my fingernails, the sun turning my shoulders pink, and the sweet taste of strawberries in my mouth as I ate them straight off the vine. I craved the purpose of it, to matter again to myself and this place.

June had a few farmhands, but not enough to keep up with the sprawling acres she stubbornly refused to scale back. Work piled up everywhere, work that June wouldn't have been handling all on her own if I hadn't left.

I was already mapping out all the projects I would tackle, but the berries came first. I gathered them quickly, my fingers moving on autopilot and staining red from the fruit.

Pluck, drop.

Pluck, toss out the bad fruit.

I'd feared I might have forgotten how, but my hands remembered. The repetitive motion calmed me in a way nothing else had since I packed up my life. I had gone to my dad's while I tried to sort things out this past week, but I'd known it was a bad idea.

Each berry that landed in the basket felt like a quiet act of defiance, a step away from the person I'd left behind in Raleigh.

That girl had let herself be consumed by a man who looked good in a suit but couldn't hold on to a promise, even if he stitched it into his skin.

That girl had been so desperate to be wanted, she shrank herself down into someone easier. But here, with my knees pressed into the warm soil, my father and Grant seemed so insignificant. If it weren't for my phone vibrating in my pocket for the fifth time since I'd arrived at June's, I might not have thought of them at all.

They didn't matter. Not on this dirt.

I yanked the phone from my pocket. Seven missed calls from Grant and another two from my father's secretary. Voice mails stacked up, but I left them to rot. I had no interest in hearing what they had to say, not anymore.

I looked up and spotted Hunter casually leaning against the newly mended section of fence on his side of the property line. He held his gloves loosely in one hand, and he watched me like he didn't care that I caught him.

I shielded my eyes and shot him my best withering look, though it lacked bite after the last couple hours in the heat. Working on the farm did that. It bled the venom right out of me and left nothing but the soft underbelly I tried to keep hidden.

"Aren't you supposed to be working?" I called, and he grinned.

"If anyone asks, I'm on my break." He turned toward the driveway as tires crunched over gravel. "You've only been here a couple hours, and you're already killing yourself. Maybe you should take one too."

I wiped my hair out of my face, tracking a blue pickup as it made its way up to the house. "I think I've had a long enough break." I didn't mean from the work. "Don't you?"

He raised an eyebrow. "That's not—The farm isn't going anywhere. You've got time."

But I didn't.

Time felt like a debt I owed this place, one which kept

growing interest while I was off pretending to belong somewhere else, only to come crawling back when it all fell apart.

Hunter watched the truck as it got closer to the house, then he pushed off the fence. He walked through the gate separating June's property from the Calloway's with the casual air of someone who had all day to do nothing but bother me.

"You going to ignore those calls forever?" He nodded toward my phone, still in my hand and vibrating once again.

I quickly hit the ignore button before I shoved it back in my pocket. "It's not important."

The blue truck came to a stop in front of June's house and idled in the small turnaround. The door swung open, and a woman jumped out. She bounded up the porch, her blonde hair half falling out of her messy bun.

Hunter stiffened beside me; his gaze snagged on her for a heartbeat too long before he dragged it away.

"Who is that?" I motioned to the woman as June walked out of the house to greet her.

"Huh?" Hunter muttered, looking out over the fields, avoiding her entirely.

She stood there, seemingly oblivious to our presence, her attention on June as she threw her head back and laughed. The sun caught in her blonde hair, turning it almost white at the edges. She was effortlessly pretty in a way that made me self-conscious of the sweat dampening my shirt and the dirt caked under my fingernails.

"That girl you won't look at. Who is she?"

Hunter didn't answer right away. He ran his hand over the back of his neck and tilted it from one side to the next as if trying to ease his tension.

"That's Maggie Dawson," he replied, before quietly clearing his throat.

I quickly cycled through my memories, searching for the name, but came up blank. "Did she go to school with us?"

Hunter made a sound between a grunt and a sigh. "No. She moved here a few years ago. Runs the bakery on Main."

He glanced back in her direction for a few long seconds, his jaw clenched before he tore his gaze away.

"What's going on there?" I circled my finger between them, like I was connecting invisible dots in the air.

"There's nothing going on."

I raised a brow as I studied him. "You just stare at everyone like that?"

He let out a low whistle and shook his head. "What about you, Blaire?" His voice dropped low enough to land the jab. "Should we talk about your love life next?"

I laughed, but even I knew how hollow it sounded. "What love life?" I turned, moving down the row of strawberries.

"I've heard some things through the grapevine." His footsteps crunched behind me as he followed. "You've been gone, what? Ten years now?"

I kept my eyes fixed on the berries nestled among their thick leaves. "Shouldn't you be doing something?" I nodded toward his chestnut mare, who stood tethered to the fence post, watching us with liquid eyes that missed nothing. "Your horse looks thirsty."

"I'm just saying," he continued, his voice more careful now. "It's a little wild seeing you after all this time. Especially after the way you left, after you and Colt—"

"Don't." The word came out sharper than I intended.

Hunter stiffened, his hands stilling at his sides.

I turned to face him fully, tension crawling up my spine. "You want to talk about Colt?" I forced his name past my lips, the syllable catching in my throat. "Then do it over there on your property. Not mine."

Hunter blinked, taken aback, and for the first time, he looked like he regretted opening his mouth.

"You're gonna see him, you know?" The way he said it, resigned like he already saw the collision coming, made something hot twist beneath my ribs. "I don't know how long you're planning on staying, but there's no way around it."

"I'm not worried about him." The lie tasted bitter on my

tongue as my pulse thrummed against my neck. "I'm back here for June and for this farm."

Hunter shifted, like he might say something else, but then Maggie's laugh rang out from the porch again and we both turned toward the sound.

June lifted a hand, beckoning us toward the porch. "Y'all going to stand out there all day? Blaire, there's someone I want you to meet."

I didn't move at first. Not until Hunter opened the gate that led out of the strawberry fields and held it, waiting. I slipped past him without a word, but he cleared his throat. "I'm going to get back to work."

But June ruined his plans. "Hunter, turn off Maggie's truck on your way up here, will ya?"

"Shit," Hunter mumbled under his breath, his shoulders tensing.

I snickered as he trudged toward the idling truck, kicking up little puffs of dust with each reluctant step.

I headed up the worn path to meet the girl who had reduced the always charming Hunter Calloway to a tense, distracted mess.

Maggie sat in one of the rocking chairs, long legs crossed and a glass of tea sweating in her hands. She glanced up as I made my way onto the porch, and the smile that spread across her face was warm and genuine.

"There she is." June wrapped her arm around mine, drawing me closer to the woman. "This is my granddaughter, Blaire. The one I've told you about."

Maggie stood and extended her hand. "I was beginning to think you were a myth."

I shook her hand, even as I winced. "More like a cautionary tale."

"Aren't we all?" Maggie laughed. "It's so nice to finally meet you after everything June's told me."

"Please don't believe everything she says." I dropped her hand and leaned back against the porch railing.

"Ms. June would never lie," Hunter huffed, shifting his weight onto the first step, his dusty boot scuffing against the weathered wood. His eyes darted from the porch to the fields beyond, then to Maggie for a fleeting second before fixing on some invisible point in the distance.

June dropped my arm and moved to him so she could pat his cheek. "That's because you're a sweet boy, Hunter."

Maggie scoffed, an unladylike sound that she immediately tried to muffle with her palm pressed against her lips, and I couldn't help but smile.

"Or he's full of shit." I shrugged. "Either one."

Maggie's laughter bubbled up. "I see you've met him before."

"Nice to see you too, Mags." Hunter clapped his hand across the porch post, rattling the lattice beneath.

"Always a pleasure, Calloway," Maggie quipped, though the glint in her eye suggested otherwise.

June gave Hunter's cheek one last pat before turning toward the door. "Let me grab your berries, darlin'. I've got them boxed and labeled in the cooler."

"Thanks, June." Maggie set her glass down with a soft clink on the porch railing as the screen door clicked shut behind my grandmother. Then she turned to me. "So, what brought you back to Tennessee?"

I hesitated, feeling the weight of Hunter's gaze on me. "Needed a change," I finally answered. *That was the understatement of the year.* "City life was getting old, and I missed this place."

Maggie didn't push me for more. She nodded as her fingers absentmindedly traced the fraying edge of her shorts. So I wasn't sure why I felt compelled to continue, but the words tumbled out.

"And there might've been a guy," I said, the admission lingering in the hot afternoon air.

A guy who turned out to be the opposite of what I should have wanted.

She laughed, and her nose scrunched. "Isn't there always?"

"Unfortunately." I looked over at Hunter and finally met his familiar brown eyes that had witnessed the rise and fall of Colt and me from the bleachers at football games to the late-night bonfires on the lake bank where our properties met. Hunter had been there through it all, a kid with a front-row seat to our tangled history.

"Well, we're glad you're here. June's been needing the help." Maggie's voice was warm and kind, but it made guilt dig its claws deeper into my chest. "And I know she's been dying to have you home. She talks about you like you hung the moon and stars over this farm."

"I'm glad I'm here too," I told her honestly. "I've been gone too long. I think the country air might do me some good."

"A girl needs time to remember who she is." She laughed as she crossed her arms, fingers digging into her elbows, and her gaze flickered to Hunter.

I recognized the look in her eyes, and I pitied her. I knew how easy it was to fall for a Calloway brother, how their slow smiles and calloused hands could undo a girl piece by piece, but I also knew how it felt to have your heart broken by them as well.

"What are you doing tonight?"

I blinked, surprised by her question. "Uh, probably unpacking."

"I'll make you a deal." She smiled at me, but her fingers tapped nervously against her thigh. "I'll help you unpack if you come with me to meet a few friends at The Dusty Spur."

I opened my mouth to decline, the refusal already forming on my tongue, but Hunter let out a dry snort.

Maggie tilted her head toward him. "Problem, Calloway?"

He leaned one broad shoulder against the porch post, arms folded loosely across his chest. "No problem. But there's no way you're going to convince this one to go to The Dusty Spur. She left the cowboy bars behind a long time ago."

I could feel something hot and rebellious stir inside me at his words, and I caught my reflection in the window. My hair was a mess of curls that Grant would never approve of, my shoulders were already a little red from the sun, and I looked more like myself than I had in a very long time.

"I'll go," I said, because I wanted to.

"Hell yeah." Maggie grinned and rubbed her hands together. "This is going to be so much fun."

I deserved to have fun.

"All right, let's get you unpacked, then get ready to go find you a cowboy to dance with." Maggie looked genuinely excited about this plan. "I'll run the strawberries by the bakery after. My apartment is right above it, and I can get ready in no time."

"I have no interest in any cowboys. I've sworn them off."

Hunter laughed again, but we both ignored him.

"Me too," Maggie said around her soft laughter. "But then they keep making more cowboys and I keep drinking tequila. It's exhausting."

I laughed, a little of my tension easing, and I decided right then and there that I liked this girl. I liked her enough that I was going back to The Dusty Spur with her when it was the last thing I should do.

Because the last time I'd stepped foot in The Dusty Spur I was still a teenager, and I was drunk on the feel of Colt and the shot of vodka he'd talked one of the men at the table next to us into buying.

But so much had changed since that night.

The neon beer signs of The Dusty Spur belonged to a different lifetime, one where my lips tasted of cherry ChapStick and *him*.

Hunter was right.

I had left cowboy bars behind, but I was tired of letting men like Grant with his control, my father with his disapproving frown, and even Colt Calloway with his broken promises decide who I got to be.

I would walk into that bar tonight and try not to flinch when every head turned. There would be whispers and questions I didn't want to answer, but for the first time in a long time, I couldn't bring myself to care.

I brushed the dirt off my jeans, squared my shoulders, and let the smallest smile curve along my lips as I met Maggie's eyes.

"I can't make any promises on the cowboys but count me in for the tequila."

CHAPTER 4

COLT

The Dusty Spur smelled like spilled beer, stale smoke, and a whole lot of memories I'd rather leave buried.

This place had always been exactly the same, but it was comforting in its predictability.

I leaned back in the worn, creaky chair and let the beer cool my palm, feeling the condensation trickle down my fingers as I tipped it to my lips. I let the alcohol be a welcome reprieve after one hell of a day on the ranch, a day that had kicked my ass harder than I'd admit. But I was grateful for a rare evening to relax. Even if I knew I'd regret it when the sun rose in the morning.

But McCoy had practically begged me to come out after we left my parents', and even though he wasn't blood, he might as well have been. He'd been my best friend since we were kids, and my parents loved him like he was their son. If it weren't for my inability to say no to him, I would've already been in bed by now.

The jukebox in the corner was crooning an old George Strait ballad about a woman who'd left and taken his heart with her, and a group of old men sat at the end of the bar, same as always. The tension in my shoulders was just starting to unwind when I caught sight of Hunter's six-foot-two frame cutting through the small crowd of people on the scuffed-up dance floor.

My brother's jaw was set in the stubborn Calloway way we'd inherited from our father as he plopped into the chair opposite mine with enough force to make the rickety table wobble. The lines etched around his eyes told me his day on the ranch had been every bit as rough as mine.

"What's wrong with you?" I asked, before taking another long drag of my beer.

"Where the hell have you been?" He flipped a coaster between his fingers. The cardboard disk cut through the air with each snap of his wrist, his movements quick and agitated.

"What crawled up your ass?" McCoy leaned forward, his eyes narrowing as he shot a pointed look at my brother, but I wasn't sure Hunter even heard him. His posture was stiff, every muscle wound tight, and it was such a rare display from someone who rarely let anything bother him.

"Cattle don't feed themselves, Hunter." I took another slow sip of my beer as I studied him. "That's where I've been."

His eyes cut back to me, the same shade of brown as our father's. "I'm well aware of that, asshole. Where is your phone?"

"Right here." I pulled it out of my pocket, and sure as shit, I had five missed calls from Hunter. "I didn't realize I was required to check in with you like a damn parole officer."

He leaned back in his chair, and the wood creaked under his weight. "You know, you can be a real dick sometimes."

"Hear, hear," McCoy chimed in, raising his beer in toast and clinking it against mine.

He was an ass, but Reid McCoy was like a brother to us.

Which is why I didn't take offense to the way he laughed at my scowl.

I studied Hunter more closely, the twitch in his jaw, the way he wouldn't meet my eyes now that I was really looking. Something had shaken him, and there weren't many things in this town that could.

"Seriously, what's going on?" I set my beer down, the glass clinking a little too loud against the uneven wood. "You look like you've seen a ghost."

He gave a bitter huff, his eyes still locked on that coaster like it held the answer to whatever the hell was eating him alive. "Might've."

"Quit talking in riddles." My voice came out rougher than I intended, a warning curled beneath the words. "Spit it out."

"I was trying to call you to warn you she'd be here tonight." He looked up then, studying my face, and whatever he saw made him hesitate. Long enough that my stomach twisted. "Blaire's back."

Two words. That's all it took.

Everything inside me went still. My lungs betrayed me, seizing up, and my fingers tensed around the neck of my beer, wishing I could shatter the thing into a million damn pieces.

Blaire Monroe.

It had been a goddamn decade since I saw her last, but she was still carved into my bones like she'd never left.

Back then, this whole town had whispered our names as if they belonged together, but that was a different lifetime.

I leaned back in my chair, crossing my ankle over my knee and trying desperately not to let them see how affected I was by what he'd said. "Didn't realize she planned on coming back."

"I didn't either, but I saw her at June's when I was working on the western fence line," Hunter muttered. "She was already out working in the fields by the time I was done."

I stared straight ahead, jaw locked, while my pulse beat a furious rhythm at the base of my throat. I could picture her too easily. Knees in the dirt. Hair tangled from the wind. Mouth too quick for her own damn good.

"How'd she look?" I hated the question as soon as it left my mouth.

Hunter's face was almost sympathetic. Almost. "She looked good." He cleared his throat. "Hot as hell."

I grunted, tossed back the rest of my beer, and slammed the empty bottle down harder than necessary. "Good to know some things don't change."

He opened his mouth to say something else but froze as his

gaze caught near the entrance of the bar. "Don't say I didn't warn you."

I followed his gaze as the front doors swung open, and there she was. She stepped into The Spur and the neon lights flashed against her fair skin.

Her hair had deepened in color, the curls I remembered smoothed into waves. Every bit of her looked different, but I would know her anywhere.

Before my mind could fully process what was happening, my body had already reacted. My skin buzzed with the memory of her touch, yearning to feel it again, and my heart pounded so hard in my chest that all I could hear was the thundering beat in my ears.

The years she'd been gone had transformed the girl I knew into something far more dangerous. Her legs stretched endlessly beneath those denim shorts, toned and so much longer than I remembered. The soft swell of her hips caught in the neon lights, casting shadows I'd never traced before, highlighting contours on a body I'd once known better than my own land.

She didn't see me at first. She was too busy laughing at something Maggie Dawson said beside her.

"Breathe, Colt," Hunter mumbled under his breath. "Jesus, and you thought *I* looked like I'd seen a ghost."

I managed another breath, slow and heavy, even though it felt like my chest couldn't find the room to expand. "I'm fine."

But I wasn't. Not with her moving through the crowd, her eyes flicking over the room with a quick, practiced sweep. Her fingers absently tucked a strand of her hair behind her ear, revealing the constellation of freckles along her jawline. She smiled gently and tilted her chin as she passed old faces like she didn't know she'd sent the whole damn bar into a slow spin.

And just like that, I was eighteen again—drunk on her laugh, chasing her through fields where time seemed to slip away, desperate to keep up with the way she saw the world. Back then, I thought I'd spend my life chasing her chaos, but then she walked away because I'd told her to. And somehow the world had kept moving on without her.

But time hadn't dulled a damn thing. Not for me.

And now she was back in my town, on land that ran through my blood, and under my skin like she'd never fucking left.

The last time I'd heard her name had been a little over a year ago. June had dropped it into conversation as if it wouldn't tear me apart.

"She's getting married, you know."

I'd merely grunted in response, feigning indifference, and changed the subject so quickly that June hadn't dared bring her up again.

But I agonized over every damn word as I got piss drunk off a bottle of Jack. I'd spent half the night imagining what she'd look like with a white dress wrapped around her body and her curls swept up to reveal the freckles that scattered over the curve of her neck.

I shouldn't have cared, but I couldn't get the picture out of my head. I couldn't shake the thought of some other man slipping a ring onto her finger, getting every part of her I had once believed was mine.

I'd only spent one night looking her up online, but that was enough to tear me in half.

I blinked, trying to clear my head, but I couldn't force myself to look away from her. Instead, my eyes wandered slowly down the line of her arm, past the curve of her waist, until they finally fixed on her left hand. Her slender fingers were wrapped around a glass and completely bare.

There was no ring in sight, only a hint of a tan line circling her fourth finger where one might have been.

I should have felt guilty about the way relief surged through me at the sight of her naked hand, but I didn't.

Maggie leaned in close and whispered something to Blaire, causing her to cover her mouth as laughter fell from her lips. The sound hit me like whiskey, warm, burning, and intoxicating all at once.

She shook her head softly and flashed a smile at the bartender. Her lips moved, probably ordering a drink, and despite the loud music and the space between us, I couldn't look away.

Then she turned her head, her eyes scanning the bar once more, and the collision of us was inevitable.

Her gaze snagged on mine, and I swear the whole goddamn world stilled. The music faded, the crowd disappeared, and for one breath, one single heartbeat, our past and present crashed into each other.

Her lips parted, her smile vanishing, and her brown eyes widened. Her throat worked once, twice, the delicate muscles tensing so hard beneath her freckled skin I could track the movement.

And when our eyes locked again, the pain bleeding through her carefully composed exterior was unmistakable. It cracked across her face like lightning splitting a midnight sky, spreading to the slight quiver of her full bottom lip.

She caught that lip between her teeth until the pink flesh blanched white, and the movement struck me like a hook snagging deep beneath my ribs. It tore through old scar tissue, and a familiar pain climbed up from my gut like wildfire, scorching through my chest before settling into the hollow of my throat.

Because I remembered that look. I had been the one to carve it into her expression so long ago.

Her shoulders stiffened as she lifted her chin and finally released her lip. One blink, and the vulnerability was gone. When her gaze found mine again, it burned with anger that seemed to simmer beneath her skin.

She was fire, and I was fucking drowning in her.

I exhaled slowly, grateful for her anger. It was the only part of her I knew I could handle.

I half expected her to storm over to our table, to put me in my place before I even had a chance to speak, but the Blaire standing at the bar wasn't the same one who'd left. I could still see that recklessness in her eyes, could practically taste her desire to act on it, but she held back.

She took a deep breath, her chest visibly rising and falling before she blinked slowly, as if clearing away the remnants of that girl. She turned back toward Maggie, an easy smile slipping back onto her lips, and she didn't spare me another glance.

But I couldn't take my eyes off her.

The bartender slid shot glasses across the bar, and she didn't hesitate. She gripped the glass overflowing with clear liquid, tipped it back, and swallowed without so much as a flinch. And then she grabbed the next.

She threw it back hard and fast like the liquor could burn the memory of me off her tongue.

Good fucking luck, sweetheart.

I forced myself to look away from her as our server dropped a bucket of beer on our table. I grabbed one, twisted off the cap, and brought it to my lips before McCoy could mutter, "Thanks, Haley."

"You're welcome." She smiled, her eyes meeting mine, and I should have thought about how pretty she was. I should have returned her smile or done anything other than take a swig of my beer and look past her to find Blaire.

I'd known Haley since high school. I'd flirted with her at this very bar where she'd served for years, but that was as far as it had ever gone. She'd have to give me a pass for being an asshole tonight. She didn't deserve it, but it was all I had to offer.

"Can we go ahead and get another bucket?" McCoy asked with a wink that brought Haley's smile back to life.

She shifted her weight to one leg, her stance practically an invitation that would've drawn any man's eye to the curve of her body, but I was too busy glancing back over to the bar. "Anything for you three."

I dropped my gaze to the scuffed toe of my boots, tapping my fingers against my beer bottle as she walked away. "I think I'm going to head out."

"What?" Hunter's brow furrowed as he reached for the bucket, ice clinking as he fished out a beer. "You never come out anymore."

"For good reason," I said, meeting his stare.

"Of course it's for a good reason," McCoy cut in, nudging my knee beneath the table. "I think what Hunter's trying to say is maybe you should finish your beer, stop glaring at the bar, and try to relax."

"Exactly." Hunter shrugged, but I didn't miss the way he tried to hide his smirk. "Plus, there's no way we're letting you walk out of here right now looking like a lovesick puppy over a girl you haven't seen in years."

"Such a good brother." I raised my beer in a salute, and he grinned.

"All I'm saying is that you don't want her to see you leave just because she walked in."

Heat crawled up my neck, settling below my hairline. I knew coming out tonight was a bad idea. I should have been at home. I should have been with Ruby where I belonged.

"She doesn't matter," I lied. "We've got a herd to move in the morning, and then Ruby and I have plans."

McCoy made a scoffing sound, arms crossing as a shit-eating grin stretched across his face. One that made me want to knock his head into the table. "Please. If that was my ex, I'd be on my knees barking like a damn dog. I know you've been staring, but did you actually see her?" He let out a low whistle that turned half the bar in our direction. "She's only gotten hotter with time."

"I fucking hate you both." I drained the rest of my beer while their laughter echoed around me.

Assholes.

Two of my favorite people in the world, but still assholes.

"You love us, and you know it," McCoy said as he grabbed another beer from the bucket and placed it in front of me.

"Do I?" I dragged my thumb across the label but left the bottle untouched. I already felt out of control, and more alcohol would only make the situation worse. "Because I was thinking about giving the ranch hands the day off from cleaning the horse stalls tomorrow. Looks like you two need something to do with your free time."

McCoy rolled his eyes. "Whatever you say, boss."

"Are you ever going to let us start calling you daddy instead of boss?" Hunter batted his eyelashes at me. "You've been running the ranch for over five years now. I think it's about time."

"It's weird for you to have a daddy kink over a man you share a father with," I said.

McCoy chuckled, grinning like the devil. "He has a point." He took a long pull from his beer, then added, "Still, I bet Blaire wouldn't mind calling you daddy."

I shot him a glare. "I swear to God, if you say her name again—"

"Relax," McCoy said, still grinning. "We're not the ones you should be worried about."

He tipped his chin toward the bar, and I followed his gaze to where some wannabe cowboy I didn't recognize leaned against it, far too close to Blaire. His belt buckle caught the light, all shine and no scuffs, and the brim of his hat curved in that perfect factory arc you only get from a box, not rain or sweat or sun.

He leaned in, saying something near her ear, and Blaire shifted back enough to put a little space between them. Her fingers tightened on the empty shot glass in her hand, her eyes narrowing slightly as she studied him.

I clenched my jaw until my molars ached.

"Okay, for real, man. You need to relax," McCoy muttered beside me, his voice dropping to the same low warning tone he used on a spooked horse. His hand clamped over my forearm where the muscle had gone rigid.

My throat locked tight as she tilted her head up to the jackass with an almost shy smile playing on her lips.

"Aw, hell," Hunter groaned, dragging a hand over his face. "This is gonna be bad."

The music shifted to another slow song, and the bastard moved in closer, splaying his hand across her hip like he owned it.

Her spine went rigid. She caught his wrist, pried his fingers off her like she'd done it a hundred times before, then pressed her empty shot glass into his palm with a forced smile. Whatever she said made him chuckle, but he still leaned forward, his face hovering near the curve of her neck like he was breathing her in.

I wanted to get the hell out of here, and I would have if it weren't for the way her eyes found mine over his shoulder.

"Colt," McCoy warned, his grip tightening on my arm. "Don't."

"I'm not doing anything," I muttered, though my eyes never left her.

She smiled up at him again, nodding at whatever bullshit he was feeding her. Then his hand slid back to her hip, his thumb brushing along the hem of her shirt, and her eyes snapped back to mine like they always had, like some part of her still knew I'd be the one to get her out of it.

Something in my chest went tight, old instincts flaring hotter than the alcohol burning in my gut. I shoved my chair back, the legs scraping against the scuffed floor, and I cut through the small crowd without a second thought.

Blaire tracked me as I closed the distance, her lips parting on a sharp inhale. Her eyes darted toward the exit, fingers twitching at her sides like she was calculating the fastest way out.

She said something low to the cowboy, stepping back just enough to pass for polite, but he either didn't notice or didn't give a damn. His hand still hovered over her hip, then slid lower.

Then he took off his hat, spinning it between his fingers before aiming it toward her head like he planned to set it right on top of her auburn hair.

My vision tunneled, and I caught his wrist.

"I wouldn't do that if I were you," I said, low and edged with warning.

"What the hell?" he snarled, yanking against my grip. "Get your hand off me, you son of a bitch."

Up close, I placed him. He was one of the new summer hands over on Warner Ranch. I'd seen him around a few times, and when he looked up to see exactly who he called a son of a bitch, he froze.

Smart.

I released his wrist and stepped closer to Blaire, instinct drawing me in until she had to tilt her chin to meet my gaze. Whiskey brown eyes flecked with gold, same as they'd always been, hit me like a punch to the gut. All those years hadn't dulled a damn thing about them.

She blinked, glanced past me, then back. "What the hell are you doing, Calloway?"

Calloway. That was new. She'd called my brother that plenty of times, but never me. I'd always been Colt, and never in that flat, guarded tone she used now.

"Blaire," I drawled, letting her name roll off my tongue like my spine wasn't locked tight just standing this close.

"Didn't realize this one was yours," the cowboy said, squaring his shoulders like he was trying to look dangerous.

I didn't answer. I was too busy watching her.

Blaire's fingers curled around the edge of the bar, her body edging back an inch. "I'm not his." Each word was clipped, but there was a small tremor in her voice.

The cowboy slid in closer, dipping his head between us as he stuck out a hand. "You're Colt, right?" His breath reeked of whiskey. "You took over Calloway Ranch from your dad."

My neck was tight, but I refused to look over at him. "The one and only."

Blaire scoffed, and it was like looking at the girl I used to know.

"You slumming it tonight?" I asked her as I nodded my head toward him. "Don't you have a fiancé somewhere?"

I glanced around the bar like I was looking for him, though I knew damn well she came here alone. A flicker of something crossed her eyes, pain or maybe regret, before her nostrils flared and a flush crept up her throat.

She leaned in enough for the scent of strawberries with the slightest hint of coconut to hit me, familiar and intoxicating. Her right hand moved over her left, the movement almost unconscious, but my gaze caught on it, drawn to the bare finger she tried to hide.

"Is that why you came over here?" she asked, her voice edged in sarcasm. "To protect the honor of some man you've never met?"

I let out a short, humorless laugh. "Nobody can protect a man from you, Strawberry. I know that better than most."

Her shoulders tightened, and a sharp breath slipped past her lips.

"It's been years, Colt," she said, slightly breathless as her chest rose and fell. "You don't know shit about me anymore."

I stepped in until there was no space left, the brim of my hat casting her face in shadow. I could still feel the cowboy lingering nearby, watching like an idiot.

"I know you, Blaire," I murmured, my voice low and gritty. "It doesn't matter how hard I tried to forget."

Her hands curled into fists before loosening again. Her right hand rose an inch before she forced it back down, and I almost wished she'd slap me.

It would've been easier than this slow, steady burn that was eating me alive.

Blaire lifted her chin, her throat working as she swallowed, then she took a step back, but all it did was make me want to close the distance.

"Relax, Calloway." Her smile was pure sugar laced with poison. "Wouldn't want you straining yourself. Take your hero complex elsewhere. I'm perfectly fine over here."

"Calloway, really?" I dragged my hand over my jaw, feeling the rough scratch of stubble. "Did you forget my name that easily? I figured it'd take you longer to forget about me. Or is that how you handled your fiancé too?"

Her eyes widened, pain flickering once more before she smothered it, and I watched the spark of the Blaire I knew fade right in front of me. I wished I could take back every damn word I'd just said.

"Don't flatter yourself." The corners of her mouth lifted back into a smile, but it never touched her eyes. "You're not that hard to forget."

We both knew that was a lie, but if she wanted to pretend, I'd let her.

"Keep tellin' yourself that, Strawberry." I tipped my hat, flashing her the laziest grin I could manage. "Whatever helps you sleep at night."

"Don't call me that," she snapped, a real fire sparking in her eyes for the first time since she walked in.

I held her gaze, memorizing every shift in her expression and every subtle change that the years had caused before I forced myself to look away. The cowboy was still there, still waiting. I should have told him she was all his. I should have walked away, let them dance, and let her leave this bar with him and make whatever mistakes she wanted.

But my mouth had other plans. "Put your hands on her again, and I'll fucking break them."

I watched fear fill his eyes. His gaze flicked back and forth between me and Blaire before it settled back on me. Then I tipped my hat at him before I walked away.

I didn't look back. I didn't have to. I could feel her eyes on me, her anger burning beneath my skin as I made my way back to my table.

If I wasn't careful, Blaire Monroe was gonna finish what she started all those years ago, and there'd be nothing left of me when she did.

CHAPTER 5
BLAIRE

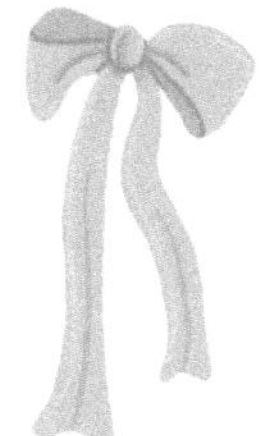

I should've left.

The moment I walked into this bar and felt the weight of his stare, I should've run right back to my grandmother's house.

Instead, I was still leaning against the bar, staring down at yet another empty shot of tequila.

Colt Calloway.

My pulse hadn't settled since the moment our eyes met, and my skin still prickled where his gaze had touched it. He had mapped out every inch of me in those few minutes, sliding past my defenses and noting every way I'd changed.

He didn't have to say a word. His eyes tracked over me, and I became hyperaware of my hair, my shorts, the flush in my cheeks.

Did he see it? The way I'd traded pieces of myself until I barely recognized the woman staring back at me?

I tossed back the shot, the burn not nearly enough to erase the sound of his voice or the way my stomach had flipped when he called me Strawberry.

I had practically lived a lifetime without him, yet he still had the power to unravel me completely.

I was more affected by him than I had ever been with Grant.

If Grant had been here, he wouldn't have told that cowboy he would break his hands if he touched me again.

But he would have had plenty to say to me.

He wouldn't have come over here if you didn't dress like such a whore.

You wanted him to hit on you, didn't you? Did you want him to fuck you, too?

His accusations echoed in my mind like a record stuck on repeat, each play making them harder to dismiss as the lies they were. He had trained my doubt to surge forward before anything else could.

I raised my hand and motioned for the bartender to bring me another.

I glanced toward the door and considered slipping out, but then Maggie leaned closer to me, her shoulder bumping into mine. "You okay?"

The urge to tell her the truth was overwhelming. I'd only known Maggie for a few hours, but being around her tonight made me realize just how lonely I'd been. In Raleigh, I didn't have my own friends. Only Grant's. There was no one for me to call when everything happened, no one to turn to. "I'm fine."

"Are you sure?" She glanced over my shoulder, and I knew exactly where she was looking without turning around. "That was —" She motioned her hand back and forth between me and the space Colt had been. "—intense."

"It's history." I shrugged as the bartender slipped another shot in front of me. "History that I'd rather not bring back up."

"So you've been caught up with a Calloway?" She was still looking over my shoulder, and I wondered if she was looking at Colt or Hunter.

"Unfortunately." I finally spared a glance in their direction, and all three of them were looking at us. Colt, Hunter, and McCoy had been inseparable when we were kids, and there was a time when I wanted nothing more than to be around all of them.

It didn't matter that McCoy wasn't a Calloway brother by

blood. He had been one of them for as long as I could remember. Ever since his mother passed away.

"You ever wonder what it would've been like if you stayed?" Maggie's voice was soft, but her words cut through me.

"There isn't enough alcohol in this bar for that conversation." I lifted my next shot and tapped it against hers. I was already feeling tipsy, but it wasn't enough.

Maggie grinned before she lifted her own and threw it back. I followed suit, and this time I winced as the burn hit my throat.

I wiped my mouth with the back of my hand, and Maggie's gaze slid away from me and back to them. "So what about you? What's going on with you and Hunter?"

She jolted as if my question shocked her. "What? There's nothing going on there."

"Be for real." I laughed and turned until I could press my back against the bar. "You two had so much tension on June's porch I started sweating a little."

She scoffed, but it was weak. "Hunter and I are friends."

"And why is that?" I glanced in Hunter's direction, careful not to look at Colt. His fingers toyed with the label on his beer bottle, but it was unmistakable where his focus was. "He's not looking at you like you're friends."

"Well, he should. Considering he's my sister's ex."

"Oh, shit." The way he was looking at her was like he wanted to eat her alive. Not like a man who used to date her sister.

"Yeah." She shook her head. "Hunter Calloway is off-limits. It doesn't matter that he's insanely hot or charming or has the best ass in the state."

I wanted to ask more, but I didn't. Fair was fair. I didn't want to talk about my history, so I had no right to ask about hers. She fiddled with the ring on her pointer finger, twisting it round and round.

"Fuck the Calloway brothers." I grinned at her, feeling the tequila's warmth in my veins. "They are not worth all this head-space we're giving them."

"That's so true," she laughed, "but it's also hard when they won't quit staring at us."

I turned back to see them, and my eyes locked with Colt's. I thought he'd look away once he realized I caught him staring, but he didn't. Instead, he let his gaze travel over me slowly, lingering at my throat where my pulse hammered traitorously beneath my skin, then lower still, leaving a trail of heat that made me forget how to breathe. The corner of his mouth lifted in a knowing half-smile that said he remembered exactly how my body responded to him.

"Should we leave? Maybe this was a bad idea," Maggie asked, but I couldn't tear my eyes away from Colt's challenge. The tequila had turned my blood warm and reckless, and I found myself shaking my head.

"We're not leaving." I grabbed Maggie's hand in mine before I pushed off the bar. "Come on."

"Where are we going?" she asked as her laughter trailed behind us.

"If they're going to stare at us all night, we might as well go over there." I sounded braver than I felt, but my adrenaline surged with each step we took toward their table. Especially when Colt's gaze lifted to mine again, and I saw surprise flicker in his eyes.

The three of them looked untouchable sitting there. Hunter leaned back in his chair, his eyes tracking Maggie. McCoy's easy grin made him look too damn charming, and Colt looked like a storm. The sun had browned his throat where his collar opened, and I wondered if the rest of his skin was that tanned.

I almost turned back, but I didn't.

Colt lifted his chin, his gaze skimming over my face, and my pulse thundered as I forced a smile and dropped into the chair beside him.

"These seats taken?"

"Apparently they are now," McCoy drawled with a grin as he leaned forward and placed his elbows on the table. He looked up at Maggie before gesturing toward the empty chair. "By all means."

Maggie slid in beside me, her chair scraping against the floor as she pulled it closer until our shoulders touched. She flashed me a look, like she couldn't believe we were really doing this, but I smiled at her, letting the tequila fuel me.

"To what do we owe this pleasure?" McCoy's eyes flicked toward Colt before settling back on me. "Never thought I'd see the day you'd come back to Willow Grove."

"I needed a bit of fresh air." I crossed my arms and raised my chin. "Plus, June needs help with the farm."

Colt's scoff cut through the air, and my gaze snapped to his.

"Is there a problem?" I asked, plucking a beer from their ice bucket at the center of the table. I held his gaze as I twisted off the top and brought the bottle to my lips, the cold liquid sliding down my throat while a muscle in his jaw ticked.

"I just can't imagine that June's farm is really what brought you back." He watched me as if he was sizing up every part of me. "She's been needing help for years. Didn't see you rushing home then."

I flinched, his words hitting their mark, and my guilt rushed through me. "Well, I'm here now."

"That you are." Colt nodded, and the way he watched me made me want to crawl out of my skin.

"How long are you staying, Blaire?" McCoy asked, and even though his question was harmless, my chest tightened.

"I'm not sure yet. As long as June needs me." I lifted my chin, and I knew I shouldn't have said the next words before they even left my lips. "Why? Are any of you planning to tell me to leave like last time?"

McCoy let a curse slip past his lips, and Hunter practically choked on his beer. But Colt hardly looked affected by my words or by me.

"I guess that depends." Colt watched me carefully.

"On what, exactly?" I leaned forward, closer to him, and I took another slow sip of my beer, swallowing the words burning on my tongue.

Maggie's knee pressed hard against mine beneath the table, but all I could feel was the weight of Colt's gaze.

"Is your fiancé going to be joining you, or did you leave him back in the city?" Colt cocked his head slightly, one corner of his mouth lifting, but his fingers tapped against the table as he studied my face.

Heat crept up my neck as I watched that calculated look in his eyes. He was baiting me—the same push and pull that used to light me up and set me off.

My fingers shook around my beer as I swallowed the urge to snap back at him. I needed to lay out the truth now, so he'd stop looking at me like he knew all my secrets.

"What's your obsession with that?" I watched him carefully. "Are you dying for me to tell you I'm no longer engaged?"

His smirk faltered, the cocky edge dissolving into something softer, more vulnerable. I couldn't stop looking at the curve of his lips. His bottom one was fuller than the top, and they parted enough to reveal the edge of his teeth. The bar seemed to fade away until I could focus on nothing else. But then Hunter's voice cut through.

"You two still fight like an old married couple." Hunter laughed, and I jerked my gaze away from Colt's mouth. "It's like you never left."

"Except I did leave."

"And we were never a couple," Colt chimed in, and his words affected me far more than they should've.

I could still feel the phantom weight of his hands tangled in my hair as we lay beneath the stars, still hear the words he'd breathed against my collarbone when he thought I was asleep. The memory of his gaze, tender and reverent like I was something precious, burned behind my eyelids. Whatever label he wanted to slap on it now couldn't erase what we'd been.

I had been in love with him, and this whole town had called me his girl.

Hunter snorted. "Not a couple? Buddy, you carved y'all's

initials in the tree by Mom and Dad's house. Y'all were joined at the hip from junior year through the summer she left."

"Honestly, even before then," McCoy muttered into his beer.

Hunter chuckled as he reached for a beer out of the ice bucket, twisting the top off and sliding it in front of Maggie without a word.

"I think I forgot how insufferable y'all are," I shot back, reaching for my beer. The bottle was lighter than I expected, and the fizz went down smoother than it should have. My limbs felt loose and my head a little floaty.

"Insufferable is generous for these three," Maggie teased as she leaned against me. "I'm not sure what the word for them is."

"Hey." Hunter pouted, his gaze flicking between me and Maggie before it finally landed on her. "I'm not that bad."

"It's a group project kind of thing." I twirled my finger in a circle, motioning among the three of them. "It doesn't matter how fun you are, Hunter. You all have been a group for a long time, and you're evaluated on your group's performance."

McCoy laughed, and even Colt's mouth twitched like he was trying not to smile.

"Well, maybe I should join y'all's group instead." Hunter moved his chair closer to Maggie's, but she quickly raised her foot, pressing her boot against his seat between his legs to stop him.

"We're currently closed to new members." Maggie grinned, and Hunter pressed his hand to his chest as if she'd wounded him.

"You two met today."

"Right." Maggie nodded. "And now we're closed."

I laughed as another round of beers appeared. I blinked up at the girl I knew from high school. "Hi, Haley."

"Blaire! Wow." Haley looked me over. "How are you?"

"I'm good. How are you?"

"Good." She nodded, but then she turned in Colt's direction and lingered.

I reached for another beer, letting the alcohol ease my tension as the others started talking. Hunter and Maggie teased one another while McCoy threw in comments here and there that had me laughing.

Colt said nothing, but his silence felt louder than the laughter around us. I tried my hardest not to look in his direction, staring at my beer label until the edges frayed beneath my fingernail. His cologne drifted across the table every time he shifted in his seat, and I swore I could feel the heat radiating from his body even though he sat just beyond arm's reach.

By the time I finished my beer, the room was hazy, the music was too loud, and my skin was flushed warm.

That's when Colt stood. His chair scraped back, and his shadow fell over me. He plucked the bottle from my hand and set it firmly on the table.

I tipped my chin up to look at him. "What if I wasn't done with that?"

"You're done." His voice was low and final, and his eyes lingered on my mouth long enough to make me wet my lips with my tongue. "Come on. I'm taking you and Maggie home."

"Maggie drove," I argued, leaning back farther in my seat, like maybe that small amount of distance would keep him from noticing how fast my pulse was beating.

"And she's had too much to drink." His gaze slid to my friend before landing right back on me. "You both have."

I folded my arms across my chest, the wooden chair back pressing into my spine as I tilted my face up to meet his gaze. "I don't need a babysitter, Colt."

"Are we back to Colt now?" He leaned closer, one hand resting on the back of my chair and the other bracing against the table in front of me. "Are we done with the formalities?"

Hunter whistled low. "Man, some things never change."

"Shut up, Hunter." Colt didn't even look his way. His knuckles grazed my shoulder absently, and heat bloomed beneath my skin, a slow burn that traveled down my spine and pooled low in my belly.

My body reacted to him before my brain could catch up, years of muscle memory responding to the way his focus was locked entirely on me, his body hovering so close to mine that I caught the faint scent of leather.

"I'm not ready to go."

"You've had enough." His words came softer, but they held an edge of command that sent a shiver down my spine. "I've got work on the ranch in the morning, and I'm not leaving you two here without a ride."

"I can handle myself." I let my gaze roam over his face and that stupid, slutty mustache that he didn't have before. It was a mustache that turned a smart, sensible woman into a fool. "You realize I've been doing just that since I left, right?"

"I'm well aware, Blaire." His gaze dropped to my mouth for the briefest second before locking on mine again. "But you're back in my town now, and I'm not leaving you here while you're drunk and every other man in this bar can't keep their eyes off you."

"Maybe I like their attention."

His jaw flexed, a muscle ticking in his cheek. He leaned in closer, his knuckles brushing against my bare skin, deliberate this time. "Is attention what you're looking for?" His voice was low and rough. "You know you can always tell me what it is you need."

Heat shot through me, my pulse stuttering, and I sucked in a sharp breath as memories crashed over me.

"Get up, Blaire." His mouth curved into a dangerous smile that made my stomach ache in a way it hadn't in a very long time. "Or I'll throw you over my shoulder and carry you out of this place. Your choice. Do you want the whole town talking about how I carried you out of here tomorrow?"

"Kiss my ass, cowboy." I held his stare, willing myself not to move, not to give him the satisfaction. But he smiled as his fingers ghosted over my skin, something in his expression told me he wasn't bluffing. The Colt I used to know would do exactly as he threatened, because protecting me had always been the one thing he took too seriously.

With a deep exhale, I leaned forward, closing the distance between us until I could feel his warm breath against my lips. "Fine, but only because I want Maggie to get home safely."

Colt's laugh was low and far too smug as he stepped back enough to let me stand. I grabbed Maggie's hand, pulling her to her feet as she giggled, and Colt jerked his chin toward the exit.

"You good?" he asked McCoy and Hunter.

"Yeah," McCoy said, gaze flicking between us. "Good night, ladies."

"I'm coming with you." Hunter threw down some cash on the table before standing and trailing after us.

Colt's hand hovered over the small of my back as he guided us toward the door, and even though he didn't touch me, I could feel myself burning beneath his hand.

I should've pulled away. Instead, I foolishly let the whole bar watch me walk out with Colt Calloway.

CHAPTER 6
BLAIRE

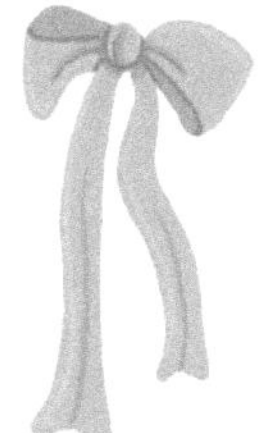

June's farmhouse used to be filled with the sound of laughter.

Every morning, June would drop the needle on vinyl, and Dolly Parton's voice would pour up the stairs, seeping under my door until the sound forced me to burrow deeper under my blankets.

But my mama would always appear shortly after the music started, singing off-key, and finding my ankles beneath the covers. She'd tug until the morning light washed over my face, and I'd play possum until her fingers moved to my ribs, turning my pretend sleep into helpless giggles.

Then up I'd go, eyes still crusted with sleep and hair a mess of curls, until my bare feet balanced on the tops of hers. She'd spin me in circles across the worn floors until I was dizzy and happiness bubbled up from my belly.

But that had been years ago. Those mornings had unraveled into an emptiness, no matter how hard June tried not to let them.

It was laughter that reached me now, high-pitched and sweet, and it felt so foreign I thought I might be dreaming. But then the pounding in my head jolted me back to reality—to this bed, this room, and the string of bad decisions I'd made last night.

A groan passed my lips as I buried my face into my pillow,

trying to escape the sunlight flooding my old bedroom and the rush of memories from the night before. The Dusty Spur had been a mistake. I knew it was a risk that Colt would be there, and if I was being honest with myself, there was a small, foolish part of me that had hoped he would be.

That part of me had been desperate to see how much he'd changed and what parts of him had stayed the same. But Colt was still smug, bossy, and desire still hung between us.

My phone buzzed on my dresser, and I quickly grabbed it and flipped it over.

Maggie: You alive?

I smiled as I squinted at the screen and typed out a message.

Blaire: Barely. You?

Her next message was almost instant.

Maggie: It's going to be a day. Come by the bakery. I'll fill you up on coffee and sweets.

Blaire: You know the way to my heart already.

Colt had insisted he take me and Maggie home last night, and I should have fought against him instead of letting my stomach flip when he opened the passenger door and helped me climb into his truck. He had said little on the drive, just gripped the wheel with those rough, calloused hands while I tried not to notice his forearm flexing every time he glanced my way.

We'd dropped Maggie off first, and I'd watched as Hunter walked her to her door. The silence in the truck grew thick as Colt's jaw stayed clenched and his eyes fixed on the road ahead. I almost wished he'd snap at me, give me something to push back against. Instead, I sat drowning in the scent of him while liquor-soaked memories I'd spent years burying rose to the surface.

When we finally pulled into June's driveway, Colt put the truck in park but let the engine idle. I could feel his stare as I gathered my things, and then I cursed under my breath when his door creaked open.

I opened my door before he could get to it, and he scowled as I climbed out and closed it softly. All the lights were off in June's house except for the porch light I knew she'd left on for me, and I didn't speak to Colt as I made my way toward the house.

Colt stood at the bottom of the stairs, and I paused halfway to the door. The world shifted ever so slightly on its axis before, "Thank you for the ride," slipped out.

His eyes glinted beneath the porch light, searching in a way that made my skin prickle. "You good, Strawberry?" The nickname rolled off his tongue, slow as honey, and I hated the way it melted straight down my spine.

That was the trouble with nostalgia. My mind could recall every bit of hurt that he'd ever caused, but my body only remembered the brush of his fingertips, how they'd traced me as if I was territory he'd once claimed, how they'd left trails of heat I could still feel years later.

I should have hated him but standing in the porch light with him looking up at me like that, his focus tracing over the hollow of my throat and down the curve of my hips, made the hate slip through my fingers so easily.

Maybe that's why, when I finally climbed into bed after peeling off my bar-tinged clothes, my skin still burned with an old, intimate ache of him.

A fresh peal of laughter drifted up the stairs, pulling me from my thoughts, and I frowned. I pushed up on my elbows as my hangover pulsed behind my eyes. That wasn't June's laugh. Hers was a smoky rasp, not this soft giggle chased by the patter of little feet.

My head throbbed as I dragged myself out of bed and grabbed a T-shirt from the floor, yanking it over my head before stumbling into a pair of shorts and out into the hallway. My mouth was dry, and I could smell traces of the night before clinging to my skin.

I let one hand trail over the faded wallpaper as I peered down the stairwell, but I saw no one. I climbed down the stairs with the smell of biscuits and bacon pulling me forward, and I followed the sounds of laughter into the kitchen. I nearly tripped over a bright pink sneaker, but when I looked up, I saw her.

A little girl stood on one of my grandma's kitchen chairs near the stove, and she had a spoon dripping with a heaping spoonful of strawberry jam.

"Well, put it on the biscuit before you drop it all over the floor. You know I hate to mop." June didn't look up from where she stood, a small knife in one hand as she hulled a strawberry before grabbing another from the flat in front of her.

The girl couldn't have been more than five years old, with dark brown hair pulled back in a lopsided ponytail. Wisps had escaped to frame her round face, and white puffs of flour coated the strands.

Freckles dusted across her cheeks and smears of strawberry jam clung to the corners of her mouth. She leaned forward as she balanced the wobbling, ruby-red mountain of jam on her spoon.

"Don't make a mess, Ruby," June cautioned before she finally noticed me. "Look who finally rolled out of bed."

The little girl, Ruby, looked up at me then, and the moment her blue eyes met mine, blue eyes that were so achingly familiar, the ground tilted beneath me. Those eyes, framed by dark lashes that matched her messy ponytail, widened with curiosity and her fair cheeks flushed pink as she took me in.

June set her knife down on the scarred butcher block as she turned to the girl, but I barely registered it. All I could do was stare at the child, at the impossible riot of recognition as Colt's eyes blinked back at me from that tiny, heart-shaped face.

I must have been standing there too long because June cleared her throat and slid a coffee cup across the island to me. I pulled my eyes away from the girl, and I gripped the mug in my trembling hands and forced myself to take a sip.

The jam finally tumbled from her spoon, slopping onto the biscuit, and Ruby grinned, dimples flashing in her cheeks mirroring the pair I'd spent years trying to forget on Colt's face.

"Perfect," June said, her posture softening a fraction. "Now take it over to the table so you can eat."

Ruby clambered down from the chair, and June handed her the plate. She moved to the table, glancing over her shoulder at me before plopping into the seat I'd sat in my whole life.

June slid me a plate with two biscuits and a stack of crispy bacon. "Eat," she commanded with a tilt of her chin toward the table.

Before I could protest, she'd already turned back to her strawberries, leaving me no choice but to face Ruby, who was cramming half a biscuit into her tiny mouth.

I moved to the table and took the seat across from her. She held the biscuit in both hands, and she didn't look away from me as she took another giant bite.

There was only one question on my mind as we watched each other, and it blared so loud I was sure June could hear it rattling between my ears. But her back was still to us as she rinsed her hands in the sink, humming to herself.

Ruby licked the last of the jam from her fingers, then cocked her head at me. "Are you Ms. June's granddaughter?"

"Yes." I nodded, tearing off a small piece of bacon. "I'm Blaire."

Ruby blinked slowly, as if weighing my answer. "But you're big." Her dark eyebrows scrunched together.

"Never said she was little, Ruby. Just that she was my granddaughter," June called over her shoulder as she twisted the faucet handle.

"This blows." Ruby huffed, folding her little arms tight across her chest.

I nearly inhaled my bacon. "What—"

"Ruby Louise." June's voice cut through before I could finish. "Your uncles need to have their mouths washed out with soap."

"They told me I could say that." Her blue eyes went round as she glanced toward my grandmother.

Ruby Louise.

"Your middle name is Louise?" I asked, my heart racing. The only Louise I'd ever known was Colt and Hunter's mother. Everyone called her Lou, except their father whenever he was trying to sweet talk her into something.

Ruby nodded as she looked back and forth between me and June. "After my nana. Daddy says I'm named after the prettiest girl in the world." She paused, dimples deepening. "But now I'm the prettiest."

Her words hung in the air, and I shot a look at June, who suddenly found something fascinating about the strawberry she was turning over in her fingers, refusing to meet my gaze, though I knew she could feel it burning into her.

I forced a shaky laugh, my pulse thundering in my ears. "And who's your daddy, Ruby?"

She beamed, as if it was the easiest answer in the world. "Colt Calloway."

Heat flared hot and fast in my chest, searing through my ribs until I could barely breathe. How dare he look at me the way he had last night, eyes hungry with memories and want, when all this time he'd been building a life?

A family.

My breath caught in my throat as the room seemed to tilt. The coffee mug trembled in my hands, liquid sloshing dangerously close to the rim. Of course I had been building a life too, *but he had a daughter.*

He had a daughter with someone else.

I tried to picture him as a father—tying her little pink sneakers, pulling her hair into the sloppy ponytail, wiping jam from the corners of her mouth with the same calloused fingers I used to trace with my own.

The image tore through me.

There had been a time, there had been so many years, when I'd imagined it would be us. His hand on my belly. His laugh chasing through a house filled with our children.

Now I sat drowning in the blue of Ruby's eyes, in the future that would never be mine. The dreams I thought I'd buried beneath years and miles clawed their way back up just to gut me.

And the cruelest part was that the life I had pictured for us still fit him so perfectly.

He was living the life I had always wanted while I'd spent years with a man whose touch never once made me imagine the swell of my belly or whose eye color our children would have.

"Do you know my daddy?" Ruby's voice was so sweet, so trusting.

I cleared my throat, forcing a smile. "Yeah. I've known your dad a long time."

Her eyes lit up. "Are you friends?"

"Ah." I tilted my head from side to side. "I wouldn't exactly say that."

"They used to be," June cut in, her voice too bright. "The two of them were inseparable."

Ruby bounced up onto her knees in the chair, her eyes wide. "Really?"

I shook my head. "That was a lifetime ago."

June slid a bowl of hulled strawberries onto the counter. "Colt is working this morning, and I thought you might want to take Ruby down to the lake for a swim. The water should be perfect today."

My head snapped toward her so fast pain lanced through my temples. "What?"

Ruby clapped her hands together, biscuit crumbs scattering across the table. "Yes, please!"

"Ruby had a sleepover with her grandparents last night, but today is my turn with my girl. Lou said she was up before sunrise and already talking about the lake." *My girl.* A girl June had never told me about because I'd always shut her down when it came to talking about Colt.

June walked to the table, her weathered hand smoothing Ruby's wild flyaways before she leaned down to press her lips against the crown of her head. Then she straightened, fixing me with a glare I'd known since childhood.

It was on the tip of my tongue to ask where her mother was, but I bit it back, swallowing hard. I had no right. I had no business trying to picture the woman who stood where I once thought I'd be.

"I don't think that's a good idea." I shook my head softly, trying to think of what to say without upsetting her.

"Go get washed up," June spoke softly to Ruby, and the girl

darted off to the sink before dragging a chair across the floor so she could reach the faucet.

June moved closer, her words low and meant only for me. "She's a good girl," she said, her eyes softening as they followed Ruby. "It's been a tough couple years. Lots of changes."

Her gaze locked on mine, and I felt the weight of it settle over me.

"She's Colt's daughter," I said the only thing I knew to say, the only thing I needed to. "Why didn't you tell me?"

June's mouth pressed into a thin line. "Like you would have listened? I've tried to tell you a million things about that boy over the years, but every time I said his name, you shut it down. You told me you didn't want to hear about his life here."

Shame crawled up my neck. It was true.

"She needs...kindness." June glanced over at Ruby before looking back at me.

I swallowed, my throat tight. I was so damn angry. Not with Ruby, but with the part of myself that still wanted what I'd buried. I was irrationally angry with June for not telling me, even when I'd made it impossible for her to do so. "And you think I'm the one to give it to her?"

"I think you're the one who's here." June's voice was firm again, but there was a glint of something behind it. "She was begging Colt to take her swimming when he dropped her off this morning, but that man has been buried in work at the ranch. Take her down to the lake. It'll do you both some good."

The lake where I'd spent my summers with Colt, where I'd given him every part of me when I still believed I'd always be his.

I wanted to protest, to remind her exactly why this was a terrible idea, but then Ruby came skipping back to the table, pony-tail bouncing. And when she looked up at me with those wide blue eyes, Colt's eyes, the words died in my throat.

"Are we going swimming?" she asked, her voice so hopeful.

I forced a smile and prayed she couldn't see the way my chest ached when I looked at her. "Well, Ruby. It looks like we don't have any other choice."

CHAPTER 7

COLT

I pulled up June's drive and killed the engine. My truck ticked and popped as I sat there with my pulse drumming against my temples.

I came to June's so often I could navigate her land with my eyes closed, but today I couldn't seem to make myself get out of the truck. June had been helping with Ruby for the last two years, stepping in when Dad's heart attack forced Mom to take over his care and me to take on even more responsibility at the ranch.

Turns out, it really does take a village to raise a kid. Between June, my parents, Hunter, and McCoy, we'd figured out something that worked. Most days, anyway.

But I still went to bed most nights feeling like I was letting my little girl down.

I groaned as I climbed from my truck, my body aching and stiff. I flexed my hands, working out the pain in my knuckles.

I walked up the porch steps and paused at the screen door. I'd long ago stopped knocking on June's weathered, blue front door, so used to following after Ruby who ran barefoot into her house without so much as an announcement that we were here.

Today, though, I knocked.

I'd been nervous as hell when I dropped Ruby off this

morning too, knowing Blaire would be here, and I was still anxious as I shifted my weight from one boot to the other while June's voice floated from somewhere inside.

"One second!"

The day was already fading, the golden light of the sun touching every bit of the surrounding land, and I leaned back against the rail as I took it in. This town and my family's ranch lying beyond that fence line, it was all I had ever known. It was all I'd ever wanted.

Besides her.

I'd always known taking over the ranch would be my duty, but it had never once felt like a hardship. My parents had blessed us with this land, with this life, and I knew in my gut that I was made to do this.

Dad had poured his soul into this dirt, and now it was bleeding me dry too. We'd always known it would be mine and Hunter's one day, a thousand acres of responsibility I both craved and resented coming at me far faster than I'd ever expected.

June swung the door open, half her silver-streaked hair escaping the twin braids she always wore, and her smile was wider than normal. The scent of something warm and sweet wafted out with her.

"Well, ain't you a sight," she said, eyeing me up and down, her gaze stopping on my mud-caked boots. "Rough day?"

"You could say that." I crossed my arms over my chest, my heart still hammering against my ribs, and nodded toward the door. Part of me wanted to scoop Ruby up and disappear in my truck until the memory of last night blurred into nothing. But another part, the part that had my palms sweating and a hard pull under my ribs, wanted to barrel past June and tear through every room in this house until I found Blaire. All day her face had haunted me, the way her lips had parted slightly when our eyes met, and how I'd nearly lost my mind fighting the urge to close the distance between us. "Where's my girl?"

June's grin only widened. "Which one?" she asked, her voice

teasing as she leaned against the doorframe, hands resting on her hips.

"Very funny," I shot back, and forced myself to take a breath, trying to keep my voice steady. "Where's Ruby?"

"We made you a strawberry shortcake," June announced, turning on her heel and letting the screen door bang shut behind her.

I knocked my boots against the steps before following her inside, where the warm scent of vanilla and sugar enveloped me. It smelled like my childhood, and I couldn't help thinking about racing Blaire through this doorway whenever June would call out that she'd been baking and coming up with a new creation with her mountains of strawberries.

June emerged from the kitchen holding a white bakery box. "Thought y'all might enjoy this after dinner. Ruby helped for about ten minutes, right until Blaire whipped out the sunscreen, then I lost my little assistant before the timer went off."

She handed me the box, her hands lingering over mine. "She's down at the lake. They've been there all afternoon." June's gaze settled on my face, and I swear the woman could see straight through me.

"What?" My grip tightened around the box at the thought of Ruby with Blaire.

I owed June and half this town a debt I could never repay for stepping in when Ruby needed someone steady in her life, someone to fill the gaps I couldn't seem to close no matter how hard I tried. But Blaire wasn't part of that arrangement. She'd never been part of the plan.

Not for a long time.

Blaire had once been my world, but that was Ruby now. My daughter was the only light I had some days, the only reason to drag myself out of bed when the weight of the ranch and everything else felt like it was going to crush me.

The thought of Blaire being back in my world, being anywhere near Ruby, made something sharp and primal rear up inside me. I feared anything that might ruin the bit of steadiness I'd built for my girl.

I tried to imagine the moment she found out I had a daughter. Had she already known? Did June tell her the news over the phone like she had with me about Blaire's engagement?

I'd spent years building up a wall between the moment I pushed her away and the world she lived in. Almost everything I knew about her had come from June or from seeing her on the news with her father.

"Ruby's been wanting to swim all day, and I'm too old for it." June huffed, and guilt settled in my chest. "She talked Blaire right into it, though."

June's eyes met mine with a look that was half apology, half challenge. Like she was daring me to say what I was really thinking, but there wasn't a chance in hell.

"She get anything to eat?" I asked, rocking back on my heels as my eyes scanned over her living room.

"Oh, for heaven's sake," June rolled her eyes. "No, Colt. I starved her."

A laugh escaped me as I rolled my shoulders, the tightness refusing to budge.

"What kind of bonus grandma do you take me for?" June crossed her arms, one eyebrow raised.

"I appreciate you, June. Don't know what we'd do without you."

"Damn straight," she huffed, and I couldn't help but chuckle.

"I'm going to head down there and get her." I took a step back, boots scraping against her floorboards as I headed for the door. "I'll probably have to wrangle her out of the water."

"Good luck!" June chuckled as she called after me, her voice fading behind the slam of the screen door. I was already striding across the yard, reaching through my passenger side window to set the cake down on the seat.

I glanced back at the tailgate of my truck, and memories of Blaire and me stretched out together on a different one slammed into me. I had tucked her head against my shoulder, and we'd talked about everything we wanted out of life like it was already ours. She'd laughed as she imagined a little girl with her curls and my eyes, a boy with dark hair and my stubborn streak. I'd listened to every word, clung to them and carved those dreams into plans of my own.

Ruby wasn't that dream. She was something else entirely. She was my new dream, with my dark hair and blue eyes. She was better than anything I'd ever pictured, better than I deserved, and some days, I'd catch myself watching her sleep and feel a love so fierce that it lit me up.

But still, my chest ached with the thought of what could have been if Blaire had been the one cradling Ruby on her hip, teaching her to braid her hair like June's. But that wasn't Ruby's reality, and I'd be damned if I let anyone, especially Blaire Monroe, breeze through my daughter's world only to vanish again.

Not after everything she'd already been through.

I started across the field, my worn leather boots sinking into the ground that was still soft and yielding from the rain we'd had earlier in the week. The late afternoon sun hung low in the sky and cast long shadows through the tall grass that brushed across my jeans.

June's property was much smaller than the sprawling acres of the Calloway Ranch, but it was no less breathtaking. Both our lands butted up to the edge of Willow Lake with twin weathered docks that had stood beside one another since before I was born. When I looked to the left, my gaze swept over June's pride: row after row of strawberry fields, the plants dotted with white blossoms and ripening fruit that peeked through the green leaves.

June was our only neighbor for miles, nothing but rolling hills, the wide lake, and open sky between us and town, and I'd always liked it that way. I loved the vastness of it all, the quiet.

A cluster of ancient oak trees marked the boundary of June's property, their gnarled branches reaching toward the water. The leaves rustled gently in the breeze, and the closer I got, the tighter everything cinched under my ribs, each step heavier than the last, like my body already knew what was waiting for me beyond those trees.

But then I heard it.

Ruby's laughter reached me first, that bubbling, unfiltered joy that always loosened something in my chest. But then it mingled with another, a sound I hadn't allowed myself to think about in years.

I slowed as I broke through the cover of the trees and saw them both at the end of the dock. Blaire sat in the sunlight, her bare feet skimming the water's surface, and Ruby clung to her calves, half submerged, kicking up a storm of tiny splashes behind her.

Blaire lifted her legs, and Ruby rose from the lake like a giggling fish on a line before dropping back with a splash and a delighted shriek. Blaire was facing away from me, but I could make out her grin before she gently swept wet strands of hair from my daughter's forehead.

I steadied myself against the nearest tree, feeling the rough bark dig into my palm, and I watched them for a long moment. Ruby whispered something, and Blaire's head tipped back in laughter. Ruby pressed closer to her, and the muscles in my jaw locked tight as I listened, taking another step forward.

"We should race!" Ruby giggled.

"You swim like a fish." Blaire snorted as she tossed her hair over her shoulder. Her skin glistened as lake water trailed down her back, and I couldn't stop myself from following the path with my eyes. "I don't think I could ever beat you in a race."

"That's 'cause you're scared!" Ruby laughed and splashed some water up at Blaire.

"Me? Scared?" Blaire made a show of clutching her chest. "I'll have you know I was the queen of this lake before you were even born." She gently kicked her legs back and forth, and I could see the way Ruby clung to her and soaked up every word she said.

"You were not." Ruby laughed, her wet hair plastering against her sun-pinked cheeks.

Blaire gasped dramatically. "Excuse me? I definitely was. You can ask your dad. I used to outswim him all over this lake."

The casual way she spoke about me caught me off guard.

"No way!" Ruby giggled so hard she had to cover her mouth with both wet hands.

"Way." Blaire leaned down like she was sharing a secret between the two of them. "I don't know if you know this or not, but your dad is a very sore loser."

Ruby's smile dropped the tiniest bit, the corners of her mouth tightening. "Is that why y'all aren't friends anymore?"

Blaire's spine straightened as she shifted. "I didn't say we weren't friends."

"You said not exactly." Ruby tilted her head, her eyes narrowing as if she were trying to make sense of what they were saying.

"You're awfully smart for a five-year-old." Blaire's voice softened as she reached forward and pressed her finger to the tip of Ruby's nose. "Has anyone ever told you that?"

Ruby grinned up at her, and it was too much, the way her eyes lit up, the way Blaire was looking down at her. I pushed away from the rough bark, moving closer to the water's edge, and made my presence known as I cleared my throat.

Ruby spotted me first, her eyes widening before a smile took over her face. "Daddy!"

She released her grip on Blaire's legs and kicked through the water toward the ladder, hauling herself up from the lake as the wooden planks creaked under my boots. She barreled into me, water dripping down her arms and legs as I bent to scoop her up. Her little arms looped around my neck, and I clamped my eyes closed as I breathed her in.

"You okay?" I asked before I lifted the hem of my T-shirt and dried off her face.

"Yes!" She giggled and tried to pull her face out of my reach. "Blaire taught me how to do a backflip underwater, and we counted all the minnows!"

I crouched down so I was eye level with her, brushing wet hair back out of her eyes, but my gaze caught on Blaire behind her.

She was standing now, water trailing down the curve of her thigh from the hem of her bathing suit. The sunlight worshipped her fair skin, stealing the air from my lungs.

Our eyes locked and something passed between us, an old dangerous current I'd spent years trying to forget. She held my gaze as she reached for her T-shirt, and I watched, unable to look away, as she pulled it down over her breasts, the now damp fabric clinging to every contour before settling against her stomach.

"We had fun, Daddy." Ruby twisted in my arms to point back at Blaire. "We're friends now!"

"I saw." The words scraped out of my throat, giving away more than I wanted to.

"But she's not your friend." The words fell from Ruby's lips so easily, and I cocked a brow at Blaire.

"Ruby!" Blaire hissed out a laugh, but her smile faltered as something flickered across her face. I couldn't tell if it was guilt or hesitation, but her cheeks flushed pink as she shifted her weight to one hip, arms crossing as if she could shield herself from me. "That's not...I never said..." Blaire's words tumbled over each other as she took a step forward on the dock. "Look, June was supposed to call when she needed Ruby back at the house. I didn't mean to—"

"It's okay," I cut in, forcing my tone to steady, like I wasn't unraveling from the inside out. "Ruby's been asking to go swimming all week. Thank you for taking her."

I raked a hand through Ruby's wet hair, the fine strands knotting around my fingers, as I tried to ignore the way Blaire's attention raked over me.

I steadied Ruby on her feet before I stood, running my hands over my jeans.

"It was nothing." She gestured to Ruby, who was glancing back and forth between the two of us. "She's so sweet, and she got me out of work at June's."

She laughed softly, and I joined in despite myself. "She is really good at getting out of work."

Ruby stuck her tongue out at me, and I reached for her, making her squeal as I lifted her back into my arms. My fingers found the ticklish spot beneath her ribs, and her laughter erupted around us, and she cried out, "Daddy, stop!"

I heard Blaire's breath hitch, and I looked back over at her to find her hands twisted in the hem of her shirt, wringing it tighter and tighter until her knuckles paled. Her tongue darted over her bottom lip, and she looked like she wanted to say a hundred different things but couldn't settle on one.

Ruby squirmed down from my arms, moving to Blaire's side, and she grabbed her hand before Blaire could stop her. "Daddy, can Blaire come to Sunday dinner tomorrow?"

Blaire's lips parted, and she looked completely caught off guard. "Oh, I couldn't." Her hand tightened around Ruby's. "That's family time."

Ruby turned her eyes on Blaire then back to me. "Grandma June comes every Sunday," Ruby said, looking up at Blaire like this was the most obvious fact in the world, and maybe to her, it was. "She always brings dessert."

Blaire's eyes darted up to me before she looked back at Ruby. "Ruby, I'm not sure—"

"She's right," I confirmed. I ran my tongue along the back of my teeth as Blaire's gaze snapped back to mine with a scowl. "June never misses a Sunday."

"You have to come," Ruby insisted, tugging at her hand until Blaire gave in and crouched beside her on the dock, their fingers linked. "Please?"

I should've told Ruby to quit pestering Blaire about it, but I couldn't get the words out. Not when Blaire's smile was so small and uncertain as she looked at my daughter. I could see her weighing her words, the careful calculation behind her eyes as she searched for the gentlest way to let Ruby down.

"Come to dinner, Blaire." I offered her a smile even as I shifted on my feet. "Mom makes enough food to feed an army, and both she and Dad haven't stopped asking about you ever since they heard you were back."

"I got back yesterday." A laugh escaped her.

"Trust me, I'm well aware." The words were sharper than I intended. "Did you forget how small towns worked? Half the county probably had a group chat the minute you crossed the county line."

Blaire's throat bobbed before she asked, "But not you?"

"No." I barked out a laugh, dragging my palm across the back of my neck. "Apparently, they saved that particular bombshell for you to deliver on your own last night."

She snorted softly, but her eyes flitted away from mine.

"Blaire, please come," Ruby begged, tugging on her hand again. "I want to have fun."

"Ouch." I clutched at my chest, rubbing my hand over my heart, but they were both ignoring me, eyes fixed on each other.

Blaire studied Ruby for a long moment, and I braced myself for her rejection. Ruby would be upset, but we'd survive it just like we did when her mom left.

"All right." Blaire nodded, shocking the shit out of me. "Only because I can't have you hanging out with your lame dad all the time, but you have to promise you'll paint my nails like we talked about."

She extended her pinkie finger, and Ruby didn't hesitate. She locked pinkies with Blaire, and both of them smiled. "I promise!"

My normally guarded girl looked up at Blaire like she was half in love with her already, and something twisted in my chest. It was part joy at seeing her open up, part instinct to shield her from what might come. Ruby had already weathered more storms than any five-year-old should, and I'd be damned if I let another one roll in on my watch.

CHAPTER 8
BLAIRE

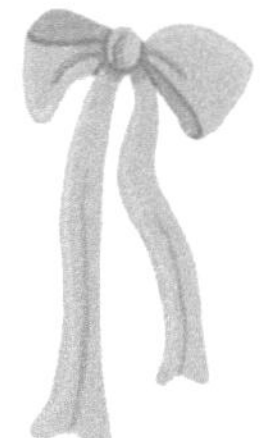

I'd spent all day trying to talk myself out of it.

A reasonable person would have already called Colt by now and claimed food poisoning, a migraine, anything to get out of going to dinner at his parents' house.

I came back to Willow Grove with only one certainty. I needed to avoid Colt Calloway at all costs. Yet three days in, I was on his parents' porch with a giant bowl of banana pudding in my arms while June knocked on their door.

The arguments I'd made for why this was a mistake hadn't been enough. Not when all I could think about was Ruby's little hand in mine as she leaned in, eyes bright with hope. I could have disappointed Colt, who I was sure didn't actually want me here, but I couldn't stomach the thought of letting her down.

Coming tonight wasn't about Colt. It was about walking back into the life I left and choosing what I wanted from it.

I wasn't prepared to meet Ruby's mother. I'd built her in my mind in a hundred different ways—soft and steady enough to ease Colt's edges or wild enough to keep pace with him.

Either way, I hated her for it, and I hadn't even met her.

Ruby hadn't spoken of her mother at all while we were swimming. We'd spent the afternoon in fits of giggles, with Ruby showing me all her moves in the water and her cannonball off the end of the dock. She'd surfaced with a smile that scrunched her nose and showed her dimples. When her small fingers found mine underwater, I didn't stop her. Her hand wrapped around mine, small and trusting, as if we'd been friends for a lifetime instead of only a few hours.

I'd expected it to be awkward, maybe even a little forced, but I genuinely enjoyed her company. Her quick wit and silly questions disarmed me, but I shouldn't have been surprised by how charming she was for a five-year-old.

She was a Calloway, after all.

Questions burned on my tongue. There were so many things I wanted to know about her life and her father, but I had no right to ask them. And what if she had said something I wasn't ready to hear?

I'd let the questions fall away, and Ruby and I swam and laughed and floated side by side as we argued over the shapes we found in the clouds.

When I'd walked back into June's still damp from the lake, I had swallowed every question clawing at my throat. "I assume that means Colt found you." June waved her cell phone. "I tried to call you, but this damn thing had no service." Her lips curled in a knowing smile I'd seen a thousand times before.

I knew she was baiting me, dangling information about Colt and waiting for me to ask. But June and I were cut from the same cloth, both too stubborn for our own good. I should have swallowed my pride and begged her for every detail, so I would've had some armor against whatever I was about to walk into.

The Calloways' door swung open, and goosebumps raced up my arms. June stood just in front of me, and I took a deep breath as I looked past her and into the doorway.

All at once, I was fifteen again, standing on these same weathered floorboards while waiting for Colt to hurry down the stairs so we could disappear into the sprawling acres of the ranch until sunset called us home.

"Don't let Blaire get hurt!" His mom would yell the same thing after us every single time, but we'd barely heard her.

Lou Calloway had always worried about us, and she was just as I remembered her. She stood in the doorway, barely over five feet tall, and she'd pulled her dark hair back out of her face with a clip. There were more streaks of silver there than I remembered, but those piercing blue eyes that both Colt and Ruby had inherited were exactly the same. A smile spread across her face as she looked up at me, and she radiated that same kindness that had once made this house feel more like home than my own.

"Blaire." She said my name as she wrapped me in a hug so tight I nearly dropped the pudding. She squeezed me into her as if she were trying to make up for all the lost time in one embrace. "Lord, I've missed you, my girl."

Guilt flooded me, yet, "I've missed you too, Lou," passed through my lips as I melted into her.

She finally let go and cupped my face, thumbs gentle along my cheeks as she studied me. "Prettier than ever."

"Let the girl in the house, Louise!" I heard Mr. Calloway's voice from deeper in the house. "You can smother her in your love and questions once she's inside."

"Oh, hush!" Lou hollered before rolling her eyes and pulling me in the door behind June. She took the pudding from my hands, but she hadn't stopped smiling.

"This looks good, June." She closed the door. "Owen's been asking for your famous banana pudding."

She ushered me forward, her hand pressed to the small of my back, and the smell of vanilla, roasted meat, and warm rolls were so familiar that I couldn't stop the longing that crept through me. The Calloway house looked almost exactly the same as it did a decade ago, down to the hooks by the door that were covered in hats and the small bench that sat above a line of worn boots.

"As long as his doctor says it's okay, I'll bring whatever the man wants," June laughed.

"Come on, Blaire. Everyone's out on the back porch. They can't wait to see you."

I followed her down the hallway, past the wall of family photos, and my steps faltered as I spotted a faded picture of me, Colt, Hunter, and McCoy down by the lake. We were all gangly limbs and carefree smiles, and the photo still hung in a wooden frame exactly where it had always been.

We crossed the living room into the kitchen, and Lou set the pudding on the food-packed island as we passed. Through the glass doors that framed the porch, I saw them already gathered. Hunter had his boots propped on the railing as he talked to his father, who was leaning back in a faded rocking chair. McCoy was opening a beer and smiling down at the yard, and I followed his gaze as we finally stepped outside.

Ruby was barefoot and her hair was flying behind her as Colt chased her through the grass. They curved around Lou's flower garden that was filled to the brim with flowers of every color, and Ruby squealed as Colt closed the distance between them. She ran toward the porch, but then she spotted us at the threshold.

"Blaire!" she shrieked, never slowing as her arms spread wide and she launched herself at me.

I dropped low, bracing for impact, and she collided against me, her weight nearly knocking me off my feet. I caught her, curling my arms around her small body, as she squeezed her arms around my neck.

"I'm so happy you're here." She pulled back, and her cheeks were flushed. "Look what I made you!"

She lifted one of her hands between us, revealing two bracelets, one snug against her wrist and the other barely hanging on. She pulled the large one off before she slid it on mine. The bracelet was a riot of pink beads of every shape and size, and I loved it.

"They're friendship bracelets. I didn't have any letter beads, but Daddy said they don't have to have letters to be friendship bracelets. And both of our favorite colors are pink!" Ruby's words tumbled out in a breathless rush, and my gaze drifted over her head to find Colt standing at the edge of the porch, catching his breath, his hands on his hips as he watched us.

His hair was a mess from running, one lock falling across his forehead, sweat making his white T-shirt cling to the cut of his shoulders, and I forced myself to look away from him and back to her.

"Thank you, Ruby." I spun the bracelet on my wrist, taking in all the different beads. "I've never had a friendship bracelet before."

Tonight, I'd planned to be careful with her, not to get too close, but she'd already made that impossible in under a minute.

"Neither have I." Ruby grinned as she ran her fingers over her own beads.

"You did a wonderful job picking out the beads," I whispered, lowering my voice like it was a secret just for the two of us. "We both know that pink is the best."

"Daddy helped me pick them." Ruby reached forward and traced her finger over my wrist. "This one's a strawberry. And see this yellow one? It's a sunflower. Daddy said we had to put it on even though it's not pink because it's your favorite."

My fingers ran over the beads she pointed to, the misshapen red oval with its green cap passing for a strawberry, and beside it, that little yellow sunflower. Something caught in my throat as I ran my thumb across each uneven ridge and smooth plastic curve, memorizing their shapes beneath my skin.

"He did good," I whispered, the words nearly lost in the sudden tightness of my chest.

I brushed the hair out of her eyes as she beamed at the bracelet, but I was acutely aware of the Calloway family on the porch behind her. Lou stood to my left, watching us carefully, and when I scooted Ruby back a step, I rose to my feet to face them.

Hunter was the first to break the silence. "Well, hell. I was a little worried you might run out on us after the other night." He grinned with his eyes full of mischief.

"What happened the other night?" Lou asked, and Hunter's grin only widened.

"Blaire had all the cowboys in an uproar. Right, Colt?" Hunter winked at me.

"That's not true," I answered before Colt could. "I think Hunter is getting confused because I had to watch your son here—" I motioned to Hunter "—act like an idiot while he pined after my friend, Maggie. You would think his game would get better with age, but somehow, he's still resorting to being a jerk if he likes a girl."

"Hunter Owen Calloway," his mother scolded, and I couldn't stop the smirk spreading across my face as I watched his eyes widen. "Maggie, as in Ella's sister?"

A blush crept up Hunter's cheeks, and he slid his hand behind his neck. I was desperate to know the story there, but I would find out from Maggie eventually.

"Yes, Ella's Maggie. We're friends." He widened his eyes at me, but he started it.

Lou sighed, still as exasperated by her son as she was when he was a teen. "June, I'm not sure how you raised such a well-behaved granddaughter when she spent so much time with this crew growing up."

Colt snorted, and my gaze snapped to him. His eyes met mine, and the corner of his mouth twitched upward in a way that made my stomach flutter traitorously. "I'm sorry," he chuckled as he picked Ruby up into his arms and rested her on his hip. "We all know that's bullshit, though."

"Language," Lou tsked, but her voice was warm as she swept past me, pressing a kiss to Ruby's forehead. "We're trying to raise another well-behaved girl over here."

"And I'll have you know I am perfectly well-behaved." I crossed my arms and faced off with Colt.

"Sure." He nodded, his lips pressed together in a tight line below that damn mustache, like he was trying not to smile. "I'm sure you've changed so much since you've been gone. That's why The Dusty Spur is clear out of tequila?"

McCoy spat out his beer as a laugh tore from his throat. I felt heat crawl up my neck, unable to look away from the way Colt was watching me, but Mr. Calloway saved me.

"Leave the girl alone," he cut in before turning to me. "Blaire

Monroe, are you gonna stand over there and deal with my fool sons, or are you gonna give an old man a proper hello?"

He smiled, and I saw the man I remembered—broad-shouldered, calloused hands that had taught me to ride a horse, with a laugh that had boomed across these fields every summer of my childhood. But time had worked him over in ways I hadn't expected. His shoulders were hunched now, his once-imposing frame diminished as if the weight of all those years on this ranch had finally settled into his bones.

I crossed the porch, my pulse thudding loud in my ears, and bent down to wrap Mr. Calloway in a hug. He still smelled of leather.

When I hesitated to pull him into me, he squeezed me against him, breathing me in and wrapping one hand around the back of my head. He was still Owen Calloway, but my heart twisted at how thin he felt in my arms.

When I pulled away, his fingers lingered on my arm. I tried not to stare, but I couldn't help cataloging the new frailty in him. His knuckles were swollen, his skin pulled tight over the blue map of veins that hid beneath, and there was bruising along his forearms.

"Don't look so glum." His voice was still full of that gravel I'd always loved. "I can't die off yet. Can you imagine these boys running this ranch on their own if I couldn't at least be here for tech support."

"Jesus, Dad," Colt groaned, and I looked back at him, really looked at him for the first time since I'd been home. He adjusted Ruby on his hip with practiced ease, and his hand splayed protectively across her small back as his thumb soothed small circles against her.

When I thought about facing Colt again, I had braced myself for a stranger, but he was still the same as he'd always been, just a bit steadier, softer, and harder all at once.

When he glanced down at his daughter, I could see the subtle dark shadows that hung below those eyes. His jaw worked beneath his stubbled skin, and his shoulders were rigid and tense beneath his worn cotton shirt.

I wondered how long he'd been taking over for his father on the ranch. He'd always known that was what he wanted, that this ranch would always be his life, but neither of us thought it would happen this soon.

"What?" Mr. Calloway's eyes narrowed as his gaze darted between me and Colt. "She was looking at me like I'm already in the ground, but I'll have you know, bad heart or not, I can still throw your mama around the bedroom whenever I need to." He punctuated this with a wink and a grin that pulled at the deep lines around his eyes.

All three Calloway boys let out groans of disgust, McCoy covering his ears with his palms, and I pressed my fingers against my lips as laughter bubbled up from my chest.

Lou swatted at Owen's arm. "That's enough out of you."

She was reprimanding him, but his grin only spread wider as he wrapped his arm around her, his reach barely higher than her thighs from where he sat. He pulled her toward him with a gentle tug. "Oh, you love me."

Lou rolled her eyes, but the corners of her mouth twitched upward, softening her entire face. Her gaze flicked over him with the practiced precision of a woman who had spent a lifetime anticipating another's needs.

When I was young, I'd watch them from across the dinner table—the way his hand would find hers without looking, how she'd refill his tea before he realized it was empty. My own parents had divorced when I was four, and I'd never seen parents who had such unguarded affection, and I used to lie in my bed at the end of the night and wish for a love like that to find me one day.

Now, I wished it would hit me like a Mack truck instead of the type of love I had been attracting.

I'd always dreamed of finding a man with steady hands and unwavering devotion like Owen Calloway, but when a diamond had been placed on my left hand, it came from a man who was so much more like my own father.

I'd given up that easy love I'd always dreamed of the moment I said yes to Grant.

"Now." Owen's voice dropped into a whisper only meant for her. "Give me a kiss."

Lou leaned down and pressed her lips to Owen's, then ran her hand over his cheek, her thumb lingering at the corner of his mouth before she straightened. "I'd better finish up dinner before my sons starve to death."

"Thank God." McCoy huffed, patting his flat stomach. "I've only been thinking about your cooking since last Sunday."

"You can come over when it's not Sunday and eat. You know that, right?" Lou cocked an eyebrow at McCoy, and he simply pointed to Colt.

"Tell that to your precious baby boy over there who can do no wrong. He doesn't let me rest!"

"Shit is getting deep out here." Colt groaned as he set Ruby back on her feet. His eyes met mine over her head, and I wanted to look away from him but couldn't. I hated how my body still responded to him, even while my mind screamed at me to remember all the reasons I'd left.

"Can I help?" The words tumbled out of me, too quick, too eager.

"Of course you can. Come on." Lou waved me in after her, and relief swept through me at the excuse to move, to step away from the porch and the weight of Colt's stare.

Ruby darted toward me and grabbed my hand, her palm warm against mine. "I'll help too!"

We walked inside hand in hand before Ruby hopped onto a wooden stool at the island, her feet thumping against the rungs as she swung her legs back and forth. I rolled up my sleeves and washed my hands as I tried to take a deep breath.

"Where do you want me?" I asked Lou, and she set a large ceramic bowl of steaming potatoes in front of me and Ruby.

"Will you mash those and add in the milk and butter for me? Ruby's great at it." Lou smiled at her granddaughter, and Ruby grabbed the wooden spoon, her face scrunching in concentration.

Together we stirred the bowl of potatoes, watching the yellow butter melt and splash over the rim. Ruby laughed so hard she snorted when a bit of potato landed on my shirt, and we argued over who was better.

"Better stirrer?" I raised a brow, nudging her side with my elbow as I wiped at my shirt. "Tell that to the mashed potatoes you got all over the counter and—" I pointed to the dark mark on my T-shirt. "—my clothes."

Ruby's eyes went big and mischievous. "That wasn't my fault! I have nothing on me." She smirked, her dimpled cheeks creasing, and her expression looked so much like Colt that my breath caught.

"Oh really." I dipped my finger into the potatoes, and I lifted a dollop that slowly dripped down my knuckle, hovering it inches from Ruby's face. "Say I'm the best!"

Ruby squealed and tried to back away from me, her body twisting toward Lou, but it was no use. There was nowhere for her to escape between me and the island, so she held up her hands, fingers splayed wide, as her laugh rang out around us.

"Never!" she laughed harder, her chest heaving with it as I moved my potato-covered finger forward with exaggerated menace.

"This is your last chance, Ruby Louise, or it's going right on that pretty little nose of yours."

Ruby stuck her tongue out at me, and I was smiling so hard my cheeks ached as I swiped my finger over her button nose, smearing the buttery potatoes over her little freckles.

"Blaire!" she shrieked with laughter, the sound so bright and full that all I could do was join in with her. She reached for the bowl of potatoes to get me back, her small fingers grasping the ceramic rim, but Lou pulled it out of our reach with a swift, practiced motion.

"Oh no, you don't!" Lou shook her head as she moved the bowl to the far side of the counter. "You two aren't making a mess in my kitchen."

Lou's eyes sparkled as she watched us, her hands never still as she swept a dish towel along the countertop, cleaning up the mess we'd made. "You better go wash those potatoes off your face before your uncle Coy comes in and tries to have a bite of you."

Ruby giggled and hopped down from the stool. She ran from the kitchen but stopped before she made it to the hall. "I'll be right back, Blaire." Her eyes met mine, needing reassurance that I wouldn't leave, so I gave it to her.

"I'll be right here." I smiled as she scrunched up her little potato-covered nose. "Thinking about how much better of a stirrer I am."

Her returning smile made my grip tighten on the counter, and she started running again, her footsteps pounding through the house.

"You know," Lou said, glancing over at me as she pulled rolls from the oven and set them on the counter. "I've never seen Ruby take to someone the way she has with you." She leaned her hip against the counter, her arms folded over her apron. "It's nice to hear her laugh like that."

Something in her tone pulled me up short, and I turned to fully face her. "She seems like a really good kid." I wiped the last of the potato from my finger, feeling too exposed under the weight of her gaze.

"She is," Lou replied as she gathered up a handful of silverware and arranged it into neat bundles. "She's the sweetest girl, but she hasn't had the easiest go of it these last couple of years." Her hands moved quickly, lining up forks and knives, but her voice slowed and softened. "Even with all of us here fussing over her."

I didn't know what to say or what she meant, but I looked over my shoulder at the direction Ruby had disappeared. "It's easy to see how loved she is," I finally offered, glancing back to find Lou watching me.

"She is," she said again, her lips pressing together. "But that doesn't always make up for what's missing."

"What's missing?" I asked, even when I knew I shouldn't.

Lou didn't answer right away. She gathered a small bowl in

her hands and began brushing butter across the tops of the rolls with a careful, methodical hand. Silence stretched until I wished I hadn't asked.

"I'm sorry." I shook my head. "I shouldn't have—"

"Her mama left," she said quietly, glancing down the hall. "It's just been Colt and Ruby since she was three."

The words dropped between us with the weight of an anchor, and I could only stare at her, unable to make sense of what I'd heard.

Her mother left.

Lou's words hit me hard, the ache radiating until it settled in my chest. Ruby hadn't spoken a word about her mother, and I hadn't asked. We had laughed, she'd clung to me, and I hadn't even considered that her mom wasn't in the picture. I'd spent the last twenty-four hours preparing to hate this woman, to resent her for this life she'd created with Colt and Ruby, and she wasn't even here. I had been jealous of this life she'd never stayed to build.

Shame dragged through me, but right behind it came something I didn't expect. Protectiveness.

She had left Ruby just as my father had left.

Like I'd left people who loved me, too.

My mouth opened and closed. "I— I didn't know."

Lou gave me a look full of sadness. "Colt didn't tell you?"

I winced and chanced a look over my shoulder at the back porch. They were all still out there, June sitting in the middle of them and making them laugh, but Colt was watching me through the glass, his expression unreadable. Our eyes locked as he lifted a beer to his lips, and I turned away, my stomach twisting. "Colt and I haven't really talked."

Lou pressed her palm to the countertop, steadying herself. "It hasn't been easy," she said, her voice so quiet I stepped closer to hear her. "Colt does everything he can, but he's had the weight of this whole family on his shoulders for years now. Owen's had heart issues, and then...well, we all thought maybe she'd come back. But she's—" Lou's lips pressed together so tight they disappeared. "She called once since she's been gone. They hadn't planned to get married, and she apparently wasn't ready to be a mother." She sighed. "Ruby doesn't remember her much, but that doesn't mean she doesn't feel it."

Hunter's deep roll of laughter came from the porch. But in here, Lou and I stared at one another. Her hands shook as she reached for a stack of plates, and I quickly moved around the island and took them from her. "I—" I closed my eyes, my throat tight with anger. "How could she leave her?"

Lou let out a slow exhale, the kind that sounded like she'd held it for years. "Some people aren't built for staying," she said as her eyes searched mine, "and sometimes the best thing you can do for someone is love them while they go." She wiped her hands on her apron with more force than necessary and glanced toward the porch. "It's taken every one of us to make it work with Colt having so much responsibility around the ranch now, but we make sure that Ruby never wonders if she's enough."

Guilt twisted through me not only for Ruby, but for Lou, for June, for all the people I'd left behind. I hadn't even been able to pick up the phone and call Lou after everything she'd always done for me. I was a coward, and I had spent so long running that I hadn't thought about how much I'd left. It had been so easy to convince myself that leaving was only about Colt and me, but I'd run from them, too.

Lou's eyes flickered over my face, and I could almost feel her reading the thoughts as they passed through me.

"I'm sorry." The words slipped out. "I should have called or written or—" I swallowed. "You didn't deserve that."

Her face fell, and she reached out to take my hand in hers. Her palm was warm against mine, and her grip was firm. "Oh, my girl. That's not what I meant. You have nothing to apologize for, not to me, anyway." She squeezed my hand, and I tried not to crumble under it all. "We all have to do what we have to do to survive this world."

I looked down at her hand, at the gold band wrapped around her finger, and that ache in my chest felt like it was pressing down on me. It pulsed in my lungs until I felt like I was drowning on nothing but air.

"I missed you," I said, my voice shaking. "I missed everyone so much, but I—" I choked on the next words, feeling suddenly so small and so foolish. "Colt and I—"

Lou let go of my hand only to pull me in, wrapping her arms around my shoulders and rocking me gently. "I know." Her breath was warm against my cheek.

I sucked in a deep breath, and Lou let go enough to see my face.

"Can I ask you something?" she asked softly, and I nodded. "Why'd you listen to your dad after everything you went through to stay here? Why did you leave?"

There was hope in her eyes, like I'd still tell her it had all been a big misunderstanding, some cosmic joke, and I could have lied. But I'd never been able to lie to her.

"Colt told me to go." My voice broke around the words, and there was no masking the hurt in them. "He said it would be better for us, that we both needed space, and that I—" My chest ached, like all the years I'd spent trying to forget that night had collapsed inside me. "That my father could give me things I would never find here. He could pay for college and take care of me."

I swallowed hard, blinking fast, but the heat behind my eyes refused to go away. The memory of that night—the way I'd screamed at him and begged him not to do it, the way he just stood there with his jaw clenched, letting us burn to ash—would never go away despite how hard I tried to forget it.

"He told me he couldn't be the one to do it anymore." I sucked in a breath until my lungs burned. "That I was holding him back."

The glass door to the porch pushed open with a loud screech, and I jumped back from Lou as footsteps sounded behind us. A tear fell down my cheek, and I swiped my hand over it frantically, forcing my lips into a smile.

"Blaire," Lou called, her voice soft with concern, but I was already retreating, each step carrying me further from the truth I'd spilled across her kitchen floor.

"I'll be right back," I called over my shoulder, my voice wavering despite my desperate attempt to sound normal. "I need to use the bathroom really quick." I fled down the hallway where Ruby had disappeared, my vision blurring with each step.

The hallway was dimmer, cooler, but I didn't make it more than a few steps before I nearly collided with a broad chest.

Colt.

His hands shot out, steadying me, and I couldn't breathe. Of course he was the one who'd come inside. His scent surrounded me as he bent down enough to search my eyes, and I prayed he couldn't see the tears that were threatening to spill over.

I tried to slip past him, but he didn't let go. He stood there, his hands cupped around the backs of my arms, where his thumbs traced small, invisible circles. The pressure was nothing, barely there, but every drag of his thumbs felt like a brand I couldn't escape.

"What's wrong?" His voice was soft but demanding. I tried to look away from him, but he ducked his head so his eyes could find mine again.

"Nothing," I lied, sinking my teeth into the inside of my cheek. "Your mom was working me to death, and I need a minute."

My body betrayed me, leaning toward him even as I tried to pull away.

"You were never a good liar." The blue of his eyes held too much concern, and I couldn't stand to look into them.

"I'm fine. I'm not your concern." I forced myself to pull out of his hold, and he didn't stop me.

CHAPTER 9

COLT

I slammed the post driver down, my shoulders burning in protest. The fence post sank another quarter inch into the hard ground, then stopped cold.

The section of barbed wire that should have been repaired last week was now a full-blown replacement, and I'd already cut myself half a dozen times as I hauled the damaged section from the ground. Sweat traced a salty path between my eyes and stung like hell, but I was grateful for it. I was grateful for anything that pushed Blaire out of my mind.

I exhaled, wiped my brow, and rolled my shoulders. Then I slammed the post driver again, and it budged a little more. The post finally gave in, sinking deep enough that I could move to the next one. I flexed my hands and let the soreness ground me. It was the only thing that made sense.

Fences were simple math. The rest wasn't. The feed bill was due Friday, diesel had gone up in cost again, and I needed to call the vet and have him come out to look at one of our horses. Dad's cardiologist appointment loomed like a storm cloud on Mom's calendar, each of us pretending we weren't terrified of what they might find this time. And Ruby—Christ, Ruby's dance class started soon.

Last night, Ruby was almost asleep before she whispered, "Can Blaire come to my dance class with me?" Not demanding, just hoping in that fragile way that made me want to promise her the world and tear myself apart when I couldn't deliver it.

Ruby's mother walked out when she was three, leaving my daughter with a wariness in her eyes no kid should have. Yet, she'd clung to Blaire without second thought. I wanted to hate Blaire for it, for already carving herself into Ruby's life like she was already meant to be there, knowing damn well she'd hurt her when she inevitably left.

But then I'd remember her in my mother's kitchen, shoulders rigid, eyes haunted by something she wouldn't name, and I could feel my anger dissolve into something worse. This desperate need to protect her too. There had been so much hurt in her eyes, then she blinked, and her mask slid back into place, all easy smiles as she sat beside Ruby at dinner. The transformation was so perfect it made my hands shake—half with frustration that she could hide so well, half with the urge to reach across the table and touch her face, to see if I could feel the seam where the real Blaire disappeared.

Memories of her stalked me, ambushing me at every fence post, every water trough, every patch of dirt where I'd once chased her through these fields. There wasn't a single acre of this ranch that didn't remember her name.

I couldn't shake her. Not from my head or the thin space behind my ribs where all the anger I'd ever carried got swapped out for something more desperate.

I wanted to pull Ruby back from hope. I could survive another break if I had to. I'd survived Blaire before, but I wasn't sure my girl could.

The next post came easier. My palms were already numb, and my mind finally slipped into that cool nothingness that came from hard labor. I relished the sense of control, the reliability of the wood and the wire.

No one could mistake a fence's purpose. Keep things in, keep things out.

I knew how to build a fence, and how to keep things locked up tight. I kept Ruby safely tucked behind the wire while I took the barbs. It worked fine until Blaire walked back into town. She'd always found the gaps in my senses, slipping through them before I'd even realized she'd done so.

When we were kids, the world seemed so simple. There was this land, my family, Blaire, and a future so vivid I could close my eyes and see every goddamn detail. We'd drive down the back roads with the windows down and my hand on her bare thigh. She'd rested her head on my shoulder and said she'd never wanted to be anywhere else.

I'd believed her because I wanted it, too.

I wanted it more than I'd ever wanted anything, but that was before everything got complicated. Before our land started slipping from my hands, before my dad's body had weakened, before I realized that love alone couldn't keep her here.

I hit the post again, setting the second one in place, before I lowered the driver to the ground and lifted the hem of my shirt to wipe my face. I moved on to the wire, pulling it taut and twisting it with my pliers. A barb bit into my wrist as I worked carelessly, but I welcomed the bite of pain. I welcomed anything that kept me in the present and didn't let me linger on what could have been.

But my mind was a mean bastard, and it didn't care that I didn't want to think about her. I couldn't stop it no matter what I did. I could still see myself at seventeen, wrestling with a length of wire just like this one, except back then, I had Blaire in cutoff shorts balanced on the hood of my truck. She stretched her legs out in front of her, and her laughter floated around me. She'd heckle me for every curse, every sour mood, and when I'd finally snapped and told her to come over and prove she could do it better than me, she'd do just that.

But somehow the fence would never get fixed because I'd grabbed her by the waist before she could do anything and kiss her senseless.

We'd spent a thousand afternoons like that and a thousand

nights beneath the same stars with her skin pressed against mine, her curls tangled in my fingers, and both of us promising to never let the world pull us apart.

But promises were just words, and those words fell apart when her father showed up with an offer of a life I could never give her and threats to take everything away.

I closed my eyes, and I was back in that summer, the one where Blaire's world and mine got turned inside out.

Her mother had only been in the ground for a few weeks when her father called and wanted her to move in with him. He didn't want Blaire in the way a father should want a daughter. He'd spent most of her life somewhere else, and he didn't start calling until his campaign for senator began. First every other week, then every Sunday, always asking Blaire what her plans were after graduation, always trying to convince her to come live with him, to enroll in school.

And she would always look over at me as she told him no.

He didn't give a shit about her, not really. He cared about how she looked at his side. He cared about the stories that were printed in the paper that smeared his perfect family man image. He wanted Blaire because she was his, and because in the tight, cold world of politics, that's all family ever really was—possessions to leverage, assets to display.

Blaire had believed that if she kept saying no, kept holding on to me and this place, he'd drop the legal battle for custody against June and disappear like he always had before.

But that summer he came in person, all expensive suits and calculated smiles, and he didn't waste a minute before making it clear what he wanted. She was going to college, and she was going with him. And when that still hadn't been enough, the threats began.

That was when I learned how little power I really had in this world. Dad was already in and out of doctors' offices back then though we hadn't realized how serious things would get, and every day on the ranch felt like I was waiting for the next bad thing to tip us over the edge. I was barely keeping myself together, barely handling the pressures I knew my family needed me to take on, and then Blaire's father showed up on my land with a deed in his hand and a smug smile on his face.

I'd never forget the way he looked, leaning against my fence as he tapped the folded paperwork against the wood.

"You know, Colt," he drawled. "It would be a shame if anything happened to all this." He turned his head, looking out over the horizon at the land my dad had practically killed himself for.

"It doesn't matter what you say." I had been so sure then, so foolish. "Blaire will never go with you. Willow Grove is her home. I am her home. She's almost eighteen. It's her choice."

He tapped the papers again before he held them out to me, my hands shaking as I took them.

"One lawsuit, one challenge to Mae's will, and it all gets tied up in court. June's place, your parents' too, the land Blaire is supposed to inherit."

I stared down at the deed to June's property and a lien that had my parents' signatures right under June's. Dated shortly after Blaire's mother had gotten sick, right before her treatments started.

I felt the blood leave my face as it all made sense. My parents had co-signed on the loan, probably to keep June and Mae afloat during the worst of her cancer. It all fell into place right before me: the tightness in my father's voice, and the acreage to the west they'd sold when they swore they never would.

Blaire's mama and mine had been friends for a lifetime, and my parents had done whatever they could to help her until the very end. But it hadn't been enough.

That night, I started running numbers nobody asked me to. Extra calves, second shifts, and quiet deposits against a note that wasn't mine.

"You will not win this, Colt." He shook his head as if it hurt him to say it. "How long do you think Blaire will stay once I'm through with this place? You've got nothing to offer her but a dying ranch. She wants to go to college. She wants a future, and, son, you can't give her that." He took the paperwork back from my hands and slipped it into his jacket. "Blaire is coming with me. It's just a matter of whether you make it easy or I make it hell."

And God help me, I believed him.

Her voice had shrunk to a whisper as I told her she should go with him. Then came the screaming, the pleading for me not to do this as her fingers dug into my arms like she could anchor herself to me. But what haunted me most, what still jolted me awake in the dead of the night, was how the light in her eyes vanished when I finally said the words I knew would hurt her the most.

The ones I could never take back.

She'd left after that, my truck door slamming so hard I feared it would break. She ripped the necklace I'd given her the year before off her neck and threw it at me, the thin metal strawberry cutting me just below my jaw, before she ran into June's house.

I had put my head down and worked this ranch until my hands bled and my muscles screamed. I had broken her that night, shattered everything between us. For years, the weight of what I'd done pressed down on me until I couldn't breathe.

Back then I only had myself and Blaire to lose. Now there was Ruby, too, and she changed the equation entirely.

I yanked the wire tighter, arms burning, but I didn't stop.

It didn't matter how many times I ran it over in my mind, I couldn't rationalize the decision, couldn't make it sound noble instead of cowardly. I'd told myself I was protecting her, that I was saving my family, but it wasn't enough.

I'd convinced myself if I worked hard and sacrificed for those I loved, it would all work out and I'd stop hearing the echo of her voice in my head.

But it never ended. I'd never stopped wanting her.

And no matter how much I tried, no matter how many seasons I pushed through, I couldn't make myself want anything else.

Not for more than a night, anyway.

Ruby was a result of one of those nights, and even though Becca and I tried to make things work for the sake of my girl, I fucked that up, too. Then I'd wake in the middle of the night with

Blaire's name half-whispered in my sleep, and Becca would be lying there, eyes open, staring at the ceiling. She couldn't stand living with a ghost, and hell, I couldn't blame her.

After Becca walked out, I swore Ruby would never find a stranger in our home. No other woman would leave traces for my daughter to find. I'd keep my longing for Blaire locked away where it belonged—in the dark, where I faced it alone, night after night.

I'd nearly finished the run when my phone rang, vibrating so hard against my thigh it startled me. I fumbled my gloves off and yanked it loose, expecting McCoy or Hunter with an update about the eastern pasture.

Instead, it was Ruby's elementary school.

My heart slammed against my ribs as I pressed the phone to my ear. The silence between my hello and their response stretched like the barbed wire in front of me, catching every terrible possibility.

"Hi, Mr. Calloway? It's Suzie from Willow Grove Elementary. I'm sorry to bother you."

"Is Ruby all right?" I asked.

"She's fine," she rushed to say. "Just feeling a little under the weather. She's running a fever and said that her throat hurts. She's resting in the nurse's office, but she's a little upset. I think she just wants her dad."

"Tell her either I or her nana will be there as soon as we can."

"Of course, Mr. Calloway. I'm going to go grab her a Popsicle while we wait."

"Thank you." I ended the call and looked over at the next section of fence that was still crushed to the ground, then back out at the cattle grazing nearby.

Fuck.

If I left it like this, we'd be chasing cattle for a week.

I tried Hunter first to have him come handle this fence, but his phone went straight to voice mail. I wasn't surprised. He and McCoy were headed to the east side of our property when I left them early this morning, and there wasn't cell service there for shit.

I quickly hung up and dialed my mom. She answered on the third ring.

"Hey, sweetheart." Her voice was quiet.

"Hey, Mom." I pulled off my hat and wiped at my forehead with my forearm. "The school called. Ruby's running a fever. I'm stuck up at the north field, and Hunter's out of reach. Any chance you can pick her up?"

She hesitated, which meant she couldn't. "I took your dad to his appointment in town. We won't make it back until three." I could hear the disappointment in her voice. She didn't want to let either of us down, and she never could. "I could leave your dad here, run and get her, and—"

"Mom, stop. It's okay." I forced a lightness into my voice I didn't really feel, caught between the broken fence, the scattered cattle, and my little girl asking for me. My mother must have heard the strain beneath my words because she let out one of those sighs, the kind that said she knew I was drowning, but she didn't know how to fix it.

"Call June," she suggested. Her voice was brisk, falling into the rhythm of fixing that mothers were so good at.

"I will, but I'm going to go ahead and head that way." I was already walking to Buck and running my hand down his neck. I'd leave the damn fence and get to Ruby, cattle be damned. That would be tomorrow's problem.

"Okay, sweetheart. I can pick her up as soon as we're back, and I'll make her some soup."

"Thanks, Mom." I hung up before untying Buck's lead rope and swinging myself up into the saddle.

I clicked on my phone, calling June's number as I kicked into Buck's sides, getting him to move while we waited for her to answer. I was about to hang up when she finally did.

"Hello." *Fuck, that wasn't June.*

"Uh, hi. Is June there?" *Why the hell was I stumbling over my words?*

"Hi," Blaire said hesitantly, and I could hear her moving. "No. She went out to bingo and left her phone at the house. That has to be a safety issue for someone her age, right?" She chuckled.

I sat frozen with the phone pressed to my ear like a goddamn idiot, Buck shifting restlessly beneath me. Every emotion I'd spent the day sweating out rushed back in with the sound of her voice on the other line.

"Sorry," I grunted. "I didn't mean to bother you. I'll—"

"Is everything okay?" she interrupted, the warmth in her voice a sucker punch.

"Are you okay, Blaire?"

She sucked in a breath, and I imagined her narrowing her eyes and biting down on her bottom lip as her frustration with me grew. "You're the one who called. What's wrong? You sound off."

God, I hated how easily she could hear it, how easily she could read me after all these years, even through a phone.

"Ruby's sick. I was going to ask June to pick her up, but I'm already headed that way."

"Oh. I— I can get her," she said with a hesitation that made my chest ache, but her offer made me stop short.

"No, it's fine. I'm out working, but I can get back to the big house in fifteen." I hated how defeated I sounded. "I'll call the school and—"

"Let them know I'll be there in ten minutes to pick her up." There was a steadiness in her tone that reminded me so much of the old Blaire.

My pulse jumped, and I opened my mouth to object. I tried to picture Blaire stepping back into the halls of Willow Grove Elementary and walking out with my daughter.

"Blaire—"

"I'm not arguing about this, Colt. You need help. June's not here, and I'm not leaving Ruby at school sick. I'm doing this for her, not you." There was a pause, and I could practically see the stubborn lift of her chin I'd always admired and hated in equal measure.

"I don't think that's a good idea," I said finally. There were rules to keep things safe for my girl. Blaire had only met my daughter at her best, but sick Ruby was different. She was needy and raw. Her brave face would be replaced with fever-flushed cheeks and trembling lips.

In one afternoon, Blaire would glimpse what I'd spent five years protecting.

She scoffed on the other end of the line. "Well, Colt, if my memory serves me, sometimes you don't have the best ideas, and right now, I'm the only option you have."

She was right.

I could either let her do this, or I'd be leaving twelve feet of fence down with cattle ready to wander. Fatherhood was a constant tug-of-war with Ruby pulling one arm and this ranch yanking the other. I'd inherited more responsibility than I thought I would at twenty-four, and it didn't matter that I'd been pretty much running the ranch for the last five years. It didn't get any easier.

Everyone was counting on me, and the thought of letting them down scared me to death.

My little girl most of all, especially after her mother left.

That was the thing no one told you when you became a parent. The guilt was always beneath your skin, a raw nerve, always pulsing. My muscles could ache from dawn to dusk, my clothes caked with mud, my hands crosshatched with barbed wire cuts, and I'd still saddle up tomorrow. But the thought of Ruby needing me and not being able to give her everything cut me bone deep.

I'd convinced myself we were making it work. We had our sunrise pancake rituals, and she giggled when I tossed her onto her bed at night. Sunday dinners at my parents' were her favorite, and she had two uncles who spoiled her rotten.

I'd hoped it would somehow patch the hole her mother left when she decided we weren't enough. But sometimes, like now, when the world moved faster than my boots could, I'd catch that look in Ruby's eyes, and I would hate myself for letting her down.

"Okay." I nodded, even though Blaire couldn't see me. "Thank you, Blaire." The words were tight in my throat. "I owe you."

The line went quiet for so long I checked my phone to see if she'd hung up, but then I heard the roar of her engine. "You don't owe me anything, Colt." She sounded tired. "Ruby and I will be fine. I'll call you once I get her."

She hung up, and I quickly called the school to let them know she was coming and that Blaire had my permission to get her.

I stared at the broken run of fence, jagged and useless like the promises I'd made to myself. Ruby came before everything, I knew that much. But I couldn't ignore the way my chest had lightened at the sound of Blaire's voice. I wanted to keep her at a distance, needed to, and yet part of me wondered what it would be like if she slipped through the gaps I couldn't seem to mend.

CHAPTER 10
BLAIRE

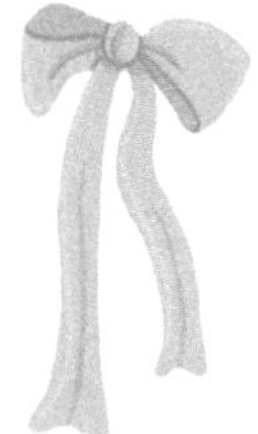

Ruby clung to me with her breath hot against my collarbone as I carried her into June's house. The booster seat I'd found in June's mudroom was still in my car.

"Come on, sweetheart." I shifted her higher on my hip as I kicked the door shut behind me. "Let's get you to the couch."

She didn't argue. Her hands wrapped around my neck as I moved through June's living room and laid her down against the worn cushions.

I dropped down beside her, brushing her hair out of her face. Her skin was warm, too warm, and I caught myself smoothing my palm over her temple as if it would draw the fever out of her.

"I'm going to get the thermometer and some Tylenol," I said softly.

Shit. I hoped June had children's Tylenol. What if she didn't? What if Ruby's fever got worse? I'd never been responsible for a sick child before, and June still wasn't home.

I wiped my sweaty palms on my shorts and pulled the worn, threadbare blanket off the back of the couch and draped it over Ruby's small frame. She burrowed deeper into the couch, her flushed cheek laying against her curled fingers.

I moved quickly and ducked into the downstairs bathroom, yanking open the medicine cabinet. I pushed aside scattered Band-Aids, a crusty tub of Vicks, and a collection of ancient lipsticks before landing on a digital thermometer.

Digging deeper, I finally found a bottle of children's Tylenol, half gone, with "Ruby" scrawled across the label in June's handwriting.

In the kitchen, I poured apple juice into a small cup and soaked a washcloth under the cold tap before I moved back to Ruby's side. I kneeled beside her and laid my hand against her cheek. The heat radiating from her skin made me anxious.

I pressed the thermometer to her forehead, tucking a stray strand of hair behind her ear as it beeped to life. Ruby's eyes were on mine as it beeped again, and I pulled it away to look at the small screen. One hundred and two point six.

My pulse spiked.

I wasn't her mother. I was just the girl who happened to answer the phone, the girl dumb enough to go pick up her ex's sick kid.

I grabbed the Tylenol, flipped it over, and scanned the dosing chart. I cursed under my breath. The dosage was by weight, not age, and I had no idea how much Ruby weighed. The bottle was a blur of numbers and warnings, and my hands shook as I pulled out my phone along with June's that she'd left behind when she went to bingo.

I bit my lip as I scrolled through June's contacts, finding Colt's number and copying it into my own phone.

Blaire: Hey, it's Blaire. Ruby and I are back at June's. Her temp is 102.6. How much Tylenol do I give her?

I pressed send, then stared at my phone. The text bubbles appeared, and I pressed the back of my hand to Ruby's cheek again, while I waited for him to answer. Her skin was still so hot, and her lashes fluttered as she looked up at me, wanting comfort I barely knew how to give.

Ruby's bright blue eyes locked with mine, and without thinking, a half-forgotten lullaby of "You Are My Sunshine" slipped from my lips. The same one my mama had hummed whenever I'd needed her. My fingertips traced along her hairline, mimicking a touch I hadn't felt in years, and I startled when my phone finally vibrated in my hand.

Colt: 7.5 ml. Is she okay? I'll be there soon.

I stared down at the screen, relief flooding me so fast my fingers trembled, before I squeezed the medicine into that little plastic cup.

"All right, Ruby girl. Open up for me, okay?"

She clamped her mouth shut and shook her head.

"Don't do that." I rested my elbows against the couch and held up my right pinkie. "I pinkie promise it will make you feel better."

Ruby hesitated for another moment before she wrapped her small pinkie around mine and we shook.

Then I slid my hand around the back of her head, helping her sit up a little, and she opened her mouth as I tipped the thick red syrup in. She swallowed, then grimaced.

Relief rushed through me. I felt out of my depth, and I didn't want to mess this up.

"That stuff tastes like butts," she groaned, and I couldn't help but laugh.

"Here. I got you some juice." I held the cup up to her, and she took a small sip before letting her head fall back against the pillow. I pressed the cool washcloth to her head before I tucked the blanket tighter around her.

"Can we watch a movie?" Her voice sounded so small, and I hated it.

"Of course." I climbed up onto the couch beside her and found the remote. "Do you want to pick?"

"*Tangled*," she said without a second thought, and I quickly found the movie and hit play.

I picked up my phone and texted Colt back, not wanting him to worry more than he already was.

Blaire: She's okay. We're watching *Tangled*. There's no rush, Colt.

The three blue dots bounced across my screen, but they disappeared before they bounced again.

Colt: Thank you. I'm about to head back to the big house to get my truck.

I let the phone fall to my chest, my anxiety easing a little as I listened to Ruby hum along to the opening song. I rotated the washcloth after a few minutes, trying to keep it cool, and Ruby stared up at me with sleepy eyes.

"Can I come by you?" she whispered, voice hoarse and hesitant.

"Of course," I said and stretched out an arm.

Ruby wriggled herself upright, the blanket trailing behind her, and shuffled to where I sat. She tucked herself into my side so naturally it almost hurt. She curled up, her knees against my thigh and her head against my chest, and her fever warmed through my shirt.

I soaked in the small shudders of her breaths. Her body was so small and tired in my arms, but she melted into me like she belonged there. I pressed my lips to her temple hesitantly, and she sighed.

I could hear the movie playing, but it faded behind the sound of her breathing and the way my heart thumped a little too fast.

She wrapped her hand around mine, the two of us linking fingers, and we watched the movie together until she finally drifted off to sleep against me. I rotated the washcloth again, cooling in slow cycles, before I'd smooth the hair off her forehead over and over.

Every so often, she'd twitch in her sleep, her small fingers clutching at my shirt like she was afraid I might disappear. I shifted carefully, lifting her higher against my chest, and swung my legs up on the couch. I settled us down, careful not to move too much and risk waking her. My arm was going numb beneath her, but I didn't care.

My palm skimmed over her forehead, cooler now than before.

The scent of her shampoo filled my lungs as I rested my cheek on the top of her head. I barely knew Ruby. It had only been three days, for crying out loud, but I already felt fiercely protective of her in a way that made me want to hold her until there was no room left between us. I'd spent years building walls, and this girl had somehow slipped right through them.

I had no claim to her, but my body was reacting as if I did. I was reaching for her, soothing her, and every part of me wanted to make sure that no part of her was hurt.

Ruby shifted restlessly in her sleep, and I trailed my finger gently down the bridge of her nose like my mama used to do to me. Her nose twitched once before she settled, a tiny whistling snore escaping with each breath.

I grinned as I watched her and ran my finger over her nose repeatedly, tracing the tiny freckles scattered across the bridge. Her mouth popped open, pink lips forming a perfect little 'O' that puffed warm breath against my wrist with each slow exhale. The sun still poured in through the living room windows, and it seemed to draw out every little line and marking on her face that my gaze drank in eagerly.

My phone buzzed on the armrest, the vibration loud enough to make me jump, and I snatched it up before it could wake Ruby. I hugged her against me, one arm curled protectively around her small shoulders as I shifted us slightly.

Senator Monroe flashed across my screen, and a photo of my father popped up with the same smugness on his face I'd always hated. I hadn't spoken to him since I left North Carolina, and I'd ignored every call, every text, and every email.

But as I stared down at his face now, I froze, torn between the urge to hurl my phone across the room and the desperate need to answer it. Wanting my father's approval felt like a bad habit I'd never quite kicked, a reminder of the years of longing when he'd wanted nothing to do with me.

I didn't need his approval anymore, and I reminded myself that I didn't want it. But I also knew exactly how loud my father could get when he didn't get what he wanted, when he thought he was being ignored.

I hit the green button with my thumb, steeling myself. "Hello."

"Blaire." His voice traveled down the line with a snap, and my spine stiffened. "It's about time you finally answered. We've been worried sick."

My father's sigh raked down the line, a long, measured sound, and I heard the faint clink of ice in a glass. Always a drink, always this slow orchestration of his disappointment.

"I'm fine. I'm at June's." I repositioned Ruby, holding her so close I could feel her slight breathing against my chest.

The silence that fell was surgical, precise, the kind that builds and builds until you'd do anything to break it. I knew that silence. My father wielded it like a weapon often, and I could feel his disapproval through it now.

My being at June's was like salt in an old wound. They made their mutual hatred for one another crystal clear when my father appeared on June's doorstep after years of absence. He had demanded I pack my things and leave with him, and I could still hear June's voice cracking as she stood in the doorway, arms spread like she could physically block him from taking me.

But I hadn't understood my father's reach back then—the way his donations opened doors, how judges played golf at his country club, how easily he made problems vanish and appear. I only learned that lesson after I'd already agreed to go with him, after I'd made him swear to drop the legal custody threats against June, after Colt had looked at me and told me to leave.

I learned it much better once I became his employee.

He exhaled once, the sigh a slow toxin, and I could picture him perfectly, sitting at his large desk, fingers tapping against the rim of his whiskey glass, assembling his words like ammunition.

"Your fiancé has called my office three times today. He says you're not answering him either. I told him you needed a little time to breathe, but, Blaire, this is not how adults handle things."

I could feel myself shrinking, making room for his voice, even as something inside me bristled. "Dad, Grant cheated on me. There's nothing to talk about. You saw the photos."

The cheating was just the final straw. I'd endured worse from Grant, things I was ashamed I allowed, but seeing those photos had finally jolted me awake, like cold water to the face after years of sleepwalking.

"Don't be dramatic," he snapped. "Every relationship has its problems, especially under stress. You can't throw away a good man because of one mistake."

A good man.

The words sounded hollow coming from my father, who wouldn't recognize genuine goodness if it introduced itself with a business card. Grant wasn't good. He was polished. He remembered my drink order, but he forgot my birthday. But he also had a bank account that made powerful men lean in when he spoke.

Grant was handsome and charming, and for a fleeting moment, I'd let myself believe I could breathe without thinking about Colt. But six months in, that charm had changed to his hand pressing firmly against my lower back when important men approached. He'd interrupt me mid-sentence to "clarify" what I was saying and asked me to change if he didn't like my dress.

He had once looked at me with admiration, but as the months passed, I recognized the same clinical appraisal I'd seen my father and his friends wear when assessing thoroughbreds at the races. He was calculating my value and checking for flaws.

He liked that I fit so well in the crook of his arm and looked good doing it. And he loved my father, while I— *I had been starved for their approval.*

After leaving Willow Grove, I was heartbroken. I had molded myself to be exactly what they wanted. I wore dresses that made my father nod with approval. I laughed at Grant's jokes with practiced timing, desperate for them to see the polished version of myself I'd created.

I hadn't realized how easily I was losing myself. Each day I'd grown more agreeable, more digestible, for the sake of earning their love. But love wasn't something they gave in return.

Grant's cheating hadn't been a crisis of character; it was a minor strategic error. A mistake that could easily be swept away as if it had never happened.

My father and Grant were not good men. They were men who had always gotten their way, and somewhere along the line, they convinced themselves that was the same thing.

"One mistake?" I could feel my anger rising and forced it down, glancing at Ruby's sleeping form to make sure my volume hadn't disturbed her. "He was sleeping with his assistant for over a year, Dad. That's not a mistake."

"Regardless," he tutted with the sharp click of his pen in the background. "Grant is willing to move past it. One bad decision shouldn't destroy what you've built together."

I nearly laughed. "What we built? You've got to be kidding me."

"You're being childish." His voice was harder now, the veneer of civility cracking enough to reveal the rage beneath, and I remembered how Grant had said the very same to me. "Grant will provide for you. What is it you think you're going to find back in Willow Grove?" He laughed, but there wasn't a trace of humor. "What kind of life do you think you'll have there?"

I bit into my bottom lip to stop myself from saying what I really wanted to. "I'm going to help June with the farm. I think I'm going to come up with a plan to sell her jams online and market them."

"The farm?" he sneered, disgust dripping from his words. "You have a marketing degree from Duke. Instead of working on my staff like we planned, you're going to waste it by selling jams on a dying farm?"

A slow burn built in my chest, and I clamped my eyes closed. I wanted to scream. I wanted to reach through the phone and shake him until he rattled, until all the years of me swallowing my own voice came up and flooded every inch of this house.

Instead, I pressed my nose to the top of Ruby's head and breathed. "I love this farm, and when I'm thirty, a piece of it's legally mine. My mama saw to that."

He paused for a long second before he spoke again.

"You're missing the point, Blaire." His words sliced through the line before he cleared his throat. "The wedding venue is still reserved. If it's canceled, people are going to ask questions. Reporters are already sniffing around waiting for any story they can find. You need to fix this before it gets out of hand. I will call Grant's father—"

There it was. He didn't even try to hide the truth of what he cared about. Not my heartbreak, not the way Grant had betrayed and humiliated me. Grant's father was a far more powerful man than Grant, and my father needed him. And he needed his perfectly painted image to keep things exactly where he wanted them.

A carefully crafted facade I helped him create.

He'd been a shit father for most of my childhood, nothing but a ghost as he walked away from my mother and me without a backward glance. He hadn't even come to her funeral.

But when he came, when he took me from Willow Grove, he wore fatherhood like a tailored suit. He dragged me to every donor gala and country club function that would have me. I learned how to walk in heels, how to smile and hold my tongue when he wanted me to, how to make myself a perfect extension of his ambition.

I had wanted so badly to make him proud. I wanted him to see me, to choose me. I told myself that if I did everything exactly right, he'd soften, and maybe even apologize for the wreckage he'd left behind.

But he never did.

He taught me how to be useful, and right now, I was not useful to him.

"I'm not marrying Grant."

He was so quiet I could hear my pulse in my ears, but then he exhaled, his disappointment raking over every inch of me.

"You're making things unnecessarily difficult." His voice was even colder now, more precise and damning. "Do you understand what you're giving up?"

My eyes flicked to Ruby as she shifted, her hand twisting into the fabric of my shirt, and I suddenly felt equal parts pity and anger for my father.

"I do."

"I'll let you sleep on it," he said, his voice tight with forced patience. "Don't throw away everything because Grant didn't live up to your expectations. I expect you to answer when I call next time." The line went dead, and I let my phone slide off my shoulder and onto the cushion beside me.

Ruby stirred, breathing a little harder than before, and I realized I must have tightened my grip around her. Her face squished against my arm as she blinked up at me, her blue eyes still glassy with fever and sleep. "Are you leaving?"

"No." The word poured out of me, and I hated myself for the panic in my own voice. I softened it, ducking down to brush her sweaty hair back from her cheek. "I'm here."

She blinked again, her eyelids fluttering twice before falling closed. I watched her as sleep claimed her again, and Lou's words from last night rose like a tide. *Some people aren't built for staying.* My father and Ruby's mother were the same. It didn't matter how they left, they still left behind the same emptiness. I couldn't draw in a full breath as I realized I never wanted to be someone who created that feeling in her.

I sat there for a long time, the light outside the window pooling across the living room. I watched it crawl up Ruby's arm and over the gentle curve of her lips. I traced my finger over her face before I reached for the thermometer, checking again.

I pressed it gently to Ruby's forehead and let my focus narrow in on her, on the way the numbers ticked across the screen.

Finally, it beeped. One hundred point two.

Blaire: Her temp is down to 100.2. She's asleep. Call me when you're close.

I clutched the phone like it was the only rope in a rising flood, hating myself for needing his response, for caring what he thought. Yet, I still checked every few seconds to see if those three dots would appear.

I wrapped my arms around her, pulling her tighter into my chest, one hand running slow and steady down her spine while the other still gripped my phone. I focused on her steady breaths until mine settled with them. The afternoon wrapped around us both, and I was already fast asleep before the phone buzzed in my hand again.

CHAPTER 11
COLT

It was still daylight outside, but the house was dark except for the flickering of the TV. I didn't spot them at first. They were a tangle of arms and legs on the couch, sleeping so deeply that neither of them shifted as I entered the house.

I stood there watching my daughter. She was sprawled across Blaire's chest, face mashed in her neck, blanket tangled around them both. Blaire's arm was slung protectively over her, while the other cupped Ruby's cheek.

I could have stood there forever soaking in the image of the two of them, but that would do me no good. They looked too natural, like Blaire was always meant to fit there, and that scared the hell out of me.

And there it was, the reason I'd set hard rules for myself. I'd never let Ruby get attached to any of my fleeting relationships. Not the women who saw me as a rescue project, and not the ones who offered to help just so they could peek inside our life.

So, I let no one in, not really. No introductions. No sleepovers. Nothing that might make Ruby think someone could stay, or worse, make her hope they would.

But watching Blaire with her, I could feel that line start to blur. I'd spent years protecting Ruby, and in just days, I could see how easily Blaire could ruin it all.

I tried to swallow the dry, hot longing rising in my throat as I moved closer. Ruby's breaths were steady, and she let out the tiniest snore in her sleep. Her skin was cool under my fingertips.

I crouched at the edge of the couch in front of them, and even though I knew I shouldn't, I let myself look at Blaire. For the first time since she left, I let myself really see her. Her hair was longer than it had been before, and I noted more freckles across her face now that she wasn't wearing makeup.

I reached for her shoulder but hesitated. The memory of her falling asleep just like this, curled into me with her hair fanned out over my chest, hit me, and all the years apart fell away in an instant.

My body betrayed me with every heartbeat—muscles remembering her curves, lungs craving her scent, fingertips burning to trace her collarbone. The rise and fall of her chest hypnotized me, and I wanted to drown in her.

I finally pressed my fingers against her shoulder, feeling the warmth of her skin through the thin cotton of her shirt, and shook her gently. She blinked a few times, her dark lashes fluttering against her cheeks, and snuggled closer to Ruby. I shook her again, my fingertips lingering longer than necessary.

Her head turned toward me, eyes unfocused as they locked on me. Her face was unguarded, and her gaze traveled across mine like fingers tracing a half-forgotten map.

But then her body went rigid beneath my daughter, and Ruby's face scrunched in protest as she let out a sleepy groan and burrowed deeper into Blaire's neck.

"I'm sorry." She shook her head, looking away from me. "I didn't mean to fall asleep."

"Don't apologize." My voice came out hoarse, so I cleared my throat. "Has she been asleep long?"

Blaire's eyes flicked to Ruby, then back to me.

"Maybe an hour." Her expression softened as she brushed

hair from Ruby's cheek. "Honestly, I'm not sure how long I've been asleep. Her fever broke, and we were watching *Tangled*."

She'd taken care of my daughter so well when she'd needed her, and I hated how much I liked it. The sight of Blaire touching my kid with so much gentleness made me want to crawl out of my skin. It felt right and wrong at the same damn time, and all I could do was nod and pretend it wasn't unraveling me on the inside.

I opened my mouth, searching for words to cut through the heavy quiet, when Blaire's voice found me first.

"You look different."

"Different?" The word came out with a nervous laugh as her gaze traveled over my jaw, my lips, my eyes.

"Yeah." She nodded as her gaze snagged on my lips.

"It has been ten years. You can't really blame a man for looking older."

"It's not that." She shook her head and finally met my eyes again. "You look tired."

"Wow, Blaire," I laughed. "You're great for a man's ego."

Her words were raw, real, and not untrue. *I was tired.*

"You don't need my help for that." Her gaze fell back to my mouth. "You grew a mustache."

This time I did laugh, unable to hold it back. "I did. Do you not like it?"

She narrowed her eyes, and everything about this moment, about the way she was looking at me, reminded me of the Blaire that had been mine.

"I didn't say that." A ghost of a smile played on her lips. "But I'm sure all the ladies around here love it. Is that how you get them?"

I felt the corners of my mouth twitch up. "What ladies? I'm a little busy for ladies, Blaire."

Her hand ran over the back of Ruby's head. "Could've fooled me," Blaire whispered as she tugged the blanket higher over Ruby. "But she is cute."

Her eyes didn't linger on mine long enough for me to figure

out what she was actually thinking, but my throat tightened as I traced my thumb across Ruby's cheek.

"Are you talking about my mustache or my kid?" I asked, lowering my voice so I wouldn't wake Ruby.

Blaire's eyes caught the dim light from the TV, reflecting it back with a challenge I hadn't seen in a long time.

"I was talking about Ruby. That thing on your face..." She squinted at me, like she needed to see it from all angles. "It's a little slutty."

A laugh burst from my chest. "Slutty?"

Blaire shrugged as her lips twitched, but I knew damn well she was fighting back a real smile. "That's what I said."

"How the hell can a mustache be slutty?" I ran my fingers over the facial hair and her eyes tracked the movement.

"I don't make the rules, Colt. It just makes you look—" She trailed off, so I finished her sentence for her.

"Slutty?" I cocked a brow.

"Exactly." She lifted one of her hands and motioned to my entire face. "Slutty."

I laughed again, and she looked so lost in the movement that she allowed her eyes to track over every part of me. "I may be giving off the wrong impression as a single dad. Maybe I should shave it."

"No." The word rushed out of her before she pressed her lips together and her cheeks flushed pink. "It suits you."

"It suits me to look slutty? I'm not sure if you're insulting me or not."

She shrugged again, eyes flicking away from me. "I guess you'll never know."

My chest ached with how easy this felt, and I was so fucking glad she couldn't see inside my head. My thoughts were a mess, colliding so fast I couldn't catch one before the next hit. Every laugh, every smile, every second only made it worse, stirring up this hunger for someone who wasn't mine anymore.

"You look different too, you know?"

Her eyes darted up to mine, startled, like she'd thought only she'd been allowed to notice the changes time had carved into a person.

"I look exactly the same," she said, tone flat but too quick, a bluff called out with the cards already on the table.

I shook my head, refusing to let her wriggle out of it. "No, you don't."

She pressed her lips together, and I could see it in every small twitch of her mouth. She wanted to argue, but she didn't. Blaire had always had something to say, but the silence between us now was more fraught than any fight we'd ever had.

There was a hardness around her eyes that hadn't been there before, a narrowing, like the world had taught her to expect the worst and she'd learned the lesson a little too well.

"You've got more freckles on the bridge of your nose," I said. "And here," I added, reaching out before I could think twice. I traced my fingers over the line of her jaw and the cluster of new freckles.

She held her breath as if afraid to inhale me. Her eyes flicked to my hand, then back to my face, and for a second, everything else faded out. She shivered, just a little, and I should have pulled back. I should have remembered all the reasons this was a bad idea.

But I let my thumb rest against her skin, just below her ear. "And here."

She tilted her chin up, almost imperceptibly, and her breath caught in her throat. My heart thudded so loud I was certain she could hear it through the bone and flesh between us.

"We've changed, but so much has stayed the same, hasn't it?" I met her eyes, and the air between us thickened until it felt like she was the only thing I could breathe in. Her pupils dilated slightly, and I watched her throat work as she swallowed, neither of us willing to be the first to look away.

"Colt," she whispered my name, and I knew I had to stop this.

"Thank you for picking her up." I dragged my gaze away from

Blaire and focused on the faint freckles that bloomed across Ruby's nose that always reminded me of her. "I should get her home."

"Of course." She shifted slightly beneath Ruby.

I moved forward, my hands sliding beneath my daughter's small frame, fingers brushing against the cotton of Blaire's shirt as I lifted Ruby's dead weight from her chest. She was heavy with sleep, and her clothes were damp where her fever had broken. Her head lolled against my shoulder as she wrapped her arms around my neck. I leaned in, touched my cheek to her temple, and even though I tried not to, my gaze drifted back to Blaire.

She looked away fast, as if I had caught her intruding. Her hands curled into the couch cushion, and then she stood as I adjusted Ruby in my arms. Blaire's body brushed against mine for the briefest moment, and the contact shot heat straight through me, so sudden and damning I stumbled over my next words.

"She really likes you, you know?"

Blaire's face went still. "I like her too."

Her words came out barely above a whisper, and I let myself read between the lines, hunting for all the maybes and almosts and what-ifs that might have been hidden between the syllables.

Her brown eyes burned into mine, traveling over every line and shadow of my face with such intensity that my skin warmed beneath her gaze.

I hitched Ruby higher against my chest, her weight settling into me like she'd been designed to fit there. The silence stretched between us, and my throat closed around everything I knew I should have said, leaving only her name to pass through my lips.

"Blaire."

Her eyes lifted to mine, heavy-lidded but unmistakably alive in a way that made my pulse quicken. "Yeah?"

God, she was beautiful.

She looked exactly like she did at night when I closed my eyes and dreams of her were the only thing I could see.

I couldn't look away as she stood there with parted lips,

waiting for me to find words that seemed trapped somewhere between my racing heart and my throat.

Say something, you idiot. Anything.

"This feels too damn easy." My throat worked as I looked over every inch of her my eyes could trace. "You're dangerous."

I could hear the wind press against the wood siding of the house, the tick of the clock in the kitchen, the inhale and exhale of Ruby's breath against my shoulder. The rest of the world faded to nothing but the two of us standing there, and the truth of what I'd said. Blaire was dangerous. Not like a loaded gun or a gathering storm. Her danger lay in the quiet persistence of hope. It was a splinter beneath my skin that worked deeper with every heartbeat, impossible to dig out no matter how desperately I tried.

She flinched, and her eyes widened before her lashes swept down, then up again. "That's not true."

"It is." For one careless second, I let myself lean closer, close enough to catch the faint trace of strawberries clinging to her skin, close enough to remember the way we'd burned for each other when it was us and no one else. My gaze dropped to her mouth, and her lips parted as she exhaled.

"Ruby's been through a lot."

She looked at my daughter, her gaze softening as it traced Ruby's sleeping form, and when she looked back to me, that softness lingered. "I was only helping, Colt. I don't know what you think I'm capable of."

I swallowed, feeling that old, reckless want surge up before I could fight it down. "I know exactly what you're capable of. That's the damn problem."

Her head moved slowly from side to side. "Colt," she breathed, and the sound of my name on her lips crawled beneath my skin.

Her eyes held shadows I'd never seen before, a hesitation that made me wonder what had happened in the years we'd been apart. I thought of her father's voice when he'd called her that summer, the way he was cold and detached even when asking her to come with him.

I thought of the diamond she must have worn, picked by a man who'd never seen her climb on the roof of his truck at midnight, making up names of constellations as she pointed them out. I wondered if he'd ever seen her doubled over with laughter, gasping for air, or watched her float in a lake, talking about her dreams, while he treaded water beside her and held on to every word.

Her father had told her I was a phase, something wild to burn through before she settled down and made herself useful, and standing here now, I could see what that had cost her. The walls she'd built around herself were so visible, brick by careful brick, and something in me raged against them.

I hated myself for ever letting her believe she was hard to love when loving her had been the easiest thing I'd ever done.

Ruby shifted between us, her small voice breaking the spell. "Blaire," she mumbled against my shoulder, her arms squeezing around my neck.

I ran my palm down Ruby's back, trying to soothe her. "Hey, darlin'. I've got you," I whispered, and she pulled back slightly to look up at me.

"Daddy?" Her voice was small and thick with sleep.

"I'm here, baby girl." I brushed her hair from her flushed cheek.

Ruby blinked slowly before she pressed her face back into my shirt, her fingers clinging to me, but her sleepy little eyes searched until they landed on Blaire.

"Can Blaire come with us?" she whispered, words slurred with sleep but still sharp enough to cut clean through me.

I hesitated, caught in the crossfire between Ruby's sleepy plea and the way Blaire swayed, uncertain, like she was fighting the reflex to say yes. I wanted to give Ruby the world, but if I let Blaire in, if I let her take even one more step past the defenses I'd built, there would be no going back. That pain behind my ribs, the one I'd spent the last decade trying to cauterize, flared hot and wild.

Blaire's throat worked as she reached out and ran her fingers over Ruby's hand. "Your daddy's got you now. Why don't you get some rest, and I'll check on you later?"

Ruby's head bobbed once, her eyelids already falling shut again. "Okay," she mumbled into my collar. "But you make me feel better."

I caught Blaire's eyes over the top of Ruby's head, and the naked tenderness there made my body stiffen with wanting and warning all at once. I should have looked away, but I couldn't break the connection, not even when guilt shadowed Blaire's face and she finally dropped her gaze.

She moved to the rocking chair in the corner of the living room, lifting a sweatshirt that was draped over the back. The blue fabric was worn and faded, and "Duke University" was written across the chest in peeling white letters. Her fingers lingered on the worn cotton, tracing some invisible memory before she extended it in our direction, the fabric hanging loose from her outstretched hand.

"Do you want to take this with you?" she said, voice cautious. "It's too big for you, but it's—" She paused, swallowing hard. "It's gotten me through some rough nights."

Ruby blinked, then reached out and fisted one sleeve in her hand. "It's soft," she said, already rubbing her cheek against the cotton like a security blanket. "It's yours?"

Blaire nodded, her eyes shining in drifting sunlight. "Yeah, but you can borrow it until you don't need it anymore."

A little more of the tension in Ruby's body dissolved, and she slackened her grip around my neck enough to let me hold her out from my body a bit. Blaire pulled the sweatshirt over Ruby's head, the fabric swallowing her whole. I wanted to step back, to put distance between us, but my feet wouldn't move. Ruby's arms only reached the elbows of the shirt as she wrapped it tightly around herself, breathing in the fabric deeply before falling back against me.

"Thank you," Ruby whispered.

Blaire's scent wrapped around us both, it wrapped my child in warmth, and I was caught between gratitude that it offered Ruby comfort and so much damn regret.

"You're welcome," Blaire said, her hand hovering over Ruby's back before finally settling on the sweatshirt. "I'll check on you tonight, okay? I'll text your daddy."

Ruby's head bobbed once, her eyelids already falling shut again. "Pinkie promise?" she mumbled against my neck, but she held up her hand in Blaire's direction.

Blaire looked at my baby girl with such tenderness in her eyes that it made me want to both shield Ruby from her and beg her never to look away.

"Pinkie promise," Blaire said, her voice catching slightly as she linked her finger with Ruby's and gave it a little squeeze. The simple gesture carried the weight of a thousand unspoken complications.

Blaire stared up at me, and it was like a whole conversation happened in the space between us that neither of us would say out loud. Ruby's breaths went slow and steady against my neck while my own caught in my throat. I couldn't stop looking at Blaire even as I told myself to look away.

She'd been back in town for only a handful of days, and it was like two halves of me colliding—the life I had to build and the one I'd never stopped wanting. "I really appreciate this."

She gave a quick nod, and I turned to the door before the temptation of her could override my better judgment. My feet carried me forward while every other part of me strained for her. For the first time in years, the distance between us was measured in breaths rather than miles.

I gripped the door handle, its metal cool beneath my palm, and I told myself not to turn around.

I turned anyway.

Blaire hadn't moved an inch, fingers twisted in the fabric bunched at her waist, gaze burning into mine like she couldn't look anywhere else.

I almost walked back to her. I wanted it so badly my bones

ached with it, the same way they'd ached that summer when she left, even as my mind screamed at me to keep walking.

One step toward her and I'd be lost again. My daughter's warm weight against me was the only anchor keeping me from drifting into the treacherous pull of Blaire Monroe's gravity. It reminded me why I shouldn't, couldn't, stay.

So, I pushed the door open and forced myself to leave.

CHAPTER 12
BLAIRE

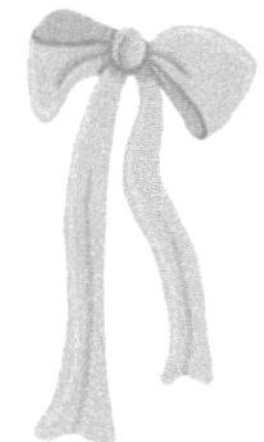

Whatever had been left of my manicure was gone by the time I finished the north field. June had given me gloves before I walked out this morning, but I'd left them on the porch rail. There was something about feeling the dirt on my hands, watching it wedge itself beneath my nails until I could barely recognize them. The work felt necessary, and each time my fingers sank into the soil, my chest settled and rooted itself back to this place.

I couldn't stop thinking about the idea of selling June's jams online. I'd pulled out my laptop last night, started building a website and designing labels.

"I'm calling it June's Jams," I'd said to June, and she snorted like it was the silliest thing she'd ever heard. But she didn't fight me.

By the time I finally dragged myself into June's kitchen, my hands were coated in dirt up to my wrists and every muscle in my body hummed with a satisfying, bone-deep exhaustion.

I moved to the sink, scrubbing my hands, and downed two glasses of water before I turned to look at my grandmother.

June sat at the table that was covered in chaotic piles of paperwork. Her reading glasses were perched high on her head, and she was glowering down at the papers in front of her.

"What are you doing over there?" I asked as I leaned back against the counter.

June glanced up with so much exasperation that it made me choke back a laugh. "I might as well be planning my funeral. It will be here before I sort through all this for my accountant." She snatched a sticky note off the counter, crumpled it, then threw it over her shoulder and nowhere near the trash can. "He's been calling for papers for my taxes, but I told him he's gonna have to wait."

My legs ached as I crossed the kitchen and dropped into the chair opposite her. "Want help?"

June's eyebrows knitted together, her mouth tilting sideways. "Sweet of you to offer, but there's no use trying to untangle this mess. It's a lost cause."

"It's not a lost cause," I said, reaching for the nearest pile. I picked up an ancient water bill and held it up to her. "What's the system here? Do you have them by date or subject?"

"System?" June huffed, tugging off her glasses. "That's cute. I just throw everything in a box."

"Jesus, June." I flipped through the stack and found a yellowed warranty for a fridge I knew for a fact she no longer owned. "You know you don't have to keep every single piece of paper you ever come across. Some people even have these things called computers." I wiggled my fingers in the air between us, like a stage magician conjuring up some rare artifact.

"Don't need one," she answered stubbornly, lifting her hands and showing me her calloused palms. "Computers are for people who don't know how to use their hands."

"Yet, filing cabinets are for everyone." I thumbed through a stack of faded receipts and bank statements so old the ink was hard to read. "Please let me take over here before this paper avalanche buries us both. You're going to crush June's Jams before we even get it up and running."

June snorted and crossed her arms. "All right, city girl, have at it. But remember when you 'fixed' my refrigerator, and I couldn't find a damn thing." She nodded toward her fridge. "I never found my mustard."

"You're going to thank this *city girl* when the IRS isn't banging on your door, and that mustard was expired."

June laughed, a throaty sound that seemed to fill every inch of her kitchen, and the warmth of it loosened something in my shoulders as I dug in and began sorting.

An hour passed, maybe more, as we sifted through decades of letters, bills, and records. There was a newspaper clipping with my name circled where I'd made the honor roll. Then there was a picture of me and Hunter, and I couldn't have been more than twelve. Hunter was scrawny and gangly, and he had braces covering his teeth as he smiled wide at the camera. I pulled out my phone and snapped a picture of it before I sent it to Maggie.

Blaire: Here you go. Just in case you ever need blackmail.

Maggie's response was almost instant.

Maggie: Holy shit. Please tell me that's Hunter and not Colt.

Blaire: That's him, all right.

I pushed the photo to the side only to find old birthday cards from my mom, her handwriting still recognizable despite the years. I ran my fingers over the familiar loop of her letters and the slight smear of the ink where she dragged her pinkie when she wrote.

My eyes prickled with tears, and I'd almost forgotten June was there until she cleared her throat.

"Ruby's doing better. No fever since late last night."

"Yeah." I nodded, focusing intently on aligning the corners of a stack of receipts. "I texted Colt this morning."

June's eyes caught mine over her reading glasses, one eyebrow arching upward. "You've been texting Colt?"

My fingers fumbled with the papers, sending several sliding across the table, but I quickly snatched them back up. "It's not— I wanted to check on Ruby. I got his number from your phone when I picked her up yesterday."

"Mmhmm." June's knowing hum filled the room, and I prayed she wouldn't press further, not when my own thoughts were a mess.

I'd texted Colt more than just this morning. I'd checked on Ruby multiple times through the night, and each reply from him sent a confusing rush of warmth and dread through me. I could still feel the ghost of his hand on my neck when he'd pointed out the new freckles on my skin. He hadn't touched me in the same way that he used to, with that easy, absentminded possession that made me feel like the only girl in the world. He was careful now, not letting his fingers linger too long.

The scene from yesterday kept flickering through my mind like a skipping record. He'd peeled Ruby off my chest and carefully lifted her into his arms. The whole time, his eyes had never left my face, watching me like I was something dangerous that he needed to protect himself from.

Dangerous.

He'd called me that before, back in his truck our junior year. After I'd grown tired of us circling each other with a tension that built day by day until I could barely breathe. I'd climbed across that worn bench seat, settled my knees on either side of him, and watched his eyes go dark.

"Christ, Blaire," he'd whispered, his hands hovering at my hips, not quite touching. "You're so fucking dangerous."

But this was different. Now, he saw me as a threat to the fragile world he'd patched together for him and Ruby.

The word stuck to my insides, and I didn't know what to do with it. Part of me wanted to be risky with him again, wanted to feel the heat in his gaze for all the right reasons, the old reasons.

But there was another part of me, the one that had learned to keep my heart guarded, that knew how quickly all that heat could burn everything around it, and I refused to let Ruby get hurt because of me.

I'd spent years becoming the girl who didn't fall for men in a pair of boots with thick thighs and a damn mustache, but a single look from him had me back at square one.

Colt was a bad habit I'd slide right back into if I wasn't careful.

I pretended not to notice June studying me. Reaching for another stack of papers, I began sorting mechanically, my thumb flipping through each document as I arranged them into tidy categories. But then a thick envelope caught my attention, and I slid my fingers under the flap and pulled out the papers from inside.

Deed of Trust.

The date stamped across the top was the year my mom got sick, and I quickly skimmed the page, not really absorbing the details until two names jumped out at me. *Owen and Louise Calloway.*

I stared at the names of Colt's parents, typed neatly at the bottom of the page next to June's, with all three of their signatures above them. The black ink blurred, and I had to blink to bring it back into focus.

Why were they on the deed to my grandmother's property?

I tried to dig up some memory of this happening, but there'd never been so much as a whisper. But I had been a teenager then, and I was so wrapped up in losing my mother.

I was so consumed in Colt and how he seemed to be the only thing that held me together.

I flipped through the next page, and my mother's name appeared, sandwiched between legal jargon and notary stamps. This wasn't just a deed. It was a loan. Not a small one either. The numbers ran well into six figures, and I felt my jaw clench as I realized how much it must have taken to keep our house, our lives, from falling apart when my mom got sick.

And the Calloways had co-signed. They'd put their land up alongside ours as collateral.

How had I not known? Of course I knew that my mother's treatments were expensive, but neither my mother nor June had ever let on how bad it was.

I thought of all the times my mama had sat at this kitchen table, staring out the window with a smile that didn't quite reach her eyes, telling me not to worry. Part of me had believed her then, needed to believe her, while another part had seen the truth in the way her fingers trembled around her coffee mug. I'd chosen the comfort of the lie over the terror of what might be coming.

And it was foolish.

I held the papers as anger and gratitude wrestled inside me. I tried to imagine June, proud and stubborn to her marrow, asking the Calloways for help. I knew that both Mr. Calloway and Lou had agreed without a moment of hesitation. It wouldn't have mattered that Colt's mother and mine had been friends most of their lives; the Calloways were good all the way down to their core.

They had signed their names to that document, risked the ranch they'd poured their lives into, all so my family could survive, so my mother could have a chance. The Calloways had tied their entire legacy to ours. They'd staked every fencepost, every acre of their own future, and I could hardly breathe as it hit me. If anything had gone wrong, their land was on the line too.

I wondered if Colt had known, if he'd realized what his family had wagered for mine.

The weight of everything I hadn't known or wanted to know pressed down on me, spreading through my chest and up into my throat. I thought of all those years since, about how I'd been gone, building my new life, while June and the Calloways had continued shouldering a debt I didn't know existed.

That realization knocked the air from my lungs. I glanced up at June, my fingers gripping the edge of the papers so hard they crumpled. I wanted to scream at her for keeping this from me, for taking this on all on her own, but the words tangled with such fierce gratitude. Because of her and the Calloways, I'd spent those last months with my mom with the illusion that we'd be okay.

I pressed the papers flat on the table, smoothing them with my fingers until they lay perfectly aligned. The gesture felt pointless, but I couldn't control the shame that hit me because I hadn't known or the relief that flooded me because June had protected me.

"What is this?" I finally managed, my voice cracking between accusation and plea.

June didn't answer right away. She leaned forward, elbows braced on the edge of the table, staring down at the papers in front of me. "That," she said finally, reaching for the deed, "is the reason this place is still ours."

"I didn't know," I said, because what else was there to say? "You should have told me."

June's mouth tugged into a sad smile. "You were fifteen when we did this, Blaire. What would telling you have done?" She pushed her glasses up, her gaze pinning me in place. "Your mother and I tried to figure it all out on our own, but sometimes, you take help when it's offered. Especially from people who love you."

"I wouldn't have left," I admitted as I shook my head. "You should have told me, and I would have stayed. I would have helped."

June let out a long, exaggerated sigh. "You wanted to go, Blaire, and your father—" Her mouth twisted like she'd bitten into something sour. "That man may not be my favorite person in the world, but he gave you opportunities I couldn't. A college education. A future beyond these fences. If you'd wanted to stay, I would have moved heaven and earth to make it work, but you wanted to go."

Because of Colt.

I thought of the way I'd spent my whole life in orbit around Colt Calloway, how every plan I made was shaped by him. It was true. I had wanted to go, but only because he'd told me to. I'd told myself I was protecting my heart, building a life beyond the girl I'd been in Willow Grove.

I hadn't been thinking about what I left behind beyond him. I didn't consider how much my grandmother needed me or how much his family had given. I had spent all those years selfishly trying to create a new life, and for nothing. It slipped away so easily because it had never really been mine.

"Your mama's Trust protected the acres in it specifically for you. She made sure her part of the land would be waiting when you turn thirty, no matter what happened with the rest." June's eyes held mine.

I nodded slowly. I had found out about my inheritance shortly after she died, but the Trust had been a distant fact in the back of my mind all these years. But the rest of it, the loans, the Calloways, the desperation, that had been kept from me entirely.

I wanted to ask June if she regretted it, if she ever sat in the quiet of this kitchen and wondered if the cost had been worth it. But my phone buzzed against the table so suddenly I nearly jumped. The sound ricocheted through the kitchen, and I watched the screen light up, the name Senator Monroe flashing across my screen over and over.

June's eyes flicked to the phone, then to me, and back to the phone again. "You gonna get that?" Her tone was casual, but I could tell she was already bracing for whatever I might say next.

"It's—" I trailed off, rubbing my palm flat against the paperwork and wishing the world would slow down for a few seconds. "It's my dad." I picked up my phone and hit the button to send it to voice mail. "He'll be fine. I talked to him yesterday."

She stilled, watching me carefully. "What did he want?"

"He wants me to come back and salvage my relationship," I said with a bitter laugh. "He thinks I should patch things up with Grant, pretend everything is fine, and stop 'embarrassing' myself by giving up such a 'good man'." The words "good man" fell from my mouth like a curse, dripping with all the venom I couldn't contain.

June grunted as she crossed her arms. "I hate that man."

"He doesn't get it." I shook my head. "He thinks if I talk to Grant again, I'll realize I'm throwing away the best thing that's ever happened to me."

"You're not," June commented without hesitation. "That asshole never deserved you. He's nothing but a rich prick, and I never liked him."

I couldn't stop the chuckle that bubbled up out of me. "You never even met Grant."

I had begged her to come so many times to meet me, but she'd always found an excuse.

"I didn't need to." She leaned back in her chair. "I could see it in the photos you sent. In the way you talked about him. There are men who are good and men who are good at pretending. Your daddy was always the latter, and I could tell Grant is the same."

I tried to laugh it off, but she was right.

"If you ever think about going back to that man, you better bring me with you so I can knock some sense into you first."

June's words landed heavy because I knew my father and Grant wouldn't stop trying to pull me back into that life, no matter what it cost me.

"There's not a chance in hell." I shook my head. "I'm not going back."

The thought of permanently settling into my grandmother's house and helping her tend the farm day after day seemed both impossible and comforting. But then I thought about June's Jams and how we could make it work.

Then there was Mama's Trust, those acres she'd set aside just for me. I'd spent years not thinking about the inheritance, that safety net, but now I felt something settle in my chest. This wasn't just land. It was roots. It was hers, and mine, and it was home.

I wiped my hands down the front of my shorts, gathering myself before I spoke again. "I think I'm gonna stick around here for a while, if that's okay."

June's smile was so wide, it revealed the slight gap between her front teeth before she reached across the table and squeezed my hand, her fingers warm against mine. "Baby," she said, her voice thick with emotion, "there's nowhere else I'd want you to be."

CHAPTER 13
COLT

The hammering hit me before we even made it up the porch steps. A steady *pound, pound, pound,* like somebody was trying to dismantle the house from within.

I squeezed Ruby's hand in mine and knocked against June's door, but the racket inside drowned it out. I was about to do it again when Blaire's voice rang out over the noise.

"It's open!"

I pulled open the door and watched Ruby's little nose scrunch up. The stench of mildew and stale water was thick, like a damp basement that hadn't been aired out in months, and the place was a mess. There were blue tarps strung across the ceiling, boxes stacked up against the far wall, and a metal ladder rising from the living room floor straight up to a jagged hole overhead.

The whine of a power saw cut through the air from somewhere upstairs before it cut off with a pop, and there, standing in the middle of the chaos, was Blaire.

She darted from the kitchen sink back to the table, hair knotted on top of her head, dust streaked across one of her cheeks. A roll of paper towels was tucked under one arm, and she was muttering to herself when she finally looked up and saw us.

"Blaire!" Ruby squealed, ready to take off in her direction, but I caught her before she could.

"What the hell happened in here?" I asked as I scanned the room, trying to figure out what was going on.

"Shit," Blaire cursed under her breath, dropping the paper towels on the table and blowing a loose strand of hair out of her face. "Did June not call you? She's at your parents'."

"June didn't call." I blinked, taking in the mess again, then met her eyes. "Did a tornado come through that I wasn't aware of?"

"Ha ha." Blaire moved into the living room, carefully stepping over things on the floor. "Apparently, we've had a slow water leak, which turned into a very big leak in the middle of the night last night."

As if to prove her point, another thud landed, and the whole house seemed to shudder, a few puffs of pink insulation floating to the ground from the hole in the ceiling.

"Have you been up all night?" I look around the living room, noticing pillows and blankets strewn across the couch, two suitcases half closed on the floor, and an entire trash bag filled with wet towels near the doorway.

She wiped her hands down her shirt and gave an exhausted laugh. "I slept a little."

"Is it safe?" I pushed Ruby behind me as I took a cautious step farther in and peered up at the blue tarp that appeared to be barely holding on.

"I unplugged everything. The contractors have been up there since around six. He said it's not structural, whatever that means." Her eyes flicked around the room before they landed on Ruby. "Sorry it's a disaster. June really was supposed to call you."

I eyed the ladder, the unsteady blue tarp overhead, and the dripping insulation visible through the gap in the ceiling. The hammering started up again, echoing down the walls. But Ruby was undeterred by the mess and ducked around my hip, making a beeline for Blaire. She nearly tripped over a cord on the floor but caught herself, then flung her arms around Blaire's legs.

"Ruby!" I called after her, but Blaire grinned as she bent, ruffling Ruby's hair.

"Did you sleep here?" I asked as I nodded to the couch, and I was pretty sure one arm was damp. I tipped my chin to the ceiling above it, and sure enough, watermarks.

"For a few hours." She gestured toward the ceiling without meeting my eyes. "The leak started in my room, which is right above June's." *I already knew that.* "Part of the ceiling gave way in the middle of the night, and water leaked straight through the floor. They said we've got multiple bad pipes, old and rusty, and need to be replaced. June's room caught the worst of it, I think."

"She's at Mom and Dad's now?" I was still taking stock of all the damage, but fuck, there was a lot.

"Yeah. Your mom came by this morning and practically dragged her out of here in her pajamas." Blaire smiled, but she looked wrung out. "She's going to stay there until we get this fixed."

Ruby peeled herself off Blaire's leg and started climbing onto the couch, or I guess I should say, Blaire's bed. "This is fun!"

"This is not fun, Ruby." I turned back to Blaire, but her eyes were anywhere but on me. "This isn't safe."

Blaire's eyes darted up as the hammering started again. "It's just water, Colt. They said it's under control." She moved to the couch and started tucking the sheets and pillows into a tighter pile as if that would somehow make things feel less dire.

"They may have this under control, but this is a lot." I glanced up the stairwell before I started climbing them two at a time. "Ruby, stay with Blaire."

"Colt! It's fine!" Blaire yelled after me, but I wasn't listening.

The stairs creaked under my weight, and I paused at the top, peering down the hall. The hallway carpet was soaked to hell and back, darkening the walls where the water had trailed downward. Every few steps, I had to maneuver around bits of soggy drywall or old insulation until I finally heard voices coming from Blaire's room.

I stepped inside to find Cal and one of his men ripping out a huge chunk of wet drywall as they shined a flashlight behind it to get a better look. Cal had lived in this town his whole life, and he'd probably worked on our property at least a hundred times. He was a good man, and I trusted his work, but then he cursed under his breath and clenched his jaw.

I cleared my throat. "Morning, Cal."

"Mornin'," he grumbled and wiped some gunk from his hand onto his jeans.

He barely gave me a nod before slicing another strip of drywall and moving it aside. The stuff was soggy enough that it slumped over itself like wet bread, and the smell coming off the insulation behind it was, if possible, even worse than the living room.

"Any idea what caused it?" I leaned on the doorframe and folded my arms, watching as Cal's assistant started pulling out sodden insulation by the handful.

Cal shook his head at the mess before cutting his gaze back at me. "They built this house before the good stuff. Galvanized pipes, old as hell. I think she's had a slow leak for months at least, but one of these pinholes finally gave out and pushed it over." He jabbed a thumb at the cavity in the wall. "Water's everywhere. We'll have to clear most of this out, rip up the carpet, and half of these walls before we can even replace the pipes."

"How long?" I asked, trying to keep the edge out of my voice.

Cal ran a hand over his jaw, eyes not leaving the mess in front of him. "Weeks, maybe more. I can patch her up livable, but we're looking at a full re-pipe and a lot of drywall. If it rotted the subfloor through—" His eyes widened.

I tried not to imagine what else could go wrong, but my mind cycled through all of it anyway. Mold, the framing, the floors. June could barely handle her farm, let alone all of this.

"All right," I said, forcing a steadiness I didn't feel. "Let me know if you need anything."

Cal grunted, already lost in the next section of wall, and I backed down the hallway carefully before heading back downstairs.

From the bottom of the stairs, I caught Blaire pacing in the kitchen, her thumb tapping rapidly across her phone screen, while Ruby talked her ear off from where Blaire had perched her on the counter.

"You have got to be kidding me," Blaire muttered, her shoulders slumping as she stared at her phone.

Ruby leaned forward on the counter, nearly toppling over. "Is it bad news?"

"Every hotel within twenty miles is full. Even the two Airbnbs on the lake are booked." Blaire's thumb scrolled frantically. "Damn tourists. Can't they go see something besides our mountains for once?"

"Yeah." Ruby folded her arms and furrowed her brow in a perfect imitation of Blaire's frustrated expression. "Damn tourists."

Blaire's head snapped up, and she stepped toward Ruby. "Oh my god, Ruby. Don't say that."

"But you said it," Ruby pointed out as she shifted and sat cross-legged on the counter.

"I know." Blaire winced. "That doesn't make it okay. Your dad would kill us."

"Kill you for what?" I asked, stepping away from the staircase and toward the kitchen.

"Damn tourists!" Ruby announced with so much frustration in her voice that a laugh escaped me.

Blaire, however, pressed her fingers against her temples and closed her eyes. If she didn't look so exhausted, I would have kept laughing.

"Hey, baby girl. Maybe dang is the word we're looking for." I smiled at Blaire and allowed myself to watch her for longer than I should have. "Damn isn't a very kind word."

"I'm sorry. Ruby was copying me, and all the hotels are booked up—"

"Because of the damn tourists?" I cut her off.

"Yes, because of the tourists." Her gaze flicked to Ruby. "And I was frustrated."

"Did you try the bed-and-breakfast off Myrtle?" I tried to think of any others that may not have been on whatever website she was scrolling.

"Yes. I called there first," she said, straightening her shoulders as if she were bracing herself. "I can run down to the hardware store and get some more tarps to block off the living room and kitchen. Cal said—"

"Cal said that this is going to take weeks to fix, and that's only if the subfloor isn't damaged," I cut in, and she winced. "Blaire, you can't live in this."

Blaire drew herself up taller, but I could see her chin trembling a little. "I'm fine. I've slept on that couch dozens of times growing up."

"That's not the point." I set my jaw. "There is water everywhere, probably mold. Who knows when Cal will get the water turned back on. You're not living in a house without water."

"I'm fine."

If she said that one more time, I was going to lose my shit. "You'll come stay with me and Ruby at our house on the ranch until the repairs are done. You're not sleeping under a goddamn tarp with toilets that won't flush."

She stared at me, her mouth falling open, eyes wide with shock. My heart hammered against my ribs as the weight of what I'd done crashed over me. I hadn't planned to say it until the words were already out.

Neither of us spoke as the hammering continued upstairs, but then Ruby let out a squeal so loud I winced.

"Can she really?" she shrieked, twisting on the counter and nearly sending herself flying. "Can she stay in my room? Please say yes, please say yes, please say yes!" The words tumbled out, and she jumped down from the counter before Blaire or I could answer.

"No. I couldn't." Blaire shook her head, but Ruby wasn't listening.

"Blaire, pleeeeeease," Ruby begged, arms wrapped around Blaire's hips as she stared up at her. "We can paint our nails and do sleepovers and watch movies, and I'll even let you use my special blanket and sleep in my bed!"

"Ruby." Blaire said her name gently as she shot me a helpless look. "I swear I'm okay here."

"We have a spare room," I said before I could stop myself. "And I'm rarely there during the day. Once Ruby and I leave for school, I'm out on the ranch until the evening. You won't even have to see me."

Blaire snorted, the sound so familiar it hit somewhere below my ribs. "Is that supposed to make it more tempting?"

I shrugged. "You can come stay with us, or I'll call my mom and she'll force you to come stay with them. Would you rather have a bed to yourself or share a bed with June in my old room?"

I let the threat dangle in the air because we both knew how badly June snored. Plus, I was sure Blaire hated the idea of my mom fussing over her for the next few weeks.

She squinted at me, jaw tense. "So, those are my options? Sleep in this mess, deal with June's snoring, or Calloway charity?"

"It's not charity," I shot back, palming the edge of the counter to keep from saying something I'd regret. "And you only have two of those options. I'll drag your ass out of this house over my shoulder before I let you stay here."

Blaire's eyes narrowed, and I could see the argument building inside her, could practically taste the way she was about to tell me to go to hell. So I used the only thing I had to use against her.

"Besides, Ruby's already got her hopes up. You don't want to let her down, do you?"

Blaire glanced at Ruby, who was holding her breath with her hands balled up in front of her chest like she could will Blaire to say yes. I watched the fight play out on Blaire's face, the old stubbornness going toe to toe with something softer, something tired.

But in the end, it was Ruby that won out.

Blaire's shoulders sagged a fraction, and she huffed, her eyes darting from the battered ceiling to Ruby and finally, grudgingly, to me. "Fine," she muttered, and I could tell it nearly killed her to say it. "But only until the water's back on."

Ruby let out a whoop and started doing a little victory dance in a circle around Blaire. I couldn't help but grin, even as I tried to figure out what the hell I'd done.

CHAPTER 14
BLAIRE

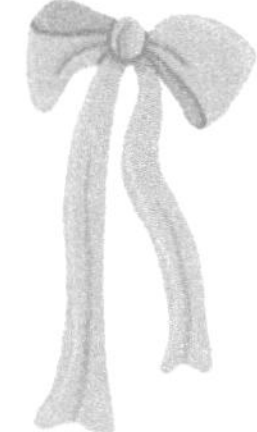

I've made a lot of stupid decisions in my life but driving up Colt's driveway with my suitcase in my trunk might be the worst.

It had been almost a week since I picked up Ruby from school, and I'd spent every day avoiding him. I'd finished helping June sort through her mountains of paperwork, we finally decided on the labels for June's Jams, and I'd laughed hysterically when I tried to get her to do a dance for June's Jams new social media accounts.

All the while, I tried like hell not to think about Colt.

But somehow, his name kept slipping into conversation. Ruby had been over twice since I decided I was avoiding him. She was feeling much better, and even if she wasn't constantly telling me stories about her daddy, I couldn't look at her without thinking about him.

I was losing my mind.

I was supposed to hate Colt Calloway.

It was the one thing I was certain of, the one constant that I could count on, and yet, I sat in my car with my palms sweating around the steering wheel as I stared up at his house.

The big house on the Calloway Ranch stood tall, all weathered siding and river stone, with a sprawling wraparound porch. White rocking chairs lined the eastern side, positioned perfectly to catch both the sunrise and the sweeping view of golden wheat fields that stretched toward the mountains on the horizon.

But Colt's place was a whole different world. It sat much farther back on the property, almost hidden by a wall of trees, and it was so close to the lake that the water seemed to lap right up to his back steps.

It was beautiful and unmistakably his.

Wildflowers spilled from the flower beds that lined his porch, all of them slightly untamed, as if allowed to grow however they pleased. And there were small sunflowers everywhere I looked.

Ruby's pink bike lay tipped against the bottom step, training wheels caked in mud and sparkling tassels streaming from the handlebars. A helmet decorated in butterfly stickers lay upside down farther up the porch as if tossed there mid-adventure.

The wraparound porch itself was nothing like the grand, sweeping one of the big house. This was smaller with mismatched chairs and a porch swing that overlooked the lake.

Where the big house was grand and open, Colt and Ruby's felt like a secret hideaway meant just for them.

Except now I was here too.

But this was temporary. I had no other choice. I could have asked to stay in the main house with June, but the Calloways were already juggling enough. I had seen how exhausted Lou looked, and after what I'd learned about the loan, I couldn't bear to be another burden they had to shoulder.

I killed the engine and took a long, steadying breath before opening the door. The air was warm, and I could hear the soft lapping of the lake beyond the house. My hands trembled as I grabbed my suitcase from the back seat and forced my legs to move toward the house before what little courage I had disappeared.

The flagstone walkway leading to the porch was a riot of color. There were chalk rainbows arched between the stepping stones, unicorns with impossible proportions smiling up at me, and two stick figures holding hands with a giant sunshine above their heads. "Ruby" and "Daddy" were written above them, and I paused, picturing Colt crouched here, gripping the pink chalk and writing their names as Ruby instructed.

The front door opened before I even made it up the steps, and Colt was there in the doorway, leaning a shoulder against the frame as he watched me. His damp hair was pushed out of his face and curling against the nape of his neck as if he'd just stepped out of the shower.

I tore my eyes from his face, only to stare at a threadbare white T-shirt and a pair of gray sweatpants hanging low on his hips. I became acutely aware of the dust and debris that still caked my clothes and the musty scent that clung to me from the disaster at June's, and he stood in the doorway like some domestic god in sweatpants.

"Hey," he said as he wiped his hands on a dishtowel, but he was drinking me in. "You find the place okay?"

"Yeah." I laughed, feeling so out of my depth. "You told me your house was down near the lake, and I did practically live on this ranch once upon a time."

"I remember," he said quietly, his gaze skimmed down, then back up. Heat slid under my skin.

"Did you build this?" I asked, nodding to his house to avoid looking at him.

"Yeah." He nodded, and I wondered if he could see how affected I was by him. "You want a hand with that?" He glanced down at my luggage.

"I've got it," I answered quickly, and I climbed up the steps, my heavy suitcase thunking along behind me.

He didn't move as I reached the threshold. Standing this close, I caught the scent of him, spiced cedar and worn leather that used to cling to my skin, and my traitorous body tensed with the recognition of what it was like to be wrapped in that scent until I was drunk on it.

"Are you just going to stand there and block the door?" I

huffed, my pulse quickening as his eyes drifted down to my lips, lingering there.

He leaned forward slightly, his forearm braced on the doorframe above his head. "Just taking you in, Strawberry," he murmured, voice dropping to a rasp. "I didn't think your stubborn ass would actually show up."

That nickname slid through me like warm honey, pooling low in my belly even as I rolled my eyes. "Yeah, well," I stammered, suddenly aware of how close we were standing. "I could come here or succumb to death by black mold. It took me a while to decide."

He chuckled as he finally stepped back enough for me to slip past. I had to turn sideways to squeeze past him, my stomach tightening as my breasts grazed his chest. My gaze caught on the tiny scar below his jaw, the one I'd given him the night he pushed me away, when I hurled the necklace he'd given me years before back in his face. His eyes darkened as they snagged on my parted lips, and when he swallowed, I watched the movement in his throat with a hunger that terrified me.

His lips twitched as he looked down at me, as if he knew exactly what I was thinking, and I darted past him before I did anything both of us would regret.

His soft chuckle trailed after me. "Need me to grab anything else from your car?" he asked, and I could feel him still watching me.

"No, this is it," I said, my voice betraying me with a slight tremor. I tried to seem unaffected as he finally closed the door with a soft click that jolted through me.

His house was so viscerally domestic—*and so him*. This was where he lived and slept, and I couldn't stop my eyes from tracking over every inch.

His work boots stood beside her tiny pink sneakers near the door, while a pair of fairy wings hung from a hook beside Ruby's rain jacket. The entryway opened up directly into the living room and kitchen, with no walls between them. There were exposed beams and sunlight pouring in from the large windows that had a breathtaking view of the lake.

Ruby's drawings covered the fridge, pinned between mismatched magnets and a photo of her and Colt by the water. Children's books were stacked haphazardly on the coffee table next to a teacup set, and a stuffed unicorn was sprawled across the couch.

Everywhere I turned, there were signs of happiness.

My chest tightened as Colt's eyes tracked me as I took in his home, and his jaw flexed before he retreated to the kitchen.

"Ruby should be out here in a minute," he said, lifting a wooden spoon from the counter and giving a quick stir to the pot on the stove. "I'm going to apologize in advance for all the stuffed animals she moved to your room. She said it looked boring in there."

He laughed as he turned back to face me. I was still standing exactly where he'd left me, white knuckling my suitcase handle. His gaze traveled over me slowly, like he was trying to figure me out.

"This is weird, right?" I blurted out, and heat crawled up my neck as his smile grew until his dimples appeared.

"It's so weird." He nodded, leaning back against the counter, his T-shirt pulled taut against his chest.

He gripped the edge of the counter behind him, the veins in his forearms standing out beneath tanned skin, and I couldn't stop myself from imagining what it would be like if he wrapped his hands around my hips and lifted me onto that very counter.

"We don't have to do this," I said, suddenly desperate for air. "If you'll let me shower, I'll head back to June's for the night. I can come up with a new plan tomorrow."

He snorted. "You're not running back to that mess. I'd catch hell from June and my mom, and Ruby would be devastated." He fixed me with a look that was half amusement, half warning. "And we are both adults."

"Who hate each other," I interjected, and he cocked his head, a muscle in his cheek twitching. His eyes traced over my face, lingering on my mouth, and I bit down on my lip to stop the plea that wanted to escape.

"Do we hate each other?" His voice dropped to a rasp that vibrated through me.

My skin prickled with goosebumps, and I shifted my weight, hands twisting on my suitcase handle until I feared it would break.

"We do," I whispered, but even I could hear the want beneath my words. "We absolutely do."

"You sure about that, Strawberry?" The nickname slid from his lips like a caress.

"Stop calling me that," I snapped, but my stomach fluttered.

"I don't hate you, Blaire." His eyes darkened, and I hated how my body responded, how I swayed toward him without permission. "Things just got complicated."

"Right," I said, my voice sharp. "My world was turned upside down because things got complicated."

The words tasted like acid, and I watched them land. Colt's jaw clenched, and a muscle ticked beneath the stubble. But it wasn't anger in his eyes. It was worse—regret.

"You think I don't know that?" His voice dropped so low it lit every nerve. "That I don't live with that every damn day?" He ran his hand through his hair, tugging at the ends. "Blaire, I—"

"It doesn't matter," I cut him off, raising a hand between us. "It was a long time ago, and it's not—" I swallowed hard, my throat suddenly dry. "It's not something I want to remember or talk about."

He pushed off the counter, each step toward me, stealing my breath until the heat of his body radiated against mine. I had to tilt my head back to meet his gaze.

"Of course it matters," he said, his eyes flicking to my mouth. "Of course it—" He caught himself, chest rising with a deep breath.

I shifted back, my body humming with awareness, every nerve alive and screaming his name.

"We're adults, Blaire." He repeated his words from earlier as if he needed to hear them again. "This isn't complicated. You need a place to stay, and I've got a house with an extra room. We can be cordial. We don't have to do whatever the hell this is."

My heart thundered as he took another half-step closer, close enough that I could feel his breath warm against my lips as he said, "And when June's house is fixed, we can both pretend this whole thing never happened."

I parted my lips to argue, but nothing came out but a shaky exhale that made his pupils dilate.

"Unpack your bag." He swallowed hard and a shiver ran down my spine. "Eat the damn dinner I cooked, and for both our sakes..." His gaze lowered to my lips again. "Let's not make this any harder than it already is."

I opened my mouth to respond, but footsteps thundered down the hallway behind him.

"Daddy, she's here! She's here!" Ruby ran into the room and beelined for me. She was about to slam into me when Colt bent and intercepted her. He scooped her up with one arm and spun her around as she laughed.

I let myself be grateful for the distraction, but I couldn't tear my eyes from the way his arms flexed around her small body, couldn't stop the way my breath hitched as he buried his face in her neck and blew raspberries against her skin until she squealed.

Colt lowered Ruby back to the floor, and she darted to my side, small fingers wrapping around mine as she pulled me forward. There were damp patches on her shoulders from her wet hair, and her pajamas were covered in tiny pink and purple unicorns.

"Come see your room!" She yanked me down the hallway, and I had to move my suitcase out of the way so she wouldn't trip over it.

I glanced back at Colt and caught him watching us with a look that set a low burn across my skin. His gaze dropped to where Ruby's small fingers were wrapped around mine, then slowly traveled back up to meet my eyes with a flash of longing so intense it sent electricity crackling down my spine.

Ruby and I moved down the hall, and she stopped at the first door and pushed the door wide open.

"Oh wow," I said, and Ruby beamed.

"This is my room." She did a twirl in the doorway before she pointed out every single detail she could.

Her comforter was covered in every Disney princess you could imagine, and the bed itself was a fortress of stuffed animals. Bunnies, unicorns, cats, and bears lined her pillows, and I wondered where Ruby slept. Her walls were covered with hand-drawn rainbows and construction paper hearts, and she had a collection of painted rocks neatly lined up on her windowsill, each one done up with glitter and googly eyes.

She had princess dresses exploding out of her closet, and a fairy village constructed from Popsicle sticks on one of her night-stands. There were toys everywhere, organized in a system that felt a bit chaotic, but she moved from one object to the next, telling me all of her favorite things and the names of her dolls.

It was a mess of a happy childhood crammed into one small room, and I couldn't help but stare at the photo on her dresser which stood out among the tiaras and necklaces she had piled there. There was a giant snowman in the background, and all of the Calloways—Hunter, McCoy, Lou, Mr. Calloway, and Colt—were huddled together in front of it, all of them grinning. Ruby was perched on Colt's shoulders, her tiny, gloved hands thrown up in the air. They all looked so happy it made my stomach ache.

Ruby took a quick breath and darted across the room, pulling open the doors of a pink canopy in the corner to show off her "secret fort" inside. She climbed in ahead of me, sitting cross-legged on a pile of blankets and pillows she'd stashed in the back, and gestured for me to join her. I crouched awkwardly in the doorway, peering inside, and I noticed my Duke sweatshirt I'd let her borrow tucked in the corner.

"You can try my fort," she said. "Daddy says even adults can use it if they need to get away from stuff."

I gave her a shaky smile. "I'll keep that in mind."

"Let's go see your room!" She crawled out of her fort and past me before she climbed to her feet, and I followed.

Ruby skipped ahead of me down the hallway, stopping at a door right down from hers. "This is your room." She twisted and pointed to the door directly across the narrow space. "And that's Daddy's. My bathroom is down there." She pointed to the last door at the very end of the hall. "You can share with me, so you don't have to go in Daddy's room."

"Perfect," I said, trying to ignore the way my stomach tightened at the thought.

She flung the door open to the room where I'd be staying, and as Colt promised, the bed was half buried in stuffed animals just like hers. There were more drawings taped unevenly across the walls, and I stared at the one right above the bed that had two stick figures that looked more like giant circles with arms and legs. Both mine and Ruby's names were written across the top.

"It's not boring in here anymore." Ruby quickly climbed on the bed and threw herself down on the pile of animals. "You can sleep with my stuffies, but if you get scared, you can come to my room."

I smiled and moved my suitcase to the end of the bed. "Thank you."

She rolled onto her stomach, propping herself up on her elbows as she watched me take in the room. The bed was queen-sized with a thick white comforter, and there was a dresser along one wall. There was a window near the bed, and when I looked out, I could see the lake glimmering in the last of the evening sun.

"Dinner's ready!" Colt's deep voice echoed down the hall.

I jumped, but Ruby was already tumbling off the bed.

"Hurry! Daddy made spaghetti. It's my favorite." She darted for the door, but I hesitated. "Come on!"

Ruby waved me forward with both hands, and I swallowed hard before trailing after her, toward the smell of garlic and the soft clink of plates as Colt moved around the kitchen, bracing myself for whatever came next.

I pulled out my phone as I followed Ruby and quickly texted

Maggie. We had talked on my way over here. She had offered to share her full-size bed with me, but I'd still come here.

I wasn't backing out after telling Ruby I would.

Maggie had only teased me when I told her that. "Oh, for sure. It's definitely all about Ruby. I'm sure seeing the cowboy half naked in his own home has no appeal at all."

I opened my text messages, and there was one waiting from her.

Maggie: Well?!?!

I shook my head, smiling, and typed.

Blaire: I made it. He opened the door in gray sweatpants.

Maggie: I'll be praying for you.

Maggie: Godspeed, cowgirl. Make sure you hydrate. Mustache burn is REAL.

CHAPTER 15

COLT

I was putting away the last of the dishes when I heard the shower cut off. My hands fumbled a glass, nearly dropping it, but I could hardly focus when I knew she was down the hallway with her bare feet padding across my tile and water beading down her spine.

I gripped the counter edge as I thought of her dragging one of my towels across her skin with her damp hair clinging to her neck and a flush spreading across her collarbones.

"Daddy," Ruby called from the couch, and I jerked so hard I nearly broke the glass.

I wiped my hands on a kitchen towel and tried to tell myself to chill the fuck out. Blaire was going to be here for weeks, and this was only day one.

"Yeah, baby?" I glanced up at Ruby and tried to look like I wasn't a twenty-nine-year-old man freaking out over a girl in his house.

She was curled up on the far end of the couch with both her feet poking out from under an old quilt.

"Are you listening?" she asked as she climbed to her knees and looked over the back of the couch at me.

"I'm sorry," I said, rubbing a hand over my face and managing a weak laugh. "It's been a long day."

"Are we still having a movie night? You and Blaire are taking forever." She pouted before pointing to the TV, where *Tangled* was already queued up. It was Ruby's favorite movie, and the only one we watched most of the time, with the exception of *Moana*.

"Okay, okay." I held up my hands in surrender. "Why don't you go ahead and start it, and I'll go wrangle the guest of honor?"

She nodded, hitting play, and I cracked my neck as I left the kitchen.

I barely stepped into the hallway before the bathroom door opened, and Blaire stepped out with a cloud of steam behind her. She was in an old T-shirt that hung uneven and too wide at the neck and a pair of sleep shorts that barely grazed the tops of her thighs. Her bare legs caught the light and the urge to move toward her and trail a hand along her skin to see if it was as warm as it looked was overwhelming.

She went still when she saw me, hand braced on the doorframe. Her hair was wet, hanging down in perfect spirals, and she blinked at me through those thick lashes, her mouth set in a soft line like she was bracing for a fight.

"Ruby is looking for you," I said, because if I tried for anything else, I was going to embarrass myself.

"I think I'm gonna head to bed."

I hated the way she wouldn't meet my eyes.

"Are you sure? We've got *Tangled* ready to go, and Rapunzel is like royalty around here. We never skip out on her."

"I—" Blaire trailed off, shaking her head as if she were shaking off whatever was going through it.

"It's just a movie, Blaire." I crossed my arms. "You're going to break Ruby's heart if you don't join us." It was a low blow and I knew it, but I wasn't ready for her to go to bed. Logically, I knew she was going to be here for weeks, but there was a part of me that feared she would go into that room and when we woke up tomorrow, she'd be gone.

Her eyes narrowed, suspicion flickering there. "Pretty sure she'll survive one movie night without me."

"Pretty sure she won't," I countered, unable to stop the smile that crept across my face. "If Ruby got anything from me, it's my stubbornness, and trust me, she won't stop until she gets what she wants."

I could already hear the sounds of *Tangled* coming from the living room, followed by Ruby's soft giggle.

Blaire studied me, and I thought she was going to refuse. But then she let out a sigh, rolling her eyes. "Fine, but if I want popcorn, you're making me popcorn."

"Yes, ma'am." I saluted her, and she moved past me in the hall, closer than she had to, and I caught the scent of bodywash on her skin. It was warm, woodsy, and unmistakably mine.

Without thinking, I reached out and caught her wrist, halting her in the narrow space between my bedroom door and hers. She stopped instantly, her pulse thudding under my thumb and goose-bumps rising on her forearm as I leaned in.

"You used my bodywash," I murmured, and it sounded like an accusation.

She glanced up at me, her eyes wide. "I couldn't get into the bathroom at June's to grab mine, and the only other thing in there was baby shampoo. You know Ruby is five, right? I need to run to the store tomorrow or my curls aren't going to survive." Her tone was calm, but her pulse ticked away beneath my hold like a bomb.

I should have heeded the warning and let her go, but it was like having my hand on a fuse and being unable to stop myself from striking the match.

"Blaire," I uttered her name, my voice far too soft.

She blinked up at me as if she were in a daze, and I let my thumb trace a slow path on the inside of her wrist.

I lowered my head until my lips nearly brushed her skin, my voice dropping to a rough whisper that made her shiver against my grip. "You smell like me."

Her lashes fluttered, and she made a half-hearted attempt to pull back. But I didn't let her go, I couldn't.

"That wasn't on purpose," she said quickly, but there was a tremor in her voice.

"Doesn't matter." My gaze snagged on the damp curls clinging to her collarbones, to the way her shirt stuck to her skin in places the steam hadn't dried. "I love smelling me on you."

I hadn't meant to say it, not out loud, but the damage was already done. Her eyes widened and her lips parted, a flush spreading across her throat as her chest rose and fell beneath the damp cotton.

I should have let her go, but my hand slid up her arm, over the back of her neck where her pulse hammered against my palm, and into the wet tangle of her hair, my fingers curling possessively against her scalp.

Her voice broke the air between us, small and so reckless. "Colt—"

"Yeah?" I whispered as my thumb traced the pulse at her throat.

I leaned closer, close enough to feel the heat of her breath against my lips. It'd been so long since I last tasted her, and heat flared everywhere we touched, a decade of restraint unraveling with each shallow breath between us.

"You can't say things like that," she whispered, her voice catching as I pressed my thumb lightly against her neck, feeling her pulse jump wildly beneath my touch. Her eyes darkened as her lips parted. When that soft fucking gasp escaped her, I felt it vibrate through my fingertips and straight to my cock.

Ten years of wanting concentrated into a single, devastating sound.

I bit back the groan clawing up my throat, dropping my forehead to hers. "Tell me to stop." The words stuck, thick and so damn dangerous, because part of me was begging her to tell me, and the rest was praying she wouldn't.

Her breath hitched, and I felt her hand fist in the front of my shirt, bunching the cotton over my abs. "I want you to—" Her words drifted off, and it should have drained every bit of the heat raging through me, but her hand only tightened in the fabric, pulling me closer to her until all I could feel was the heat of her through my clothes.

"You want me to what, Blaire?" I whispered, and she let out the tiniest little whimper.

She lifted her chin a fraction, enough that her top lip skimmed over my bottom one, and it sent electricity crackling down my spine, pooling low and heavy in my gut. Her breath caught on a small sound that made my fingers flex involuntarily against her throat.

"I want—"

She didn't move. Not away, not forward. We hovered in that half inch of space between us, like neither of us was willing to risk what would happen if we crossed it completely. My body ached to close it, to taste her lips again and press her against the wall until she felt the hard length of me against her stomach.

But this wasn't just me and Blaire anymore.

I had Ruby, and I wouldn't let her become collateral damage because of my careless decisions.

"What was it I said earlier?" I rasped, my fingers still possessive against her skin. "That we can be cordial?"

She let out a breathless laugh that vibrated against my palm, her pupils so blown out I could drown in them. "Is this what you call cordial?"

Her hips tipped almost mindlessly against mine, and I groaned as I watched her tongue flick over her lower lip. I was desperate to lean down and drag it between my teeth. I couldn't think of anything except for the taste and feel and scent of her, so dizzy with need I was seconds away from letting every bit of my want pour out of me.

"Daddy, are y'all coming?" Ruby's voice shot down the hallway, and Blaire jerked back like she'd been hit.

She twisted out of my grip so fast I almost stumbled, and the flush in her cheeks spread all the way to her ears. She wrapped her arms around herself, shaky fingers digging into her skin, eyes fixed on some invisible point beyond my shoulder. The way she closed herself off, like she was bracing for impact, made something possessive surge inside of me.

She had been sunshine in my hands once, warm and wild and bright, and I'd thrown her to the wolves, to a world that demanded she become someone else.

"We'll be right there," I called to Ruby, trying to keep the strain out of my voice, and then I stepped into Blaire's path until I forced her to look back up at me. "Are you okay?"

She nodded, teeth sinking into her bottom lip until the skin went white. My hands twitched at my sides, wanting to pull her back into me, but Ruby's voice echoed in my head.

And Blaire—Christ, the way her eyes wouldn't meet mine, the slight tremble in her shoulders—she looked like she wanted to run.

She released her lip, and she forced a smile. "Of course I'm okay," she said. "Why wouldn't I be?"

"Blaire." I took the smallest step toward her, but she stepped back.

"We're adults, Colt." Her eyes skimmed over me with a practiced indifference. It was like watching the Blaire I knew disappear behind a mask I didn't recognize. "You said so yourself earlier. That was—" She waved her hand toward where her body had been pressed against mine moments ago. "A momentary lapse in judgment." She straightened her shoulders, voice hardening. "My ex-fiancé spent the last year of our engagement screwing his assistant, so my standards are clearly questionable."

The mention of her ex-fiancé slammed into my chest, igniting a wildfire of rage that burned through every rational thought, but beneath it lay an ocean of guilt that threatened to drown me whole. I'd done this. I'd shoved her straight into the arms of a man just like her father.

If I'd kept her here, if she had stayed mine, I wouldn't see that razor-sharp edge in her eyes now. But she'd built armor around herself to survive a world I'd abandoned her to.

"Scout's honor. It won't happen again." She smiled as she raised her hands in a mock pledge, but her words were flat, and they hit me harder than if she'd hauled off and decked me.

I froze as the urge to pull her back to me was replaced by a sick, hollow ache, and I felt every inch of the distance she'd just put between us.

"Yeah." I nodded. "You made your point."

I stepped aside, giving her a clear path, and she hesitated for the smallest moment, her face falling and a glimpse of my Blaire coming through. "Colt—"

"Ruby's waiting." I turned away, biting the inside of my cheek until I tasted copper, and just like that, the wall between us snapped back in place. We were nothing more than two strangers who had to spend a few weeks under the same roof, with years of history burning between us like a live wire, and fuck, every second near her was going to tear me apart from the inside out.

CHAPTER 16
BLAIRE

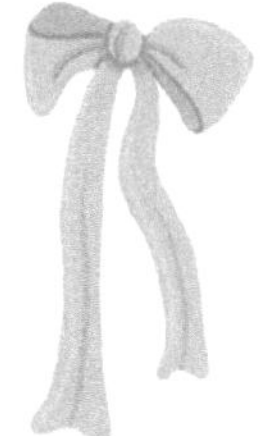

A bell jingled as I pushed through the door, and though the air was thick with vanilla and caramelized sugar, it couldn't mask the sudden hush that fell over the room. I hugged the crate of strawberries closer, the rough edges digging into me, and forced myself forward through the weight of their stares.

It had been a long time since I lived in the small town of Willow Grove, but there was one thing I was sure would never change.

The people here were nosy.

Maggie's bakery, Darlin' Delights, was packed to the brim with familiar faces at every table. I offered polite smiles as I headed toward the pie case, but it dropped the moment my gaze landed on Chelsey Leland. She was a former barrel racing queen, one grade above me, and the girl who'd made my life a living hell sophomore year.

She'd made sure everyone in our school knew my "dirty secret" that I supposedly couldn't decide between the Calloway brothers, and "brother fucker" followed me down the hallways for the rest of the year.

Chelsey was wrong though. My heart belonged to one brother, not two, and she was pissed that the boy I loved was the same one she wanted. The golden boy whose smile alone made every girl in Willow Grove stumble over their feet.

I wasn't special in loving Colt, but he'd made it so easy.

Chelsey sat with her friends, her honey-blonde ponytail swinging as she laughed. The minute she spotted me, her smile twisted and she rose. She crossed the shop in seconds, nearly knocking over a toddler in her rush to reach me.

"I'll be damned," she purred, looking me over from head to toe. "If it isn't Little Miss Strawberry herself."

I set the crate of berries down, the wood scraping against the counter, and Chelsey slid closer.

"Hey, Chelsey," I managed, jaw tight. My fingers curled around the edge of the crate. "How are you?"

"I'm good." She sipped her iced coffee, her lips leaving a perfect red rim on her straw. The ice in her cup clinked as she swirled it around, her eyes never leaving mine. "Moved back after the divorce. Daddy needed help with the horses."

She said "divorce" like it was a badge of honor.

"I heard you're back at June's." She watched me carefully as she said it. "I didn't think you'd ever come back here."

"Yeah, well." I shrugged and finally turned to fully face her. "It wasn't exactly the plan."

Chelsey's eyes dragged over every inch of me, taking in my dirty jeans and the worn T-shirt that was almost too small.

"You know," she said, dropping her voice. "I saw you on TV last year. The engagement party in Raleigh? My cousin's wife works for a company there, and we were talking about how lucky you were to land that investor guy. What happened? Are you two still engaged?"

I swallowed hard against the memory of exactly what happened, those photos still on my computer just in case. "Grant and I called it off. It didn't work out."

Chelsey's brows shot up and her eyes widened in what seemed to be actual shock. "I heard he was like a big deal. I can't believe you gave that up," she said, too loudly, so the whole shop could hear. "I guess that means you're sticking around for a while then, or are you going back?"

"I'm helping June out on the farm right now." I crossed my arms and scanned the space behind the counter. *Where the hell was Maggie?* My finger found the service bell on the counter, pressing it with more force than necessary. "We're going to be selling her jams."

"Jams?" Chelsey snorted out a laugh, and I bristled. "And here I thought maybe you'd come home for Colt. You know, now that he's single and all." Her voice dripped with mock concern. "Or did you two already—?" She made a little gesture with her fingers that could have meant anything, but her eyes said everything.

I could feel my throat tighten, but I met her gaze, refusing to give her what she wanted. "You know what? You might be the only person in this town who cares more about my love life than I do, Chelsey."

She grinned, head cocked to one side like a predator considering its prey. "Oh, I don't care at all." Her eyes flicked from my dirty boots to my untamed hair, tallying each imperfection. "Colt, on the other hand, he's supposed to take me to that new place in Belmont this weekend, but I haven't heard from him in a few days. I assumed he was busy with the ranch, but—"

My teeth clamped down on the inside of my cheek. I imagined, for one vivid second, grabbing her ponytail and yanking until those perfect blonde strands came away in my fist. Chelsey knew nothing, not one damn thing, about me and Colt, yet here she stood with his name dripping from her lips like she owned it.

She didn't know I slept under his roof, or how his fingers had traced my neck in his hallway three nights ago, until I pushed him away and told him it wouldn't happen again. She also didn't know that I'd learned to wait for the rumble of his engine each morning, hiding in my room until his tires crunched gravel. It had become a daily ritual of self-denial that my racing pulse betrayed with every passing second.

But to my credit, it worked. We barely spoke whenever Ruby wasn't involved.

"Are you two fucking?" She scrunched her nose as if the thought disgusted her, and I flinched at her question. "I'm not interested in him if—"

"If what?" I asked as a possessive heat clawed at my throat. "If he's fucking me?" I studied her, watching her reaction to my words, and I knew I should stop but was unable to dam the flood of words. "Even if he's not fucking me now," I stepped closer, lowering my voice like I was telling her a little secret just between us girls. "I've had him in ways you can only imagine, Chelsey." I leaned back just enough to watch her eyes widen. "There isn't a single piece of Colt Calloway that doesn't already know my touch."

Chelsey's mouth hung open before snapping shut, her lips flattening into a thin red line. Her nostrils flared, and her practiced bitchy composure flickered off like a dying neon sign.

She flinched when the door behind the counter swung open, and I took a step back, not believing what I'd just said. Maggie walked out from the back of the bakery, her hair leaking from its clip and a bit of flour on the side of her nose. She wore a pink apron with cherries and Darlin' Delights written across the front.

"Chelsey, girl," Maggie said, wiping her hands down her apron. "Why don't you let the woman breathe? It's barely eight thirty in the morning, and you're already on her ass about which men she's going to take off your roster."

Chelsey whirled in her direction, face pinched, but Maggie just stared her down with her hands on her hips.

"I was just welcoming her home," Chelsey lied.

Maggie snorted before she reached for the crate of strawberries. She plucked one from the top, rolling it between her fingers with a nod of approval. "These are gorgeous, Blaire."

I exhaled, tension melting from my shoulders now that Maggie was here. "Picked them this morning. I've got June's Jams in the trunk too. You're going to freak out when you see how cute the packaging is."

Maggie's eyes lit up as she took the crate. "Perfect timing. I've got a special corner all ready for them, right next to the croissants."

She winked at me before turning to Chelsey with a honeyed smile. "Some things just belong together, don't they?" Her gaze flicked meaningfully to me and then to the door. "Always have."

I turned at the sound of the bell and watched as Colt sauntered into the bakery.

"Mornin', Colt," someone called from across the bakery, and I saw Chelsey stiffen at the same moment my own body betrayed me with a jolt of awareness.

He must have come straight from the school drop-off because I'd timed my escape this morning precisely to avoid this, slipping out while his truck was still idling in the driveway.

Colt's cowboy hat was pulled low, but there was no hiding the sharp angle of his jaw or the shape of his mouth I'd memorized years ago. And that mustache, God, that mustache should be illegal.

My heart hammered against my ribs before my brain could remind it to behave. All around us, people called out good morning to him as chairs scraped against the floor, and half a dozen men rose to their feet to shake his hand.

The Willow Grove golden boy through and through.

He fit this place so well, and I wasn't sure where I belonged anymore.

His white T-shirt stretched across his shoulders that had grown broader with the years of ranch work, and he wore faded jeans tight against his thighs. One thumb hooked casually in his pocket as he laughed at whatever Mr. Chambers from the feed store was saying.

He scanned the room, not lingering on anyone for long, until it caught on me. His entire demeanor shifted. The casual air evaporated as his eyes traveled from my face down to my boots, lingering in places that made heat bloom beneath each spot his eyes touched. One corner of his mouth lifted as he murmured something to Mr. Chambers, eyes never leaving me. Then he pulled off his hat and ran his fingers through his hair before he headed in our direction, closing the distance between us with each step.

He came right up to the counter, not even glancing at Chelsey as he nodded to Maggie.

"Morning, Mags." His voice was softer than I expected, almost warm, but he wasn't looking at her. He was looking at me like I was a problem he was trying to solve.

"Morning, Colt." Maggie pulled open the cash register, the drawer's bell dinging as she slid bills back and forth. "You picking up something for Ruby again or is this a grown-up errand?"

"Grown-up," he said, his eyes still on me. "Though I suppose I should get her something too. Can I get one of those breakfast sandwiches for me, then a few of those lemon bars for Ruby?"

"Of course."

Colt's hands bracketed the counter, fingers splayed wide, and he was so close now I could see the stubble across his jaw. "Blaire, I didn't know you were running deliveries this morning." His tone was casual, but a thread of challenge ran through it.

I simply shrugged, though my shoulders felt too tight, my face too warm. "You didn't ask."

He smiled then before he ran his tongue over his bottom lip. "Fair enough," he quipped. "I guess I could've asked you this morning, but—" He cocked his head slightly, letting the silence stretch between us. "You seem to be avoiding me."

Chelsey cleared her throat, drawing Colt's attention. His eyebrows lifted slightly, as if only now realizing she was there.

"That's so funny," she said, her smile tight. "Blaire was just telling me how the two of you weren't..." She trailed off, eyes darting between us.

"Weren't what?" Colt's voice hardened.

"Together." Chelsey's laugh sounded rehearsed. "Just double-checking before our date on Saturday."

The word date sent ice down my spine, a cold trickle of dread that spread to my fingers where they were going numb in my fists.

Part of me wanted to believe Colt would never go on a date with her, but there was a bigger part of me that barely knew him anymore. And that part was so damn angry I wanted to punch Chelsey and him right in their faces.

"I mean, it would be pretty scandalous if something was happening, considering I just saw something about her wedding plans a few weeks ago." Her lips curved with satisfaction as Colt's shoulders tensed, his jaw locking into place. "But is she—" She looked back at me. "Are you staying with him?"

I was about to answer when Colt shifted beside me, his fingers drumming against the counter. "Didn't realize we had plans," he stated, and there was a bite in his voice that made Chelsey's smile falter.

"Well, Mia and Ruby have been begging to get together, and I promised Ruby that we'd make it happen this weekend." She smiled at him and pressed her hand to his chest. "We talked about it last week, Colt."

I watched her fingers curl into the fabric of his shirt, and something possessive coiled tight in my stomach. My own hands twitched at my sides as I fought the urge to peel each of her fingers off him one by one.

Maybe there wasn't a date, or maybe there was. I wanted to believe that Colt wouldn't, but then again, why not? I'd been gone so long, and he didn't owe me anything. So why did I feel like I couldn't breathe?

I felt raw and exposed, and I suddenly wanted Colt so much it left me hollow. I knew I had no right to feel this jealousy, but there was a part of me that was still rooted in this soil, in the memories of our friendship before it became more, that wanted to scream at her that he was mine first.

But the truth was, he wasn't mine at all.

He belonged to this town, he belonged to Ruby, but every part of me screamed that he did not belong to Chelsey fucking Leland.

I forced myself to look away from Chelsey's possessive grip and found Maggie. "I'll swing by later with the jams, okay?" The words caught in my throat, coming out thin and wobbly. "I can't believe I forgot those."

Maggie's brows ticked up before she glanced between me and Colt, her mouth tightening at the corners. "Of course," she said, sliding a paper bag across to Colt while ringing up his total, but she was still looking at me. "We should do dinner tonight, too."

"It's a date," I replied, putting so much emphasis on the petty, reckless word that Maggie's lips twitched with suppressed laughter.

Colt shifted toward me, and his hand hovered like he might reach for my elbow. I saw it, saw the way his mouth opened to say my name, but I didn't think I could handle it. So I spun on my heel, nearly colliding with the person waiting in line behind us, and I kept moving and forced myself not to look back.

The bell over the door jingled as I shouldered through it, and I heard Colt call my name. But I didn't stop. I kept walking past the bank, past the hardware store, desperate to get to my car.

I nearly tripped twice on my way to the parking lot. My keys slipped through my unsteady fingers before I unlocked the car. The woman in my rearview mirror looked like a stranger with her pupils wide and cheeks flushed. I jammed my finger against the ignition before I gripped the steering wheel, willing my heartbeat to slow.

I'd promised myself Colt would never affect me this way again, but here I was, angry with him for talking to the woman who used to make my life a living hell. She used to be cruel to me, and now she was having playdates with Ruby.

My Ruby.

Logically, I knew I should have been over it by now. Not just the way she'd treated me in high school, but Colt, everything about him, his absence, his daughter, the choices he'd made when I wasn't here. But logic couldn't tame the jealousy that was clawing at my ribs.

Her hand had lingered on his chest, splayed like it had been there before a thousand times, as if she owned the right to touch him in broad daylight.

Had he slept with her?

I squeezed my eyes shut, willing the image away.

I'd just made it onto the road when my phone buzzed against my thigh. I fumbled for it, heart jumping with the ridiculous hope it might be Colt, but it was Grant's face lighting up my screen instead. I almost declined the call when movement caught my attention. Colt stood outside the bakery, jaw tight as Chelsey thrust a finger into his chest. He looked away from her, and through the windshield, across the distance between us, I could have sworn our eyes locked.

My phone vibrated again, insistent, and this time, I answered, "Hello."

"Blaire." Grant said my name with so much relief that guilt twisted in my stomach, and I turned away from Colt.

CHAPTER 17

COLT

Ruby had toothpaste all over her chin, and she was making eye contact with me in the mirror, scrunching her nose as she made silly faces and grinned around her toothbrush.

She spit, making a mess, before she rinsed her mouth and turned to face me. "Daddy, when's Blaire coming home?"

I leaned against the doorframe, arms crossed, ignoring the unease twisting in my gut. "She'll be back soon. I'm pretty sure she went to dinner with Miss Maggie."

"I don't like it when she's not here." Ruby's voice shrank, the words hitting me square in the chest.

I could barely look at her as I reached for the towel, gently scrubbing at her chin while my mind raced between what I should say and what I wanted to be true.

I dabbed at a spot of toothpaste near her lip, buying seconds while my hands betrayed me with their slight tremor. I opened my mouth to warn her that Blaire was temporary, that people always left eventually, but looking into those trusting eyes, the words died somewhere between my chest and tongue.

"Me neither," I said, my voice catching. I forced a smile that felt like a grimace, searching her face while something inside me twisted between wanting to shield her from disappointment and needing to prepare her for it. I pushed her hair back from her fore-head, then ruffled the damp strands, letting my hand linger a moment.

Scooping her up, I carried her to her bedroom and dropped us onto her mattress with a huff, sending stuffed animals flying and Ruby into a fit of giggles. Ruby threw her arms around my neck, squeezing tight, then flopped backward onto her mountain of unicorns, cats, one battered, stuffed blue dog, and Blaire's Duke sweatshirt that was tucked under her pillow.

"Bedtime, baby girl." I pulled back her covers, but she hopped down and scurried to her bookshelf.

Her tiny finger ran along the spines as she deliberated which book would send us off to bed, and I watched her with a smile, though I could feel my pulse throbbing at my temples.

The house had never felt this empty before Blaire, not in all the years since it was just Ruby and me. Now her absence echoed through the rooms because I'd carved space for her in our routines. Against every instinct screaming caution, I'd invited her into the fragile rhythm we'd built. And now, with her gone for just one evening, the silence was deafening.

I checked my phone. No notifications. I should've put it away, but my thumb found Blaire's name anyway. I typed out a message, thumb hovering, before I deleted it. My thumb froze above the screen, caught between the gravity of missing her and my pride, but then I hit send.

Colt: You okay?

Ruby pulled a book from the shelf before she climbed back into the bed with *Where the Wild Things Are* clutched to her chest.

"Classic," I said as she wriggled under the covers, and I took the book. Just as I settled in, my phone vibrated against my chest. I snatched it up and stared down at the screen.

Blaire: Yes.

That was it. One word.

I glowered at the screen until Ruby started kicking her feet impatiently at my side. Then I set the phone down and opened the book. I read the story with Ruby's head on my chest, and I was about halfway through when her sleepy eyes looked up at me.

"Is Blaire mad at us?"

She was watching me with a seriousness I wasn't used to seeing on my little girl. I remembered her mother's last days, and the confusion that lingered in Ruby's gaze for months after. She had been so young, but Becca had still been her mother. It was a look I never wanted to see on her face again.

My jaw tightened. "Of course not, baby. She's spending time with her friend."

"I'm her friend." Ruby's nose scrunched, and fuck, I wanted to protect her from the world. I wanted to shield her from getting her heart broken if Blaire decided to leave again, though part of me knew I was just as terrified for myself.

"That's true, but Maggie is her boring friend and sometimes grown-ups need to talk about boring stuff for a little while."

Ruby nodded as if what I'd said made complete sense, and her eyes went heavy with sleep again. "Will you ask her to braid my hair before school?"

"I will," I whispered, and stayed like that for a while, listening to her shallow breaths and the occasional soft snore.

I set the book aside, careful not to disturb Ruby's loose grip on my arm and reached to click off the lamp. The room fell into darkness except for the moonlight sneaking through the gap in her curtains, splashing a pale glow across her cheek.

The house was quiet, leaving me with nothing but my thoughts and an uneasiness I couldn't shake. I grabbed my phone again, and the screen lit up my face. My thumb hovered as I typed out a dozen different messages and deleted every single one.

The memory of Blaire's face at the bakery this morning haunted me. Her brown eyes had widened when she saw me, enough that I could see the fleck of gold in her irises before they'd clouded with hurt. She'd rushed out after Chelsey leaned into me and asked about our playdate, and she hadn't even glanced back when I called her name.

I didn't have a date with Chelsey Leland. Christ. My stomach turned at the thought. Sure, she was pretty, but whenever she smiled at me, all I could hear was her voice bouncing off metal lockers, that vicious nickname for Blaire spreading through the halls like poison.

"Brother fucker."

The memory still made my teeth grind together. Back then, I'd wanted to stand in front of Blaire, shield her from those whispers with my body. And if I'm honest, some irrational, possessive part of me couldn't stand hearing her name linked to anyone but me—not then, not now.

Even if it was my brother.

But Mia, Chelsey's daughter, and Ruby were inseparable at school, and I couldn't deprive my daughter of that friendship because Chelsey's hand lingered too long on my arm whenever we talked.

I'd done nothing wrong, so why did I feel so guilty?

I dropped the phone on my chest, hoping the weight would pin me down and keep me from doing something stupid. Ruby squirmed in her sleep, rolled over, and mumbled something I couldn't understand. I brushed hair from her forehead, wishing I could keep her world simple and untouched by all the adult shit that kept me up at night.

The silence pressed in until my thumb was back at it, scrolling up and down the chat, searching for a less pathetic thing to say, but nothing came.

Colt: Ruby was asking for you. She misses you.

I hit send, knowing it was a cop-out to hide behind my daughter, but Blaire replied almost instantly.

Blaire: Tell her we'll hang out before school in the morning.

I glanced at Ruby's sleeping form, her chest rising and falling in the dim light, then back to the screen.

Colt: You got a shipment of labels in. They look good.

Colt: But what the hell is Saddle Up Strawberry Jam?

I'd opened the box this afternoon, not realizing it was hers, and I couldn't help but laugh at the pretty pastel label covered in little red strawberries all wearing a ten-gallon hat.

Blaire: June's Jams- Cowboy Collection. 🧋🤠

Blaire: Saddle Up Strawberry, Buckle Bunny Berry Blend, Rodeo Raspberry, Cherry Wrangler, and Giddy Up Grape.

I snorted as I read the lineup. This was the same girl who'd once set off the smoke

alarm making boxed mac and cheese, standing on a chair to wave a dish towel while cursing like a sailor. But when Blaire believed in something, she got this look in her eyes, like she could see straight through to what mattered.

I carefully climbed from Ruby's bed with my phone clutched in my hand. I looked back at my girl one last time before I quietly closed the door.

Colt: Are you making this up?

Blaire: No! We already have preorders!

Blaire: Also, June says y'all are modeling for our marketing.

Blaire: Go ahead and prepare yourself, cowboy.

A weird pang of nerves hit me. I didn't know if she was needling me, but the idea of

her thinking about my body at all made my pulse quicken.

Colt: I'm almost 30. I'm not sure anyone wants to see that.

The text bubbles appeared as she typed, and fuck, it felt good to talk to her like this.

Blaire: Oh, yes. I'm sure no one wants to see a single daddy cowboy with abs. 😊

Colt: How do you know I have abs?

Blaire: I don't. It's been a long time since I've seen you naked. That would be a sad day if they were gone.

Her words caught me off guard. A warmth spread through me that made me shift my weight and lean against the counter. I swallowed hard, suddenly aware of every inch of denim against my skin.

Blaire: Maybe I could ask that one cowboy I met at The Dusty Spur? What was his name?

My blood went hot, burning through every rational thought. She was baiting me, and damn her, it was working.

Colt: That's not fucking happening.

Blaire: That's not really up to you.

Her next text came so fast I didn't have a chance to respond to the first.

Blaire: Though I should probably see him naked too. What kind of businesswoman would I be without quality control.

I wanted to drive straight into town and throw her over my shoulder and carry her home. Instead, I clenched my jaw and sent another text.

Colt: Blaire Wilma Monroe, don't fuck with me.

Blaire: Colt Oliver Calloway, don't tell me what to do.

My neck cracked as I rotated it, trying to ease the tension coiling inside me. It was a futile attempt to quiet the hunger I felt for her and that mouth that knew exactly how to push every one of my buttons.

Colt: You going to be home soon?

Blaire: Why? Do YOU miss me?

My heart jumped in my throat, a surge of hope I immediately tried to strangle. God, she had to know that I did. But before I could decide whether to answer her honestly or play it safe, the next message came as if she regretted giving me the opening at all.

Blaire: I'm at dinner with Maggie. I'll be back soon.

I paced through the living room, my free hand raking through my hair.

Colt: Tell Maggie I said hi.

Colt: And yes, I always miss you.

I stared at what I'd sent, my pulse hammering so hard I could feel it in my fingertips. Those words burned on the screen like a confession ripped from me that I couldn't take back.

The three dots appeared, disappeared, and appeared again. I felt like I couldn't breathe while I waited for her response.

Blaire: If you needed company, you should've taken Chelsey to dinner.

"Fuck," I swore under my breath, turning to stare out the windows where moonlight spilled across the lake.

CHAPTER 18
COLT

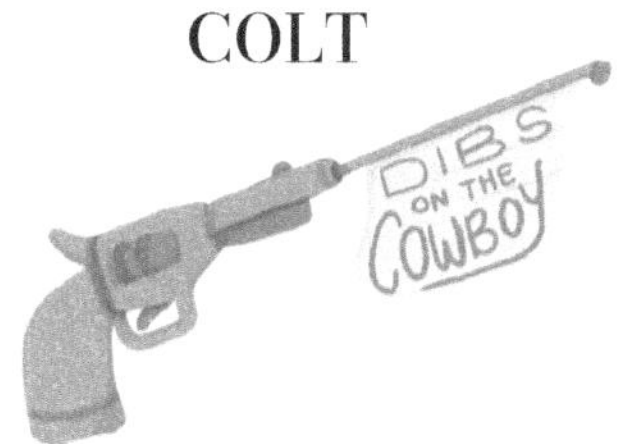

I couldn't blame her for being upset about Chelsey, but hell if I didn't have my own reasons to be pissed at her. Every time I tried to sort through my thoughts, they snagged on each other like barbed wire. She had brushed past me without a glance this morning at the bakery, and she had been avoiding me since that first night she came here.

Since that night in the hallway when I'd almost taken things too far.

But I could still feel the way her body pressed against mine and her soft gasp when my hand found her throat. The memory alone made my cock strain painfully in my jeans. She could act indifferent now, but I'd seen the truth written across her face that night. Her body yielded in all the ways her words wouldn't.

And if Ruby hadn't interrupted us when she did, I would've crossed every line, would've ripped through every boundary between us, consequences be damned.

"A lapse in judgment," she'd called me. Like I was just another mistake, no different from the asshole who'd cheated on her after he'd asked her to be his wife. Her voice had been so flat when she said it, like his infidelity was nothing more than a minor inconvenience she'd already forgotten.

I wanted to kill him.

I wanted to slam her against the wall, beg her for everything until her stubborn mouth yielded beneath mine, until her breath came in ragged gasps against my lips. I wanted her to see how fucked up what he did to her was, to obliterate every memory of that worthless asshole who hurt her. And I wanted to erase my own sins too, to burn away the years of regret with the heat of her skin against mine.

I ached for her with a hunger that silenced reason.

I should've gone to bed and let this obsession with her strangle out in the dark, but the heat spreading through my body was unbearable. I shoved my phone into my pocket, yanked open the fridge so hard bottles rattled, and grabbed a beer. I tried to breathe as I twisted off the cap, the muscles in my forearm tensing with each turn.

I needed air.

I cracked Ruby's door open one last time, watching her small chest rise and fall, then slipped outside with my pulse hammering so loud I could barely hear the door click shut behind me.

The chains groaned beneath my weight as I dropped onto the porch swing. My skin burned despite the night chill, each breath rushing out of me while the lake's silver surface mocked the chaos inside me with its perfect stillness. I dug my fingers into my thigh and told myself to chill the fuck out.

Blaire wasn't mine, not anymore, and I had no right to get this worked up over a girl who was likely to leave again when she realized this town still had nothing for her. I tried to tell myself this was nostalgia, the same kind of ache that came when you smelled freshly cut grass and remembered the nights of your childhood with fireflies and laughter.

I'd convinced myself a thousand times I was over her, and that whatever we'd once had was dead and buried beneath years of separation and hurt. We had been kids then. It wasn't real; it wasn't anything more than two people who were young, reckless, and infatuated with one another.

But that was bullshit, and even now I could feel the lie crawling beneath my skin.

I told myself I was angry for Ruby's sake; that I didn't want Blaire flitting in and out of my daughter's life, making promises she couldn't keep. But if I was honest, if I stripped it all the way back, I didn't want Blaire to slip through my fingers again.

And that scared the hell out of me. The way I'd wanted her when we were kids was one thing, but the way I wanted her now, with Ruby asleep inside, was a fault line running under my whole life.

I drank half the beer in a single pull and wiped my mouth with the back of my hand. The cold bottle sweated against my palm, anchoring me to the here and now, but my mind kept drifting to her no matter how hard I tried.

The thought of her leaving again made me sick, and I turned away from the lake, facing the long driveway snaking off into the trees. The light over the path cast everything in yellow, and beyond it, the world was black and infinite.

I forced myself to breathe in and out through clenched teeth and listened to the night. The water lapped at the dock, the wind rattled through the leaves, and finally, the sound of tires against gravel hit me.

Headlights swept a slow arc over the shadowed porch. I watched them crawl closer, engine humming low beneath the hush of crickets, and every nerve in my body went tight with anticipation.

I didn't move. I sat on the porch swing and watched her approach. Her car rolled to a stop at the edge of the gravel, her headlights spilling across the front of my house, and for a moment, nothing happened. She sat there, hands on the steering wheel, her outline barely visible through the windshield's glare.

I wondered if she saw me waiting, if she could feel the way I watched her. I took another pull from the bottle, the taste bitter, and forced myself to keep still.

Blaire finally killed the engine and opened her car door. The porch light hit her as she stepped into the cool night. She stood there, uncertainty clouding her face, before squaring her shoulders and heading my way.

She was so goddamn beautiful.

Every step she took closer to the door made my breath catch behind my ribs, and by the time she reached the first porch step, I was barely holding myself together.

She fumbled for the railing, and even the way she breathed, tight, shallow, and defiant, told me she'd been rehearsing this confrontation all the way up the drive. She still hadn't looked my way, hadn't realized that I was here, and she almost reached the door before I forced myself to speak.

"Did you have fun?"

She jumped at the sound, flinched so hard her hand flew to her chest, and I instantly regretted not warning her that I was sitting here in the dark.

"You scared the shit out of me," she heaved, looking from me back to the door.

But instead of backing down, she crossed her arms, a smirk already forming at the corner of her mouth. She looked me straight in the eye, her gaze clear and unblinking.

"Oh no. Am I in trouble?" she said, her voice low and teasing. "Never had the whole daddy waiting on the porch thing before."

The word "daddy" from her lips hit me like a live wire, the syllables vibrating between us, and I forgot how to breathe. I watched Blaire's lips as if she might say it again, as if the sound itself could break me open and bring me to my knees. My fist tightened around the bottle until I thought the glass might shatter, and I shifted in the swing, suddenly too aware of how close she was.

"Don't call me daddy unless you want me to put you on your knees." The words came out on a growl.

Blaire froze, and I watched her eyes widen while the pink flush on her cheeks spread right before my eyes. She blinked once, twice, and then her mouth opened like she was going to fire back but nothing came.

One hand curled tight around the strap of her bag, and she

looked right at me as the threat and the promise of what I'd said pooled at our feet. I watched her throat work as she swallowed hard, and I wondered if her mind, like mine, was replaying the last time I'd had her on her knees. The velvet scrape of her tongue, the desperate way I wrapped my hands in her hair, the way she looked up at me like she'd never trusted anyone more in all her life.

She licked her lips, hesitated, and then she let out a shaky breath. "You can't say things like that to me."

Neither of us moved. The night air pulsed between us, crickets and cicadas fading to the background as silence stretched. I could see her pulse flutter in her throat, and I shifted on the swing, the chains creaking.

"Why not?" I cocked my head, voice low. "You started it."

She rolled her eyes, but the flush in her cheeks only deepened. "Grow up, Colt. You don't get to say things like that because this —" she motioned back and forth between us. "—isn't a thing. The only reason I agreed to stay here was because you said we could be adults and this wasn't complicated. So don't make it complicated." She paused, swallowing hard and staring straight into me. "What happened between us was in the past. You don't want me, and I don't want you."

She wanted to play it cool, act like I hadn't gotten under her skin, but I'd seen it in the bakery. I saw how she'd lost her composure when Chelsey touched me, the way her hands had shaken when she stormed out.

I waited silently, until she looked away, blinking hard in the dark.

"You know," I said, letting the words drag between us, "for someone who doesn't want me, you did a hell of a job today acting jealous."

Her mouth twisted, and she turned back, eyes glaring. "I wasn't jealous," she snapped. "But you know how much I hate Chelsey, you know how mean she was to me before—"

Before she left.

I stood up, the swing clanging behind me, and her whole body tensed. "So you're telling me you stormed off because of Chelsey? Not because she put her hands on me right in front of you?"

Her hands dropped to her sides, fists balling. "You're such an asshole sometimes," she whispered, her voice holding the slightest tremor.

I stepped in, closing the space between us, close enough for the scent of her to wrap around me. "You think I give a single fuck about Chelsey or any other girl in this county? Do you really think I would ever be with someone who ever hurt you like that? You got pissed at me today for no reason." I searched her eyes, and there was so much vulnerability there, so much hurt. I knew exactly why Chelsey had set her off, because I felt it every time I thought about Grant. "But what pisses me off, Blaire, is thinking about you."

She bristled, but I was already burning through whatever restraint I had left.

"I can't stop thinking about him, that worthless asshole who had you." The words tore from my throat. "He cheated on you. That undeserving prick had you in his bed, had the right to touch you, had his goddamn ring on your finger, and he had the audacity to look at someone else."

She jerked her gaze away, color draining from her face.

"He had every single part of you, the parts that haunt me in the dark when I can't sleep, and he treated you like you weren't enough."

Her breath rushed out of her, and she blinked hard as she looked back at me, her eyes watery and furious. "That's none of your business, Colt. You also treated me like I wasn't enough."

Her words should have been a wall, a clear boundary I wouldn't cross, but all they did was set me on fire. I took another step forward, close enough now that the light from inside the house glinted off her cheek, close enough to feel the heat coming off her skin and to catch the slight quiver of her lips as she looked up at me.

"Maybe I did." My jaw ticked as I looked at her. "But that doesn't stop me from wanting to kill the bastard. I'm not the same kid I was when I told you to leave, when I let the world have a say in who we became. I have a daughter now, Blaire. I have this entire life." I lifted my hand and motioned to the house and property around us. "And none of it stops me from caring about you. You may not want me, but let's get real fucking clear that I have never stopped wanting you."

I leaned in slowly, giving her every chance to turn her face, to step back, to stop me before I did something I'd regret. But she didn't move. When my forehead touched hers, she closed her eyes, and we stood there, suspended between the past and the present.

My body ached with the need to close that final inch between us, to taste her again after all these years. The wanting crashed through me, and in that moment, I saw it clear as day. We were gasoline and matches, a collision that would leave nothing but a trail of ashes behind.

"Go inside, Blaire," I said, my voice rough with everything I was holding back as I took the slightest step away from her. "Before I stop pretending I've got any restraint left where you're concerned."

She looked up at me. "You can't tell me what to do."

I met her eyes, and the raw vulnerability there gutted me. Her breathing was shallow and quick, her entire body trembling with the same violent need that was tearing me apart from the inside. But beneath the desire, I caught a flash of something that froze me in place. I recognized that look. I'd put it there once before, when I shattered everything between us.

And tonight I'd prodded it again with my mouth and my temper. If I crossed that last inch between us, she would let me have everything, but when the morning came, she'd regret it.

"Go inside," I repeated, my voice dropping to a guttural command that scraped my throat raw. She held my gaze, her chest rising and falling rapidly. Then she turned and fled through the doorway, and I forced myself not to follow.

CHAPTER 19
BLAIRE

The cooler was digging into my hip by the time Ruby and I made it down to the lake. Her chatter was nonstop, talking my ear off about all the things she was going to do in the water. I was mostly trying not to trip over a tree root while balancing both the cooler and Ruby's hand in mine.

When Colt had invited me to a day on the lake, I'd almost told him no. Based on the riot of nerves in my stomach, I probably should have. But Maggie was going to be here, and I'd promised her I'd come.

Laughter and music drifted up before we even hit the edge of the trees. The inviting water stretched out before us, and I could see both the Calloways' dock and June's from where we stood. McCoy's truck had been backed up down near the water, the bed loaded with more coolers and an entire arsenal of pool noodles and floats.

Colt was standing with his back to us, barefoot at the edge of the dock, talking to McCoy and laughing at something I couldn't hear. The sun caught his shoulders, tracing every line of muscle, and my steps faltered, the cooler thumping gently against my leg while I failed to remember how to breathe. He wore dark green swim trunks, and his hair was curling at the nape of his neck from the water.

As soon as we got close to the water, Ruby immediately broke free, tearing off toward the lake. Colt turned at the sound, caught her up with one arm as soon as she made it to his side, and swung her straight in the air as she laughed. He smiled at me over her shoulder, an easy smile which made my stomach flip, and then he kissed Ruby all over her little face before he set her back down. She kicked off her flip-flops and jerked her dress over her head before she cannonballed into the water where McCoy waited.

Ruby loved like she jumped, full tilt and with no hesitation. There was no part of her that didn't go all in, no moment she hung back and considered the temperature, or the depth, or whether anyone was watching and tallying her mistakes. She was pure momentum, all hope and faith, and I envied her.

I was just like Ruby once, diving headfirst into everything without counting the cost. What I wouldn't give to bottle that courage, to press it between her palms like a firefly that wouldn't dim when life inevitably tried to steal it away from her.

My gaze caught on Colt's abs tensing as he shifted, and the corner of my mouth lifted.

So he does still have the abs.

Every slight movement he made registered like a flare in my peripheral vision. He tilted his beer to his lips, his eyes finding mine over the bottle's rim, and suddenly I was back on that porch two nights ago, the moonlight catching in his hair.

And now he stood there, shirtless and so at ease, while I felt every nerve ending in my body light up again.

Wanting Colt was easy. Wanting him where his little girl could see was reckless, but I couldn't stop.

"Uncle Coy!" Ruby screeched, and her voice drew my attention, snapping it away from her father, as McCoy lifted her in the air above him.

Maggie's voice carried across the water before I even spotted her. "Where's Blaire?" she called, all mock drama, and a second later, her head and shoulders appeared, paddling around the edge of the dock on an inflatable donut.

She was balancing a Solo cup between her knees and rowing herself with her arms.

"Oh, thank God." She stopped as soon as she saw me. "I'm so glad you and Ruby are finally here. I was about to be bro-brained into oblivion."

McCoy dropped Ruby into the water beside him and splashed Maggie so hard, lake water sloshed all over her and her drink.

"Damn it, McCoy!" She nearly capsized, clutching the float's sides, and her cup fell straight into the water. "Do you have any idea how long it took me to make that margarita? There's real lime in there, you animal!"

She flailed a leg at him, splashing wildly, and he simply wrapped his hand around her ankle and jerked her off the float.

Ruby laughed, begging McCoy to throw her again, but I looked away from them as Colt made his way over to me, pausing at the back of McCoy's truck and pulling out two beers from the cooler in one hand. He twisted off one of the beer caps and offered it to me without a word.

I took it, trying not to let our fingers brush, as he passed it over. He said nothing at first. He twisted open his own beer, tilted his head back a little, and took me in with a look that said he also remembered every single word we'd said on that porch.

"It's about time you all got here," he finally said. His voice was so low I swear it rumbled in my chest. "I thought I was going to have to come to my parents' house and haul you two out myself."

I shrugged. "Your mom was helping me and June with some ideas for the online shop, and Ruby was coloring with your dad. I didn't want to interrupt them."

Colt nodded, seeming lost in his head, before he reached out, his hand brushing against my shoulder before he wrapped it around the cooler. "Here, let me take that."

"Thanks," I said, awkward now that my hands were empty, holding the beer like a shield. I looked back at the water, where

Ruby was sprawled out across Maggie's float and Maggie was pushing her as she swam behind it.

Colt set the cooler on the tailgate, then turned back and pointed his beer directly at my middle with a little flick of his wrist. "You're overdressed."

I glanced down at my cutoff shorts and tee, and I was suddenly acutely aware of how small the bikini was underneath. I took a drink of my beer, letting the coldness wash away the sudden flush in my cheeks.

"I've got my bathing suit on," I said as I looked past him, but it was impossible to miss his grin.

"Then take the rest off." He leaned against the dropped tailgate, bracing on the edge. Everything about his posture was relaxed, but there was an edge to his focus that made me want to squirm.

"I'm going to." I hesitated, shifting my weight and glancing back down at my shorts.

"Blaire, you used to swim in this lake in your underwear. You're telling me you're shy now?" He grinned, the dimples denting his cheeks.

"Blaire! Get in!" Ruby's voice rang out from the lake. She was still on the float, now balancing on her knees, and waving her arms for me to join her. "We have to dunk uncle Coy!"

Colt's gaze flicked to the lake, then back to me. "See? You're needed in the lake."

I rolled my eyes, but that only seemed to make his smile deepen. He waited, beer bottle balanced against his thigh, watching me with an amused look that got under my skin.

"I'm coming!" I called out to Ruby, completely ignoring Colt, and I tried not to even glance in his direction as I reached for the button on my shorts.

He caught my hesitation and leaned in, dropping his voice even lower. "Do you need a hand? I'm more than happy to provide assistance." His eyes dropped to my waistband before he took another slow drink of his beer.

My stomach fluttered as I moved in front of him, and I looked anywhere but at him as I reached to his side and set my beer on the tailgate.

"I've got it handled," I muttered as I slid my thumbs into the waistband of my cutoffs. It took some wiggling to get them over my hips while Colt just leaned there in obvious amusement.

As the shorts gave way, so did the last thin pretense that I wasn't hyperaware of his eyes on me. The air was humid today and it licked right up my bare legs. I tried to keep my focus anywhere but on Colt, but he made it nearly impossible. He tracked me without apology, his head tilted a little, lips quirking at the corners, like he was watching a show meant for him alone.

I yanked my T-shirt up and over my head before I bunched the clothing together in my hands and hurled them straight at his chest.

He snatched them out of the air with one hand, laughing, the sound so damn genuine, as he pressed my tangled bundle of clothes to his side like they were some sort of trophy he'd won. He didn't bother to hide the way his gaze dragged down over me. His eyes burned over every inch, lingering at the curve of my hip, the dip of my waist, until they stopped right at the spot where my bikini top barely contained me. The heat of his stare ignited something low in my belly, and I had to squeeze my thighs together to stop the ache.

His eyes dropped to the movement, and I could see his throat work as he swallowed.

"Happy?" I crossed my arms, which only pushed my breasts higher, straining against the light blue fabric, and his eyes darkened as they jumped back up.

"Very," he said, voice rougher than before, and the word grazed down my skin. *How could he make something so innocent sound so dirty?*

I reached back beside him for my beer. I did it unhurriedly, letting the bare skin of my stomach slide across his forearm. His muscles jumped beneath my touch, and the sharp hiss of his breath catching fueled me. He held still, but I could feel the tension radiating from him.

I straightened and brought the bottle to my lips. I took a long sip before I swallowed and ran my tongue over my bottom lip. His eyes burned into me the entire time, and even though the sun was hot on my shoulders and Ruby's laughter rang out around us, all of it seemed muffled compared to the singularity of Colt's attention.

His fingers flexed around his own bottle before he lifted his other hand and ran his fingers over that damn mustache, and the effect was so heady I nearly dropped my beer.

"It's good to see you didn't actually lose your abs." I pointed the neck of my beer to his stomach which somehow was far more defined than it had been when he was eighteen.

"You really were worried about that weren't you?" He grinned as he arched an eyebrow.

"You can't have a mustache like that with no abs." I shook my head. "It's math 101. If you have that mustache, but no abs, you're creepy. But that mustache, with those—" I dropped my gaze back down to his stomach, and dear God, how deep were those lines that were disappearing beneath his shorts.

"Then I'm what?" The sound of his voice had my gaze snapping back up to his, but I simply shook my head. There was no way in hell I was going to finish that thought. I was trying to be funny, but why did he have to be so hot?

"Nothing."

"You're not looking at me like I'm nothing." He teased, watching me, and I felt like I was coming out of my skin.

"That's not what I meant."

We stared at each other, and neither of us blinked.

The air between us felt electric, charged with something dangerous and inevitable. My skin prickled with awareness as his gaze dropped to my mouth, lingering there with such naked intent that I squirmed under his attention.

I was about to turn away when he leaned in, close enough that I could feel the heat radiating from his body, his tone pitched low for just the two of us. "Blaire?"

"Yeah?" I turned my head slightly, feeling his breath on my ear, and when his gaze caught mine, there was no teasing left.

"How wet do you think you're going to get for me today?"

My brain stuttered, tripped, spun out somewhere between the slow, dangerous way he'd said "wet" and the flash in his eyes as he watched the color rise in my cheeks. Then it hit, full force, and I swear my body responded before I could even gather up a retort. A gasp, an embarrassing shiver, and the way my thighs threatened to press together to relieve the overwhelming ache, only to be caught by the solid firmness of Colt's leg as he nudged his knee between them, pinning them apart.

My pulse ricocheted. We were only twenty feet from everyone else, and the risk of them seeing us only made it worse.

It should have been humiliating, how easily he could read my body, how he stood there shamelessly taking in every reaction I had. Instead, it lit something wild in my chest, something that made my palms sweat and my heart race and my entire body spark with a reckless pulse that had me clenching my knees around his.

I couldn't care less that we were in public, forgot about Maggie and McCoy and even Ruby, floating somewhere in the expanse of the lake behind us. There was only the heat of his thigh pressing into mine, the rough edge of his breathing, and the way he watched me like he already knew exactly what it would take to push my body over the edge.

I tried to recover, to pull back, to find something sarcastic to say to diffuse my reaction, but all I could do was suck in a sharp breath, as a shameless little whimper passed through my lips.

He set his beer on the tailgate with a soft clink as he grinned, his eyes dropping to my parted lips for one heart-stopping second before his hands found my waist, palms burning against my skin. Before I could even process the movement, he ducked low, driving his shoulder into my stomach. I squealed as the world spun upside down.

He straightened to his full height, lifting me up on his shoulder, and my cheek pressed against his bare back.

"Colt!" I yelled, kicking out instinctively, but he hooked an arm behind my knees while his other hand rested on the back of my thigh.

Blood rushed to my head, but arousal pulsed between my legs. His shoulder dug into my stomach with each step, and I could feel the hot press of his skin against mine. The vibration of his laughter rippled through me as his hand slid higher on my thigh, fingers grazing the edge of my bikini bottom, leaving a trail of fire across my skin that made me want to beg him for more.

"Colt Oliver Calloway, put me down," I demanded, but my voice betrayed me, coming out as a breathless gasp.

"Did you just middle-name me again?" His voice dropped, and his palm landed quickly on my ass with a sting that shot straight through my core.

"Colt!" I said his name again, but it was drowned out by my own helpless laughter.

The aftershock of his palm lingered, tingling in a way that sent my body into mortifying overdrive. He only hoisted me higher, the world pitching with each stride, and all I could focus on was the way his hands tightened against me.

"That's for ignoring me over the last few days," he said, breathless with his own laughter, and his fingers skimmed back and forth over my thigh. I couldn't see his face, but I could imagine his smug grin, the pleasure he took in my utter help-lessness.

I could hear the delighted squeal of Ruby, and Maggie's and McCoy's laughter echoing across the water. I twisted, trying to right myself, but Colt was a wall of immovable muscle. I caught the blur of McCoy and Maggie turning to watch us as Colt stepped onto the dock.

"Look, uncle Coy!" Ruby called, abandoning her float and doggy-paddling toward the shallow water. "Daddy's going to throw Blaire in!"

McCoy cupped his hands and bellowed in encouragement, "Attaboy! Get her ass in here!"

Colt marched across the dock, and even as he laughed, I could feel the tension in his body, the anticipation winding through every muscle. Every step jostled me in ways that made it impossible not to feel the slide of his skin, the heat of his body, and the certainty that he was enjoying every second of my squirming.

"Colt, don't you dare," I managed, my voice coming out as part threat, part laughter.

He paused at the edge of the dock, feet planted wide, and shifted me slightly. His palm splayed across my thigh, possessive and steady.

"Do you promise not to ignore me again?" he asked, and I couldn't control my laughter now.

I kicked wildly, but his grip didn't budge. My hands clung desperately to his waist, wrapping my arms around his middle and holding on to him as I clamped my eyes closed.

"I'm not promising shit," I huffed and held on tighter.

"Well, you had your chance."

I barely had time to brace myself before we were airborne. I was still clinging to his waist, and he'd held on to me. The scream that tore from my lungs was filled with laughter before we plunged into the water.

We went under, deep enough I could feel the lake's chill curl around me.

We surfaced together, still tangled as he pulled me up with him, both gasping. His grip on me was firm, his fingers digging into both sides of my hips. The dock loomed above us, and I heard Ruby yelling, "Again! Again!" as her footsteps pounded against the wooden planks.

Colt's hands stayed locked on me under the water, and water droplets clung to his eyelashes and dripped from the hair trailing down his face.

"You're an ass," I coughed, trying to push away from him, but he wouldn't loosen his hold.

He yanked me closer, my chest colliding with his, and there was no mistaking the rigid heat pressing against my stomach through his wet swim trunks.

"And, you—" He paused as he looked down at me. He didn't bother trying to hide the way his eyes fell to my mouth, then lower, tracking water down my neck to the tops of my breasts. "—are a goddamn test of my will."

He finally let go of me, but not before his hands traced a lazy circle around my waist.

Ruby barreled down the dock and skidded to a stop a few feet from the edge, arms pinwheeling for balance. She looked down at Colt with her cheeks flushed and her chest heaving. "Daddy! Catch me!"

Colt's entire expression shifted so quickly, transforming from *Daddy Colt* to Colt the dad, and there was so much pride and soft devotion on his face as he stared up at his daughter. He waded toward her, holding his arms up. "Come on, baby girl. Show me what you got."

Ruby bounced on her toes. "Ready?" she asked, glancing at me.

I nodded, still floating in the water, still drowning in what the hell just happened.

Ruby launched herself off the dock, knees to her chest, and she landed right in front of Colt. His hands wrapped around her as she went under, the splash covering every inch of him. Ruby surfaced again, whooping and laughing so loudly it was impossible not to get pulled into it.

She splashed him in the face, and he pulled her into his chest before she wrapped her arms around his shoulders.

"I think that was the best cannonball I've ever seen." He pressed the tip of his finger against her nose, and she beamed.

"Did you see, Blaire?" she asked, already swimming back to the dock for another go. "I went so far!"

I found myself grinning back at her. "You did so good, Ruby. I've never seen someone go so far."

Colt's gaze tracked back over to me, his eyes still dark and hungry. He sank deeper until the lake water kissed his upper lip, his eyes not leaving mine.

I didn't move; I couldn't look away from him as Ruby scrambled up the ladder for another round.

But then Maggie swam over, her hair slicked back and her

sunglasses covering her eyes. Even still, I could see the way she looked between me and Colt. She bumped her legs into mine under the water and grinned.

"Blaire, darling," she drawled. "You, me, and margaritas, stat."

She looped her arm through mine, and together, we swam to the bank. Then she was dragging me up the embankment, the dirt and slippery rocks slick beneath our feet. As we reached the shore, I adjusted my bikini and risked a look over my shoulder.

Colt was still treading water, Ruby on his back, and McCoy had joined them, splashing at each other like they were three children. Ruby giggled as McCoy pretended to dunk them, and Colt's laughter, so deep and unguarded, rippled all the way across the surface and straight into my veins. It was the sound of *my Colt*— the one from before life got hard, before he was buried under the duties of the ranch and being a single father.

Maggie sidled closer, dropping her sunglasses enough to peer at me over the rim. "You're hopeless," she whispered. "You know that, right?"

I shook my head gently, feeling heat crawl up my neck, and she sighed before pulling me along behind her. We got to the tailgate, and I pulled one of my towels out of my bag and pressed it against my face.

Maggie pulled a large pink water cooler to the edge of the tailgate and poured herself a cup from the spigot. She dropped in a lime wedge before she took a long, dramatic sip. "This reminds me of spring break."

I chuckled as she filled another cup and passed it to me. "That's the great thing about margaritas. They're perfect for every stage of your life."

"Don't I know it." She pressed her cup against mine in a cheers, and we both drank before she turned, leaning back against the truck and looking out over the water. She was quiet for a long moment before she tapped my elbow with her cup. "No, really? How are you alive?" She nodded out to where I knew Colt still swam. "I would have spontaneously combusted if someone looked at me like that."

"Like what?" I asked, but I could still feel Colt like a live wire against my skin.

She cocked her head and fixed me with a look that made me giggle against my cup.

"Like you're his dinner and he's about to devour every inch of you." She glanced back across the water, nodding toward Colt.

He stood with his hands raised protectively as Ruby wobbled on McCoy's shoulders.

"You're telling me you didn't feel that?"

My cheeks flamed as I gulped down half my margarita. "I mean, it was—" I trailed off, searching for any words to help me describe what was happening between us. "That's how he is. It's just—Colt."

Maggie snorted, nearly choking on her margarita. "I've known him for a few years now, and I have never seen Colt Calloway look at anyone the way he looks at you."

I ran my tongue over my bottom lip, stealing another glance at him. "There's nothing happening between us," I lied. "The two of us are old history. If anything, I'm sure he's just feeling nostalgic."

She snorted again. "Honey, that wasn't nostalgia. The man looked like he was ready to fuck you right here on this tailgate while we all watched, and I'm willing to bet it would have been one hell of a show."

"Maggie!" I slapped a hand over her mouth. *Why was she being so loud?* "Colt and I are friends now," I hissed, and she grinned beneath my hand. "Or at least we're civil, friendly even," I insisted, as if saying it aloud might make it true. "That's it. He has Ruby. The ranch."

"Oh, friendly. Right." Maggie wiggled her eyebrows suggestively. "Oh, what I wouldn't give for a 'friend' who gets so hot for me, he has to throw us both in the lake to cool off. I swear y'all were like one minute away from taking someone's eye out with his boner."

"Please stop." I buried my face in my hands, but she only laughed.

"How does it feel to be God's favorite? If I had that cowboy looking at me like he was about to fuck me so good, I would beg him for it. I would have climbed him like a tree."

"Will you be quiet?" I elbowed her in the ribs, but I couldn't stop my laughter. "Ruby is, like, twenty feet away."

"Oh, suddenly you're worried about Ruby being here." She held up her hands in a playful surrender, and I downed the rest of my margarita.

Colt and McCoy stood chest deep in the water, launching Ruby between them. Each time she hit the water with a squeal and a splash, Colt's shoulders shook with laughter. McCoy threw her back in Colt's direction, and he caught her easily before she went under. He buried his face in her neck, blowing against her skin and giving little kisses, and something twisted in my chest.

What the hell was I doing?

"Shit. You really have it bad for him, don't you?" Maggie said, but this time the playfulness in her voice was gone. She watched Colt, then her eyes flicked to me.

I wanted to deny it, to make a joke, but I couldn't do it. Instead, I watched Colt and Ruby, the way his arms encircled her as if she were the most precious thing in the world, the way he seemed so unselfish in the way he loved her.

I once had that ease with him, and I hated myself for wanting it again.

"I don't," I started, but it came out as a whisper. "Colt and I were a long time ago," I said, forcing myself to look at Maggie. "And he isn't someone that you get over easily."

Maggie reached out and squeezed my hand, her palm firm and warm against mine.

"Look," she said, voice dropping. "I can mind my own business when I really have to, especially considering you've given me the bare minimum details." She frowned, and I let out the smallest laugh. "But if you need to talk about it, you know I'm here, right?"

I nodded, grateful for her. "Sometimes I wish I could undo all of it. Go back, make a different choice, and see how it all plays out."

Maggie grinned, but it was the sad kind. "I get that, I do." She nodded. "But you can't unscramble your eggs, babe. Best you can do is fry up something new and hope it doesn't burn."

I laughed, laughed from deep in my belly, and the knot in my chest loosened a little.

"Don't worry, assholes. The party is finally here!" Hunter called out, his voice reaching us as he sauntered down the grassy slope toward the lake. A twelve-pack of beer dangled from his right hand while his left was wrapped around the hand of a very leggy brunette.

Maggie sucked in a sharp breath beside me, her plastic cup crinkling in her hold. Her eyes locked on Hunter for only a few seconds before sliding to the woman at his side, her expression morphing into something carefully blank.

Her nails tapped against the rim of her cup, so quickly and so at odds with the easy smile she forced onto her face.

I turned as she drained what remained of her drink in one swift motion and reached for the cooler.

"What about you?" I said low enough for only her to hear. "Are we ever going to talk about the fact that he's your sister's ex, but you look like you've seen a ghost every time he's around?"

"Not today." She shook her head as her gaze flicked back in his direction.

"Okay," I said, passing her my empty cup. "Then let's make another margarita."

CHAPTER 20

COLT

In every way possible a man can want a woman, I wanted Blaire Monroe.

And that was so fucking dangerous.

She was so damn beautiful, and she grinned at my friends—my family, like she hadn't been tossing matches at my self-control.

I watched her now, her long, bare legs stretched out in front of her on the dock, my dock, with the late afternoon sun turning her skin to honey. I should have been thinking about the pile of work waiting for us on this ranch or the fact that I needed to finish Ruby's laundry and hit up the grocery store, but all I could focus on was Blaire's mouth, the angle of her jaw when she laughed, and the way she'd gasped against me a couple hours ago.

It was torture, the way she kept moving through the world like she didn't know what she did to me.

And all I could do was replay her shudder when I'd pressed my thigh between her knees, her desperate need for relief, and how she'd gasped when I asked her how wet she was going to get for me.

And God, I knew she had been wet.

Her body had betrayed her with every subtle quiver, every catch of her breath, and every flutter of her lashes when she looked up at me. Yet here she was acting like it never happened, and I might have believed her if I hadn't savored every one of her body's confessions.

I was a fucking wreck, but I smiled for Ruby's sake. If she weren't here, if I didn't have to keep some semblance of my control for my daughter, I didn't know what the hell I would've done.

The way she looked at Ruby was enough to do me in. My daughter's head rested in Blaire's lap, dark hair being woven into a braid by fingers that moved so tenderly against her scalp. Ruby's laughter rang out as Blaire and Maggie entertained her, and my breath caught at how perfectly Blaire fit into this moment, into our lives, like she'd always belonged there.

When she caught me watching, her lip curved into a gentle smile before her eyes darted away. She bent down, whispering something that made Ruby burst out in laughter. I didn't give a damn what secret they shared between them, even if it was at my expense, because everything felt so painfully vivid with possibility as I watched them.

And for one treacherous second, I almost forgot how hard I'd worked to make sure I'd never set myself up for that kind of heartbreak again.

Almost.

"You really need to rein your shit in," Hunter said from where he sat beside me on the grass.

"What the hell are you talking about?" I shot him a glare.

"Oh, so we're going to pretend you're not broadcasting it to the entire county?" Hunter gestured loosely toward the dock. "I don't think you've quit looking at her for even a second since we've been here."

He paused, studying me the way only someone who'd spent every day of their childhood acting as my shadow could. "Jesus, Colt, you're not even trying to hide it anymore. My money was on you at least making it three weeks before you caved."

"Fuck off," I muttered, but Hunter grinned as he knocked his shoulder into mine.

"Hey, if you want to play lovesick puppy, far be it from me to stand in your way." He shifted the beer in his hand. "But you should hold back a little before you scare her off again."

Again.

I gripped my beer bottle tighter, hating that Hunter could read me so easily. The worst part was knowing he was right about everything. I didn't have it in me to take another hit like last time. When Blaire left, she'd taken every part of the boy I'd been, and I wasn't sure there was enough man left in me to survive her if she left again.

From my other side, McCoy snorted, half listening as he lay back in the sun with his eyes closed. "You should have seen him before you got here. I thought he was going to fuck her in the bed of my truck." He blinked an eye open at me. "I would've made you clean it, by the way."

I grunted, focusing on the bottleneck in my hand rather than on their faces. They weren't wrong. I could feel it, the way my control was slipping.

Hunter laughed. "Damn, I really hate that I missed that. Blaire does have some nice fucking legs."

I slammed the back of my hand against his chest, and he only grinned as he rubbed the spot.

"Ouch, asshole. That hurt."

"Don't fucking talk about her like that," I growled and brought my beer to my lips. Sure enough, my eyes tracked straight over to the legs in question. "It's not like you can talk. Where's your little shadow, anyway?" I looked around us for the girl he'd brought with him. "You know, for a guy who brought a date, you haven't looked at her once since you got here."

McCoy let out a low whistle, rising to his elbows to take us both in. "Damn, we're getting personal now?"

Hunter's eyes narrowed, the barest flicker of defensiveness tightening his jaw. "She ran up to my truck to get something out of her bag," he said. "I don't need to babysit her." He turned his head back to the dock, and I followed his gaze. "Not that you would understand since you moved your ex in with you and are watching her like she's going to disappear."

I waited a beat, letting the silence stretch before I leveled my gaze at him. "At least I'm staring at my ex and not her little sister."

"Oh, shit," McCoy laughed, leaning forward until he was sitting up beside me. "We're going there, huh?"

"I don't know what the fuck you're talking about," Hunter growled, but he was so full of shit. Hunter and Ella, Maggie's older sister, broke up a little over two years ago, and he's spent that exact amount of time staring at Maggie like she wasn't five years younger than him or related to his ex.

"Right." I nodded before I met his eyes. "So you can see the way I'm looking at Blaire, but you're blind to your own shit?"

"I have no interest in Maggie. She's Ella's sister, for fuck's sake."

"Her very hot, very mouthy, younger sister," McCoy interjected. "Who I would have already had in my bed if it weren't for the way she looks at you."

"Fuck off, McCoy," Hunter grumbled, but he was still looking at Maggie.

McCoy, smelling blood in the water, only laughed. "Hey, Mags, you want to come over here and settle a debate?"

Maggie looked in our direction, shading her eyes. "What debate?"

"Are you kidding me?" Hunter said under his breath, and McCoy's smile widened.

"We're trying to figure something out." McCoy's voice carried over to the dock, playful and a little too loud, and all three of them looked over at us.

Maggie pulled her sunglasses slightly down her face and gave him a bored, slow blink that would make any cowboy I knew shake in his boots. "Like what?"

"Like, if you had to pick between me and Hunter, who would you choose? I'm older than Hunter, so I'm definitely the most mature, but I'm also tired." McCoy grinned, and I couldn't help but smile at the way he was baiting my brother. "Hunter is dumb, but he still has energy."

"Jesus Christ." Hunter muttered the curse, his shoulders

tensing as he ran a hand through his hair. My brother, who could sweet-talk his way in or out of anything, looked like he wanted to disappear into the grass beneath us.

"And, of course, Hunter dated your sister." McCoy slipped that in, and Maggie's spine straightened.

Ruby's curious gaze bounced among the adults, her small brow furrowed in confusion.

"That would count him out," Maggie said casually, but she looked anything but. "Plus, I prefer older men, but if your old age is affecting your stamina, I'm out."

McCoy licked his lips as he looked Maggie up and down, and I thought my brother was going to come out of his skin. "Oh, honey. You don't have to worry about my stamina."

"What's stamina?" Ruby asked, tilting her head back to look at Blaire.

Blaire's fingers froze where she was rubbing a towel over Ruby, her eyes going wide before she glanced at me in horror.

"Really, McCoy?" I knocked his shoulder, but he only laughed.

"Uh..." Blaire cleared her throat, scrambling, and I would have saved her if it wasn't so cute to watch. "It means that your uncle Coy can't really keep a girlfriend because he doesn't really know how to make them happy."

Ruby nodded, but Maggie sputtered a laugh into her drink.

"Really, Blaire?" McCoy said, clutching at his chest as if she'd wounded him. "I bet I could make you happy." He let his gaze linger a second too long on her, always the showman, and then tipped his beer in salute. "If you have your doubts, I can prove it to you. I'm nothing if not accommodating."

I tried to play it off, but the jab of jealousy landed. Which was ridiculous because she wasn't mine. Hell, I barely had the right to want her after everything I'd done, but that didn't keep my blood from surging at the idea of Blaire with someone else. It didn't matter that I knew McCoy was joking and that he'd never go there with her.

"You're such a child, McCoy." Blaire's laughter caught on the summer air, and I felt every muscle in my body tense at the sound of it.

"I wholeheartedly agree," Hunter said before he finished his beer, wiped his mouth with the back of his hand, and climbed to his feet.

His gaze lingered on Maggie for a long moment before he finally turned, and we all watched him go. He stalked toward the truck, shoulders wound tight, and then I caught sight of his date, Alicia, making her way back down to the water. She beamed at him, completely oblivious to his mood.

He passed right by her without saying a word, and she blinked up at us before looking back in his direction. She stumbled a little in her wedges that belonged nowhere near this lake as she walked onto the dock and took a seat by the girls.

But my gaze caught on the woman next to her. The one who looked like this was exactly where she belonged.

The beer was hitting me harder than usual, my head feeling light as I looked away and caught a flicker of movement at the tree line.

My mom made her way toward us with a pink fuzzy blanket slung over one shoulder and one of Ruby's sparkly backpacks hanging from the other. She'd balanced a couple roasting sticks, a battered lantern, and a bag of marshmallows in one of her arms, and she looked like a grandma on a mission.

I looked back at Ruby, but she hadn't noticed her yet. My mom marched down to the edge of the water, looking out at the view before her, and she planted her hand above her eyes as if she were searching for something.

"Excuse me," she called out, and Ruby's head whipped in her direction. "Has anyone here seen a little girl about this tall—" She held her hand at Ruby's height "—who might want to join her nana and Ms. June on a top-secret camping adventure? I've got marshmallows and chocolate, but I can't find the little girl."

My mom shook her head dramatically and Ruby squealed. "Me! I'm the little girl!" She shot up from Blaire's lap, nearly knocking Maggie off the dock. "Can we really, Nana? Tonight?"

Mom nodded and held out all the things in her arms. "I didn't pack all of this for nothing. I'd hate for me and June to have to eat it all by ourselves."

"No! I'm coming!" Ruby ran down the dock and was halfway down the gangway before she skidded to a stop. She stared at my mom as she hesitated, then she spun all the way back around, and bolted back the way she came.

Blaire barely had time to react before Ruby crashed into her, arms winding around Blaire's neck in a tackle hug. I watched the whole thing from the grass, muscles locked and breath rushing out of me. Blaire's hands wrapped around her, holding her so gently, as she squeezed her eyes closed and buried her face against my girl. I could see her lips moving, whispering something only for Ruby, and she nodded before she climbed back out of her lap.

Ruby quickly hugged Maggie, and even Alicia, before she finally made her way back down the gangway.

"Love you, Blaire!" Ruby said without stopping.

"Love you, Ruby. Go have the best adventure." Blaire smiled at her, and I wondered if she realized what she was doing. Did she know how much power she had to fuck everything up?

"You are so fucked," McCoy said under his breath as he chuckled, but I didn't respond.

I climbed to my feet and made my way over to my mom and Ruby. Mom pulled Ruby into the biggest hug before my daughter's small hands were grabbing for her blanket and the marshmallows.

"You mean to tell me all of those girls got a hug, and you didn't save one for your dad?" I teased, but Ruby's head whipped around like she'd been caught.

She ran to me, marshmallows and all, and threw herself into my arms. I caught her, easy as breathing, and she clung to me like she knew how badly I needed the hug. I pressed her into my chest, chin on top of her head, and squeezed her tight.

"I love you, Daddy. I'm going on an adventure with Nana and Ms. June," she said, her words muffled against my neck.

I tried to memorize the weight of her, the way her hands

balled up fistfuls of my shirt, and the smell of sunscreen sticking to her skin. She wouldn't always be small enough for this, wouldn't always run back to me. A fact that hit me in the gut more and more every day.

"Papa will be there too," Mom added with a smile. "We'll get him to tell us a ghost story before he goes to bed." She wiggled her fingers like she was already preparing to scare her granddaughter.

"Mom," I chastised, but Ruby only giggled.

I set her down, crouching so we were eye to eye. "You take care of Nana and Ms. June, all right? And don't eat all the marshmallows."

Ruby gave me a quick nod.

"Go give your uncle Coy a hug." I looked over my shoulder and saw Hunter making his way back down to us. "And your uncle Hunter."

She ran straight for Hunter, and he bent to scoop her up.

"You don't have to take Ruby tonight." I looked at my mom. "You've got your hands full, Mom."

And she damn well did. She'd been the engine that kept our family running for as long as I could remember. She was the first up in the morning, the last to bed, and the one who never flinched in the face of a crisis. My dad had been sick for a while, a slow, mean sickness that ground a man down, and she'd shouldered it all with the same stubborn pride she always had. He had his first heart attack roughly five years ago, and it's been a slow grind since. She cared for him in the house he built, surrounded by the land he loved, and it wore her down in a thousand small, invisible ways she'd never admit.

I tried to help where I could, splitting my time between Ruby and the ranch and whatever emergencies presented themselves in a given week, but Mom held us all together. She always had.

So, when she rolled her eyes at me like she couldn't believe she'd raised a son so thickheaded that I'd question her over her own granddaughter, I wasn't surprised.

"Don't you dare try to take our night away from us." She put her hands on her hips. "I miss my girl, and we're having a sleep-over. End of discussion."

I raised my hands in surrender. "Okay, okay," I said, laughing at how stern she looked.

"Plus," she added, "you've been working yourself ragged. You could use a night off."

I started to argue, but what was the point? She saw through me, always had. I was working a lot, but I couldn't stand the thought of losing ground, letting the work or the worry catch up to me, admitting that I might not be enough for any of this. Maybe she saw that, too.

I nodded, but the admission stung. "Yeah, maybe I could."

Ruby made her way back to us, and my mom squeezed her hand before they set off across the grass, the blanket dragging behind them. They climbed into the battered side-by-side my mom always used to get around the property, and she fired it up. Ruby scrambled into the shotgun seat, still clutching her marshmallows, and as they pulled away, she twisted back to wave at me.

I turned back to the water, blinking against the sunlight and the silence that followed Ruby's absence. The air felt too still without her chatter. I'd gotten used to the way Ruby made everything bearable, her presence like an insulating layer against all the ways I didn't know how to be around Blaire. With her gone, every edge in me was exposed.

Blaire kneeled on a towel, gathering up her things, tucking sunscreen and a book into her bag. Maggie was sitting on the edge of the dock, feet trailing in the water, head tipped back toward the sun, and Alicia was glancing back and forth between her and my brother.

Hunter, of course, had shrugged off every bit of his discomfort, and he was now near the dock with McCoy, both of them on a float with a beer in their hands.

I stayed back, trying like hell not to think about Blaire being in my house tonight with Ruby gone. I picked up the empties and tossed them into the trash as I tried to figure out what the hell I was supposed to do.

I was on my own damn land, but without Ruby here, I felt out of place.

Blaire zipped her bag and stood. Her white tank top was clinging to her, transparent in places so you could clearly see her bikini underneath, and it rode up high on her bare stomach. "I think I'm gonna go shower."

"Oh, hell no," Hunter said as he paddled over to the ladder. "Nobody's bailing now. We rarely get nights with just us, and you're gonna run off to wash your hair?"

She looked at him, then Maggie, then at the open path back to the house. "We've been in the sun all day. I'm tired."

Hunter hauled himself up the ladder and reached for the towel that was bunched at Blaire's feet. He flicked it at her legs, grinning when she yelped and jumped back. "That's the problem with you city girls," he said. "You can't hang."

"I am not a city girl," Blaire shot back, rolling her eyes and crossing her arms, "and I can hang just fine."

Maggie perked up, turning to look at her friend. "I'm with Hunter. You're not allowed to leave. Consider yourself kidnapped."

Blaire's laugh was light, but the way she clutched her arms around herself told a different story. "You're all insane."

"We have rules here," Hunter said, draping the towel around his neck and sitting down beside Maggie.

Alicia watched his every move.

"Nobody leaves the dock until at least one round of drinking games is played. Colt, back me up here."

I shrugged, grabbing the cooler and making my way out to the dock. I tried to act like I wasn't eager to find out if she'd stay. "He's not lying."

Blaire looked at me as I crossed the gangway, and I saw the same panic in her eyes that I felt. But then she set her bag down and dropped back to her towel, arms braced behind her.

"Fine," she said, but she didn't sound fine. "What are we playing?"

Hunter rubbed his hands together as McCoy climbed up the ladder. "That's more like it."

CHAPTER 21
BLAIRE

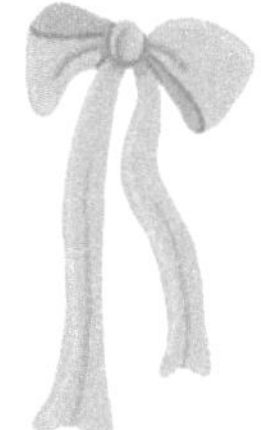

Twenty-eight years old and here I was, playing Never Have I Ever like we were kids again.

The sun had disappeared behind the ridge, turning the lake into black glass that caught the first pinpricks of stars.

Maggie's knee bumped mine with each burst of laughter, her legs folded beneath her. McCoy was sprawled out beside her, and Hunter sat on my other side with Alicia molded against him like she was afraid someone might steal her spot.

Then there was Colt. He'd taken the spot directly across the circle from me. His long legs stretched out, beer bottle dangling from his fingers, his mouth curved in a way that made me forget every reason I'd ever had for staying away.

When he tipped his beer back, I couldn't help but watch the slow bob of his throat, the way his jaw tensed just slightly as he swallowed.

Hunter lifted his beer bottle and flicked a smirk around the circle before his eyes lingered on Maggie. "Never have I ever gone skinny dipping in this lake."

The string lights strung along the dock posts cast just enough glow to really take each other in as night settled over the lake.

The dock went silent for one suspended breath. Then, Colt's gaze met mine, and I rolled my eyes as both of us lifted our drinks and took a sip. Maggie followed, then Hunter, then McCoy. Only Alicia's bottle stayed firmly planted on the wooden planks.

McCoy's jaw dropped in theatrical shock. "Hold up. Maggie skinny dipped in our lake? Without me?"

Maggie grinned and patted his leg. "You weren't invited, McCoy. Maybe next time."

"It's the very first round, and I'm already feeling left out," McCoy said, his mouth twisting into a mock pout.

"Don't worry, McCoy." Hunter leaned forward with a lazy grin, tapping his finger against his temple. "I could tell you all about it. I replay it all the time up here."

"Are you serious right now?" Maggie's voice went razor-sharp.

Beside Hunter, Alicia shifted, creating a sliver of space between their bodies that hadn't been there before.

I choked on a laugh, earning a sharp look from Maggie, but even her mouth twitched on the corners.

"Go. It's your turn," she said.

I tapped my fingers against my beer bottle, a slow rhythm that matched my heartbeat. I looked around the circle, but my gaze snagged on Colt like it always did. Like gravity. There was a hint of amusement in his eyes that made me smile. "Never have I ever ridden a bull."

All three guys tipped their bottles back. McCoy sighed dramatically. "So we're playing 'make the cowboys drink,' huh?"

"Hey, Alicia could've ridden one too," I said, but he just snorted.

Maggie leaned forward, the string lights dancing along her face. "Never have I ever been in love."

All I could hear was the soft lap of water against wood. I lifted my bottle slowly, feeling the weight of every inch. Across the circle, Colt's bottle stayed motionless in his lap, his eyes locked on mine. One heartbeat. Two. Then his fingers tightened around the glass and he raised it to his lips, taking a long, deliberate sip without breaking his gaze.

"Okay," McCoy announced, his grin spreading slow across his face. "Never have I ever called off an engagement."

"Damn," Hunter muttered under his breath, and I shot McCoy a look that could've frozen the lake.

"So we're playing 'make Blaire drink,' huh?" I mocked him as I brought my beer to my lips.

He leaned back, satisfied. "Just needed confirmation."

"You could've just asked me," I said, then gestured across the circle without meeting those eyes I could feel burning into me. "Colt, you're up."

He hesitated for a second before he finally spoke, his voice dropping so low it seemed to vibrate through the wooden planks beneath us, and my gaze snapped to him. "Never have I ever thought about kissing someone here tonight." His tongue briefly touched his lower lip as he finished the sentence, and his eyes held mine with such naked hunger that I forgot to breathe.

I inhaled sharply, the dock creaking beneath me as I shifted. Five pairs of eyes burned into us, but I couldn't look away from Colt. His gaze dropped to my lips, lingering there, and arousal pulsed between my legs. He lifted his beer with deliberate slowness, the muscles in his forearm flexing as he tipped the bottle back. I watched his throat work and remembered how his skin had once tasted on my tongue.

I shouldn't have done it. I should have lied. My fingers trembled so violently against the cold bottle I feared I would drop it, but I raised it anyway. One swallow. Two. The carbonation fizzed on my tongue while memories flooded back—the rough scrape of his stubble, the way he'd groan when I bit his bottom lip, how kissing him had always felt like a freefall.

McCoy let out a low whistle. "Well, shit. This game has taken a turn."

Alicia cleared her throat, a little too loud, and tucked a strand of her hair behind her ear. We all looked at her as she spoke. "Never have I ever," she started, her eyes flicking to Maggie for just a second then to me, "been cheated on."

"Wow. Y'all are really going for the jugular today," I said, and the laugh that tumbled out of me was just tipsy enough to sound lighter than I felt. I lifted my bottle.

"Sorry," Alicia said with a wince, as her nails clicked lightly against her drink.

"Zero stars." I held up a zero on my hand. "I don't recommend it."

"Me either," Maggie said, but her voice had the slightest edge to it. She leaned in, and we clinked beers, a little too hard. The fizz slopped onto my hand and I licked it off. I caught Colt watching me, his eyes dark and intent beneath the string lights.

"Ditto," McCoy said, and for once he didn't ham it up. He leaned forward and gave us solemn cheers.

Hunter was flat on his side now, propped on an elbow, the bottle balanced on his chest. He hoisted it up and leaned across my knee until he could tap his bottle with the rest of ours. "I also give it zero stars," he announced, then paused, thinking. "Negative stars if that's allowed."

"Baby, Hunter," I crooned, leaning over to ruffle his hair with my free hand. His dark strands were still a bit damp from swimming, and my fingers moved through his hair like they had a hundred times before, a habit from when we were kids. While Colt had been my world, Hunter had been like a little brother. "With that face? Who would dare cheat on your handsome ass?"

He grinned, a flash of teeth, and pretended to be mortally wounded by the memory. "It's my tragic origin story, Blaire. Women sense the trauma, makes me irresistible." He put the back of his hand to his forehead in a grand, swooning gesture.

"I bet that really works for you, doesn't it?" I smiled down at him.

"Kind of, yeah." He nodded, and I barely caught Alicia rolling her eyes.

"So who was the heartbreaker?" I asked playfully. "I'll have to kick her ass for you."

His eyes slid past me to Maggie then back again. "Maggie's sister," he said, and even though he said it like a punchline, I heard the old ache in the way he let the words out slow and flat.

A hush fell around the dock, and I couldn't help it, I snorted out a laugh. I slapped my hand over my mouth, trying to control the sound. "Ope. I'm sorry." I tried to swallow it, but it kept bubbling up anyway.

"No. Please, Blaire." Hunter smacked the back of his hand against my thigh. "Make fun of my misery."

"I'm not making fun of you. I swear." I was still chuckling as I patted his cheek. "You just caught me off guard." I widened my eyes and nodded toward Maggie and another laugh slid out as she pinched me. "Oh my god. Who let me play this game?"

"What about you, Colt?" Maggie asked, changing the subject. "You've never been cheated on?" There was no challenge in her voice, just simple curiosity.

Colt shook his head, slow and easy, the movement sending his hair falling forward over his forehead. "No," he said, and the word just hung there.

I let out another laugh, a quiet huff that surprised even me this time. It broke the silence, and suddenly the attention of the entire dock was back on me.

Colt's eyebrow cocked, the corner of his mouth rising in that lazy, charming way. "Is that funny, Blaire?"

A laugh slipped out before I could help myself. "No, not at all. I just... I can't picture anybody being that stupid."

He looked at me differently, then, like he was measuring something in my face, or maybe in himself. "And why's that?"

I gestured toward him with my beer. "Because you're you. You're..." I trailed off, realizing too late that I didn't actually have the words for what I meant. "I don't know. It's just obvious."

McCoy nodded his head and then pointed at Colt with both index fingers. "Our boy is a catch."

"And now he's a daddy." I arched an eyebrow, gave him a pointed look, and took a slow sip of my drink.

"What the fuck does that mean?" Colt asked, his low chuckle vibrating through the night air between us.

"Are you drunk?" Hunter laughed, tilting his head back against my knee.

"No. I'm not drunk." I shook my head. "Well, maybe a little tipsy, but tonight's just been fun." My shoulders lifted in a shrug.

Hunter smiled up at me, and I didn't dare look at Colt. "He's probably going to kill me for telling you this, but McCoy and I have been trying to get Colt to let us call him daddy on the ranch for ages."

I snorted out another laugh so hard my eyes watered, and Hunter's grin stretched wide as he watched me.

"He's our boss daddy," Hunter declared, hand over his heart like he was reciting the pledge of allegiance. "It's only right."

"Hear, hear!" McCoy raised his bottle from where he now lay flat on his back, sloshing beer onto his chest.

"Wait, I'm living in his house." I tapped my chin, pretending to consider this deeply while my heart hammered against my ribs. I finally looked up at Colt. "Maybe I should start calling him house daddy."

The smile he gave me lit up his face like the first sunrise after winter, stealing not just my breath. His eyes locked on mine, and the rest of the world fell away until there was only Colt, only this moment suspended between heartbeats. I felt myself leaning toward him without meaning to, drawn by some invisible thread that had always connected us, even when I pretended it didn't exist.

"What did I tell you about calling me daddy, Blaire?" His voice dropped to a growl, and heat flooded my body, pooling low in my belly and spreading outward until even my fingertips tingled with want.

"Jesus Christ." Maggie pushed herself up from the dock, fanning her face with exaggerated flicks of her wrist. I glanced up to find her staring at Colt and me with wide eyes. "I'm getting out of here before I burst into flames just from proximity. The sexual tension between you two is suffocating." She fanned her shirt like she needed ventilation.

"Maggie!" I laughed, my face burning hot.

She widened her eyes dramatically, unrepentant. "What? Everyone's thinking it."

McCoy hauled himself upright with a dramatic groan. "She's right," he said, tapping his forehead. "That little exchange is getting filed away for the spank bank."

"Oh my god." My entire body cringed with mortification.

Hunter and Alicia climbed to their feet too, and Hunter grabbed his things from the dock before he spoke. "Mags, you need a ride home?"

Maggie stiffened. "I'm good. McCoy's got me."

He nodded once before he grabbed Alicia's hand.

"Of course I've got you." He rolled to his feet before he dipped into a lopsided bow in Maggie's direction. "Milady."

"You're such a dork." She smiled at him as she collected her things. "Good night, guys. Don't do anything I wouldn't do." She winked at me, and I swear my entire body lit up like a flare.

I was going to kill her.

The laughter and footsteps faded up the hill as they left, leaving the dock far too quiet with just me and Colt. Ruby usually served as our buffer, her small body and endless chatter filling the space between us, but tonight that safety net was gone.

Goosebumps broke out along my skin despite the heat, and I stood, balancing on the uneven planks. I gathered up a couple empty bottles, trying to look busy, and not acknowledge that this was the first time we'd been completely alone since I came home.

My hands felt clumsy, and I could feel Colt watching me the way a coyote might watch a rabbit. My pulse thudded, and the night air pressed in until I could hardly breathe.

I'd spent a week pretending I could hide in plain sight, but the way he was looking at me now said he'd already stripped every lie I'd wrapped around myself.

"You don't have to do that. I'll get it," Colt insisted, but I didn't turn to face him. I couldn't.

I shook my head and grabbed a towel. "It's fine. I've got it."

My voice did not sound fine.

A long silence stretched between us. I could hear the water lapping against the wood, the distant ruffle as the wind moved through the trees. I was so hyperaware of everything around us that I jumped when the boards groaned beneath us. I turned in time to see him stand, stretch with a lazy roll of his muscles, and then, without so much as a word, he walked to the edge and dove off the dock.

His body cut through the moonlit surface before the lake swallowed him whole. The abruptness of it caught me off guard, and I stood with my arms full of trash, blinking at the place he'd been, uncertain what to do.

There was nothing but the night and the sound of my own heart, but then Colt surfaced, slicking his hair back with a single motion. The droplets clung to his eyelashes and shoulders, catching the moonlight, and he grinned up at me with a look that was pure challenge.

"I'm going to bed," I said before I could do or say anything I knew I'd regret.

"Wait." He stopped me, his voice low and eyes on me. "Swim with me."

I didn't answer him because I wasn't sure I could. I just shook my head.

"Come on, Blaire." He still hadn't taken his eyes off me. "You're not really going to leave me out here alone, are you?"

I rolled my eyes, but I could feel heat licking at my cheeks. "You're the one who jumped in."

"Yeah, but it's less fun alone." He stretched his arms out wide, letting his fingers ripple through the smooth surface. "C'mon. The water's perfect right now."

I turned away, putting my whole focus into stacking the bottles and tucking the towel under my arm. "I really should get inside," I protested, and I meant it. The house loomed up the hill, yet I still couldn't make myself move that way.

"Just come swimming, or are you scared?" There was laughter in his voice, but underneath it, something else, something I could feel in the way my breath hitched and my hands fumbled with the bottles.

"I'm not scared," I lied. "I'm tired."

He swam closer, the water parting around him in lazy ripples. He grabbed the dock's ladder, tipped his head back, and looked up at me. "Then at least sit with me a minute. House daddy won't bite. Promise."

CHAPTER 22
BLAIRE

I should've gone inside. My brain screamed at me that this was a bad idea, that if I stayed a second longer, something irreversible would happen. But somehow, I still found myself walking to the end of the dock like a fool. I pressed my hands against the top of the ladder, balancing myself as I took a seat right in front of him with my feet dangling over the edge.

The water rippled in slow, gentle waves, dark except for where the moon caught its surface. Colt treaded water a few feet in front of me, his shoulders just visible above the surface.

"Let's play another game," he said quietly, his gaze lingering on my face.

"Aren't we tired of games, Colt?" I asked, leaning back slightly on my hands.

He didn't answer. Instead, he sank deeper into the water, the surface lapping just above his upper lip. His expression gave nothing away, but electricity skittered across my skin as his fingers curled around the ladder rungs, drawing his body nearer to where I sat. The smile that crept across his face promised trouble I shouldn't want.

"Remember when we used to play truth or dare?" His voice danced with a challenge, light but dangerous.

A laugh tumbled from my lips, even as an ache started low in my belly. "I think we're a little old for that."

"We're a little old for Never Have I Ever too, but you had fun." The look on his face was pure mischief, but there was a nervousness underneath that caught me off guard. "Let's play. It's just for tonight. Tomorrow you can forget all about it and go right back to hating me."

God, there wasn't a single part of me that hated him.

"Fine. Truth or dare, cowboy?"

He grinned, and his whole damn face lit up. "Truth."

I leaned forward, elbows on my knees. I should have asked him something simple or something that would make us both laugh, but I didn't do either of those things. "Where's Ruby's mom?"

His expression flickered, something haunted passing over it before he answered. "She left a little over two years ago. She never really wanted to be a mother, and Ruby and I weren't enough to make her stay."

My chest ached for the way he said it, for how simple he made it seem. I wanted to tell him he was more than enough, that Ruby would never be anything less than loved, but the words caught in my throat, too fragile and terrifying to say aloud.

"Did you love her?" I whispered, my voice thin and unsteady.

He blinked, and the muscles in his jaw worked. He looked so young, so like the Colt I'd been so in love with, and my chest ached as I waited for his answer.

"You got your truth," he said, and the grin he gave me was so at odds with the way every other part of him had gone rigid. "Truth or dare?"

"Truth," I said, bracing myself.

"Did you love him?" he asked instantly. "The guy you were going to marry?"

His question hit me hard, and I hesitated, fingers digging into the dock. I could've lied. I'd been lying to myself for a very long time, but sitting here, alone with him, I couldn't bring myself to do it. "No. Not really."

He nodded once, like he'd already known my answer and only needed to hear me confirm it.

We sat there in the stillness, breathing too loudly, and I could see him running his thumb over the ladder's pitted steel, like he needed the sensation to anchor him. I wondered if he was remembering all the games of truth or dare we'd played as kids, if he remembered how none of those dares ever scared me half as much as these truths.

"Truth or dare?" I blurted, desperate to change the air between us.

"Truth," he said, and there was a challenge in the word, like he was daring me to cut deeper.

I searched his eyes, drowning in the blue I had spent years searching for in everything around me, and my heart pounded recklessly. *I felt reckless.* "Have you ever thought about what would've happened if I'd never left?"

He sucked in a breath, and the water reflected pale silver across his cheekbones, sharpening the lines of his face. "Every fucking day," he said, and there was no bravado in it this time, no careless cowboy cockiness. Just honesty, raw enough to hurt.

I swallowed hard because there was so much danger in the way he said it and in the way he was looking at me.

"My turn," he said. "Truth or dare?"

"Truth," I answered too quickly.

He dragged his hand over his mustache as he watched me, then his voice came low and rough. "When you were with him, did you ever think about me?"

His question hit like lightning through my body. Heat pooled in my body, and my fingers dug into the rough wood of the dock as an insistent need pulsed between my thighs.

"All the time," I whispered, the confession scraping my throat raw.

His pupils dilated until his eyes were nearly black, fixed on mine with predatory focus. His chest expanded with each measured breath, the water sliding down his skin with every rise and fall.

"And earlier by the truck—" His gaze dropped to my mouth. "—were you wet for me?"

My breath stuttered. My skin burned everywhere, nipples tightening painfully against my shirt. My fingers gripped the dock's edge until they ached.

"I thought we were playing a game," I managed, but I felt stripped bare.

"We are." His gaze dropped to where my thighs pressed desperately together, and I felt so exposed. His tongue traced his bottom lip, leaving it glistening. "I dare you to show me."

"What?" The word fractured between us, though we both knew exactly what he meant.

"Show me how wet you are." His voice was pure gravel, almost reverent, and his hands gripped the ladder on either side of my thighs like it was the only thing keeping him tethered. "Let me see what I still do to you, Blaire."

I wanted to tell him to fuck off, to remember that this wasn't who we were anymore, but all I could do was stare at him, lips parted, breath shallow.

Colt waited, silent except for the sound of the water around him and the steady rush of his breath through his nose.

A dare. That's what this was meant to be, but the truth hummed under my skin. If I didn't want to do it, I could walk away right now. We could both wake up in the morning, tired and a little hungover, and we could pretend like none of this ever happened.

But I didn't walk away.

Instead, my knees parted, inches at first, then wider, as if they had a will separate from my own. My skin burned everywhere his gaze touched, and the dock beneath me seemed to vibrate with each hammering beat of my heart. The night air was electric against my feverish skin, and the dark lake surrounding us became both voyeur and accomplice to what we were about to do.

"Colt." His name was a plea on my lips.

"It's just you and me, Blaire." He leaned forward, his breath scorching against my skin as he dragged his mouth along the inside of my knee.

My body jolted, a violent current shooting from that single point of contact straight to my pussy.

"Show me."

My breath came in short, desperate bursts. I could still tell him no. I should've told him no, but his voice wrapped around my throat, my wrist, between my thighs. His eyes devoured me, and whatever resistance I'd clung to shattered.

I spread my knees wider, the wood rough against my skin, and the night air hit the slick heat between my thighs only covered by my bikini. Colt's groan tore from him, the sound vibrating through my bones and pooling like liquid fire in my core.

He watched me, his eyes burning a path from my parted knees to the thin scrap of fabric between them that was already dark with want.

"Fuck," he said. "You're soaked for me, aren't you?"

I should've been embarrassed. I should've been mortified by the fact that he could see exactly what he did to me, that the simple dare to show him had my body responding so instantly, so helplessly.

But I burned with need and so many memories of the way he'd once touched me.

So I nodded, my hand sliding up my body like it belonged to someone else, someone braver. My fingertips dragged across my stomach, every touch igniting a trail of fire that spread lower, making my hips twitch in anticipation.

Colt's knuckles tightened around the ladder as he hauled himself up, water streaming off his shoulders. His breath scorched the inside of my knee, each exhale like a brand against my skin.

"Show me, baby," he growled, voice shattered with need. "Put your fingers in that pretty pussy and let me see exactly how fucking needy you are for me."

My hand shook as I dragged it lower, fingernails scraping over the curve of my hip, down to the aching heat between my thighs. I locked eyes with Colt and whimpered. His pupils had swallowed the blue entirely, his jaw clenched tight.

"That's it, Blaire. It's just you and me," he rasped.

His words ripped through me, obliterating every last shred of hesitation. I pressed my palm down hard against my drenched bikini bottoms, a moan slipping out as the pressure sent sparks shooting through me.

"Fucking perfect," Colt groaned, low and wrecked. His head tipped back, throat exposed, as one hand slid off the ladder and disappeared beneath the dark water. I could see his forearm flexing as he gripped himself.

"Slow," he commanded, his eyes devouring every desperate movement. "Make it hurt the way it does when I lie awake every night thinking about you."

I gasped, body arching against my touch. "Colt—please—"

"That's it. Right there," he coaxed me. "Every night I wrap my hand around my cock until it's throbbing, thinking about the way you used to cry out my name. Thinking about you spread out like this, begging me to let you finish."

I ground down harder, hips bucking violently against my hand, my entire body filled with need as his words branded themselves into my skin.

"You like the thought of that, don't you?" he hissed. "Do you want me to make you beg for it, Blaire?"

I nodded, unable to find my words, unable to control my reaction to him.

"Beg me to let you slide those fingers under so we can both see you dripping down your thighs as you touch yourself."

"Please, Colt." I stared up at him, and I couldn't believe what I was doing. "Please let me touch my pussy for you."

"Fuck." His hand moved faster as he fixed himself more securely on the ladder, then his other hand was on my knee, spreading me farther open until my thighs pressed into the metal.

"Move those bottoms, Blaire. Let me see what's always been mine."

My hand shook uncontrollably as I yanked the fabric aside

and slid two fingers through my pussy. My spine arched, and a sound tore from my throat I didn't recognize.

"Christ, Blaire," he snarled, his forearm flexing savagely as he worked himself beneath the water. "Look at you. So fucking wet. I'm going to come watching you fuck yourself for me."

My thighs convulsed as I drove my fingers lower, pushing them inside me, and the obscene slick sounds cut through the night.

"Do you want to fuck yourself for me, baby?"

"Yes," I exhaled, and my legs started to close, but Colt stopped them.

"Wider," he gently commanded, and I forced them back apart. "Show me everything I've been starving for."

A sound between a sob and a moan escaped me as I forced my knees apart again until I was completely exposed, vulnerable and desperate. The only thing left between us was need. Colt's whole body went taut, muscles straining from the effort of holding himself back, but he couldn't do it anymore.

A guttural, feral growl ripped from his chest, echoing over the water and making the hair stand up on every inch of my body. My fingers slid through my wetness, gently skimming my clit, and every move sent another shudder through my core.

Colt's breath came in ragged, broken gasps. His eyes were locked on me, and his hand worked furiously, sending water crashing against the dock. I could hear him, hear the slick, frantic sound of his fist, and the knowledge that he was losing it because of me made my head spin.

He dragged his gaze up from my thighs to my face, and I nearly flinched from the burn of it. "Perfect," he rasped. "Give me those fingers." He was pleading now, the arrogance stripped away, and there was something so raw and broken in the way he said it, like he needed this as much as I did.

With a shaking hand, I slid my fingers through the drenched heat of my pussy and withdrew them, glistening and slick, the air shocking on my skin. Colt reached for me so fast he almost lost his balance on the ladder, and his slick hand wrapped around my wrist like a shackle. His entire body vibrated with barely contained restraint as he yanked my hand toward him, hard enough that my body jerked forward on the dock.

Then his mouth was on my fingers, hot and soft and relentless. He sucked them between his lips, tongue swirling.

The sight of it, the feel of his mouth, the heat of his breath, the pressure of his tongue lapping the taste of me from my shaky hand, sent a pulse of molten want straight through my stomach. My hips rocked forward, chasing the friction, and my free hand clawed at the weathered planks of the dock.

Colt never took his eyes off me as his entire world narrowed to the taste of me and the need to have more. There was such a reverence in the way he looked down at me, and it undid me faster than anything else could.

He bit down softly, sending a shock of pain and pleasure up my nerves, and then dragged my fingers from his mouth with an excruciating slowness. His teeth scraped over my knuckles, and my pulse hammered wildly beneath his grip. "You have no fucking idea what that does to me," he said, voice full of hunger. "I've missed you, Blaire. Fuck, I've missed having you like this."

He let go of my wrist, then pressed his forehead to the inside of my thigh. "You taste so fucking sweet," he groaned, and I felt his tongue trace a slow, torturous line up to my knee. "I could eat you alive."

A desperate sob tore from my throat as my fingers found my swollen clit, my hips bucking hard against my touch. "Colt—"

"That's it. Say my fucking name when you come. Remind us both who you belong to." His arm flexed as he worked himself, his eyes watching me. "I'm right there with you. I'm going to come thinking about being buried deep inside this tight little pussy."

I moaned so loud it seemed impossible no one in the valley could hear us. My hand moved with desperate, clumsy need, grinding up and down, fingers finding and circling my clit, making my body jerk uncontrollably.

I couldn't look away from him. He was shaking, every muscle tensed, every breath a ragged snarl.

"Do you want that, Blaire?" he demanded, voice gone hoarse with need. "Do you want me to fuck you so deep you forget anyone else?"

"Yes," I choked, the word barely more than a gasp. My head swam with the thought of him, the memory of his body on mine, the feel of him splitting me open, slow and rough and perfect.

"Then show me how bad you want it," he panted, never looking away, hand moving fast and brutal against himself. "Show me you'll do anything for it."

I did. I wanted him so badly. I wanted to ruin him the way he ruined me. I slid my fingers down my pussy, so wet it was ridiculous, and watched him lick his lips as I dipped two fingers into myself. The sensation was overwhelming, and I cried out as I pushed them deeper and curved them just right.

I fell onto my back, and my other hand clawed at my thigh, nails digging into skin, needing an anchor as I fell apart.

Colt was losing it, his chest heaving. "That's it. I want to fuck you right now, but watching you touch yourself is making me come so goddamned hard—" He couldn't finish. He moaned, and the water around him erupted in frantic slaps as he jerked himself to the finish. "Come for me, baby. Come all over those pretty fingers while you say my fucking name."

I crashed over the edge, body bowing, mouth open with nothing but his name falling from my lips. Every muscle snapped tight as the orgasm ripped through me and left me boneless. My hand was trapped between my legs, spasming over my clit, and every wave was hotter and stronger than the last.

I could hear Colt's shattered moan, feel the echo of it pulse through the dock and up over me.

"Let me see it. Let me hear it, Blaire," Colt begged, and I wanted to give it to him, I needed to. So I forced myself to look at him, to let the pleasure twist my face, to let my hips grind against my palm. "Tell me you're mine."

"I'm yours," I sobbed, unable to hold back even though I knew in the back of my mind I shouldn't have said it.

The world blurred, my body bowing forward as heat and pressure still pulsed through me. "Colt."

He roared my name as his whole body convulsed, pumping his cock hard as he came with me.

All I could hear was the sound of our rough breathing, the cicadas droning on like nothing had changed, like we hadn't just fucked everything up.

His gaze pinned me in place, unblinking and raw, as he lowered his mouth to my knee. The brush of his lips there, so tender after everything, sent aftershocks through my limbs. I couldn't stop shaking, couldn't slow my pulse.

Loving Colt Calloway had been as easy as breathing for most of my life, and I'd convinced myself that I could breathe without him.

He'd barely touched me, yet I was split wide open, my defenses shattered, my need for him raw and exposed.

I'd spent years hiding, and in one night, he'd reduced me to the aching, desperate truth that I had always been his.

CHAPTER 23
COLT

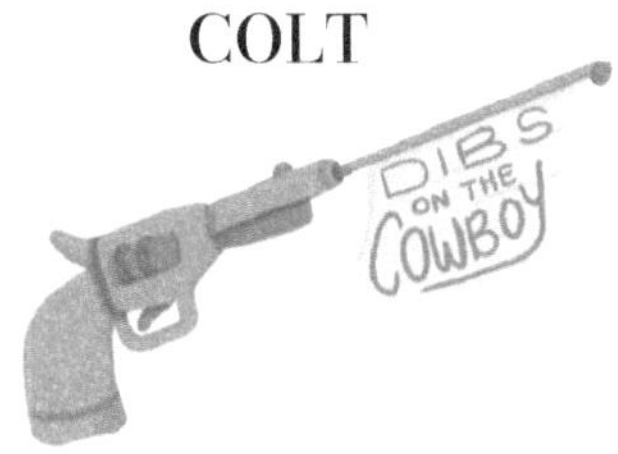

The house was too damn quiet.

There were no impatient little feet scrambling down the hall, no soft giggles, no whisper-singing the theme from *Moana* as Ruby tried and failed to sneak into my room without waking me up.

I reached out across my mattress anyway, palm sliding over the sheets as I searched for my girl. We'd stopped the crawling into my bed in the middle of the night, switched now for early hours of the morning, and even though I pretended to be exasperated when I woke up to her digging her cold feet into my stomach, mornings without her felt wrong.

My palm found only the cool, untouched sheets where her small body should have been. I blinked at the empty space, my mind still foggy with sleep, unable to recall why my daughter wasn't there beside me.

Fragments of last night slipped through the haze of sleep. Ruby was at my parents', and I should have been savoring this quiet morning all to myself.

The dull ache behind my eyes wasn't from the beer. It was the replay of last night that wouldn't stop. Blaire's skin under my fingertips, and words we couldn't take back.

She'd followed every command I'd given her, touching herself while I watched, my name breaking from her throat when she came. I'd told her she was mine, demanded she say it back.

Fuck.

My cock was already half hard from the memory, and the most damning part was that I'd known exactly what I was doing. I couldn't blame the beer when I'd spent the whole damn evening giving myself the same warning over and over. *Don't cross that line, don't let her see how much power she still has over you.*

But I'd gone and done exactly that.

That line had been obliterated the moment she laughed and called me, "house daddy."

Then I'd trampled right over it again the moment she admitted she'd never loved her fiancé and that it was me she thought of when he touched her.

And then she'd ran into the house and left me treading water and drowning in thoughts of her. I stayed until the cool water finally bit through the heat she'd lit inside me.

I rolled out of bed and stood in the middle of my room as I told myself to get it together, to be a fucking adult and not spin out over something that was never meant to happen.

I walked into my bathroom, turning on the faucet and splashing cold water onto my face with both hands. I held the water in my palms and pressed it to my neck, letting the shock run down my spine, but it didn't help. All I could think about was her.

I told myself to shower, to get dressed, to do literally anything except walk out that bedroom door and look for her. But my feet moved anyway.

The hallway was colder than my bedroom and the floorboards creaked under my bare feet. As I got closer to the kitchen, I slowed my pace. I could hear her humming softly and the scrape of a mug on the counter. There was no music playing, no TV, nothing to fill the space but her.

I leaned against the counter and watched her. She was standing with her back to me, barefoot in a pair of sweatpants that were rolled twice at the waistband, and a tank top that hugged every line of her body. Her hair was down and wild, tumbling past her shoulders, and I wanted to bury my hands in the strands.

She bent at the waist, digging through one of my lower cabinets, and I couldn't look away from the sharp little V of her shoulder blades or the line of her back.

She stood with a frying pan in her hand, and I grinned as she set it on the stove, then looked around. Things may have changed in the time since she'd been gone, but the Blaire I'd known had always been an awful cook.

I cleared my throat when it was obvious she still hadn't realized I was there. "Mornin'."

She startled a little, like she'd been expecting me but not so soon, and her eyes flickered over me and then away.

"Morning." Her tone was light and easy, and she moved to my fridge as if nothing had happened, like we hadn't spent the night breaking each other apart and putting ourselves back together in ways that couldn't be undone.

She grabbed the creamer from one of the shelves before she closed the doors, and she held it up as she smiled at me. "Coffee?"

"Sure." I nodded, and she turned away from me, busying herself with the coffeepot.

I moved to the other side of my island and took a seat as I watched her. Her shoulders were tight as she wrapped both hands around one of the mugs before she turned and set it on the island, sliding it across the counter to me.

I wondered if she remembered everything as vividly as I did, if her body still hummed with the aftershocks, or if she'd already forced herself to forget it ever happened.

I wanted to say something. I wanted to apologize or demand to know what we were supposed to do now, but I couldn't force either from my lips.

She didn't say anything either. She sipped her coffee and stared at the counter like it held all the answers.

I needed to do something, to say anything to break this awkwardness between us. "Are you about to cook?"

"Oh." She looked at the frying pan, then back at me. "I was thinking about making a grilled cheese."

"For breakfast?" I raised an eyebrow, unable to suppress the small grin that tugged at my mouth.

"Yeah, well." She bit her lip, and I could tell she was debating how much of herself to show me. "It's the only thing I know how to make."

I sipped my coffee, coffee that was exactly how I liked it, and let the silence draw out between us. "You know, they say breakfast is the most important meal of the day, but I don't think they were talking about grilled cheese."

She rolled her eyes, and a faint flush marred her cheeks. "I can do cereal too. Toast with jam."

"That won't do." I shook my head, putting down my coffee and standing. She watched me as I rounded the island and made my way to the fridge. "Have you been eating grilled cheese and cereal for the last ten years?"

She laughed, but I could hear the tension she hid behind it. "No." She shook her head. "My dad had a cook when I lived with him, and Grant—" She hesitated and our eyes met. "Grant preferred to go out."

"Hmmm," I hummed my response, hating hearing that fucker's name fall from her lips, and pulled the eggs and bacon out of the fridge.

"I'm not helpless, though." The way she said it made me want to close the distance between us, to force her to look up at me, and reassure her that there wasn't a single part of her that was helpless. There never had been.

"Well, we have two options here." I closed the door with my hip, and her gaze dragged down my bare chest. "I can either cook breakfast for you or I can teach you how."

She blinked, and something changed in the set of her jaw. It was so subtle most people would have missed it, but I'd spent years watching her. "You're going to teach me to cook?"

"Yeah," I said, keeping my voice low and easy. I slid in beside her, close enough to smell her, and set the ingredients on the counter. "If you want me to."

She looked away from me, and I could practically feel her pulling away.

"It's just bacon and eggs, Blaire." I tried to keep it light, but it sounded like I was talking about far more than our breakfast.

I opened the carton of eggs before I turned on the burner on the stove. "What are we thinking here, scrambled eggs or fried?"

She let me brush past her as I reached for the kitchen scissors, arms crossed over her chest, but she didn't move away.

"Fried, I think." She was watching me carefully, and I quickly cut open the pack of bacon before I took a step back.

I motioned her forward with my hand, and she glanced at the stove then back at me before she finally moved in front of me.

"I've made bacon before, but June used to say I'd burn all the flavor right out of the poor pig." She smiled a little at the memory.

I chuckled, picturing June's face as she said it. "The secret to bacon is all about temperature control. Too cold and it just sits there, too hot and…" I adjusted the burner dial, watching the blue flame dance beneath the pan. "Everything goes up in flames."

My mind drifted to last night and the heat that spiraled far beyond any kind of control I thought I had.

When I told her to lay the bacon away from her so the grease wouldn't pop, she nodded, doing exactly as I instructed. The sizzle rose, filling the air with a smell that made my stomach growl, and a little of my anxiety settled as I watched her move around my kitchen.

She reached for a fork and lifted the bacon after a few minutes. "Take it off now?" she asked, glancing over her shoulder at me.

"Perfect." I nodded, and I meant it. I wanted to reach over and touch the small of her back, settle her right against me the way I used to, but I didn't.

"Is June going to teach you to make your jams?" I asked with a smile, and she shook her head.

"No. I'm the straight up brains on that project. She's going to have to do the cooking."

We settled into an easy rhythm after that. Blaire cooked the bacon, and I hovered behind her before we moved on to the eggs.

"There you go," I said as I leaned forward on my elbows beside her. "Gently slide the spatula under the egg, then flip it over in one quick move."

"I hate this part." She shook her head even as she did what I'd said. The egg flipped but caught on the edge, and the yolk burst open and flooded across the pan. Blaire swore under her breath, and her face scrunched into a frown. "Well, I fucked that up."

I grinned, amused as hell. "You can't fuck it up. It's just eggs. Breaking the yolk is the worst thing that can happen, but I love my eggs like that."

I didn't, but I wasn't going to tell her that.

I could see the doubt on her face. I reached for the spatula, swiping it out of her hand and into mine, and I quickly flipped the next egg myself, making sure to break the yolk. "See? Now they're both perfect."

She laughed, her shoulders easing. "You're such a liar," she said, but she was smiling.

"I'm a cowboy, Blaire. I'll eat my eggs however they come." I shrugged, and the urge to reach out and smooth a bit of her hair out of her face was overwhelming. "If you think I'm going to be upset about a broken yolk, you don't know me very well."

Her phone buzzed on the counter, and she lunged for it with a reflex so quick I almost didn't catch the name that flashed across her lock screen. But I did.

Grant.

A picture of the two of them flashed behind his name, an engagement picture, and it felt like a punch to the gut. I watched her thumb hover over the screen, uncertainty flickering across her face as the phone shuddered in her hand.

She didn't answer. She quickly sent it to voicemail, and only the faintest tension in her shoulders betrayed her. She set the phone down, face down this time, and glanced at me with a flicker of guilt in her eyes.

"Why is he still calling you?" I asked, and I couldn't hide the anger in my voice.

"What?" She pretended her attention was solely on the food.

"Why is Grant calling you? What does he want?"

She hesitated, spatula in hand, then shrugged like she'd only just noticed the missed call. "He wants me to talk to him. Or come back to Raleigh and see him." Her voice was light, almost dismissive, but her hands were tense as she poked at the eggs.

I stared at her back. "Do you want to talk to him?"

"No." She let out a sigh. "But he and my dad apparently think if they call enough, I'll...forgive him, and everything will go back to the way it was."

I gritted my teeth and tried to calm myself down. "You mean to tell me he cheated on you for the last year, and now your dad expects you to forget it happened?"

She pulled the eggs off the burner, cutting the heat, then she finally turned to look at me. "He thinks I'm throwing away an entire life because of one mistake, and I guess I am." She shrugged, and I wanted to shake her.

"Cheating on you is not a fucking mistake, Blaire."

"I know that," she snapped. "I'm here, aren't I?" She held my stare until she let out a breath. "I'm sorry." She shook her head, hair veiling her eyes. "I— My dad keeps telling me to go back, that I owe Grant a conversation, at least. He says this isn't like me to give up on people." She let out a hollow laugh. "He called three times yesterday, and Grant called twice."

"I've always hated him," I said bluntly.

I'd wanted to teach her to cook eggs, just breathe in the smell of her skin as she stood at my stove. But the words popped out of me.

"Grant?" she asked, her voice smaller than it had been before.

I shrugged, feigning indifference I didn't feel. "Grant. Your dad. I hate them both."

She made a noise that was half laugh, half scoff, and set the spatula down. "You never liked my dad."

"For good reason." I crossed my arms. "Your dad doesn't deserve you and neither does Grant."

She glanced up at me, and there was a flicker of something vulnerable in her eyes. "And you do?"

"I didn't say that." I shook my head. Fuck, I knew I didn't deserve her. I never would.

"Well, they aren't the biggest fans of yours, either." Her hands shook enough for me to notice, and I wanted to reach out and steady her. "I'd say they definitely wouldn't be after..." The way her cheeks flushed pink, blooming up her cheekbones and across the bridge of her nose, made something in me ache.

I forced myself not to move closer, not to touch her, not to make anything harder for either of us.

I wanted to tell her I didn't give a shit about her father or Grant, not when she was standing here barefoot in my kitchen, hair mussed, and everything about her raw and real in the morning light. Instead, I took a breath and leaned back against the counter, trying to look casual, even though my heart was pounding.

I lifted my mug and cradled it in my hands so I wouldn't have to look directly at her. "So, you've been talking to him? Grant, I mean."

She didn't answer right away, just pressed her palm flat on the counter and stared at me. "I've talked to him once since I left. The other day after the bakery."

Fuck. She answered him because she was angry with me, because I hurt her again.

"And what did you tell him?" I told myself not to push her, but I needed to know if the door to Raleigh was closed or if it was still cracked, waiting for her to slip back through it.

"What?" she breathed, so soft I almost missed it.

I took a step closer, slow enough not to startle her. "When he asked you to come back to Raleigh—" I tried to keep my voice even "—what did you say?"

Her eyes met mine, and there was a flicker of panic underneath. "I told him no." She said it like a confession, voice stripped raw.

I didn't know what to do with the relief that crashed through me. It was cold and sharp and left me almost dizzy.

"Good." I nodded, my eyes dropping to her mouth. My fingers ached to reach for her, to trace the curve where her lip dipped in the center. One step, and I could taste her again. It had been so long since I last kissed her.

"Colt." The way she said my name was with more conviction than I'd heard from her since she'd been back.

"I don't want you to go, Blaire." The words weren't enough, but they were all I had.

She looked up at me, her eyes suddenly dark and unguarded. "Colt," she whispered my name again. "About last night—"

"Yeah?" I said, feeling my heart thundering in my chest. Her eyes wouldn't meet mine.

"We should forget that it happened. We were drunk." Her throat worked, but she still hadn't looked at me. "It shouldn't have happened. It won't happen again."

Her words slammed into me, and every muscle in my body went rigid as she stood there, trying to erase what had happened between us with a few careless words.

"Don't," I growled. "Don't you dare blame last night on alcohol when I can still taste your pussy on my tongue."

Her gaze snapped to mine. Fire sparked there, but it was laced with something raw and desperate. "I got off, Colt. I was wet, and you were there."

The lie hung between us, and it gutted me how fast we could switch from raw honesty to this. Her eyes refused to meet mine, both of us building walls with every breath, desperate to protect the broken parts we'd exposed to each other.

"That's why you begged me for it." I closed the distance between us until her back hit the counter. "That's why you called *my* name as you came?"

She flinched, lips parting slightly, but she didn't push me

away. "It doesn't matter what I said. It was a bad idea, and we both know it."

I bit down hard on my lip and watched the flush creep up her neck. "You don't get to rewrite what happened, Blaire. Don't make it less than what it was because you're scared."

She looked up at me, and her eyes blazed with something that made my cock twitch in my shorts. "It should scare you, Colt. What about Ruby? I'm living in your house, for God's sake." She tried to step back, but there was nowhere for her to go. "This can't happen again."

Maybe it shouldn't. Maybe the smart thing was to stop it for Ruby, for the ranch, for the small bit of peace I'd found. But looking at her, every argument I'd used to stay safe sounded like a lie. I didn't want what happened between me and Blaire to be a slipup. I wanted it all.

"The hell it can't." I crowded closer, pinning her between my body and the counter. "You think I'm just gonna sit here and pretend I don't want you?"

"That's exactly what you're going to do." She raised her chin, but her breathing was rushed and her nipples were hard against her thin shirt.

I leaned down, looking her straight in the eye to make sure she heard me. "That's not going to happen, Strawberry."

She turned like she was going to walk away, her ass grazing against me, but I couldn't let her. Not again.

I caught her wrist in a grip that made her eyes widen, yanking her back against me hard enough her breath left her in a sharp hiss. My fingers dug into the soft flesh of her hips, pinning her ass against my front. The whimper that fell from her mouth was my undoing.

I dragged my nose up the length of her neck, breathing her in, before I raked my teeth along her skin hard enough to make her gasp and arch into me.

"Colt." I didn't know if she was begging me to stop or pleading for more.

I growled against her skin and my hand shot up to grip her

jaw, turning her face toward mine, daring her to deny what was happening between us.

Her lips fell open, and the tiniest sound escaped. "We shouldn't do this," she whispered, and her breath fanned over my chin.

"I fucking want you." My thumb traced the line of her jaw. "I need to hear you say that you don't want this too."

The whole width of her body shook against mine, and her throat worked as she swallowed. "I can't."

My hand slid from her jaw to her throat, fingers pressing into her pulse point where her heartbeat hammered. Something in me snapped. It clicked into place.

Touching her didn't feel reckless, it felt like resolve. I'd spent years pretending like the risk of Blaire Monroe wasn't worth it, but she was. I wanted to take the hits, take it slow for both our sakes and for Ruby's, but I refused to let her go again.

I slammed my mouth against hers, swallowing her gasp as my teeth caught her bottom lip hard enough to make her whimper. She spun to face me, nails digging into my chest.

The kiss was frantic. Her mouth opened beneath mine, desperate and starved, and I fisted her hair at the roots, pulling her head back as she moaned.

Mine.

The thought tore through me as I devoured her, claiming every inch we'd denied each other for too long. She kissed me with a fury matching my own, her hands clawing down my abdomen, dragging me closer until there wasn't any space left between us.

My heart pounded so loud I swore she could hear it, and it scared the shit out of me how good it felt, how much more dangerous this was than watching her come apart last night.

Because this wasn't just want. This was something else entirely.

I pulled my mouth from hers, my breath hot and ragged against her flushed skin. "Tell me you don't feel that. Tell me it means nothing."

Her eyes were wild as she dragged her tongue across her

swollen lips. I could see the war raging behind them. "It's not nothing. Colt, it's—"

"Knock, knock!" My mother's voice sliced through the kitchen, followed by Ruby's thundering footsteps on the porch.

Blaire ripped herself away from me, stumbling backward as her face flushed crimson.

"Something smells good in here!"

My mom and Ruby burst into the kitchen as the door slammed shut behind them. Ruby's face lit up, her eyes shining as she ran toward me.

"Oh!" My mom stopped suddenly, her eyes darting back and forth between me and Blaire. "I texted you to let you know we were on our way. Ruby's been dying to tell you both about our night."

"Daddy! We had so much fun!" Ruby wrapped herself around my legs, clinging to me while Blaire retreated even farther.

I glanced down at my daughter and then up at Blaire, whose back was iron straight as she pretended to busy herself with the dirty dishes in the sink. She didn't once glance my way, not even as I ruffled Ruby's hair and tried to swallow the last of my own panic.

"Morning, baby." I crouched down, letting Ruby fling her arms around my neck. "Did you help Nana eat all the chocolate?"

Ruby shook her head. "No. We saved some for you and Blaire."

She looked over at Blaire, who finally turned and gave her a smile.

I stood, feeling the heat crawl up the back of my neck. "Thanks, kiddo. Y'all want some breakfast? Blaire is making bacon and eggs."

My mom smiled. "Now, Blaire, you told me yesterday morning you don't know how to cook. Were you holding out on me?"

"No." Blaire laughed, but it was weak. "Colt was teaching me."

"Oh!" My mom looked back and forth between us again. "Well, I'd say you're in pretty good hands."

I looked at Blaire, her entire face flushing, as Ruby moved to her side. "Can I help?"

"Of course." Blaire tapped her finger against the tip of Ruby's nose, making her smile. "You can be the official taste tester."

Mom set Ruby's bag on a chair and gave me a look I'd grown up with. She was seeing far more than Blaire or I wanted her to. "Well, I, for one, am starving." She took a seat at the island, and I pulled plates out of the cabinet.

I moved the two broken eggs onto my plate before I lit the burner again and placed the pan over the heat. "How do you want your eggs, Mom? Blaire's a professional now."

"That's not true." Blaire chuckled softly as she shook her head, but she took the spatula when I held it out to her. Our fingers brushed, and her eyes finally met mine for the first time since we'd been interrupted.

"I want my eggs pink!" Ruby said as she climbed up on the stool beside my mom.

"I'm not a magician, Ruby girl." Blaire widened her eyes at my daughter. "I can barely turn an egg over."

Ruby giggled, and Blaire smiled as she grabbed another egg from the carton.

This was where I wanted her—in the light of my kitchen with my daughter's laughter in the air. Not in shadows or stolen moments, but right here where everyone could see. My chest ached with a certainty so fierce it stole my breath.

"Tomorrow," I said, topping off Blaire's coffee like it was the most normal thing in the world. "We'll try pancakes."

Blaire's eyes met mine, panic flashing, but it was quickly replaced with relief.

"Low and slow," I breathed against the back of her neck as I reached around her and lowered the temperature. "So nothing gets burned."

Ruby slapped her small hands down on the counter. "Pancakes!"

I grinned at Ruby and gave her a wink as I leaned against the counter beside Blaire.

"How do you like your pancakes, Blaire?" Ruby asked, climbing to her knees on the kitchen stool to grab a banana.

"With strawberries and honey." She said it offhand, like she'd always answered that way. But I knew otherwise.

The Blaire I'd known had always piled her pancakes sky-high with whipped cream and drowned them in syrup, the whole plate a sticky mess that drove me nuts. She used to tease me about how my pancakes were blasphemous. Then she'd sneak a few bites from my plate, pretending to hate it, but always finishing what she stole.

"What?" I asked, my throat suddenly dry. I searched her face, but she wouldn't look at me. Her shoulders were tense as she tried to ignore the weight of the question she'd just answered.

Ruby gasped, eyes wide with delight. "That's how Daddy eats his pancakes too!"

Blaire went rigid then forced a smile as she turned to face Ruby and my mom. "Guess he rubbed off on me," she said, and her hand trembled as it gripped the counter.

She'd carried this piece of me, tucked it away like a secret, and now it slipped out in front of my daughter and my mom. It was nothing but a taste preference on its own, but it felt monumental, like proof that some tiny part of us had kept living even when we tried to kill it.

"Since when?" I asked and watched her throat work as she swallowed.

She turned, almost knocking her coffee cup over, but she caught it with both hands as she forced out a laugh. "I don't know. Sometime in college, I guess. June always sent me strawberries..." Her voice trailed off before she finally met my eyes. "And I was feeling homesick."

I'd been homesick too.

Not for a place, but for a moment suspended in time. I'd yearned for a feeling that lived only in my memories, and there she was, eating her pancakes like me.

CHAPTER 24
BLAIRE

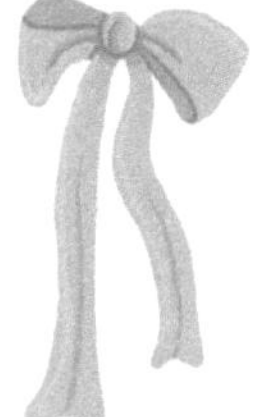

Ruby's laughter rang out around us as she clutched her cards tightly in her small fists. She bounced from one side to the other, cross-legged on the living room floor, and she was wearing my Duke sweatshirt I'd let her borrow the day she was sick. It hung past her knees, the sleeves rolled up six times to free her hands, but she refused to give it back.

"Go fish!" she shouted, nearly knocking over her pink plastic cup in her excitement.

I barely caught it before her water spilled all over us and the cards.

"Hey now!" I gasped, sending her into another fit of giggles. "Are you cheating? How are you so good at this game?"

Ruby grinned and stuck out her chin. "I'm just really awesome, and you're not."

"How dare you?" I clutched at my chest as if she'd wounded me. "I used to be the reigning Go Fish Champion of Willow Grove, two years running. No one could beat me."

She squinted at me over her cards. "You're lying." She watched me carefully before she attempted to peek over at my cards.

I made a shocked show of shielding my hand, but she lunged

forward and tried to see them. This sparked a flurry of shrieks and giggles, cards scattering everywhere as Ruby tried to wrestle them from my hands, her little fingers surprisingly strong.

"Oh my gosh." I laughed. "You really are cheating!"

Ruby squealed, scrambling onto her knees, abandoning her own cards entirely, and tried to slap a hand over my mouth to silence me. I let her, feigning defeat, before darting my tongue out and licking her palm.

She recoiled in horror. "Ewww!" Her screech reverberated through the house, and she pulled her hand away from me. "That's gross!"

She grabbed a pillow from the couch, hurling it at me, but she missed, barely hitting my hip. But I let the impact throw me sideways onto the floor, and I lay in a puddle of defeat and shielded my eyes with my arm as she continued laughing. "You're the one who put your hand over my mouth."

"You didn't have to lick me!" She pounced, pinning me beneath her and tickling my ribs. I surrendered instantly, squirming and wheezing with laughter, and both of us lay there amid a blizzard of bent playing cards as we smiled at one another.

We were still catching our breaths when I noticed Colt leaning over the back of the couch. His hair was damp and slightly curled from his shower, and I could see a patch of his bare chest above the collar of the old T-shirt he wore. He looked like he'd just stepped out of a Levi's ad with his tanned arms and muscles that only came from ranch work. And that damned mustache.

My mouth went dry as I remembered how those arms had caged me against the kitchen counter this morning, his body a solid wall of muscle that left me nowhere to run.

I was tired of running from him.

He looked at Ruby, his gaze traveling over her face, before he smiled down at me, slow and so damn confusing, and I was so caught up in watching him, in trying to figure out what was going through his head.

After Ruby got home this morning, we'd moved around each other in careful, practiced avoidance, or at least, I had.

Every time Colt passed me, he found a way to touch me. When he reached for a glass in the cabinet above my head, his chest pressed hard against my back until I could feel his heartbeat thudding between my shoulder blades, his breath scorching the sensitive spot behind my ear.

Each touch was a calculated torture until I felt like I was going crazy with how badly I needed him.

Ruby had told us all about her night with Lou and June before she turned those innocent eyes on us. "What did y'all do when I was gone?"

My cheeks burned as I mumbled something about swimming, then going to bed early. I couldn't exactly tell her we had defiled her dock while I begged her daddy dearest for things I had no business asking for.

I'd spent the rest of the day hiding in my bedroom before I snuck out to take a shower. I'd let the scalding water run over me until my skin turned pink, scrubbing at the phantom fingerprints still burning across my neck, my hips, and my knees. But the water couldn't wash away how my body still hummed for him, how every brush of the loofah made me shiver with the memory of his callused hands. I lathered my body in lotion, the slide of my palms over my skin a maddening echo of his. I dried my hair, painted mine and Ruby's nails, and did anything else to keep my hands busy and my mind from wandering down the hall to where he was.

Then we went to Sunday dinner at his parents', and my skin had been too tight, my breath too shallow, and I couldn't stop the insistent throbbing ache he'd left behind the night before.

I had slept with other men since him. There had been strangers, a couple boyfriends, and Grant. Sometimes it was good enough to make me gasp, but I'd always been chasing a ghost, my body arching for a memory, my throat swallowing his name before it could escape.

But last night, Colt hadn't even laid a finger on me, and I'd shattered for him in a way no other man had ever managed.

Sunday dinner had ended over an hour ago and Ruby was

bathed, dressed in her pajamas, and fighting with me over a game of Go Fish on Colt's living room floor, but the cards in my hands might as well have been kindling.

"Daddy!" Ruby climbed to her feet when she noticed him and jabbed a finger in my direction. "Blaire stinks at this game."

Colt's gaze cut from me to Ruby, then locked back on me, and a slow grin curled up the left side of his mouth. "Is that so?" he drawled, each word dripping like honey.

I pushed myself up on my elbows, feeling the heat of his attention even from across the room. "I don't stink," I huffed. "She's a cheater. Just like her daddy."

Ruby gasped. "I was not cheating! It's strategy. Right, Daddy?" She blinked up at him, waiting for backup, and I snorted.

"That's what a couple of cheaters would say," I said under my breath, and Ruby jumped at me like she was going to tickle me again.

Colt grinned, but he only had eyes for me. "Right," he said, barely glancing at Ruby as he moved around the couch. "But, for the record, baby girl, Blaire's not bad at cards." He crouched beside us, ruffling Ruby's hair before he started scooping up the bent, scattered cards, collecting them into a neat pile. "She was the smartest one in our whole school."

I rolled my eyes, but he kept going, laying it on thick. "Seriously. She used to win all those spelling bees, even against the big kids. She was basically a genius."

"Is that true?" Ruby narrowed her eyes, and a laugh bubbled out of me.

"Hardly. I think your daddy just doesn't remember all the times I lost."

He shook his head, and a piece of dark hair fell against his brow. "Nope. I remember you winning and scaring off every boy in Willow Grove because they knew you were smarter than them." Then he winked at me, and my stomach dropped like I was sixteen again.

Ruby's gaze bounced between us as she smiled, but then her eyebrows knitted together. "Did she scare you off?"

Colt made a show of flexing his arms, the muscles bulging beneath his shirt as he grinned down at his daughter. "Look at these guns. Do you think I would be scared of Little Miss Smarty-Pants?"

Ruby dissolved into giggles as she reached up and squeezed his biceps.

I started picking up the rest of the cards. "He was terrified of me. He's lying to himself and trying to make you think he was cooler than he really was in high school."

Colt arched an eyebrow, his voice dropping low. "You calling me a liar, Strawberry?"

I tossed a card at him, which he caught effortlessly with two fingers, and his thumb brushed over the edge in a way that made me remember those same hands on my skin. "I'm just telling it like it is."

He grinned, stacking all the cards in his hands, eyes never leaving mine as he rose to his feet. "Well, I won't tell her about how you let a frog loose in Mr. Becker's class because you wanted to save it. Then let me take the blame for it when he found out."

Ruby's jaw dropped. "What?"

I huffed a laugh as I pushed off the floor, aware of how my shirt rode up slightly with the movement. "That's not completely true either. We went in there to do it together. Your dad chickened out, and I was forced to do it." I glanced up at Colt's grinning face, catching the way his eyes flicked to my lips before I looked back at Ruby. "We were trying to set it free, not lose it in class, and we wouldn't have gotten caught if he had helped me."

Colt stepped closer, close enough that I could smell his cologne. "You always were the brave one," he said so softly, heat pooled low in my belly.

Colt made me feel seen in a way Grant never managed. Grant had never noticed all the little ways in which I changed and shifted to be at his side. He rarely noticed anything about me, but Colt's gaze made my skin prickle with awareness. A part of me wanted to hide, to make sure that he didn't see too much, but some reckless part of me craved the scorching heat that only he could give.

"I want to be brave like Blaire." Ruby's voice broke the spell, and I realized I'd been holding my breath.

"You already are." I tapped my finger against her nose, using the moment to step back from Colt, whose proximity was making it hard to think straight. "Braver than I could ever be."

"All right, Ruby." Colt held his hands out for her. "It's time for bed. We've got school in the morning."

"Ah, man," Ruby groaned, but took his hand, her tiny fingers disappearing into his palm. "I'm not ready for bed yet."

"Well, I'm not dealing with you when you're a little demon tomorrow morning because you didn't get enough sleep." He scooped her up, muscles flexing beneath his shirt as he pressed his lips against her hair.

She went limp in his arms, head lolling dramatically.

"I like being a demon." Ruby smiled with her eyes closed.

"Well, you're the only one." Colt's laugh rumbled low in his chest. His eyes caught mine over Ruby's head, and the playfulness in them shifted to something darker. "You staying up?" The question slid between us, loaded with a dangerous promise.

"For a bit." My voice betrayed me with its breathlessness. "I need to do my skincare and get ready for bed."

"Good." His gaze traveled down my body with such deliberate slowness I could almost feel it like a physical touch. "Ruby, tell Blaire good night."

"Night, Blaire!" She was still limp in his arms, but she peeked one eye open to look at me.

"Good night." I smiled, and my skin prickled where Colt's eyes lingered.

"Can we play dolls in the morning before school?" She was still looking at me upside down.

"Of course," I nodded.

"Pinkie promise." She held out her pinkie, and I stepped forward, wrapping my pinkie around hers and shaking them once.

Her pinkie was warm and certain against mine, and something in my chest went soft and terrified at the same time. This wasn't just Colt undoing me. It was the way Ruby trusted me, the way she folded me into their day like I'd always belonged here, and it made me feel chosen in a way I hadn't let myself crave in years.

I should've run to my room and swore off this weekend as if it never happened. Instead, I stood there as he carried Ruby off to bed, and the want roared back through me as he looked back over his shoulder at me before they disappeared down the hall.

Each minute alone with him would be dangerous, reckless, exactly what I'd promised myself to avoid, yet my body hummed with a need so desperate it scared me.

I couldn't walk away now even if I wanted to, and God, I didn't want to.

CHAPTER 25
BLAIRE

If I'd had the faintest amount of self-preservation, I would have taken my ass directly to bed, locked the door, and maybe even pushed a dresser in front of it for good measure.

What I wouldn't have done was wash my face, complete my skincare with unsteady hands, and brush my teeth for exactly two minutes while avoiding my flushed reflection in the mirror. I wouldn't have paced the living room like a caged animal, heart hammering against my ribs and heat prickled up my neck as I caught myself glancing at Ruby's door for the tenth time.

I foolishly tried to convince myself I didn't want Colt, didn't crave the weight of his gaze or the brush of his fingers, but my body betrayed me with each shallow breath.

Good.

The word vibrated through me as I replayed his voice in my head. That one word dripped with promise, with intent. He wanted me waiting, wanted me aching, and I shouldn't have cared what he wanted. *But I did.*

I pushed out onto the front porch, the door clicking shut behind me with a finality that made my stomach clench. The night air slid over my skin, both welcome and unbearable, as I stood there with my pulse slamming so hard against me I felt it between my thighs.

I moved across the porch as the smell of the ranch at midnight wrapped around me with sweet honeysuckle, the far-off earthiness of hay, and the freshness of the lake as it lapped against the shore.

I sank onto the porch swing, tensing as the chains creaked in protest. The seat was still warm from the sun, but I was burning up from the inside out: a low, liquid ache. I stared down at my hands and clenched and unclenched them to try to make them stop shaking.

What the hell was wrong with me?

Nothing about this felt sensible or safe, and yet I couldn't make myself pull back from it, couldn't quiet the part of me that leaned into the danger of him. Every logical part of me screamed at me to go to bed and lock myself in my room until the memory of Colt's mouth faded into something manageable. But logic meant nothing when I could still feel the print of his fingers on my skin and the ghost of his breath on my neck.

If I went to bed now, I'd only waste the night with my hands between my thighs and teeth buried in my pillow to keep from making a sound. I'd done it before, wrapped up in my want for Colt Calloway, tumbling into sleep only when the ache dulled.

But I didn't want to dull that ache tonight, and I hated myself for it.

I heard his footsteps inside the house before the handle turned, and every muscle in my body tensed at once. The door swung open and Colt leaned against the doorway, filling the frame with his body, and every nerve in mine strained toward him. His silhouette was all hard lines and shadow, but the moon caught on his face as his eyes landed on me. There was no searching, no surprise, just a low, steady heat that rolled across the porch and pinned me to the swing.

"I kind of expected you to be asleep," he admitted, voice low enough that it sank into my skin.

I fiddled with the hem of my shorts, hoping the darkness

would swallow the blush crawling up my chest. "I told you I'd still be up."

"I know." He considered me, eyes tracing the line of my jaw, the slope of my throat, like he could see right through the frantic mess beneath. "But I half expected you to run."

His eyes met mine then, and the silence stretched, taut as a wire, filled with everything neither of us wanted to say.

He finally stepped out onto the porch, pulling the door closed behind him, and the sound of it clicking shut snapped something loose inside me. He crossed the porch in a few long strides and settled onto the swing beside me, so close I could feel the heat radiating from his body.

We sat like that, side by side, both staring out into the moonlit yard as if it might offer us an answer. But all I could think about was the distance between us, the half inch of space that felt like a canyon. I could sense the tension in him, the way his leg bounced restlessly, the way his hands clenched on his thighs. I was desperate to touch him, desperate to be touched, and the ache of it was unbearable.

We didn't speak for a long time. Every second ratcheted the pressure higher, wound us tighter. My breath came shallow and fast, and I tried to steady it by matching his rhythm. It only intensified the sensation of waiting, of wanting.

It felt like it did when we were teenagers, two friends both scared to cross the line and ruin what we already had. I'd spent so many nights just like this, drowning in my want for him.

He turned to look at me, and the porch swing creaked as he shifted his weight. His gaze was almost too much to bear—hungry, dark, and unflinching.

"Why are you out here, Blaire?" he asked, voice soft but edged with something sharper. "I need to hear you say it."

I swallowed, my mouth suddenly dry, and shook my head.

He grinned as he leaned in, his eyes never leaving mine. "You know you drive me crazy, right?"

My chest hollowed out. All the sharp retorts I'd practiced in my head to keep him at arm's length disappeared. I opened my mouth to say something, but the words wouldn't come. I was tired of pretending I didn't want him, even if it was a terrible idea.

He must have felt my hesitation, or maybe he saw straight through it. He reached out slowly and tucked a strand of hair behind my ear before letting his fingers trail down the side of my neck. My skin flared under his touch, every nerve ending desperate for more. His thumb skated along my jaw, making me feel dizzy and rooted all at once.

He leaned in closer, enough to close the space that had separated us all night, and his day-old stubble followed the same path his fingers had mapped. Sparks skittered over my skin, and a shiver ran through me. My thigh jerked against the swing, and I had to anchor myself by curling my fingers around the edge of the seat.

He smelled like leather and spice and something wild I wanted to bottle up and breathe in forever.

He lowered his voice to a hush, and every word sounded like a promise and a threat. "I've had you in my house all damn week." He pressed his lips to the hollow of my throat, and the contact was so unhurried, I thought I might scream.

I clung to the edge of the swing, hot and quivering, but he was in no rush. He skimmed up my throat and across my jaw, never quite kissing, just breathing, and murmuring, "Do you have any idea what you do to me, Strawberry? The way you smell, the way you look at me." He groaned, low and guttural, and I could feel how wet I was just from his words.

I could have stopped him. I could have pushed his hand away or told him to go to hell, but every part of me was humming *yes, yes, yes.*

His mouth hovered at my ear, and I felt the smile in his whisper. "You ever think about me, Blaire? When you're alone at night in my fucking house?" He let the question hang there, a lit match tossed into the dry grass of my restraint.

I nodded once, but I couldn't find the words.

He released a breath, and it fanned across my cheek. "I think about you all the damn time," he whispered, voice rough with lust.

His hand came up to cradle my jaw, thumb dragging over my bottom lip with enough force to open my mouth. "I think about this fucking mouth and all the things I'd love to do to it. I think about you being down the hall from me, and I wrap my hand around my cock to the thought of you being in that room as desperate for me as I am for you."

His eyes were black with need, but he kept his voice low against my skin.

"I imagine you coaxing your sweet little pussy with your fingers, so much gentler than I could ever be, and I come with your name on my lips."

I made a sound in my throat, helpless and high. I squeezed my legs together, trying to wring out the ache building between them, but he was way ahead of me. His palm splayed over my throat, holding me steady, while his other hand slid with predatory patience down my bare arm, over my knee, and then up the inside of my thigh. He didn't stop until he met the trembling resistance there, and I felt my body arch toward him, desperate and exposed.

He inched my legs apart, enough to break my composure, enough to let the night air in where I was hottest. I could feel the heat of him, his body angled toward mine, the length of his thigh pressed up against my own. He held me open with one hand while his other flexed against my neck.

"Colt," I whimpered his name.

"Do you like that thought, baby?" His voice was tighter now, as if he was strangling the need with his own hands. "Does it make you hot to know that I haven't been able to get off since you left without thinking about you?"

I'd always imagined sleeping with Colt again would feel like a betrayal, like giving in to a weakness I should have grown out of years ago, but in that moment, there was no shame, only desire. I felt dizzy with it, wild with the knowledge that I was the only thing in the world that could sate him.

He pressed his forehead against my neck, and for a breathless second, we just sat there, not kissing, not moving, both of us unsteady. I could feel the shape of his restraint, the way he held himself barely in check, and it made me want to shatter that control, to see him undone.

"I think about you too," I whispered the reckless words.

His lips grazed the shell of my ear. "Tell me what you think about."

I shut my eyes tight, but the images came anyway. Late-night fantasies, the shame of wanting him when I was engaged to another man, and the echo of his hands in every man I'd let touch me since.

"I think about you touching me," I said, the words scraped raw from my throat. "I think about your mouth. I think about what it would feel like to let you do whatever you wanted to me."

He let out a low, shuddering sound, and my whole body went tight as a bow. His grip on my thigh tightened, and I felt his fingers flex, digging in hard enough to leave a memory.

"Jesus Christ, Blaire."

I swallowed and tried to keep my voice steady. "You were always so careful with me, back then. I used to imagine what it would feel like if you weren't."

He laughed, a sound so low and wicked it sent a hot pulse straight to my core. "You want me to be rough with you, baby?"

I nodded, unable to form words, and he moved his hand from my thigh to cup me through my shorts. The touch was shockingly intimate, but not even close to enough. I rocked against his hand, needing friction, and he groaned, reading my body better than I ever could myself. He pressed his thumb into the seam and stroked, slow at first, then harder when I whimpered, his other hand still anchoring me by the neck.

"You're soaked," he said, voice rough with awe and need. "Fuck, Blaire. You're so fucking wet for me I can feel it through your shorts."

I bit down on a gasp, face burning, and tried to look away, but he wouldn't let me. "Don't hide from me," he insisted, and there was something pleading in it, like he needed me to witness this as badly as I did.

He slipped his hand under the edge of my shorts, fingers dragging along the wet cotton of my underwear. "Let me make you feel good," he moaned. "Let me show you how much I want you."

I shivered under his touch, part of me still resisting the avalanche even as the rest of me was already buried. "What if Ruby wakes up?" I whispered, some distant part of me clinging to the possibility that this could be interrupted, that if I had an excuse maybe I could regain control.

He smiled against my ear, voice dark with promise. "She never wakes up, but I know how to keep you quiet if I need to."

He pressed a kiss to my jaw, then my throat, and then dragged his mouth down to the hollow at the base of my neck. He licked there, slow and claiming, all the while his fingers stroked me through the soaked cotton. I spread my legs wider, and he rewarded me with a little growl of satisfaction.

He moved his hand again, slipping under my underwear this time, and the bare skin-on-skin contact nearly made me sob. He found my clit immediately, circling it just right, and I clung to him, nails digging into his shoulders, the porch swing creaking as I ground down against his hand.

I'd been touched before, fucked before, but never undone like this. Colt's hand was still between my legs, his fingers slipping slick and easy over my clit, and every move he made drew another silent plea from my body. I didn't need to beg him because it was obvious how badly I wanted it. I was panting, rolling my hips helplessly, and I was so damn wet it covered his hand.

He watched me fall apart, dark eyes hooded and hungry, but there was a control in him that made it so much worse. Like he could tease me forever and never lose himself, like every whimper and quake made him more determined to hold the upper hand. I wanted to break him. I wanted to see him lose that iron will, even if it meant shattering myself in the process.

He pressed his thumb in tight, tiny circles, and my head fell back against the porch swing. "Do you like that, Blaire?" His voice was a low scrape against my neck, rough and intimate. "Do you feel how desperate your cunt is for me?"

I nodded, jaw slack, eyes rolling back, and the only word I

could manage was "Fuck—" as a sob. I would have done anything to keep that hand right where it was.

But he pulled away slowly, leaving my thighs shaking and my whole body on fire. He leaned back on the swing, watching me, and brought his wet fingers to his mouth. He licked them like they were coated in honey, slow and obscene, letting his head drop back with a groan. Then he spread his arms across the back of the swing and widened his thighs.

"Then show me," he commanded, voice breaking slightly. "You know how bad I want you. I need you to show me how bad you want me, too."

All the heat drained out of me and was replaced by something colder, meaner. I could see what he was doing. He was making me chase, making me prove it, making me work for every scrap. He was always in control, and somehow that made me want to be helpless for him.

But not tonight.

I stared at his hands, wide and calloused, the same hands that had built and broken things all his life, and I realized I wanted to break him back. I wanted to touch him until he was the one falling apart. Suddenly, I was so damn angry at him, at myself, at the years I'd wasted trying to be small enough to fit into someone else's life all because he'd told me to leave.

I took a shuddering breath and got off the swing, my legs barely holding me. I stood between his knees, looming over him, and he had the nerve to look up at me with a lazy smile.

"Is this what you want?" I whispered, and without waiting for an answer, I straddled his lap, knees on either side of his hips.

The swing rocked hard under the sudden weight, the chains whining. Colt grunted in surprise but didn't move to touch me, just let his hands fall to the seat, as if he was scared that one wrong move would make me vanish.

I kissed him hard, biting at his mouth as he kissed me back. There was nothing gentle or sweet about it, nothing that Grant or any other man would have recognized as desire. It was pure hunger, and Colt's hands jerked to my hips, fingers digging into my flesh as he pulled my body tighter against him.

I could feel his hard length beneath me, and I ground down against him as I raked my hands through his hair, clutching the back of his head.

He broke the kiss with a gasp, jaw clenched, eyes black with need. "Fuck, baby."

I moved my hips harder against him, needing the friction as Colt's hands clamped around my waist, rough and greedy. I reached down, grabbing the hem of my T-shirt, and pulled it over my head. The warm summer air hit my skin, and even though it was just the two of us under the night sky, it felt like the most reckless thing I'd done in a very long time.

My shirt hit the porch behind me with a soft thud, and Colt went still, staring at my bared skin. I watched the effect of it rip through him, felt the way his cock jumped beneath me.

"Goddamn," he breathed, and I could practically see his control snapping before my eyes. He leaned in, mouth already open and wet, but I shoved both palms against his shoulders, slamming him back into the swing.

"Wait," I gasped, and he blinked.

"What are you doing?" he asked, and his fingers dug hard into my hips.

I was still pushing down against him, the ache between my legs so overwhelming I could barely finish my sentence. "We need ground rules."

He let out a sound that was half snarl, half laugh, and let his head drop back, exposing his throat. I wanted to bite it. "Now? You want to talk ground rules now, Blaire?"

The swing rocked beneath us. I tried to slow down my hips, but I couldn't. "This shouldn't be happening," I said, and the words sounded hollow even to me. "We shouldn't be doing this."

He snapped his head up and caught my eyes with his. "I think it's a little late for that, don't you?"

"I'm serious, Colt." I let my hands slide up my body, over the bare skin of my ribs, and cupped my breasts. I arched into my touch, rolled my nipples between my fingers, and let my head fall back as I whimpered. "This can't be anything more than casual."

"Casual." He bit out and his hands shook against me.

I forced myself to look at him, to keep my eyes open even as the pleasure ratcheted up. "We can't do feelings," I said, and my voice broke slightly. "Not again." I kept moving on him, rolling my hips like I had all the time in the world, but I could feel my orgasm barreling toward me.

He watched my hands, his tongue darting out to wet his lips, and then he gave me a smile so slow and full of himself it set something inside me alight. "You think you're in control here, don't you?" His hands shot up, grabbing my wrists, and yanking them down behind my back in one fluid motion. I gasped, thrown off-balance, and he grinned as he forced my chest forward, his mouth latching onto my nipple with a rough, punishing hunger.

I cried out, the sensation so engulfing it made my vision blur. He sucked hard, then bit down just shy of real pain, dragging his teeth across the sensitive skin before letting go with a pop.

He hauled me in, crushing me against his chest, both hands greedy and unapologetic as they roamed from my hips to my ribs to the curve of my ass. Then he buried his face in my hair, nose pressed to my ear, and said, "You want ground rules, you got them. As long as we're fucking, this is mine." He grabbed my ass with one hand and ground his cock upward so hard I moaned as my whole body clenched. "No one else touches you. No one else gets to see you like this. No one else makes you come."

He bit my earlobe before he licked the sting away. "Do you hear me?" he asked, and there wasn't an ounce of teasing in his voice. "If you want this to be fucking casual, then fine. But you're still mine." His fingers dug into my flesh, marking me, claiming me. His eyes met mine, and there was so much possession in his gaze that it both terrified and thrilled me. "If this is the only way I get you, then I'll brand myself into your skin until you can't remember anyone else's touch."

Something inside me buckled. I hated when Grant called me his, flinched away from any trace of ownership from him, but the way Colt said it made me want to say yes to every dirty, possessive thing he demanded. I felt it in the way my hips moved, in my hands clutching at his shoulders, in the need that made my body shake.

"Yes," I whimpered. "I'm yours."

He surged up and caught my mouth with his teeth on my lip, and I kissed him back with everything I had. I ground down on him hard, and he met every movement with ruthless, perfect friction. He slipped a hand between us, fingers finding the edge of my shorts, and shoved them to the side with a single motion. His fingers skimmed gently over my clit before he buried two fingers inside me. I moaned loudly as he moved them in and out of me, fucking me with his fingers as his thumb strummed over my clit.

"Fuck, you're perfect," he muttered into my mouth, but then his lips fell away, trailing heat down my throat, jaw, and collarbone. He paused, watching goosebumps shimmer across my skin in the moonlight, and I could feel his smirk before he ran his tongue over my nipple.

His mouth was rough and greedy, sucking hard until I whimpered, then he licked the sting away slowly. His thumb moved over my clit in tight circles, and I was shaking so badly. He held me tighter, one huge hand splayed across my back, and the other was buried between my thighs, refusing to let me retreat.

My muscles tensed, straining for more, as my hands dug into his hair, yanking hard enough to make him hiss. I kissed him again, desperate for release and him, and I clamped my eyes closed as I pulled away panting.

"Eyes on me." His rough words hit me, and I blinked my eyes open to meet his stare.

His eyes were dark with hunger, but there was something else, something like awe as he watched me. I hated how much that mattered, how the thought of him being so enamored with me made my chest ache even worse than the need between my legs.

I kept my gaze locked on his, even as my orgasm built, even as my hands shook as I traced them down his neck. Every time I tried to look away, he tightened his grip, said my name in a low warning, and pulled me back into focus.

"That's it, Blaire," he murmured, and I could hear how close he was to losing control.

It was the most intimate thing I'd ever done, letting him see me like this, completely unguarded. I'd spent so many years pretending, performing for men who wanted a softer, sweeter version of me, but Colt didn't want that version.

He wanted *me*.

He wanted the messiest, most desperate, truest version of me —the Blaire who was too much, who never tempered herself, who wanted things louder and rougher and all-consuming. That fact alone thundered through me, breaking open something that Grant had tried to wall away for years.

Colt's want was a holy thing.

The proof was in the way his eyes never left me, in the way he was clearly, unashamedly fighting not to come just from the sight of me riding his hand. The proof was in the way he said my name, not as a question but a fucking invocation, like it was something to worship. I'd spent so long trying to make myself small, and now I was too big to be contained.

I wanted to take up every fucking inch of him, and something hot and aching settled in my chest.

He pressed his thumb harder, and I broke. I moaned loudly, my thighs clamping around his hand, my nails digging into his shoulders. He didn't stop, didn't let up, just fucked me through it, watching every second of my unraveling like it was the only thing he'd ever wanted.

I was shaking and boneless as Colt pulled his mouth away from mine, and in one seamless motion, he stood and took me with him. The muscles in his arms flexed as he lifted me against him, and my thighs slid open to accommodate his hips. The rough drag of his jeans against my bare skin made me gasp.

He set me down on unsteady legs, and I stumbled before I clung to his chest. He pressed his mouth to my temple, my hairline, the corner of my jaw. His hands found their way to the small of my back, then up, splaying over my ribs as he bent to murmur in my ear, "You're incredible, you know that?"

He backed me up with slow, deliberate steps until my thighs hit the porch railing and the wood dug into my ass. The porch was open to the night and the stars, but nothing about the exposure made me shy. He spun me, and I had to grab onto the railing to keep from falling forward. My pulse kicked up, and I was painfully aware of the way my body arched back into him as his fingers ran down the length of my spine.

I felt his cock straining through his jeans as he ground himself against me, like he couldn't stand to wait another second. His mouth found the side of my neck, tongue and teeth alternating nips and kisses as he bent me forward, lining my stomach flush with the porch rail. I heard the metallic clink of his belt, the quick rasp of a zipper, and then his hands were yanking the waistband of my shorts and underwear down in one impatient move. The fabric dropped to my ankles, and the immediate shock of the air on my skin made me moan.

I glanced over my shoulder, just to see his face, and the sight nearly undid me. His hair was wild from where I'd tugged it, lips swollen and red. He held his cock in one hand, stroking himself slowly, watching as I took him in. "So fucking perfect," he said, voice so low I barely recognized it. "Perfect for me, perfect for my cock."

He lined himself up behind me, and I felt the hot, blunt head of him drag through my pussy, teasing and slicking himself in my wetness.

"Wait," I breathed, barely getting the word out. "Do you want to use a condom? I'm on birth control, and I got tested right after I found out Grant was cheating on me."

He looked up at me, his eyes staring into mine. "It's been a long time for me, Blaire. I'm clean. I want to feel you without anything between us."

I could hardly breathe as I nodded my head.

He pressed the tip in, then drew back, letting me feel the

stretch and the ache. Every nerve ending in my body was awake and desperate for more.

He gripped my hips with both hands, thumbs digging into the soft flesh, and slammed forward until he was flush with me. I whimpered, the sensation overwhelming, but I didn't pull away. Instead, I pushed back against him, arching even harder.

"Fuck," he rasped as he leaned over me, his chest flush with my back. "You were made for me." One hand slipped up to curl around my throat, and the combination of pleasure and pressure sent me reeling.

I knew, in some distant rational part of my mind, that this was the worst idea I'd ever had. I knew I would pay for it tomorrow, and maybe every day after. It was impossible for this not to mean everything. But in this moment, I didn't care. I didn't want to be careful or quiet or good. I wanted him.

Colt set a relentless pace, never slowing or softening, even as his hand on my hip slid around me to find my sensitive clit. "Give me another, Blaire." His words burned against me. "I can feel how needy you are."

With every word, every movement, he branded it into me, and I could feel the truth of it hollowing me out.

"Feel how good I'm fucking you," he snarled as he slammed in harder, and I cried out when he hit a spot inside me that stole my breath. I felt him everywhere at once. He was so big it was impossible to think about anything but the way he filled me.

"Can you feel how fucking casual this is, Blaire?" he taunted, voice thick with something dangerous, and I whimpered. It should have felt cheap, the way he said it, but there was nothing casual about the way his body worshiped mine, the way he refused to let me pretend I wasn't falling apart for him.

"Colt—" I choked out and he slammed forward again, demanding everything I had left as his rough fingers pressed hard against my clit and I shattered. "Oh my god."

"That's it, baby. Give it to me." He didn't let up as I fell apart, his hands unyielding as he fucked me.

I clamped down around him as my orgasm crashed over me

harder than the last. His hands tightened, nearly bruising as he surged forward, burying himself so deep I thought I'd split open. My name tore from his lips and I felt him shudder, felt every pulse of his release as he came inside me.

He said my name again, softer this time, almost pleading, and I collapsed against the porch railing. My body was too wrung out to do anything but take whatever he gave me.

He didn't let go. He wrapped one arm across my front, gathering me to his chest as if he thought I might disappear if he loosened his grip. He leaned his forehead into the curve of my spine, breathing me in, and we were so tangled there was no telling where he ended and I began.

The night was warm and bright and indifferent to what we'd done, but I could feel it everywhere. I could still feel the ache of him inside me. My heart slammed in my chest, and my hands were numb where I gripped the rail. I blinked hard, trying to drag myself back into my own body, trying to get Colt out of my head.

But he pressed a kiss to the ridge of my shoulder, then another at the nape of my neck. His hands moved, steadying me as they smoothed over my sides before one hand pressed against the softness of my belly, fingers splayed wide. We were both breathing hard, his chest rising and falling against my back, and the raw sound of it was almost more intimate than the sex itself.

When he finally drew back, he moved so carefully before he lifted me and cradled me in his arms. I clung to his shirt as I laughed.

"I can walk," I lied, and I knew he could feel the aftershocks still rippling through my thighs beneath his palms.

"You could, but I'm not going to let you." He leaned forward and pressed his lips to my mouth one last time. "This is how us cowboys do casual."

I snorted, completely naked in his arms, and ran my thumb over his mustache. "Okay, cowboy."

CHAPTER 26

COLT

I squinted against the glare, sweat trickling down my temple and pooling at the hollow of my throat. My shirt had plastered itself between my shoulder blades, and the heat showed no signs of letting up.

I'd been on my feet since dawn, but now I let myself lean against the fence and enjoy the show.

McCoy was in the corral, and he was losing.

He'd been splitting his days lately, some working on the ranch and most weekends chasing money on the rodeo circuit. He swore he was just knocking the rust off of something he'd once loved to do, but McCoy was getting far too old to get on the back of a damn bull.

Hell, he was getting his ass handed to him right now by a two-year-old quarter horse.

The filly had a white blaze and attitude for days, and she'd just sent McCoy flying again. McCoy tried like hell to catch himself as he came off the saddle, but he still ate shit. The thunk when he landed was followed by the shrill, annoyed snort of the horse, who kicked up her heels and trotted away.

I laughed loud enough for McCoy to hear it, but he didn't look up. He sat in the dirt for a long second, catching his breath and spitting out grit. "You're real helpful. Has anyone ever told you that?" Even from a distance, I could see the flush of frustration heating his face.

"Hey—" I held up my hands in defense. "I didn't say anything. I'm just here to watch the master work."

He muttered something about being a smart-ass and climbed to his feet, flexing the wrist he always taped before a ride. The horse watched him warily from the far side of the pen, ears pinned and whole body rigid.

"Easy, girl. You're all right," he said softly as he approached her again with his hand outstretched, but she wasn't buying it. She danced away, barely letting him close the gap, and McCoy had to circle the pen twice before she'd let him lay a hand on her neck.

We'd picked up the filly through a rescue, and she didn't trust us. McCoy thought he'd have her taking a saddle within a few weeks, but I knew better. I'd seen wild before, and this girl was as wild as they came.

But McCoy was patient, and I knew she'd give in to him, eventually. "That's it, pretty girl." He nodded to her as he ran his hand down her neck.

"Now I see why all the ladies love you," I called out, folding my arms over the fence rail and watching McCoy work the filly with a kind of devotedness I'd never seen him show to any girl. "If you whispered things like that to me, I wouldn't even make you buy me dinner."

He threw a dry look over his shoulder before he turned back to her. "I like to cook them dinner, thank you very much. Keep things at the house if you know what I mean."

"With Hunter there?" I tossed back, chuckling. "I can't imagine coming home with you only to find out you live with your boyfriend."

The corners of his mouth lifted but didn't take his attention off the filly. "Jealousy doesn't suit you, Colt." He glanced back at me for only a second. "But it is nice to see, though. I thought your dick was broken, but now that Blaire's back, I can see that thing is working just fine."

The sound of her name had the muscle in my jaw flexing and my cock throbbing in my jeans. Every inch of my body responded to her, even now. I could still taste her skin lingering on my tongue, could feel her heat in my palms and smell her on my skin.

Last night replayed in my mind like a constant, slow-motion reel, and every detail was there. I shifted against the fence and tried to focus on anything else.

Blaire had still been asleep when Ruby and I left the house this morning. Her door was slightly open, and she was tangled in her sheets as she slept soundly. I'd thought about waking her up just to see how she'd look at me in the morning light, but I didn't.

I stood in her doorway for longer than was acceptable, watching her sleep as every part of me ached for her, and then I closed the door and reminded myself of what she said.

This was casual.

Bull-fucking-shit.

I would call it whatever she needed to keep her close, but there's not a single part of me that believed it.

"What the hell does that mean?" I gripped the fence rail and wiped the sweat off my brow.

McCoy stepped back from the filly, letting her move around the corral freely, as he leaned back against the gate, arms folded.

"Blaire's been dragging you around by your dick even though she barely said two words to you." He shrugged as he grinned. "It's a little pathetic, but entertaining to watch."

"I think you're reaching a little there, don't you?" I glanced away from him because I didn't need McCoy knowing how right he was.

"I don't." He pushed off the gate and turned to face me. "I seriously can't believe you let her move in with you." He shook his head.

"She's not moving in," I argued, though it sounded defensive. "She's staying with us until June's house is repaired. It was a fucking mess in there."

I would know, since I'd spent several afternoons that I should have been on the ranch over there cleaning it up.

I kicked my boot against the fence post, knocking off a dry clump of dirt.

He let out a long, huffing breath, then gave me a look. "So you're telling me," he began, drawing out the words like he was trying to put it all together, "that the girl who blew up your entire life when she left is now sleeping in your guest room like it's nothing?"

He had every right to be concerned. I'd spent my entire life circling Blaire, and when she left, I'd been destroyed. I thought about last night, about the way she'd looked at me, really looked at me, for the first time in years.

I stared past him, watching the filly circle the corral. Her chestnut coat was streaked with sweat and dust, muscles twitching beneath her skin. Every time McCoy shifted, her eyes flashed with wariness, nostrils flaring as she tracked him, coiled and ready to bolt at the slightest wrong move.

Fuck, she reminded me of Blaire. The way she watched me from beneath her lashes, how she'd lean in only to pull away the moment I reached for her, like my touch might burn. Always one step ahead, always knowing exactly how to keep me chasing, even when it felt like my heart might shatter from wanting her.

"I'm confused about what's so hard to understand about that." I stared at the horse, hoping McCoy would drop it, but he kept digging like a dog after a bone.

"Uh-huh. So you're just playing landlord. That's all it is?" He smiled, but his eyes narrowed on me.

"I'm not her landlord, but yeah. That's all it is." The words felt thin, but I said them anyway.

The filly nosed the fence near my elbow, her breath warm. I reached out without thinking, but she shied away as she watched me reluctantly.

McCoy was watching me, eyes still narrowed like he already knew everything without me saying a word. "You did it, didn't you?" he said after a long beat. "You slept with her."

My ears burned as I met his gaze. I opened my mouth to deny him, but no words came out.

"Holy shit," he laughed. "You really are a lost cause."

I wanted to deny it, to play it off, but the memory of her was too fresh, too raw. "It's not like that," I lied.

He leaned in, lowering his voice like we were fifteen years old and sneaking my dad's whiskey behind the barn. "So what's it like?"

I looked at him, tried to frame it the way I wanted, but all I could come up with was the truth. "It's..." I started, then stopped. "It's complicated."

McCoy snorted. "It's always going to be complicated with Blaire."

I rolled my shoulders back and forced the words out like they were true. "We're keeping things casual at the moment."

"Colt." He clapped me on the shoulder, a little too hard, like he was trying to knock some sense into me. "Listen, I'm not saying you can't handle it, but I think you should know exactly what you're signing up for this time. You can't just sleep with a girl you've been in love with before, and what if she goes back..." He trailed off, but the implication was obvious.

She said she'd told Grant she wasn't going back, and I wanted to believe her so badly my chest ached with it.

"I'm well aware." I nodded, jaw tight. "Don't you have work you should be doing?"

McCoy raised his hands in surrender. "Okay, okay. I'll get back to work."

I let out a curse as I turned away from his scrutiny. He was still watching me, standing at the fence with his arms hooked over the warped pine rail, and I could feel the weight of his gaze like it was a hand between my shoulder blades. I didn't want to talk about Blaire, didn't want him to see how she'd gotten under my skin in a single night and turned me inside out. Even before then.

I needed to move, to get some distance, so I stalked across the yard and reached for the lead rope of my horse. My skin burned beneath the sun, my pulse beating hard at my neck, and nothing about the day was helping. Not the sweat, not the ache in my arms, not the overwhelming thoughts of everything I needed to get done.

I swung into the saddle and jerked my hat down low, ignoring the way my hands shook as I gathered up the reins. I dug my heels in and sent him charging toward the open pasture, his hooves pounding a jarring rhythm that shook through my entire body. I wanted to outrun it, to tear myself free from the fever of her that had buried into my bones, but wherever I went, Blaire was there.

I could feel her in the hollows of my hands, could smell her on my wrists, could see her every time I blinked. The way she'd looked at me last night, not just with want but with longing. The taste of her tongue, the wildness on her face when she came apart in my lap. The memory of it was so close I couldn't breathe through it.

I kicked the gelding up into a run, the wind cutting across my cheeks and drying the sweat on my skin. The land rolled away beneath us in long, gold-green waves, and the fence lines stretched out endlessly until they dissolved against the blue haze of the mountains. I tracked along the perimeter, checking posts more out of habit than necessity. There was no one out here but me, and I let myself pretend I could ride and ride until the world fell away under the drum of hooves on dirt.

But it didn't work. It never did.

The work was supposed to tire me enough to stop thinking so much, but it only emptied me out and made more room for the mess in my head.

I wound up at the far fence line, where our land ran up against June's property. As I slowed, I caught sight of two figures in the field beyond. At first, it was a blur of color and movement, but then June's wide-brimmed straw hat came into view, and beside her the flash of red hair that could only belong to Blaire.

My hands tightened on the reins, and we slowed as I sat back in the saddle. I ran my hand down my horse's neck as he caught his breath and watched them from a distance. June was showing Blaire something in the fields of strawberries, and Blaire was laughing. The slight breeze tugged at the loose ends of her hair and tossed them around her face.

I should've looked away, let the moment pass, and gone about my business. But I couldn't.

From here, Blaire was all legs, her skin sun-kissed and golden where it disappeared into those cutoff jean shorts. My mouth went dry watching her shift her weight, one hip cocked as she listened to June. The breeze lifted the hem of her worn T-shirt, teasing glimpses of her lower back that made my fingers itch to trace the same path. She threw her head back laughing, exposing the vulnerable curve of her throat, the same spot I'd tasted last night.

This was the Blaire I remembered; wild and unrestrained, nothing like the polished photos I'd seen of her from Raleigh.

She belonged here, under this infinite sky, as natural and necessary as the sun burning against that endless blue.

I shifted in the saddle and gripped the reins harder, trying to anchor myself against the current pulling me toward her. June said something that made Blaire laugh, and the sound pooled at the base of my spine. She moved with a kind of ease that made me ache, like she already belonged here and had been waiting for the rest of us to notice.

But fuck, I noticed.

I rode farther down the fence line, and I tried to soften my expression, to play it casual when they both looked up at me. But I was almost certain I looked like I wanted to jump the fence and run my hands over every inch of Blaire in plain view of God and anyone else who wanted to watch. I took a steadying breath and tugged my hat a little lower as June watched me approach with a knowing smirk.

I almost turned the horse around right there, but I squared my shoulders and tipped my hat as I fixed my eyes on June. "Afternoon."

"Afternoon, Colt," June replied, her tone even, but her eyes sharp as tacks, flicking from me to Blaire then back again.

Blaire straightened beside her, dusting her hands off on her thighs, and she didn't look at me, not at first. But I could tell by the set of her jaw and the stubborn press of her lips that she felt me watching her.

"What brings you down this way?" June gave me a quick grin.

"Just checking the fences," I answered, which was technically true. "How are the house repairs looking today?"

June started talking, but my eyes snagged on Blaire's. I didn't hear a word she said after that. I could only focus on the way Blaire was looking at me, and the familiar electricity that was licking up my spine.

I dragged my palm across the stubble on my jaw. "Mind if I borrow Blaire for a minute?" The reins twisted in my grip as I nodded toward the barn. "There's something I need her help with."

At the word "borrow," Blaire's brows flicked up, but before she could say anything, June shot her a glance.

"Go on, honey," June said, voice gentle but edged with amusement. "We can finish this later. I needed a sweet tea break anyway." Then she looked at me, eyes sparkling. "Don't keep her too long. We've got a whole batch of jams to make this afternoon."

Blaire hesitated, hands still dirty from the strawberry runners, and her gaze flickered between June and me like she was weighing her options. But I saw the flush in her cheeks.

"C'mon," I said, softer than before, jerking my chin in the direction of the barn.

Blaire climbed over the fence. She didn't bother walking down to the gate. She hauled herself up and over like she was still sixteen, and I dismounted my horse and fidgeted with the reins as I waited.

She hesitated, eyes searching mine as she approached, but I just smiled and started walking.

Her hand grazed over mine as she caught up to me, the heat from her fingertips sending a jolt straight to my cock. I clenched my jaw so hard my teeth ached, fighting the urge to pin her to the nearest fence post. One step closer, and I'd catch her scent that had kept me hard and aching half the night. But June was still watching from the field, her knowing eyes burning holes in our backs even as she pretended to look elsewhere.

We walked side by side up the path toward the barn. Her gait was quick, almost angry, like she was trying to outpace something that was chasing her. I kept my hands to myself, even though every instinct screamed to reach out and touch her again.

The barn was maybe a hundred yards up the hill, and the walk there felt twice as long, every step brimming with the tension we'd left unresolved the night before. Neither of us spoke until we were almost at the doors, and the silence felt loaded with all the things we weren't saying.

I tied off my horse and opened the barn door, letting the warm, sweet scent of hay and leather roll out in a wave, and gestured her inside. She ducked under my arm, eyes darting everywhere except at me, and then stood in the aisle with her hands on her hips.

"Did you actually need something?" she asked.

I laughed, pulling the door almost closed. "I needed to see you."

She snorted, but her eyes softened a little. "You could have texted me or waited until I got home tonight."

Home.

The word caught me off guard and stole my breath.

"I couldn't wait," I said honestly, and she rolled her eyes as I stepped closer.

I worried she could see my pulse hammering in my neck, see how desperate I was for her, but I couldn't stand another minute of not being where she was.

At first, neither of us moved. Then, with a sigh that sounded like surrender, Blaire reached up and grabbed me by the collar before she pulled me down to her mouth. Her lips met mine, then the kiss turned hard and demanding. The barn dissolved around us, hay and dust and daylight burning away as my hands were in her hair and on her waist. They were everywhere at once, but it still wasn't enough.

I backed her up against the wooden beam, hands braced on

either side of her head, close enough to feel the heat radiating from her skin but not touching her. She arched toward me, a silent plea in the curve of her body, and I held myself still, savoring the exquisite torture of watching her. I held still just to watch her breathe and pretend I'd never lost this.

When her fingers finally dug into my shoulders through the thin cotton of my shirt, dragging me those last impossible inches against her, the sound that escaped my throat wasn't human.

If this was what casual felt like, I'd let it kill me.

"Colt," she panted my name. "You're going to get me in trouble."

"You are trouble," I answered and kissed her again, softer this time, savoring the taste of her. My heart hammered against my ribs as her body melted into mine, and I fought the urge to whisper things I couldn't take back.

The barn was empty except for the horses, and the sound of their shifting weight and gentle snuffling was the only witness to the way she pulled me closer. Her fingers burned a trail up the back of my neck, nails dragging against my skin as she pulled my hat from my head and twisted it in her hands.

She looked up at me through half-lidded eyes as she pressed her shoulders into the beam. Her tongue darted out over her bottom lip, leaving it glistening in the dim light. I dug my fingers into her hips, yanking them against me with enough force to draw a gasp from her mouth. "Do you cowboys still have the stupid hat rule?" she whispered, her voice rough with want.

She was taunting me with it, daring me to take the bait.

I braced my hand on the beam behind her, crowding her space until she had nowhere to go, but she didn't flinch. Instead, she twisted my hat between her fingers, and fuck, I could smell the hint of strawberries on her skin.

"You know damn well we do." I leaned in till my nose grazed her cheek.

Her chest heaved against mine with each ragged breath, her heartbeat hammering against my own. I slid my calloused hands back to her hips, then dragged them slowly upward until my thumbs found that strip of bare skin above her shorts.

"Remind me how it goes," she whispered as she placed my hat on her head, the brim casting shadows on her flushed face. "Something about if you wear the hat, you ride the cowboy?"

In one fluid motion, I gripped her thighs and hoisted her up, pinning her hard against the beam. Her legs wrapped around me, and she moaned as I pressed every inch of myself against her. I was hard as hell, had been since the second I'd seen her in the field, and the ache of it was only getting worse.

"Fuck," I rasped, driving my hips against her core and pinning her harder against the rough wood. "I want to watch you come, then you can take every inch of this ride."

Blaire slid her hands up into my hair, tugging at the roots just enough to make me moan. She bit my bottom lip and let it go with a snap, then dragged her tongue across it slowly, as if she could taste how I was bleeding out for her.

"I want to taste you," she whispered against my mouth, and my hips bucked so hard she slipped in my grip. The heat in her voice, the need there, stripped the last of my composure.

"Blaire," I growled her name, and my fingers dug into her thighs as she arched into me.

I wanted to throw her onto the hay and devour her, wanted to see her come apart for me right here, where anyone could walk in and find us. The need was a fever in my blood, a hunger I couldn't disguise, but she had her own ideas.

She always had her own goddamn ideas.

"Please?" That single word hung in the air like electricity before a storm, and I pulled back to look at her, my breath catching in my throat. My hat cast shadows across her flushed face, and her lips were red and swollen from kissing me. I nearly came undone at the thought of her wanting to drop to her knees for me right here in the dust and hay. I'd imagined fucking her mouth more times than I cared to admit. I'd dreamt about what she would look like when we weren't two teenagers fumbling in the dark anymore.

"Fuck, Blaire." I gripped her jaw, thumb pressing against her lips. "Take whatever you want from me. I will never tell you no."

She wriggled from my grip and slid down my body, her breasts dragging against my torso until her knees hit the barn floor with a thud that made my cock throb. Her fingernails raked down my chest and stomach in a promise of what that wicked mouth was about to do to me.

My legs nearly buckled as she looked up, her eyes almost black, and her lips already swollen and parted.

I could hardly fucking breathe.

When her palm pressed against my cock through my jeans, I nearly came right there. I grabbed her hair hard enough to make her gasp, knocking my hat off her head.

"Hey—" she started, but I shoved my thumb between her lips, pressing down on her tongue. She sucked it hard, teeth grazing my knuckle.

Her fingers attacked my belt, and she yanked it open before she popped the button of my jeans. Her knuckles grazed my cock as she tore down my zipper.

She nipped at the pad of my thumb as she blinked up at me, and even as her hands shook, she looked so sure of herself and what she wanted. Sometimes I forgot how much older she was now, how much she'd learned since the summers we used to run wild together.

"Fuck, you're so perfect," I rasped.

She freed my cock with one rough, hungry motion, her fingers so sure and tight that I had to grit my teeth not to lose it right then.

Her hot, shaky palm wrapped around the base of my cock, and the raw electricity of her touch shot through me like lightning, forcing a guttural sound from my throat as my spine bowed and my hips jerked forward involuntarily. I left one hand in her hair and braced the other against the wood behind her.

Her nails dug into my thigh as she steadied herself, then she looked up with this wicked, starved grin that made my gut twist. It was the same look she used to give me before we'd sneak out at midnight and risk everything for a taste of trouble.

I pulled my thumb from her mouth, roughly dragging it over her tongue, and she gasped. Her lips were shiny and her chin already slick from spit, and she stared at my cock. I watched the way her pupils widened and the way she swallowed hard.

The anticipation in her was a living thing, and it was the hottest fucking thing I'd ever seen.

Her breath came in pants, her chest heaving. "I've thought about doing this so many times," she whispered before her tongue darted out to wet her lips.

I twisted her hair around my fist, yanking her head back until our eyes locked. Her mouth hung open, waiting, begging. Every muscle in my body screamed to thrust deep into that wet heat.

"God," she said, voice unsteady, and her thumb running up the underside of my shaft. "You're so big." She bent her head and pressed a soft, open-mouthed kiss to the tip.

Her lips hovered, parted and ready, and I held her there as I tried to memorize what she looked like in front me.

"Open," I told her, and she did. She was so fucking obedient as I eased my cock between her lips, savoring the hot, wet feel of her as she moaned around me.

I watched her cheeks hollow as she sucked, and she didn't take her eyes off me as I pushed deeper. I wanted to take it slow, to savor the moment, but she was so greedy for it that my hips bucked almost on instinct. She pulled me almost completely out of her mouth, her tongue working the head, then the length, before she lowered her head again.

I hit the back of her throat, but she didn't flinch. Her hand moved at the base of me, pumping what she couldn't fit. With every stroke, she made these desperate little noises, and the sound of it, the sight, made me realize I had never had this with anyone else. I had never felt so desperate for anyone but her.

I pressed my free hand to her jaw, guiding her, feeling the slick stretch of her mouth around me. I could see the smudge of dirt on her cheek, the strawberry stain on her wrist, and I wanted to mark her in a way that would outlast the season.

She pulled back, gasping for air as a string of spit hung

between her lips and my cock. "You gonna fuck my mouth or just stare at it?" she rasped, wiping her mouth with the back of her hand before she dove back in.

Something feral snapped inside me. My control was gone, lost to anything but the wet heat of her mouth.

I thrust hard into her, my fingers digging into her scalp as I slammed into the back of her throat. She gagged, tears springing to the corners of her eyes, but she grabbed my ass and pulled me deeper, refusing to let me hold back. And her eyes, fuck, those eyes never wavered from mine. The raw surrender in them burned straight through me, scorching everything in its path. I was seconds from coming completely fucking undone.

Every time I'd been inside her burned through my memory like wildfire—the way she'd arch and cry my name, how she'd claw at my back until I bled, the sacred moments when she'd shatter beneath me and give me parts of herself no one else had ever touched. I needed to believe I was the only one who'd ever seen her completely surrender like that. It became a vise, crushing my ribs until I could barely breathe through the possession and need.

She moaned, sending vibrations straight through my cock, and I growled her name, feeling the pulse of it in my veins. She was sloppy and wild, spit running down her chin as one hand stroked the base and the other dug into my hip.

I watched her lips stretch around me, her eyes watering as she took me deeper. My vision blurred at the edges, knees threatening to buckle beneath me. I yanked her hair hard enough to make her whimper. "That's it, Blaire. Just like that. Fuck—"

She hummed in response, the vibration going straight to my cock. My vision blurred as I felt myself barreling toward the edge, my restraint shattering with each wet slide of her mouth.

"You look so fucking pretty like this. I wish everyone could see how good you look with my cock in your mouth." My hand tightened on her jaw, and she blinked her eyes open to look at me. The next words rolled out of me before I could stop them, and I knew I should have regretted them even though I didn't. "It makes me so goddamn angry to think about anyone else touching you, Blaire. I wish that fucking ex of yours could see you now. See what belongs to me, you on your knees, choking on my cock, with that naked ring finger wrapped around me."

The thought of his ring on her hand gutted me, but fuck if it didn't make me want to claim her harder, erase every trace of him with my hands and my mouth.

Her eyes shuddered, and she moaned so hard I felt it in my balls.

"Blaire, I'm gonna—"

She sucked me harder, whimpering as I came against the back of her throat. I roared her name as she swallowed around me, eyes never leaving mine, tears streaming down her flushed cheeks.

I pulled myself from her mouth and yanked her up before she could catch her breath. Her lips were glistening, and I crushed my mouth against hers, tasting myself on her tongue. Our teeth clashed, and she whimpered as her fingers twisted in my shirt.

When I pulled away, she blinked up at me with swollen lips and her eyes unfocused. "Was it good?" she whispered, her voice raw from taking me so deep, and the uncertainty in her tone made me go still.

There was so much hesitation in her words, a doubtfulness that made my chest tight with anger. What the fuck had happened to my girl to make her doubt herself like this? The possessiveness surged through me, and I couldn't control what I said next.

"Fuck, Blaire," I growled, gripping her chin and forcing her to meet my eyes. "Your mouth was made to take my cock. The way you swallowed every fucking drop like you were starving for it—" I dragged my thumb over her lips. "I want to wreck you. I want to fuck you until you can't remember anyone else who's ever touched you. I want to fill that perfect pussy until my cum is running down your thighs when you leave this barn. I want everyone to know you're mine."

She whimpered, pressing her thighs together, and I couldn't go another second without tasting her.

My grip was iron on her hips as I spun us around, planting her right on top of the nearest hay bale, dust and straw flying everywhere. The barn was spinning, or maybe that was my head, but I was already hauling her shorts past her knees, struggling to get them over her boots, before her breath rushed out of her.

My hands were shaking from how badly I wanted her, but I didn't slow down, didn't even try to be gentle. She laughed breathlessly as her shorts hit the floor, the sound catching in her throat and breaking into something that sounded like pleading. She leaned back on her elbows with her legs spread and boots dangling over the edge. Her face was a mess of want, all swollen lips and flushed cheeks, and her hair was tangled from my hands.

I dropped to my fucking knees and buried my face between her thighs. She let out this shattered gasp like she'd forgotten how good we were together and needed me to remind her.

So, I did.

CHAPTER 27
BLAIRE

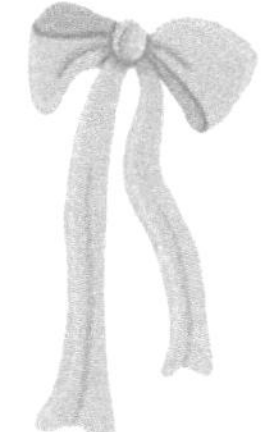

Maggie's fingers locked around mine, pulling me through the press of bodies toward the bar. I'd wanted nothing more than to collapse into bed tonight or into Colt, but Maggie was having none of it.

Instead, she'd coaxed me into wearing a tiny black satin dress that hugged my body like a second skin. The hem barely reached my fingertips, but paired with these crimson cowgirl boots, even I had to admit my legs looked longer than a country mile.

The Dusty Spur witnessed the birth of our friendship, so it was only fitting that we returned here tonight. I felt lighter after the flood of confessions I'd unleashed at Maggie's apartment after leaving June's. I worked in the fields all day, then June simmered the jams while I canned and slapped on the labels and ribbon.

But I thought of nothing but Colt.

"It's just physical," I insisted to Maggie over our second glass of cheap rosé. "We're just scratching an itch."

She'd been unconvinced, and I didn't blame her.

It hadn't even been a full week since I'd let Colt first touch me, and the tender ache between my legs became a constant companion. My inner thighs were chafed with what I'd jokingly dubbed "stache rash," and this morning I'd counted five purple blooms of perfect fingerprints on both my hips.

"That doesn't sound casual," Maggie said, and I knew she was right.

Not when I tiptoed to his bedroom after Ruby fell asleep, and he lifted me onto his dresser, his hands spreading me open like he'd thought of nothing else all day. And it definitely didn't feel casual in the mornings when he'd return from dropping Ruby at school with a look in his eyes that made me question everything.

His phone would ring and ring, but he'd let it buzz against the nightstand until I was writhing beneath him. When he finally answered, he did it so calmly, like his fingers weren't still buried inside me and my face wasn't pressed against my pillow to keep from making noises that would give us away.

"I'll be there when I get there," he'd growl, then toss his phone aside, his eyes never leaving mine as he lowered his mouth back to my skin. Colt explored my body with the focused intensity of a man reclaiming territory he'd once lost, like the ranch could burn to the ground and he wouldn't stop until I was unraveling and begging beneath him.

I told myself that keeping it casual was practical. Tactical, even. The idea of all this meaning something, of me falling for Colt Calloway again, was dangerous. So I nursed my delusion, ridiculous as it was, and tried to enjoy what I had while I had it, already counting down to the moment it slipped through my fingers.

I'd texted him earlier to let him know I wouldn't be back to his house tonight and to tell Ruby we'd have a date in the morning. Then Maggie and I finished our third glass of wine, and her eyes gleamed as she snatched my phone.

"Show him what he's missing."

We'd gone to her bathroom, and I arched against the counter, the satin riding higher as I angled the camera down my body, and my pulse throbbed between my legs as I hit send.

His response lit up my screen almost instantly, four words that made heat flood my belly.

Colt: Fuck. Look at you.

I imagined his hands sliding up my legs, pushing the dress higher. I wanted to abandon Maggie right then and there, but her fingers closed over mine as I started typing a response.

"Make that man sweat it out a little. It's good for them to yearn. It builds character."

So, that's what I was doing. I saddled up to the bar next to Maggie as she ordered us both a shot, and I was trying to pretend that his last messages weren't enough to make me fold.

Colt: Where are you?

Colt: Tell me so I can come there and make a mess of you in that dress.

Colt: Fuck, Blaire. I'm so damn obsessed with you.

"Here we go." Maggie set a shot down in front of me, with a lime wedge balanced on the rim.

I lifted it and clinked it against hers. "What are we toasting to?"

She leaned over, whispering in my ear, "To bringing the Calloway brothers to their knees."

I laughed, but my fingers trembled around the shot glass. I didn't want to bring Colt to his knees. Not really. Not in any way that would last beyond what he could do with his mouth. We'd hurt each other before, and Ruby's face flashed in my mind, her smile so much like his that my chest ached. I refused to hurt her.

Even if I knew I would end up hurt instead.

Every night I swore it would be the last; yet, every morning I woke reaching for him.

"He is awfully good there." I smiled at Maggie, then we both brought the shots to our lips.

"To men on their knees!" She clinked her shot to mine again, and I tried to match her enthusiasm as I downed my own. The tequila burned all the way down, and I was grateful for the way it helped chase away the nerves that had been building for the last week. I sucked the lime, wincing at the shock of bitterness, but it faded into something sweet and far more dangerous as I thought about how every touch, every whispered word between Colt and me felt like unlocking a door to a home I could never return to.

I felt alive in the stolen moments, in the secret touches where we wrote promises on each other's skin we had no right to make. But I knew with absolute certainty, I'd be left fighting for my life when it all came crashing down.

The thrum of the music and the press of bodies at the bar came into sharper focus, and I missed him. The urge to see him, to feel him, was a pulse beneath my skin, and I braced myself against the bar as Maggie ordered another round, her voice cutting through the music and clamor of conversation.

"Why is it so packed in here tonight?" I asked her as I looked around. I don't think I've ever seen this place this busy.

"The fair starts tomorrow, and it always brings out all the riffraff."

My phone buzzed against the wood of the bar, rattling my empty shot glass, and I reached for it.

Colt: Never mind. I found you.

I froze, the words blurring on the screen as my breath caught, and anticipation thrummed through me. My head spun with it all —the ache, the wanting, the careless way I couldn't bring myself to care about the inevitable crash when I knew he was so close.

Slowly, I lifted my gaze, heart hammering as I scanned the bar. The crowd blurred into nothing as my eyes locked with his from across the room. A jolt of heat shot straight between my thighs and my nipples tightened painfully against the satin of my dress. My body recognized him before my mind could catch up, already aching, already his.

Colt looked like sin in a pair of worn jeans and a black button-down rolled to expose forearms corded with muscle. The top three buttons were undone, revealing a triangle of tanned skin and the base of his throat, which still bore marks I'd given him the night before. His tan cowboy hat cast shadows across his face, but it did nothing to shield me from his stare.

People parted for him, and every woman in the bar stopped what they were doing and their eyes followed the broad set of his shoulders. But he moved with singular focus until he stopped right in front of me. He was close enough that the toes of his boots pressed against mine, and the smell of his cologne made my stomach flip.

He said nothing, just let his gaze drag down my body with such deliberate slowness that heat bloomed across my skin wherever his eyes lingered. His jaw tightened, the muscle there flexing as he swallowed hard. When his eyes finally returned to mine, dark and possessive, every person in that bar knew exactly who I belonged to.

"Hey, Strawberry." His voice was rough, and my skin prickled with goosebumps that raced down my spine.

"What are you doing here?" I swallowed hard.

He leaned down, his lips brushing my ear as he spoke, the feel of his breath making my eyelids flutter closed. The brim of his hat grazed my temple, and all I could focus on was his rough stubble against my cheek and the rasp of his voice. "I dropped Ruby off at Mom's the second you sent that picture. She was excited for the impromptu sleepover, but she made me pinkie promise she'd see you at the fair tomorrow." His hand found my hip, fingers digging into the satin and cinching it higher. "You really thought I could sit at home thinking about you in this?"

His hand drifted lower, the heel of his palm settling against the hem of my dress, and his fingers dug into the bare skin of my thigh. I clutched at the bar for balance because every inch of my body wanted to lean into him, to let him press me to the sticky wood and start something that would get us both banned from The Dusty Spur for life.

"What?" I barely managed the word as his thumb hooked under the edge of the satin, tracing slow circles against the bare skin he found there, the motion so gentle it felt cruel.

"Wear whatever you want, Blaire." His teeth nipped at my earlobe, hard enough to make me gasp, but it was nothing compared to the burn behind his next words, spoken so low and dirty that I felt them more than I heard them. "But if you're going to walk around in something like this, with every bastard in here wishing you were his, then I want my cum running down your thighs when you do so."

I fought to stay upright as I felt every drop of blood in my body rush south, the pulse between my legs so hot and immediate I swore he could see it.

His thumb stroked over my skin again, making me jump. "You're driving me fuckin' crazy."

Then he took the smallest step back, and my chest heaved as I gulped for air like I'd been drowning. The bass from the speakers hammered in time with my pulse between my legs. Every nerve ending screamed for his touch, but I tore my gaze away from him and caught Maggie's wide-eyed stare, her lips parted in disbelief.

I registered the tiny smile that quirked on her lips as she tried and failed to look anywhere but between me and Colt. Beyond her, Hunter and McCoy were leaning against the bar, the former smirking openly and the latter pretending to have a sudden, fascinated interest in the shelves of whiskey. I hadn't even noticed them come in.

But the real realization hit me as I looked past them and noticed the entire damn bar staring at us with shameless curiosity. I knew what I looked like. I knew they'd seen me shaking and breathless, dress rucked high, and body screaming for the man who they'd all watched break my heart once before.

Colt's voice crashed through the noise around us, low and certain, and it reeled me in like a hook in my ribs. "You want to dance?"

His hand hovered at my waist, not quite touching me, but so close I could feel the heat radiate through the thin sheen of satin. I felt the potential of that contact burning brighter than all the neon overhead, brighter than the eyes of everyone in the bar that tracked us.

"Yeah." I nodded, slipping my hand in his.

His thumb stroked the inside of my wrist as we started moving through the crowd. He didn't rush, didn't push. His body shielded mine as he led me, and I let myself fall into step behind him as if there was no other place for me to be.

Colt led us to the edge of the dance floor, where the lights dropped lower and the sound system vibrated through my body, and he pulled me in a half circle until I was facing him, the crowd swallowing us in their periphery.

He paused, studying me with an intensity that made me want to squirm. He was cataloging everything. The flush in my cheeks, the way my breath stuttered, the rigidness in my stance. His lips curled slow and wicked as he pulled me into him, pressing my body firmly against his. "I really do love this dress," he said roughly.

I felt like I was coming out of my skin as he lifted my hands and let them fall against his shoulders. "You know everyone is watching us, right?" I whispered, as his hands settled on my hips.

"Let 'em watch." He drew me impossibly closer, one hand moving to splay between my shoulder blades, and suddenly it was just the two of us in the amber light, his body hard against mine, and the music a dull roar beneath the pounding of my heart.

Colt was slow and careful, his hands firm as he guided me in a lazy two-step. Every movement was hell-bent on making me feel his body and his intent, the solid muscle under his shirt, the heat of him where our thighs brushed. It was less a dance and more a declaration, and every time I blinked, I saw the years unspooling behind his eyes—the ache, the regret, the need.

We said nothing as we danced, then the song shifted to something slower, and Colt's grip on me changed. He let his hand move lower, tracing the curve of my spine, his palm flattening over the small of my back. Our hips lined up, and it hit me that the only thing keeping me from melting into him was my own stubborn pride.

I lifted my chin and caught his eyes, dark and stormy under the brim of his hat. "We shouldn't do this."

He smiled, teeth flashing. "We already are," he said, and spun me before his arm banded tight around my waist so I landed flush against his chest. A gasp poured from my lungs as he dipped me low. He held me there for only a second as I giggled, and I felt so unlike the girl who'd sworn she would never let Colt Calloway break her heart again.

All I could see was him, the way his hair curled at the nape of his neck and that tiny little scar on his jaw. All I could remember was what it was like to trust the steady and unyielding way he held me, as if I was the only thing in the world that could break him.

That feeling terrified me, right down to the soles of my boots. It was reckless. I was spinning out, fast and wild, and I knew I should dig my heels in, pull away before we caught fire and burned us both clean through.

But he pulled me upright, lifted my feet from the ground as he pinned me to his chest, and all I could do was smile. His breath fanned out over my neck, and my eyes fluttered closed.

"I missed you. All damn day."

I wanted to tell him I'd missed him too, that I spent every minute since our last touch thinking about the next one. But I turned my head, letting the brim of his hat shadow my face from the rest of the world, and whispered, "You saw me this morning."

He laughed, and it was so warm that I found myself searching his blue eyes. "Yeah." He nodded. "But it wasn't enough."

The song shifted to something with a faster beat, drawing bodies to the dance floor like moths to a flame. Colt's fingers tightened around mine as dancers swirled around us, and I stumbled forward, my balance betrayed by the alcohol in my blood and the anticipation in my veins mixing with something far more dangerous.

A cowboy in a pearl-snap shirt whirled his partner past us, nearly knocking into us, and Colt's hand shot out to steady me, his grip firm on my elbow. When our eyes met, the naked want in his gaze burned through me.

"You wanna get out of here?" he asked, his voice rough, but I caught sight of Maggie's arm flailing above the crowd.

"We're being beckoned," I said, nodding toward the back table where she sat with the boys.

Colt's jaw tightened as he glanced over. "Damn it," he

muttered, but his hand found the small of my back as he guided me toward them. Colt didn't slow as people glanced up at us as we passed. He tightened his grip on me until we finally reached the back corner.

I slid into the booth beside Maggie, and Colt dropped into the seat on my other side, close enough that his thigh pressed against mine. He sprawled back, arm resting along the top of the booth behind me.

Across from us, McCoy and Hunter had claimed the other side of the booth for themselves, and twin grins cut across their faces as they watched us. McCoy clinked his whiskey glass against the tabletop and shot me a wry salute. "Well, hello there, Blaire. You didn't even say hi to us before you ran off to the dance floor with Colt."

Maggie slid a glass in front of me, her eyes saying everything her mouth didn't need to.

I took the shot Maggie offered and tossed it back, grateful for the burn as they stared at me. "Hi, McCoy," I said, then swung my gaze to Hunter. "Hi, Hunter."

A grin lit up Hunter's face as he leaned forward to get a better look at me. "Damn, Blaire," he drawled. "You look hot tonight." His brown eyes sparkled with a mischief I'd always loved about him. "Don't you think it's about time you gave the other Calloway brother a chance?"

There was a dull thwack beneath the table, followed by a yelp. Hunter jerked upright, his beer sloshing over the rim of his glass. "Ow! Jesus, Colt. What the fuck?"

Colt only grunted, his expression unrepentant. "Don't talk to her like that." His hand moved from the back of the booth to rest firmly on my knee under the table. My breath stuttered at the possessive heat of it, and I wondered if the others could see how I tensed, how every nerve in my thigh was suddenly tuned to the movement of his thumb on my skin.

Hunter sucked his teeth, squinting at me and then at Colt, before his face broke into a wolfish smile. "I'm just speaking the truth. She looks hot."

McCoy, who had been watching the exchange with slow amusement, cut in smoothly. "They both do," he said, tipping his head in Maggie's direction. "Hell, what was the plan here, ladies? Make every man swallow their tongues when you walked in?"

Maggie laughed as she bumped her shoulder into mine, and Hunter paused with his glass almost to his mouth, his gaze lingering on Maggie like he was memorizing the weight of her laughter. I'd never seen him look at anyone like that. Hunter was a shameless flirt, but this was different, more focused, suddenly unsure.

I couldn't help it. I needed to push back against him as I watched the way he stared at my friend. "Well, we did toast to bringing the Calloway brothers to their knees when we got here," I said with an innocent shrug, and Maggie snorted into her drink.

Colt's grip on my knee tightened, his hand sliding just a hair higher, and I felt the warning in it as much as the promise.

But it was Hunter who zeroed in on the challenge, his jaw tightening as he leaned across the table. "You may have my brother walking around like some pussy-induced zombie, but I don't fall so easily."

McCoy nearly lost his drink, choking on a laugh.

"Oh, honey. I've known you a long time," I said as I looked away from Hunter to Maggie, then back. I reached for Hunter's beer without breaking eye contact, and his jaw flexed as I pulled it toward me. But he didn't stop me as I took a long, slow sip, then set it back down in front of him. "I'd put my money on it."

McCoy was still laughing at the exchange, his shoulders shaking in silent amusement, but Hunter turned to Maggie and his normal bravado withered into something else as they stared at one another. The shift was so obvious even McCoy noticed it, his smile morphing into genuine curiosity as he watched the two of them.

Color bloomed on Maggie's cheekbones, and she brought her drink back to her lips as she looked away from him. Hunter blinked, shook himself out of whatever stupor he'd wandered into, and smirked in a way that was pure damage control.

But I barely registered it because Colt's hand had abandoned all pretense of subtlety and slid higher on my thigh, his intent torching straight through me. He squeezed, not hard, but with the easy authority of a man who knew exactly how to handle a wild thing, and everything in me went bright and tight and wordless. I leaned into him, feeling the way he canted his hips slightly to put his mouth close to my ear.

"Behave." Colt growled the warning, and the command in it made me desperate to shift in my seat.

I angled my head, met his stare, and let him see every ounce of dare in my blood. "Make me."

He squeezed my leg, hard enough that I almost moaned, but I bit down on my lip instead. The weight of Colt's hand, the closeness of his body, the way his words slid through me— I wanted it, needed it, and I wanted to push back until he lost control.

I opened my mouth to say something else, to bait him until he had no choice but to pull me from this table and put me in my place, but Maggie blurted, "I need to go to the bathroom."

Colt let out a slow exhale as I looked over at Maggie. Her gaze held mine, a silent SOS I knew by heart.

"I'll come with," I said, and Colt let his hand trail down my leg before he stood to let us out.

I could feel him watching us even though I didn't turn around, and Maggie waited until the bathroom door closed behind us, before she faced me, her voice barely a whisper and her eyes panicked.

"What's going on?" I asked, walking closer to her hesitantly. "Should I have not said what I said? I was joking."

"I almost slept with Hunter." The words tumbled from her lips, and she pressed her palm to her mouth as if she could stuff the secret back down her throat. "Holy shit. I can't believe I said that out loud." She stared at me, eyes pleading.

"Okay." I nodded. I wanted to say something to make it better, but Maggie had barely told me anything when it came to her and Hunter. "It's okay."

"It is not okay." She shook her head and moved to the sink.

She ran her hands under the cold water before pressing them to her neck, as if she could cool the heat of her shame. "He is my sister's ex, Blaire." She looked up at me in the mirror with big, haunted eyes. "It's not just that I almost slept with him. I wanted to. I still want to, and I can't."

"Okay." I stepped closer to her. "Why don't we get out of here? We can go back to your apartment and binge some movies. We can stop on the way there and get us both a tub of icing to eat our feelings."

She laughed as she straightened and turned off the tap. "No." She shook her head. "Colt would kill me if I stole you away tonight."

"Colt will be fine." I shrugged, and I meant it. As desperately as I wanted to go with him, I would leave right now with her.

"No." She shook her head again before she fixed her lipstick in the mirror. "I'm going to go back out there. I can't avoid him forever, and I don't want him to think I left because of him."

Maggie exhaled and reached for the paper towels. She tore off three, dabbed at her neck, and tried to piece herself back together. "I— I needed to get that off my chest," she said. "In case I do something stupid."

I twisted my fingers against my lips as if I were locking them with a key. "Your secret dies with me."

"And yours with me." She laughed as she reached for the door.

"Yeah. I don't think I'm doing a very good job keeping it a secret."

We both laughed, but the second we stepped out the door, we froze. Colt stood against the opposite wall, one boot propped behind him, arms crossed over his chest. His hat was tipped low, but it was impossible to miss the way his eyes were already on me.

"Excuse me, Maggie," he said, but his eyes never left mine. "I'm going to need to borrow your friend."

"All yours," Maggie murmured, slipping past him before she glanced back at me.

Her footsteps faded down the hallway, and the air between Colt and me thickened until each breath felt difficult to draw in.

His jaw tightened as he pushed off the wall, one slow step after another, until the heat of him radiated against my skin. I retreated until my back pressed against the bathroom door I'd just come through, the cool metal a shock against my feverish body.

The corner of his mouth lifted in a smile that promised both pleasure and punishment, and my pulse hammered wildly at the base of my throat where his gaze now lingered.

"What are you doing?" I asked as my eyes searched his.

"You told me to make you behave." He braced his hand on the doorframe above me. "So, I'm going to."

CHAPTER 28
BLAIRE

His fingers dug into the nape of my neck as he shoved the bathroom door open and hauled me inside. The door slammed shut, cutting off the bar noise and leaving only my thundering pulse in my ears and the rasp of his breathing.

He clicked the lock before his gaze turned back to me, and I stumbled backward.

"Colt, you're insane. We can't—" My ass hit the counter, and I grabbed the edge with both hands as he stalked toward me.

He caught my jaw, his callused thumb dragging across my bottom lip hard enough to make me whimper. "The hell we can't." His voice lacked his normal control as his grip slid down my throat while his other hand clamped around my hip. His fingers blazed a path from my neck to my collarbone before hooking beneath the thin strap of my dress.

He yanked it down my arm until my bare breast was exposed to the cool air. The groan that tore from his throat was almost unrecognizable as he cupped my breast in his rough palm, fingers digging into soft flesh.

I shuddered when his other hand gripped my waist, fingers twisting into the delicate fabric of my dress. The satin bunched between his knuckles, the hem climbing my thighs as his head dipped low. His breath was a hot caress against my exposed skin before his mouth found me. His tongue circled my nipple before drawing it between his teeth with devastating precision.

"Oh God." My head fell back as his mouth drew a long, desperate moan from my lips. Each flick of his tongue, every greedy tug of his lips, was stoking a fire in my belly until the wetness between my thighs became a slick, unignorable ache.

Colt lifted his head, breathing harshly through his nose, and he spun me around with a force that had me gasping. My palms slapped the counter, and I steadied myself, catching my own startled expression in the mirror.

And behind me, Colt looked like some kind of fucking god.

His hands closed over my hips, so damn big they nearly spanned my waist, and he held me flush to the counter until I could feel every hard ridge of him against my ass. "Look at you," he ground out as his gaze traveled down my back. His eyes met mine in the mirror, pupils blown wide with hunger. "Look at us."

I stared into the mirror, breath catching as his thumb traced slow circles on my hipbone. My dress fell from one shoulder, one breast exposed while the other strained against the fabric that suddenly felt too tight. There was a wild, desperate look in my eyes I hardly recognized.

His fingers dug into my dress, the satin crumpling in his fists, and he hauled it up inch by excruciating inch until it bunched around my waist. I felt the cool air kiss my exposed skin, felt his eyes burning into me before I heard his sharp inhale. The scrap of black lace I'd worn tonight was all that stood between us now. His palms glided up the backs of my thighs before they found my ass. His fingers pressed into my flesh before he slowly spread me open for him.

The first slap to my ass was so unexpected I gasped, more from surprise than pain, and my knees nearly gave out from under me. I'd never let anyone touch me like that, never thought I'd want it, but the sting bloomed across my skin, sharp and hot, before it ebbed into a low ache that radiated through my body like a fever.

Before I could process that he'd done it, he did it again. A second, harder blow this time before his hand instantly smoothed over the sting he'd left behind. The paradox of pain and comfort made my breath hitch, and I heard a noise from my own lips that I'd never made before, strangled and shocked and wanting.

"Jesus, Colt," I hissed, but my voice came out thin and needy.

He leaned in close, the length of him pressed against my back, his palm spanning my ribs as his mouth hovered at my ear. I felt the hard scrape of his teeth before he let out a little laugh and his gaze met mine in the mirror. "You want to behave, darlin', or are you going to keep acting like a little brat?" His drawl was rough and so low it vibrated through both of us, the words a dare and a promise and a threat.

I could see everything in the mirror, every humiliating and exhilarating detail. There was an angry flush that crept up my chest, my nipples stood out hard and aching against the air and my dress, and my lips parted around a whimper. Colt's hat was still on his head, low over his brow, his jaw flexed and eyes wild. He looked almost feral as he stared at me.

"Come on, Strawberry," he murmured against my skin as his eyes fluttered closed and he breathed me in. "What's it going to be?"

I wanted to fire back something smart, something to put him in his place, but instead, I breathed, "I'm going to be a brat."

His eyes shot open, his gaze meeting and holding mine in the mirror as one of his hands ran along my scalp before he fisted my hair. He pulled my head back, baring my throat, as he grinned.

"There's my girl."

The words hit harder than his hand.

His hand twisted deep into my hair until my scalp prickled, and he pulled my head back until I had no choice but to see my own reflection. I was panting, feral, and unrecognizable. The woman in the mirror wasn't the polished, proper version I'd crafted for men like Grant. I couldn't look away from this wild, unmasked version of myself, couldn't hide from the naked hunger in my eyes that matched Colt's. The sight stripped me bare in a way no physical nakedness ever could.

It should have thrilled me, but it scared the living hell out of me instead. I watched as I crumbled for him, watched every trace of good sense bleed out of me until nothing was left but pure need.

Colt pressed me into the edge of the sink until the cheap laminate bit into my hipbones. His hand stayed locked in my hair, keeping my face turned to the mirror and forcing me to look. The other hand slid around my waist, his palm spreading wide and flat across my stomach.

He pulled me into him, until I could feel the hard line of his cock against my ass, then he dragged his hand lower. His fingers trailed over the thin lace covering my pussy, and his touch was featherlight. It was so gentle I whimpered in frustration, and my hips jerked forward, chasing more pressure.

He pressed his hand hard against me, forcing my hips back to where he wanted them, and he tsked. His knuckles pressed hard against my thigh as his thumb caught the top of my panties and yanked them down to my knees in one hard jerk.

I made a pleading sound as he kicked my feet apart with one of his boots between mine, spreading me wider, then his hand moved between my legs. His fingers didn't move for an endless, punishing second. They just rested there, the pad of his index finger barely grazing my slickness. I held my breath, unsure if I was more afraid he'd move or that he wouldn't, and my face in the mirror twisted with the effort of not begging him out loud.

His eyes burned into mine, and the corner of his mouth curled up in a way that made my stomach drop. His finger brushed against me, so light I might have dreamed it, and my legs quivered beneath me. The gentleness was worse than any roughness could have been. My resolve crumbled with each barely-there touch, my earlier defiance dissolving into desperation.

"Fuck," I whispered, my voice breaking as I shivered against him.

His fingers moved then, and his smile was infuriating as he slid two thick fingers through my wetness, pressing them hard against my clit. My hips bucked against his hand, the counter edge cutting into my skin as a raw moan tore from my throat.

"Colt," I gasped as his fingers came down against my pussy with a gentle slap.

He ground his hips into my ass, making it impossible to ignore the thick, desperate evidence of how hard he was. The sight of him watching me so intently while he was coming apart himself made something inside me snap. I wanted to be ruined by him. I wanted him to see me until there was no part of me left that didn't belong to him.

And that scared the shit out of me. I wanted to run. I wanted to stay.

His thumb circled my clit, gently at first, then harder as he slid two fingers inside me. I was shaking, my hands slipping on the counter, my breath coming in frantic pants.

"Good girl." He leaned in, his mouth brushing my ear. "Do you want to beg me yet?"

The words sparked something in me I didn't want him to see. I tried to wrestle out of his hold, but he pressed me down harder, bending me over until my cheek nearly touched the counter.

"I hate you," I said harshly, because it was easier than admitting the truth.

He chuckled, low in his throat, and the sound traveled through his chest and into my back. "No, you don't." His teeth grazed the side of my throat. "You could never hate me."

His fingers were still working inside me, each thrust slower and more measured until it bordered on excruciating. His thumb was now featherlight, skimming over my clit with a restraint that made me ache in places I didn't know I could. He just watched me, his gaze fixing on me in the mirror, on the way my body shuddered beneath his touch. Then he leaned up and traced his other hand down the length of my spine.

I bucked against him, furious at how desperate I was. I wanted to blame the alcohol, but the truth was, I'd never wanted anyone the way I wanted Colt.

I closed my eyes as his hand wrapped around me and splayed

against my stomach, and he lifted me until the brim of his hat brushed my hair. His other hand didn't stop its assault as his words hit me. "I thought about you every goddamn day you were gone."

My eyes snapped to his, and neither of us breathed. He pressed his fingers deeper inside me, and I cried out.

His thumb pressed hard against my clit, and my orgasm gathered fast, right at the edge. "Fuck, Colt—"

His thumb vanished as the first wave hit, leaving me gasping until I nearly sobbed.

"You want something?" His eyes in the mirror were stripped of arrogance and replaced with something darker. "Ask. Nicely."

I tried to fight it, but my hips betrayed me, grinding desperately against his hand, chasing the release he dangled just beyond my reach. When his fingers stilled completely, I whimpered.

"Please." The word ripped from me, and I didn't care how needy I sounded.

He plunged his fingers back inside me, curling them with devastating precision while his palm crushed against my swollen flesh. He played my body like he owned it, drawing out each sensation until stars exploded behind my eyes and my lungs burned for air.

Sweat slicked his forearm where it pinned me like steel against the counter. My pulse hammered violently in my throat, in my chest, in my pussy. His breath came in harsh pants against my neck, hot as a brand.

"You fucking love being bad for me, don't you?" he growled, teeth grazing my earlobe.

"Yes." The admission came so easily.

His fingers never stopped their assault as he tore my panties completely off with his free hand, the fabric giving way with a sharp rip. He kicked my legs so wide I nearly lost balance.

The metallic rasp of his belt and zipper cut through my fog. I watched him in the mirror as he freed himself, his cock thick as he positioned himself behind me.

He withdrew his fingers and pressed his cock against me, the heat of him searing my skin as he rocked against my entrance, the promise of what was coming making my legs shake violently beneath me.

He let me squirm, let the anticipation stretch, and then in one rough motion he filled me, hard enough the counter bit into my hipbones. I gasped for air as my body stretched to accommodate him.

He froze, buried to the hilt, his grip bruising my hip while his other hand fisted a handful of my hair until my scalp burned. Every nerve ending in my body screamed with the dual sensations of pain and pleasure so intertwined I couldn't separate them. But it wasn't just my body unraveling. It was my mind, my defenses, everything I'd sworn I'd never give him again.

In the mirror, I saw how my body arched, shivered, and was fully possessed by the man above me.

"Look at us, Blaire," he commanded. "Look at how I can't stop needing you."

I couldn't look away if I wanted to.

He started to move, each thrust driving deeper than the last, and I watched my expression contort, my lips parting in silent pleas. His fingers dug into my hip as he slammed into me with enough force that the mirror rattled against the wall.

"Fuck, you're beautiful," he growled, and I tried to turn away.

His hand pulled my head back, forcing me to witness our collision in the mirror. He fucked me like he was trying to carve himself into my body, and the bathroom filled with the brutal sounds of flesh meeting flesh, my whimpers, his grunts, until nothing existed but this—us.

"Tell me this pussy is mine, Blaire. I need to hear it." His voice cracked with raw desperation.

I opened my mouth just as the door jolted. The cheap lock rattled in protest and threatened to give way as someone banged against it.

"Hello!" The pounding came again.

"Tell me," he growled against my ear, his voice dropping to a feral whisper. His hips never faltered, each thrust driving deeper, harder.

"It's yours," I gasped.

He snarled a curse through clenched teeth, and I watched his eyes go black with possession. He reached down, his fingers finding my clit, and my orgasm hit like lightning. It seared through every bit of me, and I couldn't stop the scream that tore from my throat.

"That's it, baby. Let them hear who it belongs to." He drove into me with a punishing force as he chased his release. When he came, his entire body went rigid, fingers digging so deep I knew I'd wear his fingerprints for days. His groan vibrated through my spine as he pulsed inside me.

We collapsed forward, chests heaving, and my hair clinging to my sweat-dampened cheeks. My body still convulsed with aftershocks, and I knew something fundamental had shifted between us, something we couldn't take back.

I looked up and caught my own reflection in the mirror. And for the first time in a long time, I saw her. The girl I'd abandoned when I left this town was staring right back at me.

CHAPTER 29

BLAIRE

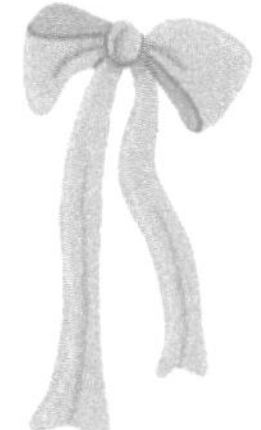

It was the hottest day we'd had since I'd been back, and I almost forgot how hot Tennessee could get as spring faded into summer. The end of spring also meant the end of strawberry season, but there was still so much work to do around the farm and for our new jam business. Even though my crazy grandmother swears it's all mine.

Under our booth tent, a hand-painted banner read June's Jams in pink script, ringed with strawberries, cherries, and raspberries and little green ribbons. Ruby helped me make it, and I couldn't help grinning at all the little smiley faces she'd added to the fruit.

Sweat trickled down the back of my neck as I stared out at the fairgrounds, but it wasn't just the heat that made me fidget. I shifted on my feet, leaning my hip against the booth while June handed a customer her change.

My body still thrummed with the memory of last night. I couldn't stop thinking about Colt's hands on me or his voice when he said he'd thought about me every day since I'd been gone. Last night hadn't felt casual, not like the stolen hours when we pretended it was only heat, but that was the problem with Colt. Even when I needed things simple, even when we both swore it

311

would be, his touch always felt like a promise neither of us had the right to make.

Because even when I told myself I no longer loved Colt Calloway, my heart beat like a liar the moment he touched me.

The hope that filled me at the possibility was a physical ache beneath my ribs, and it scared me more than anything else. With every brush of his skin against mine, the careful boundaries I had between desire and good sense crumbled a little more.

I smoothed a June's Jams sticker over one of the kraft bags and straightened the ribbon. The fairground smelled exactly like it did when I was a child, with sugar spun into cotton candy and funnel cakes frying a few booths away from us.

For years, Willow Grove's Annual Spring Fair had been our ritual. Mama would braid my hair tight so it didn't tangle in the Tilt-A-Whirl. June would bring extra napkins in her purse for when we finally made it to the funnel cake, and we'd laugh as the three of us ran all over the place, discovering what was next.

Later came summers with the boys, all of us stumbling off the Graviton we'd ridden three times in a row and laughing when Hunter threw up in a trash can. Then there was that last summer, when Colt took me by the hand and led me behind the Ferris wheel. That damn wheel kept turning like nothing had changed, and one glance at it and I could taste the sticky sweetness of caramel apples mingling with his mouth on mine all over again.

A steady stream of familiar faces stopped by our booth, each one armed with similar questions. "How are you, darlin'?" "Are you home for good?" "June wouldn't let you name her jams after you?" Their voices blended together after a while, a chorus of curiosity I deflected with warm smiles and vague answers. All the while, June studied me from behind her cash box, her eyes not missing a thing.

Only Mrs. Lee brought up Colt. She used to run a small boutique on Main before she retired, and now she spent her time gossiping at the beauty shop and playing bingo with June. Her eyes lit up when she mentioned our "unfortunate" water leak and how I'd landed myself under the same roof as "Willow Grove's most eligible cowboy."

I laughed. "Only temporarily. Repairs are underway, and we should be back at the farmhouse in a couple weeks."

My cheeks burned, but I steered the conversation to Ruby instead, keeping my voice light as I talked about her. Mrs. Lee patted my hand before she winked at June and tottered off with a large bag stamped with our new logo.

June's eyes cut to me, and she didn't bother with the polite smiles everyone else had offered all day. "You're not fooling me, sugar."

I looked up at her nervously. "What do you mean?"

June leaned across the table, closing the cash box with a decisive click, giving me that look she reserved for when she already knew the answer and wanted to see if I'd lie.

"You've been dreamy-eyed all day, and you almost jumped out of your skin when Mrs. Lee brought up Colt's name. Anyone with half a brain can see you've been knocking boots with a certain Calloway who moves like he was born in a saddle." She wiggled her eyebrows, and I couldn't help the laugh that escaped me.

"June!" I glanced nervously at the customer approaching our booth.

But she kept right on going. "Do you know how many years I've watched that man lose his sense over you, Blaire? I watched it when y'all were kids, and I'm watching it all over again."

"There's nothing going on," I lied, but heat crawled up my neck and my fingers kept fidgeting with the red-and-white checkered tablecloth, brushing away invisible crumbs. "He has Ruby. My life's a mess, and—"

"And he could help you fix it if you gave him half a chance," she huffed. "If I were your age, I'd climb him like the last ladder out of hell."

"June Wilma Cates!" I hissed through clenched teeth, but my scandalized tone betrayed me by the laughter bubbling up my throat.

"Blaire Wilma Monroe!" she mimicked, hands on her hips.

"These old eyes still work just fine, and they see exactly how that man watches you."

My smile vanished.

"We're just having fun," I protested, but the only thing going through my head was *lie, lie, lie.*

"Sure, sugar." June's eyebrows arched knowingly. "And I suppose that's why you've both spent the last ten years looking like heartbroken fools. I'm sure y'all can just bump uglies, and there won't be a single feeling involved." She let out a dramatic sigh and shook her head. "Lord, you two can pretend all you want, but bodies don't lie, even when mouths do."

I tried to focus on arranging the rows of strawberry preserves and treats, but her words clung to the inside of my skull, sticky as sap. My body sure as hell hadn't lied last night.

June watched me before she turned her gaze to a man browsing jams only a few feet away. "You've loved that boy your whole damn life," she said, softer now, picking up a basket of berries and straightening it with unnecessary care. "I don't think you'll ever stop loving him."

The words hung between us, and I didn't have the guts to answer her. But I could feel every syllable sink straight into my rib cage. If we'd been alone, maybe I'd have confessed. Maybe I'd have told her how scared I was that she was right, that there'd never be anyone else for me. That there never had been, never would be.

But the fair was bustling with nosy neighbors and customers, and I bit my tongue against the truth. I smiled at a woman who asked about prices while my heart hammered traitorously in my chest. My eyes betrayed me every few seconds, scanning the fairgrounds for him even as I silently scolded myself for looking. I didn't want to need him. I shouldn't want to need him. Yet there I was, counting the seconds between each desperate glance toward the crowd.

This thing between us was supposed to be simple, but nothing about loving Colt had ever been. The first time he kissed me, I'd been barely seventeen years old and knew in my marrow there'd never be another person who could make me feel like that again, and I'd resented him for it.

Because Colt owned a piece of me I could never take back, no matter how hard I tried.

The way Grant had touched me felt like static compared to the way Colt could burn me right through my skin, but at least with Grant I'd been able to breathe, to think.

Even after all the years I'd spent building a careful, grown-up life that should have erased Colt, I caught myself ordering pancakes at the country club with strawberries and honey drizzled on top, the way he ate his. Then hated myself for the habit I couldn't break. The scent of freshly cut grass would transport me to those July nights we spent out by the lake staring at the sky as we both danced around our feelings for the other—nights I'd spent trying to forget.

I'd convinced myself I could handle it now, that I was immune to Colt Calloway, but that was a stupid, dangerous lie.

Tonight was supposed to be easy. Just me selling strawberries at a fair booth like I'd done dozens of times before. But my skin was electric with anticipation as my eyes frantically scanned the fairground for any glimpse of him. I told myself I was looking for Ruby, due at our booth any minute, but that lie tasted bitter on my tongue. Every cowboy hat in the distance made my breath catch, and every broad-shouldered silhouette sent heat flooding through me.

There were countless cowboys roaming around, but none with his unmistakable swagger. I'd know him anywhere, and that was the problem. I couldn't stop looking, couldn't stop wanting, couldn't stop the flutter in my stomach every time I thought I spotted him.

"Blaire Monroe? Well, I'll be damned."

I turned toward the sound, nearly dropping a pint of berries as I blinked up at the man in front of me.

"Danny Watson?"

He'd been a year ahead of Colt, McCoy, and me in school, and he was known back then for being the best running back in three counties. At our graduation party, he'd danced on Colt's tailgate in nothing but boxers and cowboy boots as he sang a drunken rendition of "All My Ex's Live in Texas." But he was all grown up now. He'd traded in his shaggy blond hair for a short fade and a sharp jaw.

"Damn, it's really you." He smiled. "Heard you were back in town, but didn't believe it."

"It's me," I said with a shrug.

He stepped closer into the booth, leaning in with that same cocky charm I remembered. "You look great," he said as his eyes roamed over me. "I never thought you'd come back. Did Raleigh lose its appeal?"

I laughed and wiped my hands on my shorts. "Something like that."

His gaze moved to my mouth for the smallest moment before he met my eyes again. "You staying long?"

I hesitated then flicked my eyes back to June, who had suddenly busied herself with counting the rest of our stock. "For a while. I'm helping out with the farm."

He leaned closer to me, and his cologne, something woodsy and expensive that hadn't been part of his high school arsenal, drifted between us as he braced one hand on the edge of the table. "I'd love to take you to dinner sometime."

A flush crept up my neck as his smile hit me with the full force of that old high school charm. He had always been such a flirt.

My mind scrambled for a gentle rejection, but I only managed a single breathless word. "Dinner?"

"Yeah." His smile softened as he nodded, his eyes not leaving mine. "There's this new place in Belmont. Or, I mean, we could grab a drink." He ran his hand over his hair even though it was already perfectly in place. "Whatever works for you."

I was about to answer him when movement caught my eye, and the words died in my throat. My pulse stuttered as Colt cut through the crowd with Ruby on his shoulders. There was a paper crown tilted precariously on her head and a giant bag of cotton candy clutched in her small fist. Lou walked alongside them, her mouth curved in exasperation at whatever her granddaughter had said.

My mouth went dry as they moved closer. Colt wore a baseball hat pulled low. He wore a sleeveless T-shirt with the sides cut low, revealing arms carved from years of ranch work and offering a glimpse of obliques that made my fingertips burn with the memory of tracing them. His thighs strained against worn denim as he made his way to me, and there was something lethal about how he moved tonight. He had a predatory ease that hit me low in my belly and spread to places that had no business aching in public.

His eyes found mine, and something in them shifted. His jaw locked, a muscle twitching beneath stubbled skin as his gaze flicked to Danny then back to me. A flicker of something dangerous and possessive crossed Colt's face, turning those familiar eyes into storm clouds.

The cowboy was jealous.

"Blaire?" Danny's voice caught my attention, and I blinked back up at him.

"What?"

"Do you want to let me know or—" Danny's words trailed off as he followed my gaze.

Ruby's squeal pierced the air as she scrambled down from Colt's shoulders so fast he had to grab her ankle to keep her from falling headfirst. The second her feet hit the grass, she raced toward me.

"Blaire!" She collided with my legs and her arms wrapped around my waist. I staggered back, laughing, just as Colt stepped up to the booth.

"Watson," Colt said flatly as he nodded his head to the man without sparing him a glance.

Danny straightened, suddenly less sure of himself. "Colt, how are you?"

Colt lifted the bill of his hat with one finger, tilting it back enough that I could see the full force of his stare burning into me. "Better now."

Ruby tugged at my hand, oblivious to the tension, while Lou gave Colt a sharp warning look. Colt smirked at his mother before his gaze slid back to me. His eyes raked over me so slowly and with such raw hunger that my skin prickled and blood rushed to every place his gaze lingered.

"Wait. Are you two back together?" Danny asked, and his question shot up my spine.

I could feel both June and Lou watching us as I opened my mouth to deny it, but Colt answered before I could.

"She sleeps in my bed every night, Watson." His eyes burned into mine as he said it. "You tell me what that means."

My skin flushed hot, my pulse hammering so hard I could feel it in my fingertips. I forced out a laugh that caught in my throat. "He means the guest room."

Colt's mouth curved into a slow, dangerous smile, and his eyes darkened to a midnight blue as he cocked his head. "Do I?"

A muffled laugh escaped June behind me, and when I glanced at Lou, she was examining a jar of jam with intense interest, lips pressed together to hide her smile.

Colt moved in, crowding my space until the scent of his cologne wrapped around me. "June, do you mind if we steal Blaire for a while?"

June's eyes flicked between us, bright with amusement. "By all means. Lou and I can manage here."

I hesitantly looked back at the booth, but June rolled her eyes at me.

"Lou and I aren't going to wreck your new business within a few hours. Go have fun."

Colt's gaze sliced back to Danny, all pretense of civility gone. "You don't mind, do you? Me and my girls have plans."

My girls.

My heart stuttered. The words were so simple, and I wanted to laugh them off, but I couldn't. Part of me ached to lean into them, to be his girl again, while another part screamed to run before I got hurt.

Ruby's fingers tightened around mine, her small hand insistent as she dragged me from the booth. I stumbled slightly before finding my footing at Colt's side.

Danny's smile didn't reach his eyes as he backed away a step. "Message received, loud and clear," he said with a forced chuckle. "Rain check on that dinner, Blaire."

I offered him a smile as Colt pressed against me, the hard ridge of his belt buckle claiming territory against my side, and his body heat searing through my clothes. His hand spread wide across the small of my back, his thumb digging into my spine with such possessive pressure as he nudged me forward.

My breath caught as he bent down, his mustache tickling my sensitive skin as his lips brushed the shell of my ear. "Over my dead body," he growled, the vibration of his voice shooting straight down my spine, loud enough that Danny couldn't possibly miss it. His eyes locked with Danny's and he grinned.

"Have fun, Watson."

CHAPTER 30
BLAIRE

We spent hours following Ruby from one ride to the next, our stomachs full of fair food. Hunter and McCoy had joined us shortly after leaving June's booth, and I'd felt on edge all night as I played with Ruby and tried to ignore her dad. Now Ruby struggled under the weight of a stuffed bear that was bigger than she was, but she dragged it along with pride, refusing to let Colt help her.

"That thing is not coming home with us," Colt muttered, eyeing the bear. "We'll send it to your uncle Hunter's."

Hunter nudged his brother's shoulder. "Ruby, sweetheart, your daddy's just jealous because I knocked down those bottles first try while he wasted fifteen bucks."

Colt's jaw tightened, and I bit back a smile.

Hunter wasn't wrong. After watching Colt mutter profanities with each missed shot, Hunter sauntered up, knocked down all the bottles on his first try, and claimed the bear Colt had been trying to win for Ruby. The muscle in Colt's jaw hadn't stopped twitching since.

Ruby hugged the bear tighter against her chest, and Colt rolled his eyes.

"Let's go on the Ferris wheel, Ruby," McCoy said, reaching

for her small hand. "You and me in one car, and Hunter can babysit your bear since he doesn't have a date."

Hunter rolled his eyes. "Rich, coming from someone who also didn't come with a date."

Ruby hoisted the bear tighter against her and looked over its head at me with concern. "What about Blaire?"

"Don't worry about Blaire," Colt said, wrapping his arm around my shoulders and drawing me against him. "She's with me."

I caught three different expressions aimed my way—Hunter's raised eyebrow, McCoy's knowing smirk, and Ruby's wide smile.

"She's with you, huh?" McCoy teased.

Colt shook his head. "Shut up and go before we lose our place in line."

Ruby skipped ahead, and as soon as she fixed her gaze on the towering Ferris wheel, I drove my elbow into Colt's side.

He jerked away with a laugh, rubbing at his exposed ribs. "What was that for?"

"You know exactly what that was for," I said quietly as we approached the Ferris wheel's entrance.

Ruby scrambled into the waiting car, legs swinging freely beneath her. McCoy settled beside her, his arm curling protectively around her small shoulders as he pulled her close. When the attendant pushed the safety bar down with a metallic thunk, Ruby let out a delighted squeal and clutched the bar with both hands.

"Be good and listen to uncle Coy," Colt called out as their car jerked backward and began its ascent.

Hunter claimed the next car, wrestling the oversized bear into the seat beside him. When he caught us watching and laughing, he shot us an annoyed grin before raising his middle fingers as the ride whisked him upward.

I stepped into our car, the metal floor swaying beneath my feet. Colt followed, his shoulder brushing mine as we settled in. The attendant secured our bar with a practiced push, and our car rocked. I tilted my head back, taking in the carnival lights and the scattered stars above.

We rose, the initial movement gentle before the car lurched higher with a groan. The fairgrounds dwindled beneath us, and the carnival music and laughter faded as the wind whistled through the struts and the rhythmic mechanical hum of the motor echoed around us.

I could feel every inch of Colt beside me. His thigh pressed against mine and the denim between us felt too thin and too much at the same time. His arm rested on the back of the car, fingers threading into my hair, and his calloused thumb skimmed over my pulse point where my heartbeat betrayed me.

The car jolted to a stop, leaving us dangling above the ground while more riders climbed in below. From this height, I could still see mine and June's booth and all the others, and I smiled at the string of lights crisscrossing between the stalls like stars. I tried to memorize this moment, to match all the others that came before it, but all I could focus on was the gentle pressure of his fingers woven in my hair.

I turned toward him, and my gaze crashed into his. His blue eyes were so dark they reminded me of the sky. One corner of his mouth lifted, his mustache twitching, as his thumb brushed my skin in a silent promise, and my pulse thundered beneath his touch.

My eyes traced the hard line of his jaw, the curve of his lips, and that damn mustache. His gaze dropped to my mouth, lingered there with such raw hunger that my lips parted involuntarily, my breath coming quick and shallow.

I should have gotten this itch out of my system by now, but somehow, it was worse.

The night stretched wide and reckless. At the top of the Ferris wheel, there was no boundary left to cross. After years of pushing and pulling, fighting not to be the one who wanted more, I was suspended with him. Nobody watching, no one left to blame for the way I'd come undone but me.

My body trembled, caught between what I wanted and what I feared, suspended in midair just like this damn Ferris wheel.

His breath warmed my neck, and I leaned into him, my breath hitching when he shifted closer. Ruby's giggle cut through the fog, loud and sugar-fueled, and our heads snapped up as the wheel lurched back into motion.

As the wheel turned and we dropped back toward the earth, my stomach flipped in a free fall, and Colt's fingers slid from my hair to my shoulder. He traced a slow path over my exposed skin, and I couldn't breathe, couldn't move, couldn't do anything but surrender to the feeling of him.

The metal car groaned beneath us, the sound vibrating through the seat beneath us, matching the pulsing between my thighs. Ruby's laughter floated up from below, and a knife of guilt sliced through my haze of want.

Her happiness was the price we'd pay for this. I knew it. He knew it. But I burned for him, selfish and reckless, even knowing we would inevitably hurt each other. Because loving Colt Calloway had always felt like striking a match in a drought—consuming and impossible to survive.

"She's so good," I blurted out, nodding toward Ruby's car. "Like, deep down good."

"Yeah." Colt's face softened. "I don't know how I got so lucky."

I shook my head as my eyes met his, then focused back on the blinking carnival lights. "That's all you, you know. You're such a good dad."

His smile faltered a little, and he shifted beside me. "I worry about her all the time. Worry that I'm screwing it all up somehow. I make all these decisions, and what if I'm making the wrong ones?"

I nudged him with my shoulder, my heart skittering as I looked at him. "Ruby's the happiest kid I've ever met. She looks at you like you hung the moon."

"She is happy." He nodded, but then he hesitated. "I just want her to grow up strong and sure of herself. If I'm lucky, she'll grow up to be like you."

The words landed with a weight I wasn't ready for, and I couldn't breathe. My palms went clammy, nerves sparking under my skin. I tried to laugh it off, but it came out harsh and bitter. "No, you don't want that."

His eyes didn't waver, but they softened as the carnival lights caught in them like stars. "I mean it," he said, voice dropping to that rough whisper that always found its way under my defenses. "You're fierce. You're stubborn as hell, even when you shouldn't be." His hand found my knee, thumb tracing a small circle that sent warmth spiraling through me, and I flinched. His gaze tracked the movement, but he kept going. "That's all I want for her...to have that fire I've always seen in you."

"Fire?" The word caught in my throat. I gripped the metal bar until my knuckles ached, until I could feel the cold steel imprinting itself on my palms like a brand. "I don't have fire, Colt. I wouldn't wish any of my mistakes on Ruby."

His hand remained on my knee, heavy and so warm, a counterpoint to the ache settling into my hands. I realized I was clutching the Ferris wheel's safety bar so tightly the ridged metal pressed into my palms like a punishment, like I needed the sting to keep me from falling apart.

I stared at the fairgrounds below, at the mess of colored lights and the safe, ordinary world inside them. I wanted, just for a second, to be anyone but Blaire Monroe, the girl who ran away, the girl who loved a man who'd already broken her once.

Colt's hand flexed on my leg, anchoring me to the seat. "I wouldn't wish them on her either," he said, voice low and careful, like he was afraid he might spook me. "But you know what I wish for Ruby, every single day?" He didn't wait for my answer. "That she grows up unafraid to want things, unafraid to fix things when she's made the biggest mistake of her life."

My lungs seized. I could feel the air shudder in my chest, each breath scraping against a narrowing funnel in my throat as if the entire world was shrinking down to the Ferris wheel car and the man beside me. The strobe of carnival lights below us made everything look unreal, washed in blue and gold and red. Some small, traitorous part of me wanted to lean into his words and believe what he was saying, but the rest of me recoiled at the idea of exposing one more inch of soft skin for the world to bruise.

He leaned in slightly. "Blaire, when you left—"

"Please, don't." The sound of my voice startled me as I pleaded with him. I could still taste the memory of that day. I remembered the way my hair stuck to my face as the rain poured down around us. I remembered the words he'd thrown at me, words that left marks I'd never been able to erase. I remembered the sound of my own voice as I shouted at him, as I begged him to stop. "I can't do this tonight, Colt."

"You can't do what, Blaire?" His voice scraped against my raw skin. "You can let me fuck you any way I want to, but God forbid we talk about the past or about how I fucked everything up."

A wave of fury slammed into me, sudden and hot, and I whirled to face him. The Ferris wheel car creaked under the shift of weight, and I could feel the air charge between us, static and dangerous. All around us, the carnival blurred into a glow of spinning lights and voices and music, but inside the little metal cage, there were only the two of us and the thousand things we'd never said.

"I shouldn't have fucked you." The laugh ripped out of me, harsh and ugly. "You agreed to keep things casual. You agreed not to do this." I said it because it felt safer to deny the truth, and I motioned between us, my hand trembling so badly I had to clench it into a fist.

His eyes darkened as he clenched his jaw. "So what, you're just going to keep running? That's your answer for everything?"

"Don't." I raised a hand, palm out, hating how it shook. I wanted to slap him. I wanted to kiss him. I wanted to forget this moment ever happened and go back to the safety we'd pretended to have before—the kind where this was just sex, not the wreckage of who we used to be. "Don't act like you know me, not after all this time."

He reached for me then, his hand wrapping around the back of my neck. His touch burned through me, and I hated myself for leaning into it, for craving it. "Blaire, I never stopped knowing you. I never stopped thinking about you, not for a single day."

There was none of the cocky confidence in his eyes. There was just longing, raw and unsheltered, a mirror to the ache I'd carried for years.

For a moment, neither of us spoke. The Ferris wheel reached its apex and the car rocked gently, suspended in a hush so complete it was as if the whole world was holding its breath, waiting for us to fuck up again.

"You don't get to do this," I whispered, my voice cracking. "You don't get to fuck everything up then say shit like that." The words tasted like poison. "When I left, I swore I would never fall for anyone the way I fell for you. Never let myself be that vulnerable again."

Colt stilled, but something inside me had broken open and I couldn't stop the flood.

"My dad made sure I went to Duke, then he put me on his staff, exactly where he wanted me." I was coming apart at the seams. "Look who I became with Grant."

He didn't move, but his eyes never left mine, watching me unravel with an intensity that made me want to scream.

"I thought Grant loved me, but he loved the idea of me. He'd dress me up in clothes that cost more money than I'd ever seen, parade me around parties and dinners for his wealthy friends, and I—" My throat closed around the words. "I let him. I smiled and nodded and became this hollow thing because I thought if I became what he wanted, what my father wanted, I'd be enough for once."

Colt's free hand curled into a fist so tight I could see the tendons straining beneath his skin. Something flashed in his eyes, rage or pain, I couldn't tell which, but I couldn't stop.

"When I found out he'd been fucking his assistant for the last year of our relationship, I was relieved." The confession slammed into me. "I stormed into his office anyway. But it wasn't even about him, it was about me. I was so fucking angry at myself."

Colt's breathing had gone shallow, his face carved from stone.

"I got back to our condo, and my key wouldn't work." My laugh sounded so sad. "I lived there for two years, and he'd changed the locks within minutes. I'd spent three days at my dad's before Grant finally let me in to get my stuff, and he stood there and watched me pack my bags with this smirk on his face I'll never forget, like he was waiting for me to break down and beg."

I finally met Colt's gaze, and I wished I hadn't. Rage flicked across his face, and the intensity of it made my stomach drop, as if the Ferris wheel had suddenly plummeted twenty feet. I felt naked and exposed in front of him, like every flaw and weakness I'd tried to hide was suddenly lit up for him to see.

"I had nowhere to go, no one except my father, who wanted me to look past Grant's little mistake, and I hated him more than I could ever hate Grant. And when I called June, and I heard her voice, I wanted to die from shame."

Colt shook his head, a muscle twitching in his jaw. "You have nothing to be ashamed of."

The words tumbled between us in the rattling Ferris wheel car, and I opened my mouth to tell him how wrong he was, but the gentle fire in his eyes stopped me.

I pressed my lips together and stared over the edge of the chipped metal seat, watching the world drift by in slow, dizzying circles. "I do, though," I whispered. "I thought I had it all planned out. I thought I was—someone. But here I am, a twenty-eight-year-old woman who owns nothing and lives with her grandma—" I cut myself off, a bitter laugh ripping free. "Or should I say, living with my high school boyfriend because he felt sorry for me? And now I'm—" My stomach churned. "Now I'm spreading my legs for him like he hadn't already broken my heart once before."

I could feel myself sabotaging this, trying to break it before he could ever break me, and I didn't know how to stop it.

Colt's hand tightened on my neck, pulling me forward. "Blaire."

"I'm sorry. I shouldn't have said that." I looked anywhere but at his eyes, and every bit of me shook as the ride slowed to a stop.

"Look at me." His thumb slid beneath my jaw and forced my gaze to his. "You don't get to do that," he growled, and his fingertips dug into me. "You don't get to talk about yourself that way, not to me."

I tried to twist away as my chest tightened. "Stop—"

He released my jaw, his thumb ghosting over my bottom lip, rough and merciless. The wheel creaked back into motion, but I was paralyzed by the heat of him, the urgency in his stare. "You've always been enough, Blaire. Always. Look at how you are with Ruby. Look at what you're doing for June's farm."

He leaned so close I tasted his frustration. "You weren't the only one destroyed when you left. I was a kid. A fucking idiot who made mistakes." His voice shook. "I have a daughter now. I have everything I'd always thought I wanted, and still, I have searched for pieces of you in everyone I met."

His fingers on my neck became rougher, more desperate, as he held on to me.

"You asked me before about Ruby's mom. I was too much of a fucking coward to tell you that the real reason she left. She wasn't ready to be a mother, but she'd been willing to try for me. But no matter what I did, I couldn't make myself love her. I couldn't make it work. It never worked, because she wasn't you."

Each admission seemed to cost him, like he was skinning himself alive before me.

I tried to summon anger. I tried to remind myself of all the ways he'd hurt me, all the nights I'd spent cursing his name and every lie he'd ever told. But I felt hollowed out, a canyon of want and regret.

"What?" The word was as raw as I felt.

His next words slammed into me, one after another. "She. Wasn't. You."

I made a noise that was almost a sob, and his mouth crashed against mine. His lips claimed me with raw hunger, yet his fingers shook as they cradled my face like something sacred.

Each stroke of his tongue was reverent; each breath we shared a communion. I could feel him worshipping every inch he touched, as if kissing me was both my salvation and damnation.

We devoured each other with such desperation that the idea that this could have ever been casual seemed like madness now. We'd been fools thinking we could ever be anything other than this.

This burning, consuming thing between us.

He tasted of lemonade and something darker, something uniquely him that made me dizzy with need. His body pressed against mine, hard and wanting, his heartbeat thundering against my chest. I clawed at his hair, pulling him impossibly closer, my body arching into his as if trying to melt into him completely. I wanted to erase every second we'd spent apart, to burn away every touch that wasn't his. His groan vibrated through me as his hands slid down to grip my hips, fingers digging in with a possession that made heat pool low in my belly.

There was just me and him, his mouth on mine, and his hands branding my skin. Every part of me screamed his name as we kissed each other, the taste of him drowning out a decade of regret. I didn't feel the descent, didn't hear the machinery groaning, until the Ferris wheel slammed to a halt, jerking us apart as we reached the bottom.

His fingers dug deeper into my hips, bruising promises into my skin. My chest heaved against his, our foreheads pressed together, both of us gasping like we'd been drowning and finally found air. His pupils swallowed the blue of his eyes, leaving only a thin ring of color around the bottomless want that matched the molten need coursing through me.

"Well, well, well." McCoy's voice sliced through the moment, and I jerked back, heat flooding my cheeks as reality crashed in.

McCoy, Hunter, and Ruby stood watching us by the exit, their grins wide and knowing. Ruby's eyes shined with such naked hope it made my throat close. The weight of it crushed against my chest, and panic and longing surged through me. I wanted to make her happy. I wanted to be the one who gave her everything she ever wanted.

I was desperate to show Ruby that my love didn't come with stipulations, and I was scared to death that I would prove myself wrong.

My fingers remained twisted in Colt's shirt, the heat of his skin burning through the fabric against my knuckles. I couldn't let go. I wouldn't. Hunter's smirk followed us as Colt's grip loosened with visible reluctance, his rough fingertips dragging fire across my hipbone.

"It's about damn time."

CHAPTER 31
COLT

By the time we pulled into the drive, Ruby was already fast asleep in the back seat, her breathing slow and even, her paper crown slipping over one eye. She'd given up fighting sleep miles ago, the aftermath of too much sugar and an evening spent shrieking with laughter on rickety carnival rides. Her arms were still clamped around the neck of that ludicrously large stuffed bear, and I smiled as I watched her in the rearview mirror.

I shut the engine off and sat for a minute, listening to the hush of the night as it unfolded around us. I glanced over at Blaire, and she was staring straight ahead. She didn't look over at me, but I could see her jaw working and the way she picked at her nails.

I pushed open my door and circled around the truck, careful not to slam it shut and wake Ruby. I opened Blaire's door, and I stepped back as she finally looked up at me. She studied me, as if searching for proof this wasn't the kind of night that would fade by morning.

I waited. I could wait all night if she needed me to. The years had taught me patience in work, in loss, in knowing that nothing worth having came easy or fast, and tonight was not a night to hurry anything.

I reached my hand out, and she took it before bracing her

other hand on the seat and swinging her legs out. I fought the urge to wrap my arms around her and pull her close, even though the distance between us felt unbearable. But I stepped back, giving her space, and she climbed out of my truck before her hand slid out of mine.

I opened Ruby's door and unlatched her seat belt and pried the bear from her arms, scooping her out in one practiced motion. She barely stirred. She melted against me, her hair tickling my jawline, and the full length of her small body pressed to mine. I could feel her heartbeat, slow and steady, against my chest, and I tried to calm my own to match it as I breathed her in.

I felt Blaire at my back as I carried Ruby up the steps and through the front door. Normally I would have expected her to hang back, invent an excuse to disappear before things got too soft or too real, but she stayed close. She walked through the door right behind me and let it shut gently at her back before she locked it.

In Ruby's room, the day's chaos lay scattered over every surface, proof of a life lived with joyful abandon, and I nearly tripped over a half-finished drawing and crayons on the floor. It was a picture of me, Ruby, and Blaire, all three of us holding hands, and I couldn't stop the ache in my chest as I stepped over it.

I shifted Ruby in my arms, careful not to jostle her, and laid her on her bed. She sighed and snuggled into her pillow. Blaire bent over, quickly untying Ruby's shoes and pulling them from her feet.

"Good night, Ruby," Blaire whispered before tucking that giant stuffed bear Ruby loved beside her and her blanket over her. She smoothed the tangle of Ruby's hair from her forehead, pausing to stroke her cheek, and I saw something in Blaire's face that twisted my insides.

She loved my girl.

"She had fun tonight," she whispered.

I nodded, swallowing past the knot in my throat. "She did. Too much fun. I'm going to have to hose off her sheets tomorrow."

"You're the one who let her have the cotton candy in the

truck." Blaire jabbed her finger into my chest. I caught her wrist in my hand, holding it captive against my chest. Her skin was warm, and I could feel her pulse racing under my thumb. She tried to pull back, but I didn't let her. We stood there, bodies close, and the thin space between us became charged as her breath hitched.

"Come to my room tonight." My voice was ragged, stripped bare by the need I couldn't hide anymore. "No more sneaking. No more pretending."

Blaire's lips parted, a soft gasp escaping her, and when her tongue swept across her bottom lip, I had to clench my fist to keep from claiming her mouth right there. She nodded once, the movement barely perceptible, but the electricity that shot through me nearly brought me to my knees.

I let my fingertips graze hers, the lightest touch sending shock waves up my arm. When I tugged her toward me, the small sound that escaped her throat made my blood surge hot beneath my skin.

Each step down that hallway was torture. My heart slammed against my ribs, and her fingers tightened around mine with each step. The floorboards creaked beneath us, counting down the years of waiting and wanting. For almost a week, Blaire and I stole moments, but always ended with one foot back in reality.

Tonight, I wouldn't hold back. I wanted to consume her whole, to surrender everything I was to her until I couldn't remember where I ended and she began—until there was nothing left of me but the parts she'd marked as hers.

I pushed my bedroom door open, then forced myself to hold it for her like some goddamn charade of civility while every bit of my body screamed to claim her. She brushed past me, the curve of her hip grazing mine, and the scent of her skin made me groan. I let the door close behind us, my breath coming in ragged bursts as the lock clicked into place.

We didn't bother with the lamp. Moonlight carved Blaire's silhouette against the window, and my body ached with a hunger that had been building for years. I crossed the room in two strides, my cock already straining against my jeans. My fingers dug into the soft flesh at the nape of her neck and pulled her to me, a groan escaping me at the first contact of her body against mine. Our mouths collided with such violent need that nothing existed beyond the heat of her lips and the way she clawed at my shoulders, her hips already seeking mine.

We hit the mattress like a breaking wave, tangled in the undertow of each other. Blaire's fingers twisted in my hair, yanking my head back, her lips hungry and bruising against my mouth. There was the sharpness of her touch, the taste of her tongue, the desperate way we clawed at each other's clothes. Years of restraint had snapped like a dam giving way, and now we were drowning in each other, desperate not to come up for air.

I grabbed the hem of her shirt, ripped it over her head, and brushed my open mouth over her bare skin until I lost myself in the taste of her. She dragged her teeth down my neck, her breath shaking against my skin. I could feel her heartbeat against my chest, frantic and wild, and it made my heart pound so hard I could feel it through every inch of me.

There was no more hesitation, no carefulness left between us. It was just the fevered devotion of people who'd run out of reasons not to love each other.

And fuck, I did love her.

I'd loved her for as long as I could remember, and I'd never stopped. It was as deeply rooted in me as the old oak trees on this ranch. It weathered storms and droughts, but it still held strong.

She pushed on my shoulders, flipping me onto my back and straddling my hips as her hands braced on my chest. Her hair fell around her face, a wild curtain of auburn curls, and in the moonlight's haze, I saw her eyes. They were dark, determined, and so full of longing it split me wide open.

I fumbled with the hook of her bra, and she laughed before she reached behind her back and undid it herself.

"Fuck, you're everything." My voice broke as I seized her neck, fingers digging into her pulse before dragging down her chest, claiming every inch of her bare skin that burned beneath my palm.

She whimpered as she ground against me, and I surged

forward, teeth sinking into the curve where her neck met her shoulder. Her cry echoed through the darkness as I moved lower, my mouth closing around her nipple. She arched into me as she moaned, fingernails clawing at my scalp, pulling me harder against her as if she'd die without the pressure of my mouth.

I hooked my thumb into the waistband of her shorts and popped the button. My hand plunged beneath, finding only the thin barrier of cotton, already drenched. The heat of her pussy was intoxicating, and I couldn't stop myself as I dragged my fingers roughly along her slit through the fabric, savoring her desperate whimpers that vibrated against my mouth.

"You're still so needy for me," I growled, yanking her panties to the side. Her hips bucked against me when my fingers finally met her bare flesh. "Fuck, you're dripping for me, baby."

I parted her with my fingers, finding her clit and making her gasp against my mouth. I circled it slowly at first, teasing, and watched her eyes flutter closed as her hips strained toward me. Then I pressed harder and moved faster until she bucked against my hand.

Her body burned in my memory, but time changed her. There was so much new ground that I was desperate to claim.

"Colt," she whimpered my name, and her nails dug into my shoulders as she writhed harder against me.

I crushed my mouth to hers, savoring the taste of her, then flipped her roughly onto her back, pinning her beneath me. I raked my hands down her flushed skin, feeling the heat rise beneath my palms before I pulled her boots off one by one and dropped them to the ground. Then I hooked my fingers into the sides of her shorts and panties, tearing them down her legs.

I pulled my shirt over my head in one rough motion, tossing it blindly into the dark. Blaire's gaze turned hungry as she watched me undress, her breath coming in shallow gasps, and her thighs already parting wider for me.

I moved between those thighs, gripping them in my hands, and dragged her to the edge of the bed. Her gasp cut through the darkness as I traced my hand up her leg, skimming my fingers over her clit.

"Oh, God." Her hands dug into the sheets, and I moved my thumb hard against her clit before plunging two fingers deep inside her. I curled them upward, and her spine bowed off the mattress as a broken cry tore from her throat.

"Tell me what you need," I bit out as I circled her clit with agonizing slowness. Her hips bucked desperately against my hand, seeking more pressure. "Say it, Blaire."

I wanted to hear her say it. I needed it.

"You," she gasped, and her eyes locked with mine.

"Not. Good. Enough." I punctuated each word by dragging my fingers almost completely out of her slick heat before thrusting them back in and curling them against that spot that made her walls clench around me.

Her whole body stiffened, hips fighting for me, but I didn't let up. Her words on the Ferris wheel had cracked something open in me, and now I was starving for all of her.

I needed to hear her voice break around the words, needed her to shed the last of her armor she held up between us. By dawn, I wanted her to know that the man who claimed her body tonight was a man who would worship at her altar for as long as she'd let him.

I'd tear myself open and bleed out every last drop of pride if that's what it took for her to see the truth. Loving Blaire Monroe wasn't some choice I made. It was branded into my bones before I knew what the hell love even was.

I would burn the world down just to keep her exactly as she is. Fierce and flawed and fucking perfect.

"Tell me exactly what you need, Blaire." My breath rushed out, and my whole body burned to give in. But I wanted her as raw and exposed as I was. I felt like an addict who was on the brink of their high, and I chased it desperately.

She bit back a moan, and her back arched as she lifted her hips. Her hair fanned wildly across my bed as she shook her head, like if she didn't say it out loud, she could keep some last scrap of dignity.

"Say it," I rasped, slowing my hand, making her feel the loss, and I could see the battle of self-preservation versus her need in her eyes.

She made a strangled sound before she finally broke. "Please, Colt. I need you to fuck me. I need you to—" She moaned as I pressed down on her clit again, then eased up. "I need to feel you inside me. I need to know that you're mine, please."

The way she said mine knocked the fucking air out of my lungs. I'd be a liar if I said I didn't need it just as badly, that I didn't ache to belong to her as much as I wanted her to belong to me.

"Fuck. That's it, baby." I dropped to my knees before her, and I spread her legs wide before I hauled her to the edge, her ass nearly slipping off the bed. She squealed, the sound frantic, and I hooked my arms beneath her legs, spreading her open even farther with my hands digging into her inner thighs.

She was so completely at my mercy, and fuck if that wasn't exactly where we both wanted her.

I bent and put my mouth on her, kissing her inner thigh first, dragging my lips over the smattering of freckles there, then biting down with enough pressure to make her cry out. I could feel the tremor run through her, a shiver of anticipation that made my cock throb.

But I made her wait. I licked a slow, agonizing line from her knee toward the heat between her legs, and I savored every inch, every gasp, every shudder. When I finally reached her pussy, I brushed my mouth over the soft, soaked skin, breathing her in.

She was perfect and pink and swollen with need, and the first swipe of my tongue made her hips buck so hard she nearly knocked me off her. I held her firmly, hands gripping her thighs tight, and I ran my tongue through her slowly.

I groaned at the taste of her arousal, and I couldn't stop running my tongue over her flesh again and again, each time ending in a rough little flick over her clit. She sobbed, her hands grabbing my hair, yanking me closer, desperate for more.

"Oh fuck. Please, Colt." Her pleading was a weapon, and it made me wild.

I pulled back, my breath hot against her slick skin, and looked up at her. Blaire watched me with her lips parted as she panted, the blush on her cheeks making her look so alive I wanted to tear the world apart to keep her like this.

"Beg me for it, baby," I rasped, letting my mustache and scruff scratch at her inner thigh as I spoke. "Make me believe you'll die without it."

A whimper escaped her, high and so damn needy. "Please, I need you. I need this, Colt. Please don't stop." Her words tumbled out in a rush.

I rewarded her by plunging my tongue deep inside her, fucking her with it slowly, then flicking up to circle her clit until she whimpered. One of her hands braced herself on the mattress and the other tangled in my hair. I could feel her getting closer, her whole body tightening, her legs squeezing around my neck.

I sucked her clit into my mouth, gently at first, then harder, teasing her until she was right on the edge. Then I stopped, long enough to make her sob, before I started all over again.

She thrashed on the bed, curses and broken pleas spilling from her lips, until finally she shattered against my mouth. Her whole body went rigid, and her thighs clamped down so hard it was hard to breathe. But I didn't stop. I kept sucking and licking her through it, drawing out her orgasm until she was a mess of cries and shaking limbs.

When I finally pulled away, my mouth, chin, and mustache were slick with her, and I groaned as I crawled over her and brushed my lips against hers. She tasted herself on my lips and moaned as she squirmed beneath me. She let her thighs fall open around me, and she wrapped her arms around my neck, pulling me closer before she'd even caught her breath.

I'd never felt so alive as I did with her. The years apart, the ache of missing her, all of it collided into this reckless moment.

I knew what it was like to exist without her, and I knew I'd never survive the loss of her again.

I leaned back, lining myself up with her, and let the head of my cock brush against her soaked entrance before I dragged it through her wetness. "Look at you."

I pressed my cock against her sensitive clit, and her breath rushed out of her as she reached for me.

"Fucking desperate for me."

I gripped her hip hard enough to bruise, pinning her in place as she tried to writhe against me, and I watched my pre-cum mark her skin.

"I want to fill you up," I rasped, and my fingers dug into her thigh, spreading her wider and exposing all of her to me.

The image of her with a swollen belly sent fire racing through my veins. She would be just as she was with Ruby, tender and loving and mine. We'd been skin to skin since that first night, but tonight felt different. The way she'd let me see her wounds, shared parts of herself she usually kept hidden, it made me want to claim her in the most primal way possible.

"You're going to take everything I give you," I said and slapped her clit gently with the thick head of my cock. "Because you're mine. Say it."

She made this strangled keening sound, half frustration, half need, but she still held back. She still wanted to be in control, even as I held her open and quivering and desperate. I needed to see her break, needed to watch the moment she surrendered everything to me. I needed the words, but more than that, I needed the truth behind them.

I pushed in a fraction, just enough for her to feel it, and then stopped. I held her there on the edge while I leaned over her, forcing her to meet my eyes. "Tell me who you belong to."

Her breath hitched, and I wrapped my hand around her throat, my thumb finding her pulse.

"Tell me."

I could feel her heartbeat in her throat, in her cunt, pulsing around the head of my cock even though I hadn't given her more than the tip.

"I—" Her voice broke, and she squeezed her eyes shut, trying to fight it, but I wouldn't let her retreat. I pulled her chin up, thumb digging into her jaw until her eyes opened again and locked on mine.

"I need to hear you say it," I said, softer now, but edged with a desperation that could cut both of us wide open. "Because you are mine, Blaire. You're the first thought in my head when I wake and the last before I dream. I have never stopped thinking about you. Not for a single goddamn day."

She flinched like the force of my confession hit her somewhere nobody could see. Her mouth trembled, her bravado slipping, and I thought she might push me away. But she stared up at me with her chest rising and falling so fast I could feel her racing heart in the space between us.

"I'm yours." The words ripped from her throat like she'd dug them out of a place she'd promised she'd never open again. "I've always been yours."

The admission was a punch to the gut. It was pure and wild and so honest I wanted to fall on my knees and worship at her feet. Instead, I crashed my mouth down on hers, and I drank every broken sob like it was the only thing that could keep me alive.

Then I pushed all the way inside her, and the world narrowed to nothing but the feel of her. She was wet and tight and holding on to me like she were afraid I'd disappear if she blinked. Our bodies met in a slap of skin and heat and need, but the moment I bottomed out, it went past desperation and landed somewhere sacred. She arched up to meet me, nails raking down my back, and she whimpered my name in a voice so raw I barely recognized it.

I set a punishing rhythm, hips snapping forward and dragging back, each thrust rougher and deeper than the last. She begged, she cursed, she pleaded, and I gave her everything she asked for. Because she'd finally given me the only thing I ever wanted.

I watched her face and her eyes never left mine, even when her whole body shook. She opened for me, surrendered to me, and

I could see every ounce of fight and pride melting away, replaced by something softer and sweeter.

I leaned down, scraping my teeth over the shell of her ear, and whispered, "You're the only thing I need. The only one I've ever wanted."

She clung to me, legs locking around my waist, and I could feel how close she was. Her whole body went rigid beneath me, every muscle drawn taut, and I reached between us and found her clit, circling it in time with every thrust.

The combination made her cry out. "Don't stop, please! Colt, don't—" Her voice broke, but I swallowed the rest of her plea with my mouth.

I kissed her hard and fucked her harder. My control slipped with every second, and I could feel the edge coming for me, the pressure building white-hot in my gut.

"Come for me," I demanded against her lips, and she shattered with my name in her mouth. She came hard, her body spasming around me, and I let go at the same moment, emptying myself into her with a groan that sounded more like a prayer.

I stayed inside her, refusing to let go, even as our bodies went limp and the sweat cooled on our skin. I pressed my forehead to hers, breathing her in and memorizing the way she felt with her arms still wrapped around my neck.

I held on to her like I'd feared I'd never find my way back to her again.

She blinked up at me with wet lashes and flushed cheeks. She smiled, small and shaky, and I wanted to say a thousand things. But I just kissed her, soft and slow, and hoped she understood everything I couldn't put into words.

I pulled out of her and we lay tangled together with the sheets twisted around our legs, and my hands mapped every inch of her, relearning the shape of her ribs, the curve of her hip, the way her spine dipped right above her ass. I couldn't stop touching her. I didn't want to. I wanted her to feel me for days, wanted her to remember what it was like when nobody and nothing came between us.

CHAPTER 32
COLT

I pulled my quilt up over her, covering as much of her body as I was willing to lose.

"Colt," she whispered my name.

I looked up from the curve of her knee, lips still brushing her skin, and caught her gaze. Her eyes were clearer than I'd seen them since she came home. There were no walls left between us, no games. "Yeah, Strawberry?" I tried to soften the edge in my voice, but the term of endearment made her cheeks flush.

She reached for me, weaving her fingers through my hair, her touch light as if testing whether I might vanish under her hands. Her inhale was shaky as she searched my face and then the ceiling.

"What are we doing?" she asked. There was a wobble in her voice, a ghost of old wounds I hadn't been able to take away. Her hand stayed at my nape, as if she needed the anchor, and despite the softness of her just a few moments ago, she was now tense.

I let out a long breath and propped myself on my elbow. I took her hand from my hair and brought it to my lips. I slowly kissed the inside of her bare wrist as she watched me.

"We're doing the only thing that makes sense. You and me. It's always been that, hasn't it?" I watched her eyes shutter, watched her try to hide the relief, but it was there in the way her fist unclenched and her breathing eased.

Her fingers brushed over my jaw, and there was so much hope and fear mixed in her eyes.

"We said we wouldn't do this," she whispered, her voice cracking as her lower lip quivered. "This is why we agreed to be casual. We don't need to make each other promises we can't keep."

My gut twisted at the word *casual*. Nothing about this was casual, even if she clung to that word as if it would keep her safe. But there was nothing safe about the way I loved her.

"Why can't we keep them?" I pushed the hair off her cheek, my fingertips lingering on the fine spray of freckles.

She gave a watery, disbelieving laugh, and her gaze darted back up to the ceiling as if it could offer her the answers she was searching for. "You make it sound so easy." The words were a challenge, but I could hear the plea buried inside. "We broke our promises before."

When she finally looked back at me, the hurt in her eyes was a mirror to the hollow space I'd carried inside me. My chest ached with the weight of everything we'd lost.

"We were kids then, Blaire. We didn't know what we were doing." I swallowed hard, forcing myself to tell her the truth. "I was scared of not being enough for my family. I was too damn scared to watch you realize I'd never be enough for you."

I could see the tears in her eyes she wouldn't let fall, and even though I wanted to say more, I forced myself to wait for her. I let the silence hum between us as my hands traced slow circles over her ribs.

"I was scared too," she whispered, and her voice was so raw. "You always seemed so sure of yourself, like nothing could touch you. But you were the one person who could break me." She squeezed her eyes shut, and I felt her chest shudder under my palm. "I hated that about myself. Hated I couldn't outgrow it, that

I never stopped wondering if you'd show up on my porch one day and—"

Her voice broke on the words, and I kissed her hairline as I held her against my chest. The shape of her pain was a living thing, thumping against my ribs in sync with hers, and when her breath hitched, I felt it down to my bones. I wanted to take every bit of that hurt away from her.

But she kept talking, and I let her, even when my every instinct screamed to tell her I would spend the rest of my days making it up to her.

"I always wanted to be my own person," she whispered, and her voice was smaller than I'd ever heard it. "But it's like no matter where I went, or who I was with, there was a part of me that was always waiting for you." She exhaled, and the sound was shaky and so damn lonely it made me want to scream.

"I was so fucking sure I'd finally figured my life out, you know? I thought if I did everything right, if I kept my head down and my heart locked up, then maybe I could—" She went quiet, and I could practically feel her trying to find the right words. "But the harder I tried to move on, the less I recognized myself. I know that's not your fault. That was on me and what I allowed. I'd look in the mirror and see a stranger with my mother's face, but none of her fire." The tears finally came then, and I gently wiped them away with my thumb as I held her tighter. "My mom wouldn't recognize me."

"She would," I said, unable to control the raw edge in my voice. I cupped her face with my hand, thumb pressing under her jaw, lifting her gaze so she had no choice but to meet my eyes. "Your mama would be so proud of who you are. You've never been small, Blaire. Not one goddamn day of your life. Not when you left, not when you came back, not now."

The words tore out of me because I needed her to feel them. She blinked, and I could see the fight in her, the stubborn denial, the part of her that still believed she was all the things other people said she was. Her lips parted, and the beginnings of an argument formed, but I didn't let her speak. I pressed a kiss to her forehead, then another to the tip of her nose and the corner of her mouth, lingering there as her breath hitched.

"I should have told you this years ago. I should have grabbed your arm that day and fallen to my knees and begged you not to go." My voice broke, and I kissed her again. "Fuck, Blaire. There wasn't a single part of me that wanted you to leave, and I've been drowning every goddamn day since."

I wanted to tell her how I'd scraped myself raw trying to figure out how to keep her and keep the only home I'd ever known, but the words caught in my throat. But Blaire deserved the truth, even if it made her hate me.

"That day when I told you to leave with your father, when I said I couldn't do this anymore." I forced the words out, my voice rough. "I lied to you, Blaire. Every damn word of it was a lie."

Her eyes flashed wide, lips parting with unspoken questions, but I pushed forward before courage could desert me.

"Your father showed up at the ranch." My hand trembled as I pushed it through my hair, the memory flooding back with sickening clarity. "He was already dragging June through court, and she was barely keeping her head above water. Then he pulled out those loan papers, and I didn't even know about it until that moment. Those papers had my parents' signatures right next to June's, and he told me exactly what would happen if you stayed." I had to look away from her then, shame burning hot through my chest. "He said he'd drag June through every court in the state, that June and my parents would lose everything they worked for. And anything tied to your mama's estate? He swore he'd take that too. And I—" My voice cracked. "I was eighteen and terrified, Blaire. I thought I was protecting you, protecting everyone. I'd convinced myself that you were better off without me. I couldn't give you the life that he could."

For a moment, the only sound was the hitch in Blaire's breath and the thunder of my own heart. The words hung in the space between us, heavy as summer thunder. I felt a sick, hollow need in my gut for her to understand, and I realized I was gripping the sheet so hard it might rip. But I couldn't let go, couldn't even reach for her, because I was terrified that if I touched her now, she'd slip through my fingers for good.

"I'm so fucking sorry, Blaire. I hate what I did to us. What I did to you." The words rasped through my throat, making my chest burn as I forced myself to hold her gaze. Her brown eyes were wet with the tears she refused to let fall, but was unable to hide. "Every morning since that day, I've woken up with the weight of my regret. Your father gave me no choice, but I still should've chosen you."

I could see the impact in the way her lips trembled, the way her jaw clenched as if she could trap the ache inside her mouth before it escaped. My hand hovered inches from her cheek, desperate for contact, but I didn't touch her. I didn't have the right. Not after all I'd done.

"You deserved the truth then, and you deserve it now. When you left, I tried to put everything back the way it was. I threw myself into the ranch. I helped June. I tried to rebuild my own goddamn soul from the pieces you left behind. But no matter what I did, no matter how many times I told myself it was for the best, loving you was the one thing I never figured out how to stop." I said the last part so quietly I wasn't sure she heard it, but she did. She heard every damn word.

Her throat worked as she swallowed, then slowly, with the kind of hesitation that felt like standing at the edge of a cliff, she reached for my hand. Her fingers laced through mine, shaky at first, then with more certainty, as if she needed to anchor herself to something real.

"I spent years hating you," she whispered, her voice catching on the words. Her fingers tightened around mine until I could feel her nails pressing into my skin. "Every night I'd lie awake replaying everything, searching for the moment I became someone you couldn't love anymore."

My chest felt like it was splitting open, all the things I'd never said clawing their way out at once. I could barely breathe past the knot in my throat, but I forced the words out anyway, because if I didn't say them now, I didn't know if I would ever get the chance again.

"I know I fucked up," I said, my voice shaky and too loud in the hush of her room. "There isn't a day where I don't wish I could go back and do it all over again. Even when I hated myself for it, even when I tried to convince myself I'd moved on, or you had. But this place," I said, barely able to look at her. "This ranch, this town, all of it, means nothing if you're not in it. I didn't realize that until it was too late. But there was never a single moment I stopped loving you. Not one. Even when I was trying my damnedest to hate you, to erase you, you were still right there, under my skin."

She blinked, and I could see the fight in her, the way she wanted to call me out for the way I'd hurt her. But it was like something inside her broke. "Who else knows? About what my father did that day?"

"No one," I said, and it was the truth. "I never told June, or my parents, or anyone. He came to me, and I made the choice. And that choice was mine to live with."

She nodded, slow and jerky, as if she was still trying to process the world reassembled by my confession. I could see her lips moving, as if counting the years, trying to measure out all the time we'd lost to silence and pride.

"Ten years." She still wasn't looking at me. "Ten years of where every single move I made was him steering the course." She stopped, drawing in a breath that shook. "And all that time, you had helped him."

"Blaire—" I started, but she lifted a hand, palm flat and rigid, and the force of it made me bite my tongue.

"I need to say this," she said, and the words sounded like steel. "Because if I don't, I'll be the one choking on it forever. You stole my choice, Colt, and you never even gave me a chance to fight for it." Her chin trembled, but the rest of her was stone. "And I'm done letting men decide what I can bear. My father doesn't get one more inch of me. And you—" She swallowed. "You don't get to shield me with lies, not ever again."

I nodded, my throat raw. The sting of her words was nothing less than I deserved. "I swear," I managed. "Never again."

She looked up, and the anger in her eyes was as bright and hot as the sun at high noon. "I hate him for doing this to us," she said. "But I'm furious with you, too. I'm so damn angry at you for believing we couldn't have handled it together. And I hate that I understand why you did it." She scrubbed at her eyes with the heel of her hand, angry at herself now. "I should be angrier. But I get it, Colt. I do. I've worked for my father since the day I graduated college. I know what he's capable of. Hell, I know more about the terrible things he's done than anyone."

She blinked her eyes open, and there was a vulnerability in her then that was almost more than I could stand. Because I knew she endured years of conditional affection from her father, always tugged by invisible wires. He'd done it to her before she left, and I couldn't imagine how bad it had been when she was with him.

I'd been a coward, and I'd carried the guilt for so long. But now it was like the wound was new, raw, and pulsing between us.

"I'm sorry," I said. "I'm sorry for everything I did, and for not telling you the truth when you needed it." The words felt small, but they were the only things I had left.

She was silent, but her eyes didn't leave my face. For a moment it felt like everything in the world was balanced on the knife-edge of her forgiveness, and I didn't know which way it would tip.

"I don't know what to do with all this," she said at last, voice trembling. "It's like I've been walking around with a big empty hole inside me, and I finally know what fits in it, but that doesn't mean it hurts any less."

I reached for her hand and this time she didn't pull away. Our fingers twined together, holding on for dear life. "I can't fix the past," I said. "But I can start by telling you the truth now. Every time. Even if it scares me."

Her lips twitched, and she lifted one hand, running it over my mustache. "The Colt I know has never been scared of anything."

"I'm scared of you," I said, my entire body aching with the admission. "I'm scared of losing you."

I felt her palm quiver against mine, and tightened my grip, as if I could somehow press the memory of her hand into my skin before she pulled away.

We sat like that for a long time, not moving, not even blinking, just staring at each other across the canyon of everything we'd never said. I wanted to reach for her, to pull her into my arms and promise her the world, but I didn't dare. She needed space to decide what she wanted, who she was now. The only thing I could do was be honest, for the first time in my whole goddamn life.

"I know you have a life and a future that probably doesn't have a place for me in it. But I needed you to know. I needed you to know that it was real, Blaire. That it was always real. When you came back, I was so scared for you to get close to Ruby because I don't know if she'll survive if you leave. I won't survive it. I know I won't."

A soft sob tore from her throat, and I stroked my thumb along her cheekbone, and for a moment, she closed her eyes. She leaned into my touch like she was starved for it, like she was scared it would vanish if she looked too closely. I could feel her wild and unsteady pulse racing under my thumb.

"I know I'm not good at this," I whispered. "I know I broke every promise we ever made, and if I could go back and change any of it, I would. I'd do it a thousand times over. But I can't. So all I can do is try like hell to be better now."

I moved closer, my weight shifting until I was above her, supporting myself on one elbow while my fingertips ghosted along the curve of her cheekbone.

"You're the only thing that's ever made sense, Blaire. Only you and Ruby."

She stared up at me, her eyes glistening in the low light, and her hands rose to clutch my forearms.

"I wanted to hate you," she whispered. "I'd convinced myself for so long that I did."

"I know," I said. "You can still hate me if you need to but just don't—" I leaned closer until my words brushed her lips. "Please don't leave again."

"Colt—" She shook her head against me, and I had no idea what she was going to say, but I couldn't bear the thought that she could tell me she was going to leave.

"It would kill me, Blaire. It would kill Ruby."

I let the words hang there, let them bite and burn. Blaire just stared up at me, and her fingers dug into my arms.

"I used to pray that I could take it all back, that I could have a do over and change what happened that day. But then I wouldn't have Ruby." I let my hand drift down the line of her neck, my thumb grazing the hollow of her throat.

"When Ruby was born, they put her in my arms, and I swear to God, Blaire, the world stopped spinning. I couldn't breathe. She was this tiny, perfect thing with my eyes and dark hair, and I didn't know a man could love like that. I remember running my finger over her little lips, and it was your face that flashed in my mind. It was the greatest moment of my life, and I knew that the only thing missing was you. Always you."

Her breath caught, tears trembling on her lashes until they fell down her cheeks.

"I thought about you, and I kept seeing your smile in her face even though that was impossible. I was so happy, but I kept thinking about how you should've been there beside me." My chest ached with the admission. "That night, when the rest of the world was asleep and it was just me and her, I told her about the girl who owned every piece of me before she did." I brushed my thumb across her cheek, wiping away the moisture. "I looked you up online that night. There was a photo of you laughing in a city I'd never see, looking like everything I'd ever wanted and could never have again. And God, I'd never felt so fucking split in two. I loved her so completely while still loving the ghost of you."

I shook my head, dragging my thumb lower to the ridges and valleys of her collarbone.

"But seeing you with Ruby and watching her light up around you? I've never seen my girl so happy." My voice broke, and I had to swallow hard against the ache in my throat. "It kills me and makes me the happiest son of a bitch alive. It makes me feel like maybe I'm not failing her."

"You're not failing her," she whispered, and her fingers shook as they trailed up my arm. "You've given her everything."

I leaned in, pressing my mouth to hers, and feeling the warmth of her lips against mine. "I want to give her you." I breathed. "No more casual, Blaire. I want all of you."

CHAPTER 33
BLAIRE

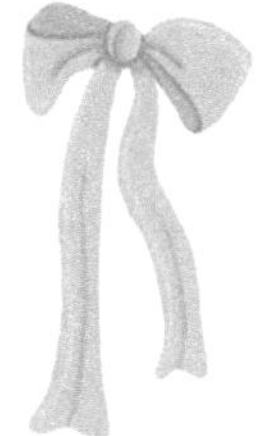

The silence in the room was suffocating.

Colt's arm was slung possessively across my waist, his hand curled loosely around my hip, as if some subconscious part of him knew I was already half gone. As if his sleeping body was already preparing for the goodbye his waking mind couldn't yet face.

I couldn't stay in here. Not with the taste of all those secrets crushing around me. I rested my hand over his fingers, just for moment, a small surrender to this man I'd always loved. My thumb traced the callus on his palm, the same roughness I'd memorized as a teenager, and something in me wanted to crawl against his chest and pretend I hadn't heard a word.

A quiet restlessness settled over me, a flutter beneath my ribs that wouldn't ease. I counted my breaths—in for four, hold for seven, out for eight—the way my mother had taught me during thunderstorms. It didn't help. The thoughts kept coming, soft but insistent, like rain against a window.

I slipped out from under the covers. The loss of his warmth hollowed me, a quiet ache spreading beneath my skin. Goose-bumps rose where his body had pressed against mine, as if each inch of me remembered and longed for his heat. I rose on trembling legs, wincing at the whispered protest of the mattress, my fingers seeking blindly for something to cover the chill that had settled into my bones.

I reached for his sweatshirt hanging from the bedpost and pulled it over my head, drowning in fabric that carried the scent of him. The floorboards creaked softly under each hesitant step as I crossed the room, my bare feet padding against the cold wood. My chest ached with something that felt like grief, and I pressed my palm flat against my sternum, feeling its wild rhythm beneath my fingertips.

Phone clutched in my hand, I eased into the hallway, pulling the door shut with barely a whisper. The screen's harsh glow made me wince. 4:32 a.m. Not even the sun was up. The world outside was covered in mist.

I knew I should step outside into the morning air, clear my head, and try to catch my breath. Instead, my feet betrayed me, carrying me down the hallway toward Ruby's room. A thin sliver of her nightlight spilled from the cracked door onto the hallway floor. I paused, my fingers hovering against the wood, before easing it open and slipping inside.

Ruby lay sprawled across her mattress, arms and legs flung outward as if she'd fallen from the sky into her pile of stuffed animals. We hadn't even changed out of yesterday's clothes, and the memory of her excited face at the fair tugged at my lips.

As I approached her bed, something on the floor caught my eye. It was the drawing Colt had carefully stepped over last night, and three stick figures hand-in-hand beneath a crooked sun.

Colt, Ruby, and me.

A small sob escaped my lips before I could stop it, and I bent down and clutched the drawing in my hand. My fingers traced the crayon lines, pressing so hard the paper crinkled at the edges. This family, these three stick figures, was everything I'd dreamed of for as long as I could remember. They stared back at me impossibly simple and devastatingly complicated all at once. I pressed it against my chest where my heart thrashed like a wild animal.

My fingers clamped around the edges of the paper until it

shook. I wanted to rip it, to tear through the fragile hope it forced in my chest, but my hands were too unsteady and my vision blurred as tears fell down my cheeks.

Of course this was what I wanted. I wanted a family, a place to belong, something that could never be taken away, but every time I reached for it, it seemed to slip from my fingers.

What if I wasn't enough for any of this?

"Blaire?"

I spun around, clutching the drawing against my chest like I'd been caught stealing. Ruby sat up in bed, one hand rubbing her eyes, the other clutching her stuffed rabbit by its ear.

"I'm sorry, sweet girl," I whispered, my voice catching. "I didn't mean to wake you."

She blinked at me, her eyes huge and solemn in the dim light. There was a pink flush on her cheeks, sleep-warm and soft, and the tangle of her dark hair reminded me so much of Colt it made something sharp twist in my chest.

"Why're you sad?" she whispered, voice rough with sleep. She hugged her rabbit tighter, gaze flicking between the drawing I still pressed to my heart and my face, like she couldn't decide which was more important.

I opened my mouth, then closed it. Part of me wanted to gather my things and slip away before dawn, before anyone could stop me. Another part wanted to crawl into that little bed and promise I'd never leave. "I'm just—" My voice cracked. "I'm not having a very brave day."

"I have those too." Ruby climbed down from her bed and clutched my hand in hers. Her small fingers felt both like an anchor and a trap. She tugged me forward, and I followed.

"Come on." She slid into her little canopy tent, and I hesitated at its entrance, before I slipped inside behind her.

Inside the tent, everything was muffled and shadowed, a world apart from everything outside. We sat cross-legged on the quilted floor, knees knocking, our faces almost touching in the cramped space.

She stared at me with an unblinking gravity that made me

want to look away. "Is this what you do in here?" I asked, an unsteady laugh breaking out of my throat.

"Yes." She nodded. "Sometimes I just sit with my stuffs." She pointed to the pile of stuffed animals that took up half the tent. "Sometimes I just play in here until I can be brave again."

I pressed my knuckles to my mouth, trying to keep the quiver out of my voice. "Does it work?"

"Not always." She shrugged. "That's why I need my brave berry."

I blinked at her. "Brave berry?"

She clambered up onto her knees and shuffled past a barricade of plush animals to the very back of the tent, where the shadow was thickest. I watched her fumble around, arms disappearing into a nest of mismatched pillows, and when they emerged again, her hands were clutching a tiny pink jewelry box.

"My daddy gave me this when my mama left."

The words landed between us with a weight I physically felt in my stomach. Five years old, and she'd already learned who stayed and those who didn't.

Ruby fumbled with the clasp of the jewelry box, a small tongue of concentration poking from the corner of her mouth. "He lets me put it on whenever I need help feeling brave." She looked up at me, seriousness radiating from every pore. "Maybe you can try?"

She pushed the jewelry box into my hands. I wasn't ready, but I opened the little lid anyway. Inside, nestled on a velvet pillow, was a thin gold chain. I dug my fingernail under the clasp and lifted it, uncertain and trembling. There, dangling at the end, was a small, gold strawberry charm.

My heart stuttered, and I felt like I couldn't breathe.

I held it up, the charm swinging gently between us, and I stared at the necklace I'd thrown back at Colt over ten years ago. The very necklace that gave him that little scar on his jaw.

"Daddy said it belonged to the bravest girl he ever knew. He said when I need it, I can put it on and borrow some of her brave."

The ache in my chest expanded, pressing against my ribs,

pushing up behind my eyes. I tried to breathe around it, but it was like swallowing a stone. The charm was warm in my palm, and I realized I was shaking.

Ruby plucked the chain from my grip with delicate fingers. "I'll put it on you." She leaned forward, tiny tongue sticking out in concentration again, and fastened it around my neck. Her hands were cool and sure. The gold strawberry settled against my throat like a brand.

"There," she said. "Now you can be brave, too."

I pressed my fingers to the charm, staring down at it as if it were a fragment of another life. I could smell Colt in the cotton of the sweatshirt I still wore, and I wondered how many times he'd held this necklace, how long he'd kept it hidden away.

"Do you feel braver?" The question was so earnest, so impossibly gentle, it nearly undid me

I looked into her big blue eyes, this little girl who I loved so much, and the bravery I felt had nothing to do with the piece of metal around my neck.

My fingers closed around the little strawberry pendant, feeling its fragile weight press into my palm. It was an absurd thing, really, to believe that courage could be conjured by a scrap of gold, but when Ruby's eyes fixed on me with that searching, loyal faith, I could almost pretend it was true.

I wanted to answer her with something grand, something worthy of the moment, but the truth was, there were no grand words left in me. I was emptied out, scraped raw by the night and by all the secrets that had come tumbling loose hours before. What I had left was the warmth of her, the steady hush of her breathing, and a memory of Colt's hands on my skin, anchoring me to a future I'd been too afraid to name.

"I do," I whispered, before I drew her into my lap and wrapped my arms around her, burying my face in her tangle of hair. She was so small, so impossibly light, and yet the gravity of her was what made me pull out my cell phone and click on my father's name.

There were so many unread messages, and the familiar suffocation of expectation and obligation clawed at me.

"What are you doing?" Ruby asked as she looked down at my phone.

"Borrowing some of this bravery." I kissed the top of her head and looked at the very last message from my father.

Senator Monroe: My patience is wearing thin, Blaire. Do you really want to handle this the hard way?

I stared at my father's message until the words blurred. Every cutting remark, every backhanded compliment, every disappointed sigh he'd ever aimed at me seemed to echo from that glowing screen. Then I looked up at Ruby's trusting face, her small fingers still touching the brave berry at my throat, and something hardened inside me.

Blaire: I know what you did to Colt and to June. I'm never coming back, dad.

Blaire: Willow Grove is my home.

CHAPTER 34
BLAIRE

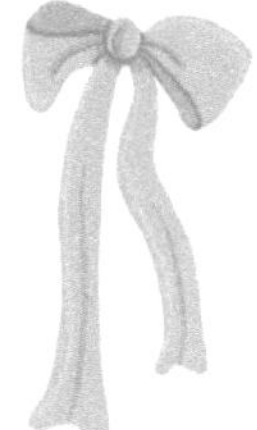

I lingered in Colt's doorway, watching the rise and fall of his chest beneath the sheets. Ruby had drifted back to sleep nearly an hour ago, and I felt desperate to get back to him.

The hinges betrayed me with a soft creak as I eased the door wider. Colt's eyes snapped open, disoriented for a heartbeat before they found me.

"What's wrong?" The question tumbled from his lips, rough with sleep but sharp with concern.

I slipped inside, closing the door behind me with a quiet click before climbing into bed to face him. Before I could speak, his hands found my waist, drawing me against the warmth of him.

"Strawberry," he whispered, his voice cracking on the word as his gaze burned across my face. "Tell me what's wrong."

"I'm not going anywhere," I whispered, and his entire body went rigid against mine. His fingers dug into my flesh hard enough to bruise.

"What?" His blue eyes widened with such raw panic that my heart stuttered in my chest.

"I'm still angry with you," I said, my voice breaking on the last word as I trailed my finger over his jaw.

"I know," he choked out.

His hands trembled violently as they clutched at me, and when his eyes darted away, I saw the fear lurking beneath his eyes that I'd vanish like smoke between his desperate fingers, leaving him alone in the wreckage of us.

My chest cracked open at the sight, a physical pain that made me gasp. His fear gutted me, a mirror reflecting back every doubt I'd ever swallowed.

What if he was right? What if staying was just another promise I couldn't keep?

The thought alone made something primal and desperate claw up my throat, threatening to tear me apart from the inside. My hands shook as I pressed them to Colt's chest, feeling his heartbeat hammer against me. I wanted to keep every promise I ever made to him, and I was so scared. But his heart kept beating beneath my palm, steady and sure where mine faltered.

Everything I needed lay within him and Ruby, and the certainty of it crashed into me like lightning.

I loved Colt Calloway with a desperation that terrified me.

I had always loved him, would always love him, even if it meant I bled for it for the rest of my life.

And I needed him to know that.

I closed my hand around the strawberry charm at my throat, squeezing until the little jagged edges bit deep into my palm. This tiny piece of metal was everything—my surrender, my homecoming, my declaration. With every heartbeat, the charm pressed against my skin like a brand, each pulse a reminder. I chose him. I chose them. And somehow, through all the years and heartbreak and impossible choices, he had always, always chosen me.

"I love you," I said, the words breaking free like a dam finally giving way. My voice cracked but didn't falter as I pressed my forehead against his. "God, Colt, I've tried so hard not to. I've run and I've hidden and I've lied to myself for years, but I love you."

He stared at me, blue eyes flaring wide with disbelief.

"Blaire." His voice cracked on that single syllable, as if it contained every prayer he'd ever whispered into the darkness.

I unclenched my fist, the strawberry charm having left angry red indentations in my palm, and dragged his calloused hand up until he could touch the necklace against my throat. His fingers shook violently as he gripped the metal, the warmth of his skin burning against my collarbone. His eyes locked with mine, raw and so exposed, silently begging me not to take this away.

"You make me brave, Colt," I whispered, my voice breaking on his name.

His face twisted, jaw clenching as if my words physically hurt him. A growl tore from his throat as his hand slid around my neck, fingers digging into my hair with bruising urgency. He yanked me toward him until we both gasped, and then his mouth crashed against mine. I welcomed the sting, the brutal pressure of his kiss branding me, claiming every breath I took. His teeth scraped my bottom lip, and I moaned, clawing at his shoulders.

"Don't ever fucking leave me again." His words burned against my skin as he dragged his mouth over my jaw. "I have never known how to love anyone but you, Blaire."

I pushed against his chest, gentle but insistent, until he fell back, his dark hair splayed across the pillow. The sweatshirt, his sweatshirt, caught on my breasts as I peeled it over my head. I hooked my thumbs into my panties, dragging them down my thighs as quickly as I could, feeling his eyes burn into every inch of newly exposed skin.

Then I slid one leg over his body, straddling him, and his fingers dug into my thighs.

I bent over him, hair falling like a curtain around our faces, and kissed him hard. I needed him to feel the truth of me, of us.

His hands tightened on my thighs, fingers digging in so hard I knew I'd wear the shape of him for hours. Our kiss was a battlefield, a prayer, a last stand. He shuddered when I bit his lower lip, and the sound he made was the kind that lingered in the air and slithered down my skin.

I broke away for air, and he followed, his hand cradling the back of my neck, needy and unashamed.

We barely surfaced between kisses. His need was frantic, but it was mine, too.

I reached down, thumbed the waistband of his boxers, and he caught my wrist, eyes blown wide. "You sure?" he whispered, and it sounded like he was asking for permission to believe in us, permission to hope.

"Always," I whispered as I kissed him again, slower this time.

I could feel every inch of him, hot and hard beneath me, and my fingers shook as I reached between us and wrapped my hand around his cock. I wanted to map the expanse of him and claim it as mine, the only place I'd ever belonged.

I didn't need acres of Tennessee soil or fields of wildflowers beneath an endless sky.

He was my home.

He groaned, deep in his chest, and every muscle in his body seemed to tense under me.

I moved my hand up and down the length of him, slow at first, dragging out the moment until I felt the tremor in his thighs, the strain of his hips fighting for more. His breath came in ragged pulls, every exhale a plea he tried to swallow. I watched his face as I stroked him, fascinated by the shifting storm behind his eyes. I'd seen Colt Calloway furious, laughing, wild, and broken, but never undone like this. Never with his defenses stripped bare.

His eyes tracked my hand's movement, his tongue sweeping across his lower lip. The raw hunger in his gaze sent a thrill of power through me. I ached to savor him slowly, to build our need until neither of us could stand it, but I was too greedy. I needed to feel him inside me, to erase the years between us and silence the whispers of doubt I still saw lingering in his eyes.

I pushed up onto my knees and lined us up.

He lifted his head off the pillow to follow the motion, his gaze dropping to where my hand met his cock, then to the soft, slick heat of me he was about to fill. His eyes devoured me, and the space between us vibrated with a hunger so visceral I could barely breathe.

I leaned forward, anchoring myself with my palms on his

chest, feeling the frantic thrum of his heart beneath my fingers. I guided him inside me, savoring the stretch and burn until I was fully seated on him, his cock buried so deep I felt it everywhere. He let out a noise, and his grip on my hips turned painful.

He tried to say something. I saw the words form, then die on his lips, replaced by a gasp as I started to move. I set the rhythm, rolling my hips in slow circles, grinding down onto him the way I knew would drive him insane. He met every motion with his own, our bodies syncing up like we'd never forgotten how to fit together.

It was blinding, the way it felt. He filled me so perfectly, every thrust scraping away another layer of fear, another lie, until all that remained was the two of us. I arched my back, taking him deeper, desperate to burn away the polished veneer my father had demanded and Grant had praised. With each movement, another piece of Senator Monroe's perfect daughter crumbled away.

I dug my nails into his chest, and he moved his hands up my ribs, thumbs grazing the curves beneath my breasts.

"Jesus, Blaire," he groaned as he watched me.

I rode him faster, grinding down until the base of him hit the spot that made me shudder. Every time I rose up and came back down, he met me with a force that showed his fraying control. He wanted to crack me open, and I wanted to let him. I felt it in the way his hands bruised my hips and the way his eyes never left my face, like he was memorizing every flinch, every sound I made.

He was watching for doubt, but he found none.

I leaned back, letting my hands settle on his thighs, hair falling in knots down my back, and he watched the way I moved. He slipped a thumb between my legs, watching with greedy focus as I shivered and clenched around him, each stroke of his thumb sending me higher until I thought I'd break apart from the inside out.

"Look at me," he said, soft but stern, and I did.

I let him see me. Stripped and ugly with need, bare of pride or shame.

All I could do was move, chasing the fire he'd set in my blood. I rocked harder, feeling the edge coming up fast, and he felt it too.

His hands tightened, his own rhythm faltering and losing control. He was close.

We'd done this before, but it had never felt so real.

"I love you, Colt." I didn't try to hide how utterly frantic I was. "I have loved you most of my life, and I will never stop."

"Fuck," he hissed as my words hit him.

I pressed my palms into his chest, anchoring myself in the thundering beat beneath my hands. I wanted him to feel it, to feel me. I rode him with a recklessness that bordered on self-destruction, grinding down until I felt him in every part of me.

"Do you hear me, Calloway?" I rasped, nails biting into his skin. "I've tried loving others, but it was always you. It will always be you."

His jaw flexed, and his hand shot up to the back of my neck, palm cradling the base of my skull. He yanked me down hard enough to steal my breath, and our mouths clashed together. I swallowed his growl, his need, and gave him everything in return.

Our bodies moved, fueled by every memory of loss and every second we'd spent pretending we could live without each other.

It was a collision, and there was no space between us for regret.

The headboard banged the wall, the mattress groaned, and the house seemed to shrink around the shape of us. He bucked up into me, his rhythm gone wild, and I clung to him, shaking with the force of my need.

"You undo me," he muttered against my mouth. "Fuck, I have always loved you."

I felt myself unraveling, every muscle drawn tight.

"Don't let go," he gasped against my mouth. "I'm not ever letting go. Never again."

The tension built and built, and his hands were nearly crushing my hips, his body shaking beneath me. We snapped at the same time. His head thrown back, my hands fisting in his hair, both of us breaking open. A desperate sound escaped my lips, and it was full of everything I'd never been able to say.

He met me, every inch, every thrust, and poured himself into me with a gasp.

For a long while, we held on to each other, slick with sweat, shaking and breathless. There was nothing but the two of us and that gold chain that still hung around my neck.

The gold chain that he'd saved after all this time.

CHAPTER 35

BLAIRE

R uby and I were in her room when Colt's phone rang over and over.

A cold dread filled me when I heard the tension in his voice from the kitchen. He moved down the hall, stepping into Ruby's doorway, and his whole body was rigid.

"Stay here," he muttered, voice already steeled for a fight.

"What's wrong?" I asked, already climbing to my feet.

I couldn't just stay there.

The thought of hiding, of cowering behind a door while chaos battered the porch, was unthinkable. Every nerve in my body shrieked at me to intercept whatever storm was about to roll through Colt's house, to shield Ruby from it.

And deep down in my gut I already knew what it was.

It had only been two days since I sent my father those texts, and he'd been blowing up my phone ever since.

Two days of me, Colt, and Ruby in a perfect little bubble, but of course he was going to ruin it.

"Your father and Grant are about to pull in," Colt said, his voice dropping to a harsh whisper as he raked his fingers through his dark hair.

A muscle jumped in his jaw, and the veins in his forearms

stood out as he clenched and unclenched his fists, like a man preparing for a fight he wasn't sure he could win.

My heart punched fast and ugly against my ribs, and I crouched to Ruby's level, my words a frantic whisper against the roar in my ears. "Ruby, I need you to stay in here, okay? Go to your tent and play with your animals for a little bit."

Ruby's eyes were wide, her small hand fisted in my sweatshirt she was currently wearing. "What's happening?"

"My daddy's here." I nodded gently. "And he's not like your daddy. I just need you to be really brave for me, okay?"

Her chin wobbled, but she nodded. "Okay."

I was almost through her doorway when she called out for me.

I stopped, turning back to look, and Ruby ran in my direction, dropping our strawberry necklace into my palm. "In case you need to borrow some brave."

"Thank you, Ruby." I closed my fingers around the necklace, feeling the small metal strawberry press into my palm.

By the time I reached the living room, Colt was already at the front door, shoulders squared, as he pulled the door open.

Hunter was there, walking in the doorway, but Mr. Calloway was too. His shoulders were squared, and his jaw was set with the quiet resolve I remembered from my childhood. I hadn't seen Mr. Calloway out of his house since I'd been back, and despite how frail he looked before, he looked far more like the sturdy rancher I remembered now.

Mr. Calloway looked straight past Colt when he saw me, and there was so much pity there that it made me flinch. "They showed up at the big house first looking for you when no one was at June's. They're on their way here."

Hunter stepped further inside, eyes flickering from me to the hallway. "June laid down behind his SUV and bought us a few minutes to get down here first."

I snorted because of fucking course she did.

Colt looked over his shoulder at me, a smile playing on his own lips.

"She really is the best fucking grandma."

"She was mooing at them too, but I wasn't going to tell you that." Owen shook his head as if the woman absolutely exasperated him.

I started to head toward the door but stopped. "Hunter, will you watch Ruby? I don't want her anywhere near my father."

"Of course." He nodded.

I stepped outside just as a black SUV came into view.

"Blaire," Colt whispered my name and tried to pull me behind him. He was trying to shield me, and I loved him for it.

But I had to face this.

I shook my head before stepping past him. The sky was dense with clouds, the air thick with the threat of rain that had not yet broken but wanted to. Every nerve in my body buzzed as I crossed the porch and let my bare feet slap the old wood. I still held the strawberry necklace in my hand, and I wrapped it around my fingers as if it could truly give me the courage to face my father.

At the top of the porch steps, I paused. The SUV crawled up the gravel, black and glossy and wholly out of place on this cracked Tennessee drive. Colt stood at my shoulder, but this time he didn't try to touch me. He just hovered, a silent, bristling presence radiating fury and fear in equal measure.

Mr. Calloway stepped outside with us, pulling the door closed behind him.

I wrapped my arms around my ribs, the gesture instinctive, and watched as the car came to a slow stop near the house. The engine idled, a heavy, juddering sound that made the whole porch seem to tremble.

Colt's fingers brushed my elbow, just as the car door opened, and my father stepped out first, as impeccable as ever, not a single hair out of place despite the humidity, his suit jacket crisp and deeply black against the dull morning. He shut the door and came up the walk like it belonged to him.

I barely registered the second figure until he rounded the front of the car. Grant, of course. He emerged in a storm-gray suit that had probably cost more than my first two years of college, but the man inside looked rumpled, poorly fitted to the role he'd been cast in. He lingered behind my father, hands in his pockets, and a thin, unsatisfied smile on his mouth.

His eyes landed on me, flicked to Colt, then right back to me.

I could feel the heat of Colt as his chest expanded against my shoulder blade, but I kept my eyes trained on my father.

His gaze never left my face. He didn't even acknowledge Colt or Mr. Calloway as he stopped at the bottom of the stairs.

"Blaire." My name fell from my father's lips, and it was loaded with every way I'd ever disappointed him.

I forced myself to meet his eyes.

"Dad," I said, my voice surprisingly steady. "What are you doing here?"

His nostrils flared. "You're coming home. Right now. Pack your things and say your goodbyes. We're done here."

This wasn't about my future or even his position in politics. This was about control. I'd spent my whole life trying to be the daughter he wanted, and now that I was slipping from his grasp, it was freeing.

Grant shifted on his feet, his smile spreading, and finally found the nerve to speak. "Blaire, you look...rested."

Colt bristled at my back, and I thought he might leap the railing and tackle Grant right there on the gravel. I could feel his heartbeat against my back, thumping louder and faster with every condescending word out of Grant's mouth.

I turned my attention back to my father. "I'm not leaving."

A crack appeared in my father's expression. He wasn't used to being told no. Not by anyone, least of all me. He took a step up, closing the space between us, but I didn't back down.

"You're making a mistake," he warned, low and irritated.

I swallowed hard, adrenaline burning in my throat, and the taste of Colt still clinging to my tongue. "No. I'm not."

Grant scoffed. "Come on, Blaire. You seriously want to throw your life away for...this?" He gestured to the house, then to Colt with a look of practiced pity. "For a worn-out cowboy and a kid who isn't yours?"

I felt Colt shift behind me, but the moment he mentioned Ruby my anger flooded me.

"Don't you dare speak about her," I spat, my voice low and shaking with restraint. "That little girl is worth a thousand of you. If you speak of her again, I'll call every reporter I can think of and tell them exactly why Grant Chandler's wedding is in shambles. Would you like me to send them the photos of you fucking your assistant who isn't even old enough to drink?"

That wiped the smile clean off his face.

Colt moved to my side, his stance rigid. "You're not welcome here." His hand pressed against my lower back as if he needed the feel of me as badly as I needed him. "You have thirty seconds to get off my land before I call the sheriff."

My father's jaw flexed, his gaze flicking between me and Colt like he was recalculating the best way to separate us. "This is about salvaging what's left of your future. You're not thinking clearly, Blaire. You never do when you're around people like—"

"Like what?" I snapped.

"Like your mother." My father turned, finally acknowledging Colt, and sneered. "You think you can protect her from me? From any of this?" He swept his hand out. "You couldn't even keep her from running away the first time."

"I've spent every day since regretting it," Colt said with a growl.

My father's mouth twisted. "Touching." His eyes slid back to me. "June's farm is hanging by a thread, Blaire. One phone call from me, and the bank forecloses tomorrow." He tilted his head, watching my reaction. "Your grandmother signed her name to numbers she couldn't possibly understand. It would be a blessing for me to take that burden off her."

My heart stuttered. The numbers on that Deed of Trust flashed in my mind. June's farm was all she had. I was all she had. "I'm going to help her pay it off." I didn't even want to think about how many jars of jams that would take. "June and I are—"

My father scoffed, cutting me off, and my legs shook beneath me. Colt's arm locked around my waist, anchoring me against the solid wall of his chest.

"That paperwork you're threatening her with?" Colt's voice rumbled through my chest. "It doesn't exist."

My father's eyebrows arched. "I beg your pardon?"

"June's loan. It's been paid in full."

That didn't make sense.

There was no way June had been able to pay off that loan already. I blinked at Colt over my shoulder, certain I'd misheard him. But his face was stone, his eyes narrowed on my father, and there was not an ounce of doubt in him.

"What did you say?" My father's voice was glacial.

Colt didn't flinch. His jaw was set, the muscle ticking just once as he tightened his hold on me. "June's loan," he repeated slowly. "The one you've been holding over her." He nodded in my direction. "It's paid off. You don't have any leverage anymore."

"That's not possible," my father sneered. "The bank—"

"It's not impossible." I felt the careful, terrifying calm in Colt's voice as it rumbled through his chest. "I worked my ass off for the last ten years to help her pay it back, then I sold a portion of my land from my father's ranch to pay the rest." He said it like it was nothing. Like it was a single stone in a wall he'd been building for years.

The silence that followed pressed against my chest until I felt like I couldn't breathe.

"Why?" I looked at Colt, my vision swimming with shock and something wild and painful that I didn't dare name. This ranch, this land, it meant everything to him. "Why would you do that for her?"

He finally looked down at me, and the world narrowed to just us standing there. His eyes, the same blue that haunted my dreams, searched mine with a rawness that made my chest ache.

"I didn't do it for her," he whispered. Then, he gently reached up and tucked a loose strand of hair behind my ear, his hand shaking just enough for me to notice. He leaned in, so close I could feel his breath on my cheek. "Always for you."

The words struck bone.

My father's face flashed with disbelief, outrage, then the cold calculation of a man who'd never known what it meant to lose. For a second, he looked older than I'd ever seen him, lines of power and privilege suddenly cut deep with panic.

"I'm going to call my lawyers," my father snarled as he reached for his phone.

"Go ahead." Colt shrugged. "I can have the paperwork couriered to your office before you get back to the city."

My father looked at me, and if Colt wasn't holding me against him, I probably would have cowered. "You think this is over?"

"All of June's land has been restructured in a new Trust for Blaire," Colt interrupted his threat, and there was a finality to his words. "We went through every step. It's untouchable."

I felt his words in my teeth, my gut, behind my breastbone.

He did that for me.

He'd cut out pieces of his own legacy, the land he'd lived and bled and breathed, just so my future could not be weaponized by the man in front of me. If there were any remaining walls between us, they would have collapsed with his words. All that remained was something terrifyingly tender, a wild hope I hardly recognized as my own.

"Bullshit," my father seethed. "I've sacrificed too much for you to just throw it all away, Blaire."

"That's enough," Mr. Calloway said, and though he didn't raise his voice, it cut through every one of us.

He shifted his weight, boots scuffing against the porch, and looked at me the way a rancher sizes up a storm, narrow-eyed and entirely without fear. Then he turned, facing my father.

"You think you know something about sacrifice?" His voice was like sandpaper and old whiskey. "I've lived on this land my whole life. I've chosen this land and my family time and time again. You think this ranch is just dirt and fence posts? It's the sum of every heartbreak and every homecoming. It's the sweat poured into the soil and the way you love your children more than you love your own damn self. You want to talk about what a man gives up for the people he loves?" Mr. Calloway looked right at Colt, before he wrapped his hand around the back of his son's neck, unflinching and real. "A man works this earth so hard he forgets how to say the things that matter. Sometimes he fumbles it. Sometimes he fucks it up so bad the only thing left is to keep going and hope he gets a second chance to do it right."

He looked at me. "There isn't a thing in this world my boy wouldn't give up for you. He's been losing sleep and about half his mind for a decade, waiting on the chance that you'd come home and let him try again."

I didn't realize I was crying until I tasted salt on my lips. I blinked hard, trying to focus on anything other than the ache in my chest that made it impossible to breathe.

"There are two different kinds of men in the world, Blaire," Mr. Calloway went on. "You've had both. One who did anything to keep you, even if it meant breaking you to fit his own design." He nodded toward Grant, but I didn't look away from him. "And the other let you go when it killed him to do it, then spent every day since working himself to the bone making sure you had solid ground to land on, even if that ground never brought you back to him." He held my gaze without wavering.

Colt's arm trembled around me as he tightened his hold. All the anger and regret and battered hope in the world was in the heat of his palm and the steadiness he tried to muster just for me. He pressed his face into my neck, his breath warm against my pulse point, and the brush of his mustache sent a shiver down my spine.

"Enough of this nonsense. Blaire, get your things." The sound of my father's voice made me flinch. "You have a job in Raleigh. We have a wedding we have to deal with. You have five minutes," he said, each word weighted with consequences.

I looked at my father, and I watched his eyes sweep over me, calculating the losses and gains like I was just another column in his ledger. Then my gaze flicked to Grant who still stood beside my father, hands in his pockets, jaw working hard as he tried to keep control of his smug, easy smile. But his gaze was zeroed in on where Colt still held me.

I laced my fingers through Colt's, gripping his hand like a lifeline. His skin told stories my father would never be able to read. Every callous was a sacrifice, each crease a burden shouldered for someone else's sake. I thought of Ruby's tiny fingers wrapped around his thumb, the way she looked up at him like she'd never questioned the way he loved her. My chest constricted, vision swimming as rage and protectiveness collided. I couldn't bear the thought of her ever standing where I stood now, desperate for a love that should've been given freely.

This was my family now. Colt, Ruby, and me, and I'd fight like hell to protect it.

I turned back to my father, and my chest cracked open with grief not just for the woman I'd become, but for the child I once was. I used to curl under my blankets after my mama tucked me in, and I would pray for him to love me enough to come back.

Ruby would never stand where I stood now, trembling with the pathetic hope that maybe this time, just this time, she might be enough.

Her mother had left just as my father had left me, but I would choose Ruby every day. I would fill her doubt with so much love that she never questioned it for even a moment.

"Get off this land," I snapped, my words hard and sure, and this time, the tremor was gone. "Don't come back."

For a heartbeat the whole world stilled, the porch and the yard and the sky itself contracting to the flash of my father's eyes and the slack-jawed shock twisting Grant's face.

My father's lips pinched, the first hint of real anger seeping into his voice as he searched for some new weapon. "You don't know what you're saying. You don't know what this will cost." There was the threat he always delivered. He'd always measured love in ledger lines, and he couldn't help but reach for it now, even as the ground fell away beneath him. I wanted to laugh. I wanted to scream.

"You can take your money and your name and go back to your

world." Every word felt like letting go of the woman I had become under his thumb. "I don't want either."

Colt's hand steadied against me.

"Blaire, you are my daughter—"

I didn't let him finish. "I am my mother's daughter. Not yours."

His head snapped back at my words, and he blinked.

I met his gaze and held it, letting him see exactly how serious I was. "I have your drafts, timelines, and every 'private matter' you made me scrub. If you ever come here and threaten my family again, I'll leak them to the press myself."

Colt's hand shuddered against me.

I watched the calculations tick behind my father's eyes, the way he weighed which of us would do the most damage if cornered. "You'll regret this, Blaire." He shook his head. "And don't come calling me when you do."

Grant let out a low chuckle, and he looked at me with a smile that would have made me cower just a few weeks ago. "You think this is noble? You think this is love? He's going to let you rot here, same as your mother did."

One second Colt's hand was on my waist, the next he was gone. A streak of rage hurtling down the porch. Colt's fist caught Grant square in the face with a sickening crack that echoed through the yard like a gunshot.

Grant went down hard, crumpling backward onto the gravel, his expensive shoes skittering up dust. His hands clutched at his nose as blood poured between his fingers.

Colt loomed over Grant, chest heaving, fists still clenched at his sides. "Don't talk about her mother," he said, and his voice was pure, undiluted fury. "Don't you dare look at my girl ever again."

Grant glared up at Colt with wild, watering eyes, then spat a bright red streak onto the dirt at Colt's boots. No one moved for a long moment then Mr. Calloway walked down the stairs and crouched beside Grant with a handkerchief outstretched.

"Here," he said quietly, voice stripped of any judgment. "It'll help slow the bleeding."

Grant batted it away, more child than man, then staggered to his feet, swaying a little. His nose was already swelling, his eyes watering with pain.

"You're both a fucking joke," he whined, the words muffled and wet.

"Go," I said, and he did, stumbling after my father like a wounded dog.

Colt stood in the dust, his shoulders rigid. His knuckles were split, a smear of Grant's blood across them. He didn't move until my father and Grant had climbed into the SUV and disappeared over the horizon in a cloud of dust.

Even then, he stared at his hands, breathing hard. I stepped down from the porch, the soles of my feet hitting the sun-warmed wood.

Colt looked up at me then, and there was so much in his eyes I thought I might drown in them. Grief and relief, yes, but also a kind of awe. Like he finally let himself believe I was real and here and his.

I walked to him, standing so close I could smell the sweat and the iron and the faint hint of his cologne. "You didn't have to do that," I said, and his mouth twitched.

"He had it coming." His gaze held mine, his eyes searching.

I reached out and traced my fingers over his hand, below his busted knuckles. "Does it hurt?"

A flicker of emotion crossed his face, vulnerability shining through. "Not anymore. Not as long as I have you."

CHAPTER 36
COLT

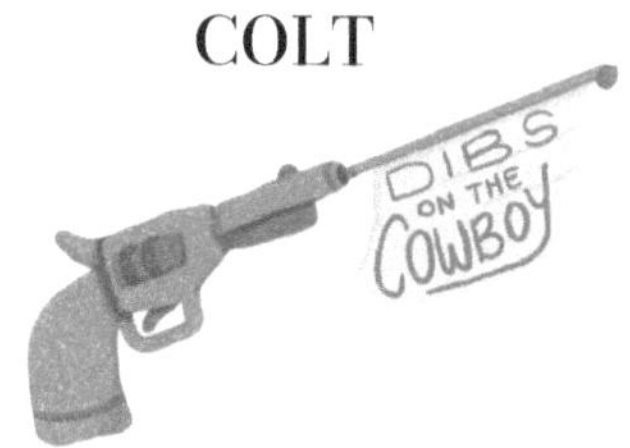

Their tires kicked up a cloud of dust that hung in the air long after the SUV had vanished down the road. My whole body shook. Breaking that bastard's nose wasn't enough. It wasn't nearly enough for what he and Blaire's father had done.

Blood dripped between my fingers as I stared at the empty road, wishing my rage had disappeared with that black vehicle. I flexed my hand, watching the blood crack across my throbbing knuckles. I would do it all over again, a million times over just to watch that asshole crumble in front of her.

Blaire's fingers brushed over my bloodied knuckles, tender where mine had been violent. I forced myself to meet her gaze, and the sight knocked the wind from my lungs.

It was just her, my Blaire, with those big brown eyes staring up at me and her curls framing her face. She scrunched her nose as she looked at my injured knuckles with her bare feet planted on my dirt, and I wanted to fall to my knees.

She was my home.

"You didn't have to do that," she said so calmly, but my lips twitched thinking about Grant's face as he climbed in the car.

"He had it coming." I searched her eyes, looking for any signs of regret, any sign of what was going on in that beautiful head of hers.

"Does it hurt?" Her fingers were still tracing my hand, careful not to touch the injured parts.

"Not anymore. Not as long as I've got you."

She stared at me head-on, and the laugh that broke from her was so sudden it startled me. It was a small, wild thing, but it meant everything. She took my hand gently, cradling the split knuckles as if willing the pain from my body into her own.

"Come on," she said, tugging me by the wrist. "Let's rinse this off before Ruby sees her daddy all bloodied up for me."

I didn't deserve her.

The porch creaked behind us, and I turned, bracing myself for Hunter or my father. But it was Ruby that stood in the doorway, clutching her bear tight against her chest.

She blinked at the two of us, at the blood on my hands and the way Blaire was holding me.

Ruby shuffled closer, bare feet padding softly over the porch as she moved to my dad's side. "Daddy?" she said, and the word was so tentative it almost broke me in half.

"Hey, baby. You okay?" I asked as Blaire finally dropped my hand, both of us turning more fully to face the porch.

Ruby looked from her to me and back again. "Did you get hurt?" she asked.

I climbed up the stairs toward her, running my uninjured hand over her head. "Just a scratch, kiddo. Nothing to worry about."

She frowned, unconvinced, and pointed a finger at my hand. "It looks gross."

"That's because your daddy's tough," I told her, forcing my lips into a smile as I flexed my hand and tried not to flinch. The pain shot up my wrist, but the sight of Ruby's lips curling at the corners made it worth it. She tried to hide her smile behind the bear, but I caught it. And a bit of the tension in my chest loosened.

Blaire stepped onto the porch behind me, and she slid that strawberry necklace over Ruby's head before she wrapped her up in her arms. I watched them together, and I could hardly breathe. Blaire kept one hand cupped gently around the back of Ruby's head and looked up at me, her brown eyes warm and clear.

"He'll be fine," she promised. "We all will."

Ruby shifted in her arms, peeking out from behind her bear. "Did you punch Blaire's daddy?"

Hunter laughed, and my gaze finally met his. "No. But he landed a hell of a shiner on her boyfriend."

Ruby scrunched up her nose, and her head whipped around to look at Blaire. "I thought Daddy's your boyfriend?"

"He is now." Hunter laughed, and Blaire blushed. "Blaire found a bigger boyfriend to beat her little boyfriend's ass."

Blaire immediately covered Ruby's ears, and I smiled at the look she gave my brother. "Really, Hunter. I swear you really are the worst sometimes."

Hunter shrugged and gave her the biggest grin. "No. You love me. You can't deny it."

My father hovered at the edge of the porch, hands stuffed deep in his pockets, gaze darting back and forth like he was tracking some invisible threat on the horizon. I recognized the anxious energy in my old man, the kind that only surfaced when he didn't have the words or tools to fix whatever was broken in one of his kids.

He hiked his finger over his shoulder as his eyes met mine. "I think me and your brother are going to get out of your hair. Want me to take our girl with me for a while? I could put Ruby to work."

Blaire's answer was so immediate it startled me. "No. Not today." Blaire's arms tightened around her. "I want her with us."

My dad's face softened. He nodded once, before he leaned forward and gave Ruby's hair a quick ruffle. "She saved you this time, Ruby. Next time, I'm going to make you clean out the stalls with me."

Ruby made a disgusted face and Blaire snorted.

Blaire shifted Ruby from hip to hip, eyes never quite leaving my father. "Thank you," she said, quietly. "For everything." Her gaze snagged on Hunter. "You too, Hunter. Thank you for being here when I needed you."

My father cleared his throat as he looked at Blaire. "You're family, Blaire. Always have been."

Blaire's eyes went glassy, and she started to reply, but Hunter swept in before she could gather her words. His usual wiseass grin was gone as he gathered her and Ruby both in a hug.

He pressed a kiss to the top of Blaire's head, and squeezed Ruby so tight she squeaked and started giggling. Blaire pressed her face into Hunter's shoulder, laughing even as she wiped her eyes. Ruby beamed, the bear mashed between her and my brother's chest.

He let them go, stepped back, and my father cleared his throat again. He reached out to squeeze my shoulder, then he and Hunter started for the truck, walking side by side. I watched them go, Hunter's arm flung over my dad's shoulders, the pair of them silhouetted against the gravel drive. They didn't look back, didn't need to.

Blaire put Ruby back down on her feet before we all drifted back into the house. Ruby trailed close behind Blaire, dragging her bear by one battered paw, her eyes fixed to Blaire like she was afraid she might vanish if she looked away.

Blaire moved around the kitchen as I turned on the sink and let the cold water run over my bloodied knuckles. She poured a glass of water and grabbed some pain relievers before setting them both in front of me.

"Take those," she ordered, and I smiled.

"Yes, ma'am."

Ruby looked up at us, gaze bouncing from my face to Blaire's, her little brow furrowed in concentration. There was a question brewing in her, but she chewed her lip before letting it out in the kind of earnest, no-nonsense voice only a child could muster.

"But Daddy really is your boyfriend, right?" my daughter asked, holding her bear close and blinking at me with that same unfiltered curiosity I'd seen on her face so many times before. "Even if he didn't beat up your other boyfriend?"

I snorted, laughter rumbling in my chest, but Blaire ignored me.

She looked at Ruby with a steady gentleness that made me wonder how the hell I'd ever let her go. "Are you okay with it if he is?" she asked. "I don't know about your daddy, but I'd like that. I'd like to be more than that. I want us to be a family."

Ruby's eyes widened, and hell, so did mine.

"Like a mom?" Ruby whispered, and my gaze slammed into Blaire.

This wasn't something we'd talked about yet, and fuck, she'd only told me she was staying a couple days ago. I didn't want this to freak her out.

But Blaire held Ruby's gaze, calm and honest, and I'd never loved anyone the way I loved the two of them.

I watched them, my daughter and the woman I loved, and I saw the shape of a future that I'd always been too scared to dream of.

"If that's what you want," Blaire said, and her voice was so gentle it was almost a whisper. "But I can just be your friend, too. It's completely up to you."

Ruby's mouth made a perfect 'O', and she looked from Blaire to me and back again, as if she was measuring us, weighing our promise against all the things she'd lost and learned in her short little life. There was a hush then, the instant before lightning strikes, and I realized I was gripping the edge of the kitchen counter, my knuckles white and raw from the fight but numb to everything except this.

Blaire's hand slid over Ruby's, small fingers tangled with bigger ones, and Ruby studied their hands as their pinkies wrapped together. Their pinkies stayed locked, a single bridge between them that linked them together, and Ruby blinked up at Blaire with her eyes full of hope.

"Yeah," she said, and her voice was so sure it almost broke me. "That's what I want."

Then she launched herself at Blaire, arms flung wide, and Blaire caught her, laughter bursting out of her. She spun Ruby around in a circle, and they both giggled, the high-pitched sound ricocheting off the kitchen cabinets and filling up all the empty places in the house.

Ruby buried her face in Blaire's neck and Blaire hugged her so tight I thought they'd fuse together. I wanted to memorize every detail—the way Blaire rocked her side to side, the way Ruby's little hand clung to Blaire's shirt, the way the sun shined gold through the windows against their skin and made it look like they'd been carved from the same streak of fire.

After a long minute, Ruby pulled back, her cheeks pink and eyes shining brightly. "We should paint each other's nails."

"Absolutely!" Blaire said, and Ruby took off running toward her room, her giggle trailing off as she vanished around the corner.

I caught Blaire before she could follow, arms finding their way around her waist, pulling her up against me so her back was pressed to my chest. She landed with a little "oof" and laughed, and her hair tickled my jaw as I buried my face in her neck. She was warm and relaxed under my hands, and I let out a shuddering breath at the feel of her in my arms.

"What just happened?" I said, voice shaky, not sure if I was asking Blaire or myself.

I felt the tremor in her too. Her breath caught in her chest like we both needed a second to process that this was real.

And goddamn it, I wanted it to be real.

Blaire leaned back into me, hands covering mine where they splayed over her stomach, and she laughed again. "I think I just got promoted," she whispered as she twisted in my arms, enough to look up at me. "You in?"

I couldn't help it. I pressed my mouth against hers, kissing her with every bit of happiness that was pulsing through me.

"I'm in," I murmured, awed by the simple truth of it. "I want this." My voice cracked a little. "I've always wanted you."

"If you keep kissing me like that, I might have to call dibs on you, Calloway."

She was trying to play it cool, but I could see the way her eyes glistened, the hope and fear and everything else we'd been carrying around for years all crashing together.

"I think you just did," I said, my voice rough.

She didn't argue. She let her head fall back to my chest, trusting me to hold her up, as Ruby's voice called from down the hallway.

"Blaire! I can't find the blue one!"

Blaire laughed, disentangling from me with a gentle pat to my hand. "I'm coming!" She lingered a second longer, her fingers brushing over my cheek, her gaze searching mine.

"You're not mad at me, Strawberry?" I asked, and my stomach ached as I waited for her answer. "A lot of shit has happened over the last few days."

"Oh, I'm plenty mad at you." She nodded and narrowed her eyes. "But I can think of a few ways for you to make it up to me."

She smiled, quick and dazzling, then slipped from my hold and hurried after Ruby.

I watched her go, and I leaned my weight against the counter, my busted hand throbbing in time with my heartbeat. I looked around my house that had belonged to Ruby and me alone for so long, and already, there were so many signs of Blaire everywhere I looked.

She was in Ruby's drawings that covered the fridge. Her sweatshirt, the one Ruby had claimed as her own, hung off one of the kitchen chairs where she tossed it. By the sink, that chipped blue mug I'd always reached for first, now belonged to her. Even the air felt different, carrying the hint of summer strawberries that hit me like a memory I'd craved half my life.

"You coming, or are you too scared to get your nails painted?" Blaire's voice floated back to me, and I glanced up to see her leaning around the hall, staring straight at me.

"Do I have a choice?" I laughed.

Blaire shook her head and crooked her finger for me to follow her. "No. I think you're stuck with us both, cowboy."

And damn if that didn't sound like the best thing I'd ever heard.

Epilogue
BLAIRE

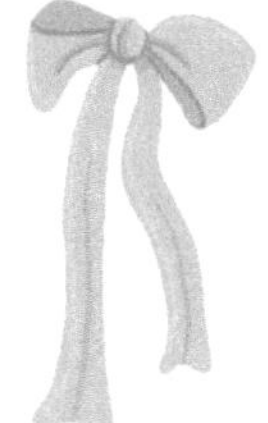

Three Months Later

Colt's silhouette carved itself against the Tennessee sky. The fading light of the sun washed over his skin, catching the proud line of his jaw where a day's worth of stubble darkened, and casting long shadows below the brim of his cowboy hat. My breath caught as I watched his shoulders flex and roll with each movement of the horse. His shirt clung to the ridge of his spine as he shifted his weight in the saddle.

He looked so wild and untamed as he rode, like he belonged to nothing and no one but the open sky above us.

But he belonged to me, and he belonged to this land.

Every muscle in his arm and thigh moved with that steady, easy confidence of a man who knew this soil the way he knew his own hands.

I'd been chasing after their dust for three miles now, my heart racing faster than my horse's hooves, the same way I'd chased that man for half my life.

Every few minutes, he'd turn back in the saddle, and when our eyes met, his smile would unfurl slowly and knowingly. Each time, that smile sent a flush of heat cascading through me like wildflowers blooming across this hillside after rain.

We'd dropped Ruby off at the main house half an hour ago. Lou had met us on the porch with a Tupperware of fresh cookies still warm from the oven. Ruby barely waved goodbye before she was sprinting inside, words tumbling out of her mouth faster than she could form them properly.

I'd felt the first pang of separation watching Ruby go, then that immediate, guilty relief that made my cheeks warm. It was followed by the unmistakable want that bloomed low in my belly when Colt's calloused fingertips found the small of my back. He'd pressed there, his thumb grazing the strip of bare skin where my shirt had ridden up. That single touch burned through my clothes like a brand.

It was hard to argue with a man like Colt when he wanted something. It was even harder when I wanted it, too.

We rode in silence toward home, *our home now*, since that night two months ago when we stood in my freshly repaired bedroom at June's. Colt had shifted his weight from one boot to the other, eyes darting around the small space.

"Ruby's gotten used to having you down the hall," he'd said, voice gruff. His eyes met mine, one hand rubbing the back of his neck. "This room's too small for all your things anyway."

"What?" I'd laughed and wrapped my arms around his waist as I looked up at him.

"Just stay with us, Blaire," he huffed, and he was so damn cute, I couldn't deny him.

At the far end of the property, the house came into view, and just beyond it, the lake stretched and shimmered with the dying sunlight.

Our horses slowed to a walk as we approached the house, and Colt glanced over, eyes dancing with something that made my stomach flutter. When we stopped, our legs nearly touched as we slid from our saddles. His fingers grazed mine as he reached for my reins.

"I've got them," he said, voice low and rough.

With quick, practiced movements, he secured both horses to the hitching post, then dragged his forearm across his forehead. I couldn't help but notice the way his muscles moved beneath tan skin, or the way a flush of color still rode high on his cheekbones from our ride.

I was halfway up the porch steps when his fingers caught my wrist. Heat bloomed beneath his fingers, and I stopped, looking over my shoulder to find him standing a foot below, his face half in shadow, half in sunlight. His grip shifted, fingers sliding between mine, his calloused thumb finding the sensitive hollow of my palm. I felt my breath hitch as his gaze traveled down my body, lingering at my throat, my chest, the curve of my hips where my jeans clung from the heat of our ride.

"What?" I asked, the word so quiet I wasn't sure he heard it.

My skin prickled with awareness as his eyes made their slow journey back up, leaving a trail of heat behind. When his gaze finally locked with mine, the unmistakable hunger I saw there made something low in my belly tighten and unfurl. He stepped closer, close enough that I could feel the warmth radiating from his body, smell the sun on his skin, but not close enough to touch.

"Swim with me," he murmured, his fingers tightening around mine as he tugged me toward him until I collided with the solid wall of his chest.

I laughed, but it came out breathless as his free hand found the small of my back. "Are you not going to let me change into my swimsuit?"

He simply shook his head, the corner of his mouth lifting in that half-smile that promised trouble. "Don't need one," he whispered, close enough now that his lips brushed my ear.

I barely had time to catch my breath before he was tugging me down the porch steps and toward the lake. He stepped in tight behind me, chest pressed to my back, and his mustache tickled my neck as he bent his head, lips grazing the shell of my ear.

"I want you like this," he murmured. "Hot from the ride. Still wild."

I shivered, and he caught the motion with a low laugh, his

hand sliding up to gently grip my throat. I twisted to face him, reckless with need, and hungry for the way he looked at me like I was the only thing in the world worth wanting.

I nodded, rising on my toes to press my mouth to his. He caught my face in his hand, fingers digging rough into my jaw, and kissed me like he'd die without it. His tongue swept against mine, stubble rough against my cheek. I whimpered into his mouth, already wild for him, but he broke away too soon, his breath burning across my face.

"Come on," he rasped and tugged me after him.

We barely made it to the side of the house before he stopped and snatched up a battered old cooler I hadn't even noticed. I blinked, breathless, and smacked his arm. "Colt Calloway, did you plan this?"

He just grinned, all cocky and devastating, and pulled me closer. "Maybe."

He tugged me so close our hips touched, and I could barely keep my balance, dizzy on the sudden shift in gravity. All I wanted was to reach up and haul him down to my mouth, but he'd already moved ahead, pulling me behind him with a greedy, unhurried certainty.

The last gold light slanted low over the mountains as we descended toward the lake. The water flared with reflections of the sky, blue and bruised and shot through with streaks of fire.

His fingers remained locked with mine as we half-ran, half-slid down the slope. When his boot caught on a slick rock, he stumbled forward but never let go, pulling me into his momentum until we both nearly toppled. My laughter bubbled up wild and unchecked, my lungs burning as I tried to match his long strides.

He glanced down at our twined hands, then up at me, and all the bravado and cockiness melted into something softer and wilder at the same time. In one sudden motion, he swung me up, arms banded beneath my thighs, and I let out a yelp that was half laughter, half unguarded joy. He just grinned and stalked the length of the old wooden gangway with me locked to his chest.

The dock creaked under his boots, the sound echoing across

the water, and all I could focus on was the flex of his arms around me and the racing tangle of my own pulse.

At the end of the dock, Colt set me down with a gentleness that was so at odds with the fire in his touch, steadying me even after my boots were firmly planted on the wood. The cooler thunked onto the dock next to us, but he didn't let me go.

Instead, his thumbs hooked into the hem of my shirt, and in one smooth motion, he drew it up and over my head, the fabric snagging for the briefest second at my elbows before I left my arms to help him.

He tossed my shirt onto the dock boards, and his hands found my bare stomach. His mouth followed, lips soft at first as they traced the hollow of my throat, then rough and hungry as he bit gently at my collarbone. I felt my knees wobble and braced both hands on his shoulders, steadying myself on the familiar slope of muscle under cotton. He was already working the button of my jeans, and I laughed as I tried to catch his hands, but he just shook his head, that wolfish smile widening.

"Didn't say you could stop me," he murmured against my skin, his voice a low rumble that vibrated straight through to my bones.

"I thought we were going for a swim," I managed, but my body was already arching into his, greedy for the heat of him. He had my jeans undone and halfway down my thighs before I could protest, and then he was kneeling to tug off my boots and pull them the rest of the way off.

He looked up at me from where he crouched, and the expression on his face was worshipful, hungry, so full of love it made my chest ache. It made me want to drop to my knees and thank the universe for delivering this man to me, even if it had taken the long, hard way around.

He stood, dropping his hat to the dock before shedding his own shirt in a single impatient yank. I took in every muscle and scar and freckle that told the story of a body built from years of hard work. He leaned in and kissed me, his hands skating up my ribs, and I felt myself go weightless again, floating even though my feet were on solid wood.

Colt's mouth was still on mine when he nudged us both backward, step by step, until the ladder pressed against my calves. He broke the kiss, and for a second, neither of us spoke. The only sounds were the lap of water against the dock, the distant whinny of one of our horses, and the wild hammering of my heart.

He grinned at me, all mischief and challenge. "Ladies first," he said, but his eyes said I could do whatever the hell I wanted, and he'd still follow me anywhere.

I reached behind me, fingers fumbling with the clasp of my bra. His eyes tracked every movement, darkening as the straps slid down my shoulders. The fabric caught for a moment between us before falling to the wood. I hesitated, suddenly shy despite everything we'd already done, then slowly hooked my thumbs into the sides of my panties. His breath hitched audibly as I pushed them down my thighs, the evening air kissing every inch of newly exposed skin.

I let my gaze wander before dropping pointedly to the part of him still confined by denim. I arched a brow, lips curling with mischief. "You're overdressed," I whispered, the words trembling on my tongue like a dare.

He followed my gaze, grinned, and opened his mouth as if to say something cocky, but I didn't give him the satisfaction. My skin already prickled with anticipation, every nerve ending live wired from his touch and the memory of his hands, his mouth. So, I spun on my heel and dove, headfirst, straight into the lake.

The shock of cold hit every inch of me as I sliced through the water, and I gasped for breath as I finally surfaced. I rolled onto my back and floated, limbs splayed, and I peeked open an eye toward the dock. Colt stood there, arms crossed over his bare chest, eyes tracking my every move.

He made a show of slowly unbuttoning his jeans as if he had all the time in the world. I watched as he tugged them and his boxers down his legs, casting them aside and kicking them, boots included, into a careless pile on the dock. Then he paused at the edge, feet planted wide, and just watched me, his eyes gone dark with intent.

My gaze drifted down to his thighs, lingered on his hard cock, then traveled slowly back to his face. Heat flooded me despite the cool water lapping at my skin. I arched my back as much as I could and let my breasts break the surface as I tilted my head. "What's taking so long, cowboy?" I teased. "You're not afraid of a little cool water, are you?"

He didn't move at first, just stood there watching me, and I could see every sharp cut of his muscles and the ravenous look in his eyes. I stretched out more, trailing a hand across my chest and let my fingers drift down, my eyes glued to his. "I could do this on my own, you know? I've done it so many times to the thought of you."

Colt's mouth ticked up, and his eyes lazily roamed over me as if he were in no hurry to break the moment. He let his eyes graze every inch of me, lingering on the places he knew could make me blush, but I refused to flinch. I wanted him to see me, all of me.

"Maybe I'm just savoring the view," he finally drawled, his voice a lazy honey that threatened to sprawl out and settle over every nerve ending I owned. "You always did look good like this. Unashamed and so fucking beautiful. Kinda makes a man wanna take his time." The words rolled off him, and I had to bite my cheek to keep from grinning.

I watched the slow tilt of his head, how his eyes roved from my throat to my waist to the place where my legs fluttered beneath the surface, and it was so boldly possessive and so very Colt that I found myself arching into the attention.

"Suit yourself." I shrugged, letting my body sink lower until the water licked just beneath my bottom lip, my eyes never leaving his as I started swimming away from the dock.

I heard his rough chuckle before the splash. Three powerful strokes and he was on me, his hand circling my ankle underwater, tugging me back through the ripples. My breath caught as he pulled me against him, water slipping between our bodies then pushed away by the heat of our skin.

"Where the hell do you think you're going?" he whispered, his lips so close I could taste his words. His thigh slid between mine beneath the surface, and I bit back a moan that threatened to betray exactly how much I wanted him.

He kept one arm locked around my back, pinning me to him, while his other hand skated up the inside of my thigh beneath the water, claiming territory with the slow confidence of a man who knew every inch, every secret, every quake I had to offer.

I tried to twist out of his grip, but all that did was grind myself against his cock. "Colt," I gasped as his fingers skimmed over my pussy.

"Yes, Strawberry?" He grinned, slow and wolfish. His fingers on my back bit into my skin while his other hand was still unbearably light. "Did you think I was just going to let you float away?"

He was moving us back toward the dock, but I was barely paying attention as his finger slid over my clit until I whimpered.

"There's not a chance in hell, Strawberry," he whispered, his mouth grazing the shell of my ear. "You're mine."

And with that, he lifted me as if I weighed nothing, and set me up on the edge of the dock, legs dangling just where the old wood met the lake. Right between the rails of the ladder, exactly like that first night when he made me come while he watched.

My skin prickled, cold and hot all at once, every inch of me exposed for him. I could feel the wild thud of my own heart, loud as thunder.

"What are you doing?" I breathed, but he was already reaching past me, the brush of his forearm sending a shudder up my spine.

He popped open the cooler then grinned as he fished out a jar of Saddle Up Strawberry Jam.

"You've been so damn successful with the launch of June's Jams." He set the cold jar between my thighs, and I hissed as the glass pressed against my overheated skin. "But as your boyfriend, I don't feel like I've done enough product testing."

I started to laugh but it caught in my throat as Colt unscrewed the lid and dipped two fingers inside, scooping a glistening ruby glob from the top. He brought it to my lips, smearing a line of jam across the seam of my mouth, and used his thumb to coax my jaw open.

"C'mon, Strawberry," he crooned, and I let my tongue dart out, licking the sweetness right from his skin.

He leaned in and licked the smudge of jam from the corner of my mouth, then kissed me until I was gasping. I drank him in, clawing at his forearms and feeling the tremor in his muscles as he held himself in check. Colt trailed a line of jam down my neck, between my breasts, each new touch a shock of cool stickiness that made my nipples pebble in the night air.

He followed each mark with his tongue, licking up every drop with a devotion that bordered on worship. I squirmed, half desperate and half delirious, the feeling of being completely devoured more intoxicating than any drug I'd ever known. When he reached my stomach, he paused and looked up, the jam-stained corner of his mouth quirking into a grin.

"Have I told you lately how proud I am of you?" he asked, and I could feel myself blush, heat racing to the very tips of my ears. "You've created something really special here, Blaire." He nodded just as he picked up the jar and set it just outside my thigh. "It's a shame I haven't figured out which one of you is sweeter though."

His hands slid up my thighs, widening me as far as I could go with the ladder on either side of me, and then he licked a slow path from my navel to the softest part of my thigh. Then he dipped back into the jar for another spoonful of jam.

This time he spread it along the inside of my thigh, sticky-sweet and cool, and the next thing I felt was the warm, careful press of his mouth as he cleaned every trace with the flat of his tongue. The sensation was dizzying.

I couldn't keep still. My body went taut, muscles fluttering, fingers digging into his hair. I arched my hips and moaned his name, not even caring if it echoed across the lake to the far pastures. He was methodical, almost tender, and he took his time, alternating between the slow, lazy strokes of his tongue and the impatient nip of his teeth.

He chased every dab of jam with reverence, until I was

shaking and begging in a way that would have made my old self blush and my new self proud.

"Colt, I can't—" I started, but he just shook his head, the motion sending another rippling shock up my thigh, and pressed his mouth right where I needed him most.

He sucked, then lapped, then sucked again, and I cried out so loud I half expected to see fireworks behind my eyes. He braced his hands around my hips, holding me steady while his tongue worked me open with single-minded determination.

Every time I thought I might shatter, he eased up, teasing the edge of my sanity, then dove right back in relentlessly until all I wanted was to come apart in his hands. He finally looked up, lips shiny with my arousal and that damn mustache covered in my jam.

"I'm still not sure," Colt drawled, shaking his head like he was genuinely disappointed in himself, though the glint in his eye told me he was anything but.

His hands bracketed my bare thighs, and he wasted no time dipping his fingers back into the jam for another glistening scoop.

"Suppose I better try again." He smeared a thick, sticky ribbon of strawberry right at the apex of my thighs, painting a line of jam just above my clit, and I jerked.

His tongue darted out, catching the edge of jam, and then his whole mouth followed, warm, soft, and hungry. He flattened his tongue and dragged it slowly through the mess he'd made, gathering every last trace of sweetness before making a show of sucking it from his own fingers.

He bent his head again and licked another stripe, this time catching my sensitive clit with a teasing, gentle flick. My hips jerked up, an involuntary plea.

He glanced up at me, his pupils dark with desire but soft around the edges with something that made my chest ache. Jam glistened on his lips, and a strand of hair clung to his damp forehead.

"I could spend the rest of my life doing this, Strawberry," he whispered, voice rough. "I want to trace every inch of you with my tongue until we've made up for all those sunsets when I was supposed to be kissing you."

I reached for him with trembling fingers, tracing the sharp line of his jaw where a hint of stubble caught against my skin. My thumb brushed the corner of his mouth where a smear of jam still glistened in the fading light. "Ten years of dreaming," I whispered, my voice breaking on the confession, "and not once did I imagine it would feel like coming home."

"I'm never letting you go again, Strawberry," he whispered, each word a vow against my skin. "I promise you that."

It was like ten years of winter, gone in an evening. I swear I could taste the sun on his fingers as they brushed my jaw, a clumsy, reverent touch, sticky with leftover sweetness. When our mouths finally met, it was all strawberries and *him*, but something more lingered underneath, a flavor thick with memory that had been waiting for us, patient and inevitable, no matter how long the cold had dragged on.

I'd been desperate to find myself, desperate to find my home, but as I stared into those bright blue eyes something bloomed in my chest, unfurling like June's strawberry blossoms after the last frost. The answer to every question I'd ever asked was written in the way he looked at me and the way his fingers trembled over my skin.

All this time, I'd been searching for something I'd already found years ago, beneath a Tennessee moon that had been waiting, patient as love itself, for me to finally come home.

Want more from the Calloway Ranch Series?

Hunter Calloway and our favorite baker are coming May 12th, 2026.

Preorder now!

Acknowledgments

Thank you to all the readers who are taking a chance on Cowboy Casual.

Thank you to my husband, Hubie. *You are the must supportive partner I could ever hope for.*

To Lauren Cox- I love you so much! Thank you for everything you do every day, and for peer pressuring me into writing my favorite book I've ever written.

To Amber Palmer- For listening to 50+ million voice notes and spirals. I love you so much!

To Brandi and Kenie Marie- The two best sisters in the world. Thank you for watching me spiral over this book every day.

To my incredible Alpha + Beta Readers: Kendra, Anna, Ashley, Lauren, Isabella, Tanya, Vee, & Salma

To Rachel Brookes- Thank you for always being there and always be willing to help. I appreciate you more than you know.

To my editing team- Rebecca's Fairest Reviews, Rumi Khan, and Olivia Winston.

Thank you to my entire team who I couldn't do this without. Lauren, Brandi, Kenie Marie, Savannah, Rumi, Rebecca: thank you, thank you, thank you.

About the Author

Holly Renee is a USA Today bestselling author of romance that crackles with tension, swoons with heat, and leaves readers giddy with delicious banter. Whether she's whisking you off to a moon-drenched fantasy kingdom or a Tennessee ranch filled with heartbreak and horses, her stories are fast-paced, emotionally charged, and undeniably fun.

Born and raised in East Tennessee, Holly is a married mom of two, a lake enthusiast, a lifelong lover of pink, and hopelessly obsessed with the kind of love that makes you scream into your pillow.